NEW YORK REVIEW BOOKS
CLASSICS

THE UNFORGIVABLE

CRISTINA CAMPO (1923–1977) was born in Bologna and brought up in Florence. A congenital heart malformation kept her out of school and away from her peers for much of her childhood. In her reclusion, she read; by her teens, she had immersed herself in Italian, French, Spanish, German, and English literature. After World War II—toward the end of which her father, a composer, was briefly imprisoned as a Fascist sympathizer—Campo moved to Rome, where she became acquainted with Eugenio Montale, Elena Croce, and Roberto Bazlen, among others. Intensely private, she almost always published under pseudonyms (Cristina Campo being one of them) and translated—Simone Weil, Katherine Mansfield, Emily Dickinson, Virginia Woolf—far more than she wrote. Although she had always been a Catholic, in the 1960s Campo's faith became more fervent; she spent long periods in convents and strongly opposed the Second Vatican Council's relinquishment of the Latin liturgy. Her heart continued to cause her serious trouble throughout her life, and she died in Rome at the age of fifty-three.

ALEX ANDRIESSE is the editor of *The Uncollected Essays of Elizabeth Hardwick* and an associate editor at New York Review Books. Among his translations are Roberto Bazlen's *Notes Without a Text* and François-René de Chateaubriand's *Memoirs from Beyond the Grave* (published by NYRB Classics).

KATHRYN DAVIS is the author of eight novels, including *The Silk Road* and *Duplex*, and one memoir, *Aurelia, Aurélia*. She is the senior fiction writer on the faculty of the writing program at Washington University.

THE UNFORGIVABLE

and Other Writings

CRISTINA CAMPO

Translated from the Italian by
ALEX ANDRIESSE

Introduction by
KATHRYN DAVIS

NEW YORK REVIEW BOOKS

New York

THIS IS A NEW YORK REVIEW BOOK
PUBLISHED BY THE NEW YORK REVIEW OF BOOKS
207 East 32nd Street, New York, NY 10016
www.nyrb.com

This book was translated, in part, thanks to a grant awarded by the Italian
Ministry of Foreign Affairs and International Cooperation.

Library of Congress Cataloging-in-Publication Data
Names: Campo, Cristina, 1923–1977, author. | Andriesse, Alex, translator.
Title: The unforgivable and other writings / by Cristina Campo; translated
  from the Italian by Alex Andriesse.
Identifiers: LCCN 2023017744 (print) | LCCN 2023017745 (ebook) |
  ISBN 9781681378022 (paperback) | ISBN 9781681378039 (ebook)
Subjects: LCGFT: Creative nonfiction. | Essays.
Classification: LCC PQ4863.A39525 U54 2024 (print) | LCC PQ4863.A39525
  (ebook) | DDC 808.84—dc23/eng/20230807
LC record available at https://lccn.loc.gov/2023017744
LC ebook record available at https://lccn.loc.gov/2023017745

ISBN 978-1-68137-802-2
Available as an electronic book; ISBN 978-1-68137-803-9

Printed in the United States of America on acid-free paper.
10 9 8 7 6 5 4 3 2 1

CONTENTS

INTRODUCTION

You approach the house, if indeed it is a house. Whatever it is, it seems impossible to touch bottom or top. Most of the time you will not get beyond the threshold. You will not get beyond the veil of leaves that glisten in the sun like fish in a veil of water. There's a doorway and just inside the door a little white cat with velvet paws. A mother and father playing piano four hands, Paisiello, Donizetti. Also that other dance, "hands clenched, wrists flexed," seen by a poet in a dying child's limbs, opening and closing slowly, like a corolla.

This is not a collection of essays. This is a dwelling place, a gathering of rooms, of turns of mind, winding hallways, *la fin du parc*, the sort of rectangular basin in which Proust contained, like a giant in a bottle, his great fluvial dream. This is the Tuscan house like a lily— all light and loftiness and renunciation, where "behind windowpanes so clear they blind us move the figures of the ones we've loved, the ones we've lost, who, behold, stand up from the piano bench or arrange fruit on a table." This is a dwelling place in which you are as likely to encounter William Carlos Williams as "pure, terrible" Frédéric Chopin, Jesus Christ, Marcel Proust, "meticulous, specious" Marianne Moore, Anton Chekhov, Simone Weil, Madame d'Aulnoy, "very attentive adders"—a dwelling place comprising the infinitely subtle and terrifying presence of the immense in the small, a place where you are granted "the almost mortal happiness of seeing without possessing."

Cristina Campo, christened Vittoria Maria Angelica Marcella Cristina Guerrini, was born on the 29th day of April 1923, in Bologna,

Italy. Her godmother told her that because she was born on a Sunday, she saw many things others did not. Creatures born on Sundays have the gift of seeing the fairies—otherwise known as the seven planets or the twelve constellations—that preside at their baptism, their gifts propitious or adverse. Mistakes can be made, a powerful fairy left uninvited, a curse leveled. Campo was born with a congenital cardiac malformation, the very condition she claims caused her to be thrown into the "thick of [her] own destiny," her deformity elevated into an unusual kind of power, the "ability to penetrate impenetrable places." A firm believer in destiny, she was also born with a yod in her chart, betokening an extraordinary and unshakable sense of purpose.

Transported at the age of five to a fairy-tale villa in Tuscany—"the heavy afternoons alive with cicadas," "the green iron table under the cedar of Lebanon already set for tea," "the pure white of the last meadowsweet"—Campo didn't so much grow up reading fairy tales, nor even so much grow up *in* a fairy tale. It's more like she grew up *as* a fairy tale, her end having been with her from the beginning, a condition she both understood and embodied in every cell of her star-crossed body and remarkable brain. "In Italian," she explains, "certain peaches are said to have a 'distinguished soul,' meaning the stone is easily dislodged from the pulp. The fairy-tale hero, likewise, is called upon to dislodge his heart from his flesh or, if you will, his soul from his heart. For no one with a heart held fast will ever make his way into the impossible."

The almost uniformly aphoristic quality of her sentences is a product of this condition, of her acute sense of the way a fairy tale—as well as everything she held most dear, really—always manages to be and to be doing two things at once, thus securing a victory over the law of necessity. "In a fairy tale, there are no roads. You start out walking, as if in a straight line, and eventually that line reveals itself to be a labyrinth, a perfect circle, a spiral, or even a star." The teller of tales, the person close to the end of a lifetime, is pointing the listening child toward a destination that isn't his own past but the child's future, the future of his memory as an adult. All time is encompassed in this transaction, hidden in a "numinous quality of the language which envelops them both in the same rapture." The realm of the fairy tale may be a realm of ecstasy, but it is above all a land of pathos and of symbols of sorrow. "Nothing, with the exception of the Scriptures, is more radically unsentimental than a fairy tale," Campo tells us.

To attempt to describe the quality of her sentences, to submit to being taken over by them, is to attempt to describe a form of possession not unlike the one her fearless and fearlessly eloquent translator, Alex Andriesse, has submitted himself to here, a true act of daring performed in the face of Campo's severity of judgment, leveled from the beyond she so firmly, inexorably inhabits. On the one hand her prose demonstrates the lightest touch, the gift of sprezzatura she revered and practiced, herself like a fairy, fata nix. "I have written little and would like to have written less," she announced. But there is also in her prose the presence of something that arouses a sort of holy terror, something "you can hold in your palm, with its menacing geometry and atrocious elegance, like Chinese armor, the first draft of life on a dead star..." Think of it like the little girl in the Tuscan fairy tale, led by the shoulder toward the tomb of her grandparents, toward "the flower bed that changed into a moat, the empty eyes, the serpentine ring, the underground realms and the blood, the silence and the prohibitions, the little girl with the rose in whom childhood and old age tacitly tied the knot of their mutual secret."

This book is a big house, a house of apparently endless proportion. You can try following the little girl into it, but as she makes clear, having "set foot in that part of life beyond which one cannot go with any hope of returning," not everyone is allowed in. That this book takes its title from the essay "The Unforgivable" is no accident. Who are they, the unforgivable ones? What, exactly, have they done or failed to do that could be considered unforgivable? Campo's message might be taken in the same spirit in which a child tapes a sign to the bedroom door: KEEP OUT AND THIS MEANS YOU—equal parts interdiction and challenge. "The passion for perfection comes late," she warns. "In an era of purely horizontal progress, in which the human group seems more and more to resemble that line of Chinese men on their way to the guillotine mentioned in chronicles of the Boxer Rebellion, the only nonfrivolous attitude seems to be that of the man in line who is reading a book."

But not just any book will do.

It's instructive to assemble the subjects of her deepest reverence, her impassioned inquiry, and attempt to assign a common denominator. "Everything that brings us joy is somehow or other divine territory," she says, including in her pantheon Madame d'Aulnoy, creator of true poems that are fairy tales; Marcel Proust, "a seer more than a witness"; Marianne Moore whose "lodestar" was perfection; William Carlos Williams, freest in his own time and space; Frédéric Chopin, mercilessly measuring "pianistic preparations for death"; "regal, ruthless" Djuna Barnes; "conscious dreamer" Jorge Luis Borges; C. P. Cavafy, "spiritual son of the great archons of destiny, Plutarch and Shakespeare"; Giacomo Leopardi, "last to examine a page as it ought to be examined, in the manner of a paleographer"; Anton Chekhov's "heroically attentive eyes" trained on the barely perceptible beauty of human grief; Scheherazade's "thoroughly, scrupulously horrifying depiction of destiny"; Katherine Mansfield's "purity worthy of a mystic"; the "hard, uncrackable nuts" that were the Desert Fathers. If there is a common denominator, I think it can be found in Campo's claim that the genius of "Beauty and the Beast," of fairy tales in general, resides in the fact that they are fundamentally about "the loving reeducation of a soul—an attention—which is elevated from sight to perception," a claim echoed in the contention that "Attention is the only path to the unsayable . . . [it frees] the genie from the bottle."

The prevailing ethos here is truth, not fantasy. Campo's disdain for the operation of mere imagination—a quality reviled by the Greeks—is of the highest order; she makes reference at one point to "the universal disaster of the Renaissance." Art nowadays, she complains, is in the grip of imagination and nothing more. "When it is confronted with reality, imagination recoils. Attention, on the other hand, grasps it, directly." Real art is to be found in poetry, in the

Bible, in a fairy tale. "To ask a man to never be distracted, to be continually turning his faculty of attention away from the errors of imagination, the laziness of habit, the hypnosis of custom, is to ask him to realize his highest form."

These essays were written over the course of an abbreviated and not obviously eventful lifetime, if by "event" we mean something along the lines of going to sea to be a writer. Due to her fragile health, Cristina Campo grew up isolated, essentially homeschooled, though her parents were both accomplished mentors, her father a musician and composer, her mother the daughter of "sculptors, patriots, and doctors." While in Florence, Campo translated into Italian the work of Virginia Woolf, Katherine Mansfield, William Carlos Williams, John Donne, and Simone Weil; Weil's work in particular had a profound effect on Campo's way of looking at the world, as well as on her art. In 1955 she followed her mother and father from Florence to no. 3 Piazza Sant'Anselmo in Rome, where her father took a position as the director of the Conservatorio di Musica Santa Cecilia, and where Campo's life as a professional writer began in earnest. She published a collection of poems, *Passo d'addio* (1956), her first collection of essays, *Fairy Tale and Mystery* (1962), and established friendships with other writers, acquiring a reputation for being a brilliant conversationalist though she had no interest in literary salons or awards.

It was also while living in Rome that Campo—who had grown up in a nominally Catholic household—underwent a religious conversion, her newfound relationship to Catholicism as uncompromising as was her relationship to everything else in her life. Together with the philosopher and religious historian, Elémire Zolla, she edited the 1963 anthology *I mistici dell'Occidente* and was among the members of Una Voce, an international group fiercely opposed to the liturgical changes made by the Second Vatican Council—changes she castigated as "leprosy." Christ's parables, the Gospels in general, Scripture, had always been mainsprings of her life and work; following her conversion they became the prime undercurrent. "Belle's prince" in initial iterations of "A Rose" became in revision "the Prince"—thus firmly securing the fairy tale's ascendancy to religious parable. In 1964 her mother died, her father the following year, their deaths deeply unsettling Campo, who had lived with them her whole life long. She was only fifty-three years old when a heart attack worse than the many heart attacks she'd endured over the years turned out to be fatal. January 10, 1977, Cristina Campo died among the furniture she'd brought with her from Florence, in the guesthouse at no. 3 Piazza Sant'Anselmo all'Aventino.

"After slowly constructing one of his Cities of God upon the keyboard, it is not unusual for Bach to bring us back once more to the cornerstone: four little notes." Back to the cornerstone: the life Campo lived as a girl with her parents in Tuscany, the one period of her life she recorded with fidelity to something resembling fact. "The Golden Nut" is the single overtly autobiographical text in this collection, though you could say that everything Campo wrote was autobiographical. It was in the Tuscan house—the house like a lily— where she formed her lifelong habit of reading fairy tales. This is also where she formed her unshakable communion with the natural world, a world with no roads in it like the world in a fairy tale, "a motionless point the soul never leaves, even as body and mind take what appears to be an arduous journey."

Consider the child—the remarkable child who was Cristina Campo—the life being breathed back into her. "I threw my tricycle down on the English lawn," she writes, "and Luigi, cassocked in his red jacket, quickly opened the little glass-paned door in its bronze arc of ivy, while my beautiful older cousins Zarina and Maria Sofia hopped down from the car like birds." There she is, alive and breathing, unaware of everything she is about to do in her short and remarkably eventful lifetime, standing there with her cousins, breathing the life into her small body, awaiting the moment when awareness arrives, "when [her] memory closes like a circle over [her] own beginnings."

The fairy tale was there, terrible and radiant, resolved for a moment and insoluble; the eternal, which is always returning in dreams, viaticum for a pilgrimage, the golden nut that must be kept in the mouth, that must be crushed between the teeth at the moment of gravest danger. I was looking for my little handkerchief, holding back my sobs, when my mother, with a faraway look in her eyes, placed her gloved hand on the back of my neck.

The infinitely subtle and terrifying presence of the immense in the small—the golden nut. ENTER YE WHO DARE!

—KATHRYN DAVIS

TRANSLATOR'S NOTE

WHEN, at the prompting of the late Roberto Calasso, I read Cristina Campo's essays for the first time, I discovered a writer of sentences unlike any I'd encountered; a student of the American modernists, Proust and Borges, the Metaphysicals and the Elizabethans, Simone Weil and Henry Corbin; a mind lit up by the sayings of the Desert Fathers, fairy tales, and magic words of all kinds—a human, a linguistic, phenomenon, I thought, completely impossible to translate into English.

This has in the most literal sense turned out to be true. Campo's knowledge of our tongue, among others, seems to have made her especially keen on Italian's nontransferable resources: the pronouns and articles implicit, the subjects deferred, the inversions abundant.... All of which means, where a translator is concerned, that Campo almost never writes a sentence that can be carried over word by word. Her phrases instead demand something more like contemplation and, after a certain spell has passed, re-creation—always a tricky proposition when dealing with a writer as aphoristic, baroque, colloquial, direct, enigmatic (and so on down to, say, yeasty and zealous) as Campo.

Should the reader come across any passages of exceptional beauty or mystical insight, those, of course, belong entirely to her. Any infelicities belong to me.

A NOTE ON THE NOTES

Campo composed a fair number of endnotes for her essays, though she conceived of these notes as a separate entity, running parallel to the essays themselves. Both her notes and mine, meant to help readers orient themselves in her library, can be found at the back of the volume, organized by essay and page number. However, they are not signaled in the text itself—an authorial decision it seemed important to honor.

—ALEX ANDRIESSE

THE FLUTE AND THE CARPET

to my father, Guido Guerrini

THIS BOOK collects writings from various periods, and there can be no doubt that some of these are rather youthful.

Yet, under different pretexts and with various colors, it seems to me that the book addresses the same subject, from beginning to end, time and again. It is or would like to be, from beginning to end, a humble attempt to dissent from the game of forces, "a profession of disbelief in the omnipotence of the visible."

For this reason, I have not even eliminated repetitions. In the "painted rooms" created by our old artists, it was common for dissimilar figures, on the different walls, to allude with the same gesture to a single center, a single guest—absent or present.

—C.C.

ONE

A ROSE

To ACCUSE the French fabulists of frivolity because they adorned their fairies with a handful of ostrich feathers is to "have sight and not perception." Perception is exactly what someone like Madame d'Aulnoy possessed. She was able to find the subtlest mysteries in the voices of the people, and she did so almost unconsciously, almost in a dream, the way you find a four-leaf clover in a meadow. (Not so the Grimm brothers, who, methodically exploring folklore leaf by leaf, found, yes, a good many of them too, but surrounded by a stultifying harvest of unmagical herbs.)

Madame d'Aulnoy composed sublime fairy tales: "The Golden Branch" and "The White Cat," for example, in which it seems impossible to touch bottom or top. But it would be enough to recall the more familiar tales of Perrault (or of that mysterious son of his who so swiftly disappeared). I mean his most-read tale, "Cinderella." Leaving aside for the moment the symbols, which have already been so sadly deflowered, of the wicked sisters and the glass shoe (but the real shoe, exquisitely, was made of vair), what revelations we find in "Cinderella." Flashes of insight that only storytellers of this sort—slightly scattered, like all seers—have the ability to capture.

Here we have the prelude to the great crisis at the court ball:

When she was thus attired, she got into the carriage; but her godmother commanded her, above all things, not to stay past midnight, warning her that if she remained at the Ball one moment too long, her carriage would turn back into a pumpkin, her horses into mice, her footmen into lizards, and that her old clothes would become just as they were before.

In these few words, the mystery of time and the laws of miracle are established with immense nonchalance and yet as firmly as can be. For what can the failure to observe a limit lead to, if not a tragic regression in time, where one awakens in the morning to cold ashes? On the third and most glorious night of the ball, Cinderella comes very close to such a precipice. And in her effort to escape it, running away like mad, she doesn't care about losing her vair slipper or giving up a shred of the freely given, ecstatic gift in which a power has garbed her. But sure enough, it will be this very thread (the vair slipper) that leads her back to the prince. Her voluntary loss will be his gain.

"Whosoever shall lose his life shall save it." Madame Leprince de Beaumont, in "Beauty and the Beast," takes the same theme to still subtler and more secret zones. Like any perfect fairy tale, this one is about the loving reeducation of a soul—an attention—which is elevated from sight to perception. To perceive is to recognize what alone has value, what alone truly exists. And what else truly exists in this world if not what is not of this world? The Beast's relationship with Belle is a long, tender, very cruel struggle against terror, superstition, judgments made by the flesh, vain nostalgia. Cinderella's lingering at the ball is not dissimilar from Belle's return home, which nearly costs the Beast his life. For both girls, there is the risk of falling back into the magic circle of the past, which can devastate, like an unseasonable frost, what has so long been waiting to bloom: the present. This is Belle's ordeal, but Belle does not know it. In fact, in essence, it is the Beast's ordeal.

And when does the Beast transform into a Prince? When the miracle has become superfluous. When the transformation has already imperceptibly occurred in Belle: washing her of every adolescent regret and every stain of fantasy, leaving her only an attentive soul stripped bare ("He no longer seems like a Beast, and even if he were one I would marry him anyway, for he is so perfectly good and I could never love anyone but him").

The Beast's transformation is in reality Belle's transformation, and it is only reasonable the Beast becomes a Prince at this point as well. Reasonable because no longer necessary. Now that Belle is no longer looking with the eyes of the flesh, the Prince's elegance is purely superfluous. It is the surplus of happiness promised to those who sought the kingdom of heaven first of all. "For unto every one that hath shall be given," says the verse that so intrigues those faithful to the letter.

To lead Belle to this triumph, the Beast came very close to death and despair. Night after night, with perfectly insane tenacity, he labored, appearing to the recluse girl, resigned and unafraid at the ceremonial hour: the hour of dinner and music. Girded in the aegis of horror and ridicule ("As well as being ugly, unfortunately I am also stupid"), he risked hatred and execration of what was dear to him: he descended into the Underworld and made her descend there too.

God does no less for us, and no less madly, night after night, day after day. It should not be forgotten, however, that it was Belle who elicited her Prince, from afar and unaware. This was when she asked her father, whose foot was already in the stirrup, to bring her, not a jewel or a sumptuous gown, but that mad gift of hers: "a rose, only a rose," in the dead of winter.

IN MEDIO COELI

the gates were at first the end of the world ...
... and something infinite
behind everything appeared

—Thomas Traherne

Everybody knows the very old, though they forget a large part of the life they have led, remember their childhoods with increasing clarity. It has been said that only children may enter the kingdom of heaven, and it seems only right that we should have to give up every other thing we own in exchange for that one possession, which will be had, perhaps, with death.

The most befuddled old man assumes the mystery of an augur the moment he starts telling stories about his childhood. Life will slow its pace around him, strange silences will enshroud him, and even the most impatient child will be unable to resist him. He seems endowed at such moments with auspicious powers. Indeed, he is pointing the child toward a destination: not his own past but the child's future, the future of his memory as an adult. Neither one is aware of it, unless they notice the numinous quality of the language which envelops them both in the same rapture. The old man's words could not be simpler. And yet you often hear the child interrupt, wanting to know more, insisting on the shape of that focaccia, the size of that garden, the color of the dress his great-grandmother was wearing during that afternoon stroll or at that party. And if such questions fail the child, if he is not gifted with poetic attention, he will still ask the old man, furrowing his brow, "How old were you then?" Such is his attempt to conquer the bewildering distance, the unimaginable journey, that lies between him and the child of the past, who waits at the far end of his future. An ageless child—an old man in disguise—like the black children in icons. "Six or seven," the old man will say. And almost as though reciting a secret responsory, he will add, "Like you, more or less." Such is the perfect, impartial kabbalah that holds the thread of the hours, the order of the days and years, suspended around them both, as around Proust's bed.

See how slowly the child blinks his eyes, as if he were hypnotized by the old man's reminiscences; see how feverishly he parts his lips and how heavily he gulps as he swallows his saliva. His expression betrays no trace of amusement; his whole body is taut against the old man's knees. He has the motionless tension of an animal in motion or an insect undergoing metamorphosis. Perhaps he is a little like the nightingale in full-throated song, when its temperature rises and its fragile feathers ruffle. In these moments, he is growing; he is drinking with great gulps and fear at the fountain of memory: the dark, flashing water that brings the subtleties of perception to life.

The objects that the child is so anxious to *see*, after all, surround him too. They are within his reach. And yet he seems unable to establish the connection; there appears to be no relationship between the things he is being told about, such as his grandmother—things so simple they scare him, and so appealing as they elude his grasp—and the things he touches and sees every day, the things he will go back to touching and seeing very soon, once the old man's stories are finished or broken off.

There is something brutal, or perhaps only animal, in the abruptness with which a child goes back to his games after one of these moments that have held the motion of the spheres in suspension overhead. As long as the story lasted, it was impossible to imagine him coming out of his trance without tears or tantrums. But almost like someone awakened from a dream, like an animal or one of those people who, after a miraculous cure, awake with an appetite, he, too, will immediately say, "I'm hungry," and greedily snatching up a slice of bread, hop off on one foot to go and eat it somewhere else. He is almost arrogant—almost flaunts his independence by shouting or singing at the top of his lungs. He will then, if he has his way, turn toward the animal world. He will drag off the dog or scoop up the cat and go running with them through the garden.

Not that the child doesn't normally live in perfect harmony with the objects around him. On the contrary. Immersed in the grace of unsullied sensuality, his hands grasp an orange or plunge into the luxuriance of fur or water with angelic speed and aplomb. But he does not know it. Only when his memory closes like a circle over his own beginnings will he know. The old man knows, however. Their dialogue transpires between a garden where everyone is naked without being aware of it and an antechamber where everyone has been stripped bare.

That is why an old man's simplest story assumes a parabolic pace. In the past, the old preferred to express themselves in parables, and the traditional teller of fairy tales—those gospels that discourse so casually on morality—was the grandmother: the doyenne of the house, the woman of good counsel, no matter whether she was a lady or a peasant. "An old man by the fireside is worth more than a young man in the field," says an Italian proverb. The truth of this is plain if we consider the image of the storyteller (whose voice my father could still hear): a mysterious man invited to the house after dinner on long winter nights, like a celebrant or haruspex, an old man with a clay pipe who lived off his tongue and around whom the whole room or kitchen divided like a chapel, with the gynoecium of spinners and embroiderers on one side and the androecium of smokers on the other.

In Tuscany, fairy tales were always called "the stories," just as the Gospels used to be. With the hearth at its center—an ancient locus of communion with the dead and with ancestral spirits—the house was reserved for the storyteller. The square was where you went to hear the balladeer, the chronicler of secular deeds. And since public spaces have always been secular spaces as far as the people are concerned, "balladeer" also took on the meaning of "fire-eater" and "charlatan." Whereas the storyteller, disdainful of end rhymes and pitiful patter, traveled mysteriously from house to house like a bearer of treasures. The children liked to picture him with a sack full of words very much like the sack of dreams parceled out by Sleep. For centuries, legends circulated about those who were no longer able to tell (or no longer wished to tell) fairy tales. For they were a gift from heaven, and always revocable.

Even as he tells his own story, the artless old man may be unaware of his secret role as a hierophant. The artful old man is well aware, and prefers parable to history. The former will say: "When I was little, they used to take us to see a certain holy cripple . . ." (or, in the worst case: "In that year of famine, we had to eat mice . . ."). The latter will begin: "On the island of the Children of Kaledan, there lived a blind king who did not believe in death . . ." Both of them, however, keep faith with a consignment of silence that is the very law of life. The first man surrounds this silence with the most familiar, everyday objects of memory, reminiscent of rustic phylacteries or treasured talismans. The other weaves it into complex, recurring figurations connected with magic numbers and symbols apposite to the secret of the story: like the reverse side of a carpet, whose design will not reveal itself until it has been unrolled.

It is no coincidence that so many fairy tales—those figurations of the journey—end like a ring right where they began. At the end of it all, beyond the seven mountains and the seven seas, there is the paternal house, the family park or garden, where, in the meantime, the grass has grown tall and the gray-haired king has been waiting to give the crown to his son, the prodigal prince. There is one fairy tale, and not even a very old one, in which the journey extends beyond the world: A little girl sets out in search of her dead mother. Beyond the forests and the oceans, the labyrinthine cities and the thunderous mountains, after crossing the cadaverous plain of the moon, the girl is led into the garden of paradise. It is the first pleasant place she has been. But then she recognizes the tall oaks and whirlwinds of purplish leaves.

For this is the forest near her house, where she had first decided to stray at the start of her pilgrimage. And it comes as no great shock, a few moments later, when she finds her mother sitting in a little antrum, a cave, near the spring where she loved to play as a child.

In a fairy tale, there are no roads. You start out walking, as if in a straight line, and eventually that line reveals itself to be a labyrinth, a perfect circle, a spiral, or even a star—or a motionless point the soul never leaves, even as body and mind take what appears to be an arduous journey. You seldom know where you are traveling, or even what you are traveling toward, for you cannot know, in reality, what the water ballerina, or the singing apple, or the fortune-telling bird may be. Or the word to conjure with: the abstract, culminating word that is stronger than any certainty. As for the Moirai (who may take the form of decrepit beggars or talking beasts), they will never be able to give you more than three or four negative rules as viaticum, rules on which everything depends and which will promptly be broken, because it is impossible to follow rules that stand for other rules that have not yet been revealed: "Do not buy meat from a condemned man," "Do not sit on the lip of a fountain." So it goes. Since the thing you start out looking for cannot and must not have a face, how can you recognize the means to reach it until you've reached it? How can the destination ever be anything but an apparent destination?

An Eastern teacher expresses himself very similarly when he says that his disciple must start walking if he wants to get anywhere—that he must set forth with all the strength of his spirit if he wants to receive his enlightenment. The dawning of enlightenment is like a lotus opening or a dreamer awakening. It isn't possible to predict the end of a dream; when the dream is over, we wake up spontaneously. Flowers don't open when they are expected to open; it will happen when the time is right. No one *arrives* at the enlightenment he sets out to seek. It will come to him in its own sweet time.

Thus the destination walks side by side with the traveler like the Archangel Raphael with Tobias. Or it hovers behind him as with Tobit the Elder. In truth, the traveler has always had it within him and is only moving toward the motionless center of his life: the antrum near the spring, the cave—where childhood and death, in one another's arms, confide the secret they share.

The idea of travel, effort, and patience is paradoxical, yes, but it is also exact. For in this paradox, we stumble on the intersection of eternity and time: the form must willingly destroy itself, but it cannot do so until it has achieved perfection.

This tenacious relationship between childhood and death seems to pervade every plane of existence. Proust is an important witness, but perhaps it's Pasternak who divulges its ultimate meaning in his notes on Chopin, when he says that the études are "essays toward a theory of childhood" and, precisely for this reason, "pianistic preparations for death," a pursuit in which "the ear is the eye of the soul."

Ancient navigators, when they regained the course they'd been blown off by the winds—often from the opposite direction—used to call the maneuver "advancing backward." At the outset, I spoke of old age. It can just as well be called exile, or precocious predestination—or it can bear both names, as it did for Chopin. One thing, in any case, is certain: Whether the zenith of a life coincides with or precedes its natural vertex, the path does not then wend toward forgetfulness, as the law of time would have it, but instead toward remembrance. All the knowledge we have acquired before we reach that point—at midheaven—afterward seems to turn back toward childhood, home, the earliest landscape, toward the mystery of origins that speak to us more and more eloquently each day. Toward an increasingly intimate dialogue between the long-vanished child and the dead—the veiled, omnipotent ministers of memory. I can easily understand how, listening to his maternal grandparents—deposed and banished by Spanish conquistadors—the half-caste Garcilaso recognized once and for all that he himself would, in the future, be known only as "El Inca," although he was a Christian, a fervent Catholic, and the son of an illustrious Spaniard. In an instant, he understood those laments he'd heard a thousand times, those old men desperately nostalgic for their dead emperors who were as terrible and sweet as the sun. Happening on the family portrait of a man we've heard mentioned a thousand times, an ancestor who has our face but who—only today is it clear—*has seen the emperors*, can be no less dramatic; he bears in his cold and tender gaze what we have been seeking since birth, within and without us. Something very like the earth, which (as an Indian once put it) was stolen from us under the pretense of giving us the heavens. An uncorrupted language, first of all: a spontaneously liturgical arrangement of words. And compared to this, as one can never say enough, an arrangement of stars is a minor matter.

The landscape, in these encounters with our own prehistory, is the primary mediator.

Whoever has had the good fortune to be born in the countryside (or at least with a garden large enough for him not to be overfamiliar with its boundaries) will carry with him, his whole life long, some sense of an arcane yet quite precise poetry, a musical unfolding of phrases that, even as it overwhelms the senses with extravagant joy, intimates to the mind an ultimate design, which is always promised and always deferred. Like the solution to a rebus, this ultimate form is sometimes suggested by a dream (in which the beloved landscape discloses unsuspected depths) and sometimes by reading what will frequently be a fairy tale (and more than ever, as we read these tales, familiar places lead us down unanticipated paths, are filled with presences, undergo increasingly subtle and sublime metamorphoses).

Childhood is a rebus of limitless limits and uncertain boundaries, magnified by the child's small stature (like the magic words he must spell out slowly in the book of fairy tales). It was the ridge, velvety with a line of sunlight and inaccessible to tiny steps, beyond which the incomparable meadow, the clearing of Brocéliande, must have stretched. It was the gate that was always closed, the grove scarcely glimpsed, the avenue without end. It was, during the twilight stroll, the ruin of a vertiginous and unmoving castle that kept changing—transmuting with each bend in the road. It was the cave, with its foretold moss and secret water. It was *la fin du parc*.

A mere photograph is enough for these golden hieroglyphs, these green ideograms of a perfect presence—ceaselessly foreseen and lost—to reassemble their signs. Only laymen of memory can look at one of these photographs and find them merely yellowed. For whoever looks at them as living pictures, that yellow is the pure honey of sunlight. It is all those dazzling and overcast mornings sweetly transfixed by calls, rustlings, buzzing bees, bright clothes in the distance, and muted voices, beneath a sky as translucent as ice. A whole network of angel hair stretched across a shimmering space.

An absolute space, one might say. Even if it is, in fact, composed precisely by those prohibitions, those invisible confines so comparable to the threads of meter and the loops of rhyme. At times memory insists so strongly it torments us, as around some ecstasy denied. And from time to time, with cruel, angelic obstinacy, a recurring dream presents it to us all at once: the walled garden we seek weeping at its gate, the house deserted or destroyed, the invisible water that might speak to us, like the river Scamander, if only we could plunge our hand into it.... For others it may be elusive music, or a voice behind a series of doors, or a perfect word, or language that is erased in the act of putting it down on paper.

We wake from such dreams in a desolation fiercer than rapture. The belief that, when we realize we are dreaming, the thread of our dream is broken, is untrue. Consciousness can hold on for a long time and lead the dream by the hand, the way a child leads an adult who can perhaps open the latch of a gate too high for him. These are the moments when Borges—a conscious dreamer, and therefore omnipotent—decides to create for himself, in his dream, what he dreamed of all through his childhood. But "Oh, incompetence!" the longed-for beast fails to materialize, looks ridiculous, or leaps over his head in a flash. So it goes. From the blindfolded, luminous eyes of childhood, all that can reach us is a filtered gaze in a dream: the gaze of Fortuna, aloft on her wheel.

The fairy tale is a ceaseless weaving of these ungraspable moments, fixed at the height of their splendor. The dervish separates a cloud of smoke with both hands, and through this opening the prisoner can go out into the garden. A small door in the trunk of an oak opens to the runaway princess, and beyond are vast fields, unpeopled and unknown.

It is no coincidence that reading fairy tales, the secret language of the old, is so often one of the indelible events of childhood. For the child who has read them in a living landscape, they will already be a first initiation, if not to the meaning, at least to the power of symbols. Corrado Alvaro, a writer graced with mystery, has likened the fairy tale to the childhood of the world, when journeys were made on foot or on the backs of animals.

> What were the caves, the woods, the underground worlds if not places glimpsed along difficult paths?...The means of travel...magnified the landscape, made for a more intimate and, at the same time, more mysterious knowledge of things... and the very animals that carried us on their backs added to the mystery with their unforeseen fears, their refusals to continue, their attention to certain paths and places, their sudden gallops and starts. In those days, the road was animated by obscure presences, horrors, hazards, happy deliverances...

This rapturous and rather slow pace of travel—this "eternal rhythm"—is native to the fairy tale, as to all those spiritual writings whose exact hyperboles and impossible precisions are the root and flower of the fairy tale. Saint John of the Cross's *Spiritual Canticle*, for example, is a classic narrative of love and the quest for a prince beyond compare. There is talk of mountains and rivers, lions' dens and strange islands, silver surfaces in which eyes appear, nuptial beds defended by golden shields. The traveler vows not to pick the flowers, not to fear the wild beasts, to cross fortresses and frontiers.

The fairy tale of all fairy tales, the journey of all journeys, the Book of Tobit, is lit by a vivid glow in the moment when the old father gives thanks for the stranger of the fish and the staff: "O thou leadest down to Hell, and bringest up again . . ."

Thus, if there were one event essential for our life—one encounter, one instant of enlightenment—we would recognize it first of all by the light, familiar from childhood and fairy tales, that suffuses it. Miraculously, for a brief spell, we find ourselves at the center of things and can decipher them. Alien landscapes seem to bear some resemblance to our first gardens, valleys, and forests; and the fairy tale is made flesh in the meshwork of symbols, the realm of emblems, that immediately inaugurates significant events. Instantly, the web of correspondences and the magnetic quality of objects have become talismans, charms, blazons. The exasperating mechanics of *Elective Affinities* are broken up by the splendor of one of these objects: the glass on which chance has interlaced the initials of Eduard and Ottilie.

But it is the landscape above all that opens its most hidden folds in these spiritual states. The geometry of time and space is abolished as if by magic. You walk for hours in a circle, or conversely, you reach the edge of the infinite in a few quick steps. It isn't our state of heightened vigilance that casts a spell on the world around us; it is a much more recondite correspondence between discovering and letting ourselves be discovered—between giving shape and taking shape. Everything already *was*, but today it truly *is*. Today any peasant, pointing in any direction, will sound like a gnome or a fairy, will gesture at the path you nearly took a thousand times without suspecting it. The path that leads to four indescribably white springs suspended on the hillside, protected, for a hundred paces or a thousand miles, by fields of tall fragrant grasses; or to the royal tomb hidden by the Etruscans in a cave now covered with brambles, out of which white hounds and a man the size of an ifrit, carrying a shotgun, emerge; or down below the ridge secretly lighted by the sun, at a bend in the riverbank so deep it casts the whole hanging tangle of pink roots into shadow.

Velvet water that looks motionless and yet moves. Water that runs off into the beyond without flowing, so that it would be enough just to follow it, for that *beyond* which is always forbidden, always intimated in our dreams, is transpiring here and now. But does that *beyond* now matter? Life appears to thrive on the contemplation of the limit—the unavoidable loss, concealment, interruption of vision—like the bird in the Upanishads that looks at the fruit without eating it. A surprising, almost excruciatingly intense taste that combines, perhaps, something of the last, lukewarm prenatal water (already mixed with the crude air of the world) and the strangely wild flavor of fresh water turning salty near an estuary.

It takes a great deal of faith to discern symbols in what has already happened. It takes even more faith to discern them in what will happen later. Because it is always today: all the vanishing lines of existence depart from it—magnetic needles oscillating in every direction, sensitive to every least breeze.

It is not uncommon, in such states, to be visited by a dream. It is the old recurring dream, but it has to some extent changed. More than a dream, it is now a precipitate of dreams in which each figure is illuminated in relation to the others, like those isolate words in a language we've just learned which enchant us without revealing what they mean. But since the meaning is now clear, of course, this time the whole dream—the whole garden of dreams—is open and beckoning to us. Quick glances direct our steps, hands point beyond the thresholds. Behind windowpanes so clear they blind us move the figures of the ones we loved, the ones we've lost, who, behold, stand up from the piano bench or arrange fruit on a table. It all unfolds like a scroll from a mouth known yet unknown, a dark and luminous sentence, an irrefutable commentary set down between past and future.... Such was, perhaps, in the morning of the world, the healing dream dreamt by Asclepius.

But will we enter those rooms? Those shadowy recesses we have awaited so long? Most of the time we won't get beyond the threshold. We won't get beyond the veil of leaves that glisten in the sun like tiny fish in a veil of water. And this time too—does it need to be said?—it's not the dream that stops us, much less waking up; it's the *non licet* of surplus plenitude, the almost mortal happiness of seeing without possessing.

Beginning with this moment (I would like to say: Beginning with this dream), our life is at stake. We have journeyed halfway across the heavens. If the series of veiled annunciations that have followed us so far, like clever talking animals, cannot now be translated into a series of inspired actions, more and more candid choices, more and more good-humored refusals—if from this dream we have not *unlearned seeking* and *learned to find*—then we will certainly never be one of those wise old men who express themselves in images, regally unfolding the fabric of the days like the magic cloak painted with "all the birds and animals and fish and trees and plants and fruits of the earth, and every rock and rarity and shell of the sea, and the sun and the moon and the stars and the planets of the firmament," which could nevertheless pass through the eye of a needle. We will be just one more old man with sweet, melancholy memories: a blind augur and yet still an augur, perhaps unable to supply the ultimate key, the little golden key that deciphers the world—unable to describe a path that isn't dark and difficult, although, in the end, all paths are the same. Still, even if he doesn't know the hidden destination, he certainly knows every pebble, every thistle, every thorn along the way. He knows the secrets of the houses, the human constructions, the animals to be encountered in the twists and turns. A few ragged ends of vision are sufficient: "An olive press, carved from the wood of one big oak. . . . In the evenings, my mother and father played piano four hands: Paisiello, Donizetti. . . . When I was eight years old, they gave me a burnt bay with three white boots. 'White boots three, king's cavalry,' said the stable boy. And they gave my sister two mute ducklings . . ."

The message contained in his words, like the messages in dreams, may seem incoherent, but the secret order that arranges these words is no less perfect.

A Renaissance prince, simply following whims nourished by dreams of power and play, is capable of creating a whole population of fantastical sculptures in his park, unaware he has designed, in that seeming chaos, the perfect initiatory itinerary—a path leading toward a treasure he did not even know existed.

A perfect poem can sometimes capture this moment when the scales are balanced, when opposites, as on the sword's edge or the oar's tip, are reconciled.

The poem reproduces it: in its unmistakable tone, its ancient wisdom, its irrepressible childlike glee. A feeling of fear blends with a feeling of certainty. Questions converse with memories. And the living being, at the central point of his three ages, can pass the time at peace with the dead. He has become like Janus with his two faces, or perhaps like certain arachnids whose multitude of eyes light the way in every direction at once.

True poems have always been rare in human history, and very few are of recent vintage. Perhaps the purest revelation of the plurality of worlds—translated not into parable but into gesture—survives in the noble dramas of Japan: folding screens of disparate landscapes unconnected by time or space, each as solitudinous as it can be, yet all as carefully arranged as a constellation. These plays are, without exception, works of memory and dramas of death. They do not seek the ways of the inexpressible; they offer the inexpressible as the sole presence, just as dreams do: in the gesture that points out a pine along the path, in a sleeve on which the snow has fallen. Yeats noted the mysterious veneration those ancient dramatists (and their public) had for the forest, the spring, the unknown abode, the abandoned sanctuary. In scene after scene, we see the return of those mutilated and yet inexpressibly meaningful images that shocked us as children, that come back to us in dreams, that fairy tales figure as enigmas and the Holy Scriptures raise into the heavens: *locus absconditus, hortus conclusus, fons signatus*. And as it is in memories and dreams, so it is in every work that partakes of the arcane. It is always the same theme we discover, again and again, first as a fragile seed, then as the tree in which a thousand birds can nest: from the *Vita Nuova* to the *Commedia*, from the first to the last pages of Hofmannsthal or Proust.

Out of this long, insatiable love affair, which is never quite broken off and never quite resumed, with the four sister sphinxes—memory, dream, landscape, tradition—comes poetry: the great sphinx whose luminous face is even more inviolable than the dark faces of the others.

At the end of the Japanese drama, destiny was fulfilled, the dead lovers were married, the boat crossed over the lake where the shades of the courtesans sang the song beyond compare. Like water in water, the apparition disappears. It will not be the one to tear away the last veil. But to the child who listens to a fairy tale, to the man who is finishing a poem, to the sleeper who, on the verge of awakening, has passed through the forbidden gate, the eternal has also granted a measure of itself. No more than a measure, of course.

> Now you will come out of sleep,
> You tread the border and nothing
> Awaits you: no, all this will wither away.
> There is nothing here but this cave in the field's midst.
> Today's wind moves in the pines;
> A wild place, unlit, and unfilled.

ON FAIRY TALES

for Cayetan

MYSTERY surrounds the teller of fairy tales. "A popular legend," we find written in a book—but we know that every perfect adventure is an adventure undergone by a single person. We know that only the precious experience that has befallen a unique human being can reflect, like an enchanted cup, the dream of a multitude. An unrepeatable event is a universal story. The greatest depth must be measured from its most superficial point.

It may be that a person who creates fairy tales is a bit like someone who finds four-leaf clovers—that, as Ernst Jünger says, he acquires clairvoyance and augural powers. He starts telling a story to entertain the children and suddenly the fairy tale becomes a magnetic field where the inexpressible secrets of his life and others' converge from every side in the form of figures and images. Then again, whoever is forced by the nature of narrative to make constant use of metaphors will have a hard time avoiding the dangerous, stupendous gift of secret contents, since "in the beginning was the image": a golden vessel awaiting an unknown liquid. As time goes by, he will be able to make better and better, and increasingly subtle, use of this gift—as it always is with gifts. (This is, I believe, the case with someone such as Madame d'Aulnoy.)

The great creator of fairy tales will bring innumerable geological deposits to the splendor of his perfect mineral: the iridescent agate, the deep malachite whose veins, marquetry, and striations seem more like the work of a goldsmith than of water and time. The assurance with which the teller chooses these materials and reassembles them will vary depending on his familiarity with the mystery that dwells at the deepest level of the tale.

That this mystery is always present, in every fairy tale worth remembering, is evident even in the smallest details.

There is, first of all, beauty, in all its measureless variety. Does anyone ever do anything in a fairy tale except for pure beauty? Most of the time this beauty isn't even described, only obliquely evoked: the three oranges that sing and dance, the daughter of the King of the Golden Roof. Beauty and fear—the tragic poles of the fairy tale—are its terms for both contradiction and conciliation. The most carnal terrors fail to distract the fairy-tale hero from the most unreal beauty, and the nature of his lunatic quest is revealed through the quality of the obstacles he must overcome, and the virtues he will need in order to do so. The three theological virtues, yes, but also all four cardinal virtues, and, what's more, the seven gifts of the Spirit.

Even a character who seems merely human, Sinbad the Sailor—that Eastern Odysseus who's already as rich as can be after his first voyage—responds, in his six subsequent voyages, to the bewitching appeal that promptly casts him back, time after time, toward the Leviathan of Fear. Seven times beauty lures him, and seven times fear captures, purges, and reforms him so that, impelled on his first voyage by a verse from Ecclesiastes, "I repented before God," finally he'll declare that "the seventh was the last of the voyages *and the end of all his passions.*"

All through the centuries, the heroes and bards of the absolute fairy tale—the tale of tales—were the saints. Or they were mysterious characters, gentlemen and ladies who graced certain courts with their intellects and, under the guise of love laments or extravagant fantasias, told stories very similar to the stories of the saints. There is no need to recall the lais of Marie de France, which amount to a long, romantic golden legend. Even in the court of the Sun King, fairy tales circulated that were really parables: "Beauty and the Beast," "The White Cat." In the nineteenth century, when the link between fairy tales and mystery had been completely broken, the case of Madame de Ségur is surprising. For after she was done admonishing her children and grandchildren with the travails of innocent, obstinate Sophie (that juvenile personification of de Sade's Justine) and virtuous Blaise, the moment they asked for a fairy tale, she was unexpectedly capable of drawing up two perfect mystical itineraries: "The Story of Blondine, Bonne-Biche, and Beau-Minon" and "Good Little Henry."

If the saga of good little Henry, who, out of filial piety, scales the insurmountable mountain in search of "the plant of life," is a climb up Carmel described with impeccable wisdom in all its seven stations, the story of Blondine is a tale of expulsion from paradise and redemption from original sin, and it makes no difference if the customary erotic reading of the figures remains quite reasonable. There is no level on which an exemplary adventure cannot be read, especially on the literal level, so that even the passage—traditional in mystical treatises—where Blondine goes to sleep one night and wakes up seven years later knowing everything it is humanly possible to know may soon be translated, or so it appears, into astronautical terms. But with one difference: the astronaut will not know any more when he wakes up than he did when he went to sleep, and the meaning of his dream—which is, if not metaphysical, certainly monstrous—will be totally lost. As swiftly as an arrow speeding from the bow, this returns us to our earlier point: the fairy tale needs to be read at every level at once, or else none of them will be entirely plausible.

The impossible awaits the hero of a fairy tale. But how is a person to reach the impossible if not, precisely, by means of the impossible? The impossible is like a word we first read from right to left and, in the next instant, from left to right. Or like a mountain with two slopes: one steep and one gentle. Like the mountain scaled by good little Henry, who on the way up *must* do the impossible time and again, and on the way down *can* do the impossible whenever he feels like doing it, since once he reaches the summit, all the obstacles are transformed into talismans.

This double movement cannot but demand of the fairy-tale hero a perfectly ascetic turn of mind: he must forget all his limits when he contends with the impossible and pay constant attention to these limits when he performs the impossible.

A hero starts down the path of the fairy tale without any earthly hope. The impossible is at first represented by the mountain, and with the simple decision to confront the mountain comes a feeling that serves as an Archimedean point outside the world. "There's nothing I wouldn't do to save my mother" is a symbolic formula, opening the gates to the fourth dimension. Its effect is comparable to what a mystic claims of prayer: it yanks up the mountain by the roots, so to speak, and turns it upside down on its summit. From this moment forward, the hero of the fairy tale is a fool in the eyes of the world.

After such a profession of faith—that is, of disbelief in the omnipotence of the visible—the different ordeals that the hero faces will be no more than means of perfecting and confirming this senseless faith. His feats of fearlessness—jumping through fire, taming dragons, competing in tournaments—are nothing much compared to the painful renunciations of the heart. Setting out in search of beauty, he must devote the tenderest mercies to monsters. If he is noble, he must dress as a beggar or a pilgrim or a servant and become his servant's servant. If he is a lover, he must cede his own nights of love to his rival, the usurper. And then there is the door that cannot be opened, the question impermissible to ask, the beloved face that, the moment one looks at it, dissolves into a scream...

In Italian, certain peaches are said to have a "distinguished soul," meaning the stone is easily dislodged from the pulp. The fairy-tale hero, likewise, is called upon to dislodge his heart from his flesh or, if you will, his soul from his heart. For no one with a heart held fast will ever make his way into the impossible.

This middle province of the fairy tale, between the trials and the liberation, is a world of mirrors par excellence. As at an old court ball, good and evil exchange their masks, and if it's true the smiling queen is really a necromancer, and if it's true a minstrel's hovel hides the magnanimous King Thrushbeard, this will not be revealed until the hero reaches the overworld of imponderable conclusions to which the fairy tale leads: only then will the figures be reassembled in the sumptuous brocade, the perfect atlas of meanings. And yet, from the first, the hero is called upon to interpret this otherworld in filigree, to second the laws implicit in his choices and refusals. No more and no less is asked of him than to dwell simultaneously, somnambulantly, in two worlds.

What will come to the aid of the mortal creature who must pass between these fires and mirrors? The ascetic and mystical writings would answer, in the first place, the memory of the supreme good into which the hero has been initiated ("he thought of his mother... he thought of the wonderful garden"). In the second place, there is no dearth of angels and patron saints, sacraments and sacramentals. Amidst the horrors of the forest, the fairy godmother and the good genie supply the lost man with delicious food and restorative drink; they offer him nuts that contain coaches and handkerchiefs that sop up seas.

Often, thanks to the good works of the past ("The beautiful bird, released, squawked as he flew away: 'I owe you one, Henry!'"), these promises come into play in moments of gravest danger: the moment when weariness is confused with the temptation to look back, to cast a glance at the road already traveled—so long, and so pointless, it seems. Voices pursue the hero along that road, and hands reach out to him. Voices and hands that trouble the mind because they beg for help, they promise tokens of love and gratitude. (The wicked parrot who guards the forbidden rose does not incite Blondine to pluck that rose, he implores her to *release it*.)

To such enticements, there can be only one response: the one that teaches for good and all how to traverse the game of forces at one stroke: "Man does not live on bread alone" or "Thou shalt not tempt..."

The inexorable, inexhaustible moral of the fairy tale is thus victory over the law of necessity, the constant transition to a new order of relationships, and absolutely nothing else, for there is absolutely nothing else to learn on this earth.

The brave little tailor, to beat the horrible giant capable of breaking all his bones with a single breath, throws a bird instead of a stone into the air...

For there is no giant, in the game of forces, that an even bigger giant cannot face down. No treasure is sure to be the only treasure. And is there anything more possible than upstaging one marvelous princess, if the king promises the throne to whoever finds her, with another princess even more alluring?

More ruinous still are the rigged scales—my enemy opened the chest, so I will not open it; my rival was poor, so I will be rich—in the pendulum-like and inevitably ironic motion of the law of necessity, whose oldest ally is ingenuous cunning.

When the cadet prince makes his entrance into the throne room and says, "In all my travels I did not find one princess worthy of my attention, but I have here a little white cat *qui fait si bien patte de velours*," we know right away that he will get the crown.

Anyone who has met a spiritual man, even just once, will recognize this method.

Like the Gospels, the fairy tale is a golden needle suspended from an imponderable, oscillating north, which is continually tilting in different directions, like the mainmast of a ship on a storm-tossed sea.

From time to time, it offers a choice—but a choice hidden behind veils that are never twice the same—between simplicity and wisdom, hardness and softness, memory and salutary forgetfulness. One wins because in a country of dupes and schemers, he was skeptical and secretive; the other because he childishly put his trust in the first person to come along, or even in a band of criminals. "Prudence," the fairy tale exhorts in each line, but the princess who falls into a magical hundred-year slumber can thank the jealous terror of her father the king, and we know that, if we flee from Baghdad, we will find ourselves in Samarkand. No scripture offers precepts that are good forever, or else it would deny life. The enigma is new every time and every time takes a new form; it is never solved except in the decisive moment, the pure gesture—definitively liberated from indigent experience and nourished, day after day, on vision and silence.

Every fairy tale, and every life, is freighted with one central, impenetrable enigma: destiny, election, error. The most glorious adventure may befall the innocent: the meek shepherd, the girl locked in a tower. An imperative force pushes others, the restless ones, to go on journeys with no hope of return, to divest themselves of every possible possession for that other impossible good. Inscrutably, it pushes some toward transgression—toward that "providential error" that clears Blondine's path to victory.

A great number of fairy tales center on such a transgression, but the Comtesse de Ségur described it as no one had before her. Although it appears inextricable, this is one of those terrible false knots that can only be undone by pulling hard on both ends at once. So says the good deer, who has regained the appearance of a fairy godmother thanks to Blondine's error, which is also her redemption:

> Blondine! Blondine!...We could never have resumed our natural appearance if you hadn't plucked the Rose, which I, knowing it was your evil genius, held captive. I placed it as far as possible from the castle in order to shield it from your eyes.... But Heaven is my witness, my son and I would gladly have remained a Deer and a Cat forever in your eyes to spare you the cruel tortures you have had to undergo...

An exchange takes place, in this disaster in the blessed garden, between suffering and liberation, appeal and intercession. Both the deer and the cat, subjugated spirits, sweetly try to avoid it, but they require the redemptive passion of a living creature if they're to be set free.

Oblique and subtle, the fairy tale is obstinately horoscopic as well. Almost as though surging up from a horizon, the fairy godmothers come one after another to the baptism of the newborn princess. Seven planets, twelve constellations, propitious or adverse depending on the parents' merits. Did the queen send out all the invitations she should have? Did she remember the fairy who had shown herself to be a true friend and not pass her over in favor of more powerful fairies?

The planets and constellations seem promising at first. But soon an evil Saturn— the neglected, spiteful fairy—will come darken the sky with her bat-drawn carriage. And what good will the exquisite gifts of the others do if she delivers an inauspicious verdict: The princess will die when she is twenty years old.

Supplications are useless, everything seems lost, when one last fairy—a jovial being who, as it happens, hasn't yet had her say—intervenes with her own little promise. She will not be able to undo the curse, but she will alleviate it by changing its nature. The princess will not die, she will remain mired in a magic sleep for one hundred years before her destiny is fulfilled. Delay, then, not disaster, will preside over the princess's life.

Such is the relationship between the errors of parents and the destiny of children, the imponderable time necessary for a vocation.

Just as horoscopic is the scene of the round dance—what Madame d'Aulnoy, in a popular and arcane turn of phrase, calls "*le branle des fées*." This may be the young fairies' celebration at the vernal equinox or, on the contrary, it may be the Secular Counsel held every hundred years in the clearing of Brocéliande: fate renewing its ties with nature, or a sort of conjunction of spectacular stars.

Fairy-tale heroes, born deformed or very small, are thrown by their mothers, who are determined to obtain the unobtainable, into the center of the round dance, into the thick of their own destiny. Usually the child, after a few moments of foreboding perplexity, is picked up by the fairies. His deformity will not be removed, only elevated to a power. The little man will be granted the ability to penetrate impenetrable places; the armless to discover treasures, auriferous veins, and the whole extent of the underworld, a mirror of the heavens.

The moment the misfortunate one is dedicated—offered up—to the powers, his misfortune is transformed, for himself and for the world, into a key.

Down among the roots and up in the heavens: never have the two directions in which life is sought appeared so exquisite, so outrageously complementary, as in fairy tales.

And yet the aristocratic fairy tale (for what else does "prince" or "princess" mean except a soul singled out?) does not stoop to arrangements of opposites or Jungian androgynies. Nothing, with the exception of the Scriptures, is more radically unsentimental than a fairy tale. In the faces of the twins—the sublime and the abject—the realm of shadow and the realm of light seem densely intermixed. But it's always the contemplative one, the faithful one, who rescues the other:

with his tears that restore sight, his blood that makes thorns bloom, reanimates statues, or reassembles mutilated bodies. Mystical substitution, once so common among the Trappists and the Carmelites, is always, in fairy tales too, the ineluctable premise of the miracle.

Sinbad made it plain: A fairy tale works solely with the raw material of existence, its natural alchemical field. This material is the mystery of character—traceable to the humors, or the stars, or an atavistic inheritance from another fairy tale—which maintains its traits to the end, and can only be transformed by repeating the same errors, suffering the same defeats.

The nature of this mystery is sometimes suggested with enchanting ambiguity. The cadet prince, the last of nine bewitched swans, will, like his brothers, receive a tunic of nettles that can restore him to human form, but it will have only one sleeve: there was no time to finish the other. . . . So he will keep a swan wing his whole life long. He will be one of those rare, disquieting beings who permanently retain the memory of their dark night and their spiritual totem: the painful, regal wing of a swan.

Maturity is, after all, an unforeseeable, lightning-quick, conclusive moment that no man arrives at before his time, even if all the angels of heaven swoop down to help him. In the fairy tale, the hero encounters a series of apparitions that speak eloquently but nevertheless ineffectually. The dove, the little vixen, the old woman with the bundle of brushwood: Do they not all pronounce, one after the other, a single sentence? Do they not reiterate a single warning? How can no one glimpse between the feathers, the red fur, the rags, the blue flash of the Moirai's gowns?

But maturity is not the result of persuasion, much less an intellectual epiphany. It is a sudden, I would almost like to say *biological*, collapse. It is a point that must be reached by all the senses at once if truth is going to be turned into nature.

It is to wake up one morning knowing a new language: signs, seen again and again, become speech. It is Blondine who comes to the end of her long night of slumber knowing everything that can be known. Or: "*Est-ce vous mon prince? Vous vous-êtes bien fait attendre!...*"

And yet children have mysterious senses, attuned to omens and correspondences. At the age of six, it is possible to read fairy tales all day long, but why should there be this stubborn, spellbound circling back to certain images that, later, we will recognize—the recurrent emblems, the veritable blazons, of a life? Beauty and fear. The dialogue, under the dark city gate, between the goose girl and the severed head of a horse:

> "Oh! Falada, 'tis you hang there!"
> "'Tis you, pass under, Princess fair:
> If your mother only knew,
> Her heart would surely break in two..."

A story that may continue to appear in every corner of a life, opened to a new page or unlocked with a new key.

> A tale obscure, a medlar hard,
> Both will be ripened by time and straw.

(Thus, in poetry, the image preexists the idea that will slowly seep into it. For years it may haunt the poet, whatever it may be: fabulous or domestic, dismaying or familiar. Almost always it is an image from early childhood: the bewitching label on an old tree in the park; the return, in waking life and in dreams, of the figure of a woman arranging fruit on a table. Sweet and inscrutable, it patiently waits for a revelation—a destiny—to suffuse it.)

It is worth noting that a writer who attempts a fairy tale unfailingly produces his best prose, becoming a writer even if he has never been one before: almost as if language, when it comes into contact with symbols so universal and particular, so sublime and palpable, cannot help but distill its purest flavor. So that a classic book of fairy tales opens not only the atlas of life for a child but also the atlas of language.

Or perhaps those symbols can only be fully mastered by those who have a feeling for their own language as liturgical as the rite of the Eucharist and as familiar as an ordinary meal?

In this light, the "daily bread" of Luke, which in Matthew tolls as "supersubstantial bread," would cease to seem a philological obscurity and reveal itself as a natural ambiguity. Just as in the rite: where the bread becomes "supersubstantial," the absolute substance.

"The man tossed some incense on a brazier, separated the smoke with both hands, and through that opening the prisoners went out into the garden."

"The old woman approached her and passed the rock before her eyes, moving it from left to right in the air, and the girl saw a wooded valley and a familiar clearing and her lover lying on the grass."

"I dreamed that a word rose up from under the ground. It came from below and passed before me: I looked at it and my hair stood on end."

"When he wandered over the mountains, he ordinarily assumed the appearance of a half-rotted mule. He trotted on his forelegs, his head and neck still covered with skin, dragging the skeletal remains of all his other parts behind him."

Examples of pure creation—of a transmutation of the species by means of the word.

Whom does a marvelous fate befall in fairy tales? He who trusts hopelessly in what is beyond hope. Hope and trust must not be confused. They are different things, as the expectation of fortune here on earth is different from the second theological virtue. He who blindly, obstinately repeats "let us hope" does not trust; he is really only hoping for a lucky break in the momentarily propitious game governed by the law of necessity. Those who trust, on the other hand, do not count on particular events, for they are sure there is an economy that encompasses all events and surpasses their meaning the way a tapestry, a symbolic carpet, surpasses the flowers and animals that compose it.

In the fairy tale, the victor is the madman who reasons backward, who reverses the masks, who discerns the secret thread in the fabric, the inexplicable play of echoes in a melody; he who moves with ecstatic precision in the labyrinth of formulas, numbers, antiphons, and rituals common to the Gospels, fairy tales, and poetry. He believes, like the saint, that a person can walk on water, that a fervent spirit can leap over walls. He believes, like the poet, in the word, from which he can conjure concrete wonders. *Et in Deo meo transgrediar murum.*

At first the madman's faith may be ascetic or mystical, but over time it at last becomes apostolic. After his descent into the inferno or his ascent of Carmel, "good measure . . . running over" awaits him, and the whole world too. Not only the object of his impossible love but all the other objects he was able to renounce in his quest. Not only his own life, which he does not wish to save, but the lives of all those who have taken part—for good or ill—in the holy adventure. When the spell is broken, the forest comes alive with figures. Bluebeard's wives emerge, pale as ghosts, from their bath of blood. Even the clever little animals, who have served the hero like so many subtle instincts, reacquire human grace and dignity. . . . A new world, and new heavens, come into being around a spirit that has been transformed.

TWO

LES SOURCES DE LA VIVONNE

AMONG the innumerable disappointments whose black threads crisscross the carpet of his poem, Marcel Proust, as many readers will know, includes a destination: *les sources de la Vivonne*. He arrives there with his friend Gilberte (they are both past forty) after a lifetime of dreams revolving around those springs, and instead of something supernatural—say the entrance to the underworld—what does he see? "A sort of rectangular basin in which bubbles rose to the surface."

This glacial phrase, in which Proust seems to want to compress, or contain, like a giant in a bottle, his great fluvial dream, may have the opposite effect. It may, indeed, arouse a sort of holy terror. The presence of the immense in the small is infinitely subtler and more terrifying than the dilation of the small into the immense. Leopardi must have thought as much when he shivered at the extreme smallness—and precisely because of the extreme smallness—of Tasso's tomb.

I recall an image arguably akin to Proust's basin: an old photograph of the source of the Tiber. Two mountain boots flank, like the feet of the Colossus of Rhodes, the tiny vein that gushes, a tender bud, from a cleft between crystalline snow and black stones. Such an image is inexhaustibly wonderful. I think the little gate of Mycenae must look just as wonderful after Aeschylus and above all *The Iliad*, in which a warrior's sandal can overshadow a whole page. Most terrifying in *The Iliad* is the wild fig tree that marks the edge of the three mortal circles that the crown prince describes around his kingdom, or the deserted washing pools "of smooth-laid stone" near the gates of that kingdom—not the catalogues of great lifeless bodies or the beloved friend's funeral pyre.

In his treatise on the art of making gardens, an English gentleman gave the palm to the Italians for the beauty and harmony of proportions they nobly conceal behind modest walls. "If care has been taken," he observes, "to make the expectation less than the reality, we shall have the added thrill of wonder." In every country, this is a golden rule, but what if we turn it on its head? "If care has been taken to make the reality less than the expectation..." Here lies the magic threshold, the silk thread that no sword can cut and that, in the sagas of King Laurin, defends his priceless realms. The three greats of the Medici family understood this completely. After impressive welcoming ceremonies, they would astonish Byzantines, Lombards, and Romans alike with the sublime austerity of their rustic palace. The "north star" that guided that mysterious dynasty could be called, in a certain sense, the genius of litotes.

A child reading a book is promised he is going to see a king: luminous word. But the shrewd, sibylline fairy tale knows better than he: "The heralds blew their trumpets, the golden doors flew open, and the king appeared, pale and sad, without scepter or crown, all dressed in mourning."

(The realm of the fairy tale, as someone has said, may be a realm of ecstasy, but it is above all a land of pathos and of symbols of sorrow.)

To seek out the first earthly form of a mythical image, to trace its long, rather vague lines back to the incorruptible solidity of the real, is a road to truth that turns into pathos as soon as one starts unwinding, like threads of mist, the dreams that the generations have wound. The entrance to the workshops of the wizard Mandrone, on I know not which peak of the Adamello Alps, or to King Laurin's mines in the Rosengarten—places beyond which whole clans of shepherds have gone missing, which have been versified in octets, which have made their way into fables told around the fire—have, also, been photographed. The first is a diamond-shaped hole whose almost mystical walls, blocks of pure ice, are darkened by the black firmament of the mountain above. The other is a horizontal fissure almost level with the ground, half hidden by a spur and blocked up with debris (which legend has it King Laurin amassed there in the days of his disdain for mankind). One must imagine the ancient climber ascending those peaks. One must imagine the moment when he stops, suspended on the rock face, swaying near the last cliff, and his brief, intoxicated vision of those recesses—the subject of so many painful dreams—among the gusting mists and the black mantle of the storms...

In the books that collect what still remain of these sagas, the passages that most fascinate a child are often, strangely enough, the mournful conclusions: "Today, only two piles of stones mark the place on the plateau where the atrium of the Vaglianella Palace once stood..." Or: "Today, the hut among the forget-me-nots no longer exists. The shepherds who pass through the Val Travegnòl point to the blue meadow and say to one another: 'Look, in the old days that's where the *tambra de selièttes* (the hut among the forget-me-nots) used to be...'"

At an exhibition of Eastern treasures, it is still plausible to think the eye might wander from the ceramics, statues, and invincible swords over to a glass case where, scorched and mutilated from the torso down, looking like a lizard without a tail, sits the little lion made of lapis lazuli "salvaged from the ruins of the palace of Persepolis, after the fire set by Alexander the Macedonian." Almost as unlikely as this, after all, is the fact that, on a plain in Sicily, a truck driver in his overalls still brakes in the middle of a desert stretch of land and points out to the stranger, on an ancient wall, "the hoofprint of Rinaldo di Montalbano's horse." What does this man see in that little crater? The charismatic presence of the past? The token of a perfect vision never to be seen again, but consigned to a stone by the dead? Certainly, in such signs, something was cast forever, with a subtle smile, like Prospero's wand into the depths of the sea.

Somewhere in Europe, one can visit the wobbly, peeling schoolboy's table on which a great poet wrote the bulk of his work. That table rests in a little wrought-iron hut, a "solitude" several meters from a hunting lodge, under the thick foliage of some peach trees. Anyone who looks at it seems to see the pillar of that poet's universe rising up from under those three inches of wood and towering majestically: its palaces like inexhaustible enigmas, its mazes and merchants, its prisoners "of the highest station." Exactly like a pillar of oil, spouting from the corner of a peach orchard, capable of setting whole fleets and cities into motion.

Not everyone has seen the holy places, and yet everyone can imagine the pious man's encounter with the four stones that were the Temple of Solomon, the tower from which the Redeemer was tempted to throw himself. Or the rock (which was venerated in I forget which sacred enclosure) where his divine feet left their mark as if in moist clay.

That the Valley of Josaphat, the theater of the extreme responses reported by Joel, is in reality a modest basin to the east of Jerusalem, crossed by the fragile thread of the Kidron, makes it no less terrifying than the "rolled-up scroll" to which Joel himself, taking the opposite approach and shrinking it down to what can be held in two hands, compares the heavens in the hour when space will cease to be.

(These, I suppose, are the vertices of the pyramid. At whose base, perhaps—blind, petrified, and equally terrifying—lies the trilobite of the Primary Era. Here, you can hold in your palm, with its menacing geometry and atrocious elegance, like Chinese armor, the first draft of life on a dead star...)

Little sites in ruins, battered by every wind and corroded by millennia of rain. Silhouetted cliffs, gateways to forests that sent forth, in bolts of lightning, and maelstroms of mist, and bright full moons, the apparitions that gave the old world its terrors and songs. Cocoons of perennial wisdom, tiny icons of immense ceremonies: What was their mission? Life undoubtedly sprang from them if the pilgrims and crusaders proclaimed them from one end of the earth to the other—if monks wrote about them for centuries, on pale animal skins, in large letters of gold. The poet fixed his gaze on them the way one might stare at a red wax figurine pierced by a pin: to invest it with the suppliant energies of love, or to elicit from it whatever lies between all that cannot be said and all that man, once again, is going to try to say...

Proust's painful inability to savor the true face of wonderment is typical of a modern poet. He cannot follow that inverse path from the infinite to the finite—from the deserts that the wind is always wearing away to the little Black Stone in the forbidden enclosure at Mecca. He codifies the laws (already in effect for more than a century) of *rêverie*: the incapable and culpable longing that "is greater than the real." But only the true is greater than the real, and still the real makes us tremble when we see it: so small, so touchable, so corruptible. It is, besides, the only envelope granted to vision. Vision alone does not let itself be dreamed of but only venerated with tears of joy, when it deigns to appear. (How small and strange, intense and imperfect, the face of the Countess of Tripoli must have been, for Jaufré Rudel to die with a smile on his lips!)

We open Dante's book searching for the passage that, in our memory, is a Mosaic tablet explaining and sealing certain destinies on this earth and beyond, and we discover it contained in a tercet. After slowly constructing one of his Cities of God upon the keyboard, it is not unusual for Bach to bring us back once more to the cornerstone: four little notes.

Today one is constantly hearing the naive phrase, "I can't tell you how big it is." And in fact it cannot be told. Can the mind take in the colossal? Does it mean anything to the imagination (that sleeping flower which suddenly opens such pitiless valves) that the thermal radiation radius around the atomic blast at X measures twenty kilometers, that the missile launched from the base of Y weighs ninety tons, that the stadium of Z is capable of holding half a million spectators?

A few inches tall, with stern, knowing eyes, King Laurin terrifies and moves us, while the fate of Goliath or Polyphemus makes us laugh.

"I can't tell you how small it is," said my friend, perplexed and ecstatic after coming back from the shore of Cumae that Virgil described so exactly, down to its "foul-smelling" gorge.

"I can't tell you how big it is," is what he meant. He was thinking of the eternity contained in that small patch of sand and nauseating earth: the entrance to the underworld, the matrix of poetry, and the first root of a race.

Proust is the first historian of an unhappy era—the era of "bigger, and even bigger, but by how much? I don't know…" And there's no doubt his poem wouldn't be what it is without his lament for the sense of wonder now lost. (A lament that a past master of misfortune, Tasso for example, would not have been able to comprehend: he who, in the madhouse, harkened once more to the wondrous, innocent music of the *Della famiglia*.)

How can a masterpiece take root and grow on such an illusory measure of the universe—on this blind prerequisite mourning of the heart?

And yet Proust, a man mutilated from the first, continues to be implacably a poet. He understands, like all the poets who preceded him (as Leopardi, a man mutilated in a different fashion, understood), that the way of poetry is one and goes only one way. That it is nothing other than reverence for the theological meaning of the limit: the directive to work in imitation of God—from Sinai to the burning bush, from Tabor to a little bite of Bread.

(What is a dogma finally if not a circle traced, as if by a diamond point, by the seven-times purified word, around something that cannot be said?)

The only guarantee of mystery is the unrepeatable luminosity of a real object in which a spirit has momentarily taken up residence. And if it may be said yet again, what is Proust's poetry if not infinitely unrelenting reticular analysis, galactic thought, applied to the singular and concrete object: the *metaphor*, the precise, incandescent similitude? "The Guermantes never seemed so boundless," one writer has recalled, "as in that simple red G on the black cloth into which Robert de Saint-Loup disappears at the end, like a pagan god wrapping himself in his cloud…"

By expanding the boundaries of the object, by snipping the silk thread that encircled the kingdom, man has sent his sublime guests packing. But this is another act of violence that no one is very eager to discuss.

NIGHTS

I. THE STORY OF THE CITY OF BRASS*

> In the seventh century of the Hegira, in the outskirts of
> Bulaq, I transcribed in careful calligraphy, in a language
> I have forgotten, in an alphabet I do not know, the seven
> adventures of Sinbad and the story of the City of Brass ...
> —JORGE LUIS BORGES, "The Immortal"

> I am not sure if I ever believed in the City. . . . I think that
> at the time the task of seeking it was enough.
> —JORGE LUIS BORGES, "The Immortal"

THE BOOK called *The Thousand and One Nights* is, as everyone
knows, a labyrinth with a thousand entrances. At times this labyrinth
seems concentric, and one center might be—as in the labyrinths of
long ago it was the enigma of the mirror—the desolate and sibylline
legend of the City of Brass.

It is strangely difficult to arrive at this story that, according to the
numbering now generally accepted, was recounted by Scheherazade
late on the 556th night. After having perused five or six copies of the
old book, you may still not find it. There is always an exquisite comic
tale or a delightful moral fable not far away; and after you finish "The
Seventh Voyage of Sinbad," which directly precedes the legend of the

---

*The title of this tale is in reality "The Story of the Djinns and the Demons Sealed
in the Bottles from the Time of Solomon (Blessing and Health Be Upon Him)."

city, it is only natural to close the volume lost in thought. On the other hand it seems some of these tales shift around at night, as in certain unfinished canvases by Leonardo on which the marvelous white horse never appears to be quite where we left him the previous evening. Borges mentions, for example, a terribly circular 602nd night during which Scheherazade tells the king her own story, thereby rendering the book infinite. And the atrocious adventure that Hofmannsthal refers to as the "Tale of the 672nd Night" is well known. But if we look for these great parables where the two poets found them, it will be in vain.

Many other Nights seem deliberately to lead us through the labyrinth to this possible center in the City of Brass, although some Nights lengthen and others shorten the way. We encounter mirages and omens of the city several times before we reach it. There is "Iram of the Pillars," which the Koran also mentions, perfect and white in the middle of the desert—and next to it the tomb of the melancholy king who wished to make it a mirror of the delights of paradise but died, struck by lightning, before he set foot in it. There are the halls of the forbidden castle in the city of Toledo where the motionless horde of Arab horsemen, all made of stone, "with their eyes turned toward the west," prophesizes the invasion of Spain. In there, in the darkness, lie Solomon's treasures: the emerald table, the magic mirror, the book of Psalms written in Greek on golden pages, the unfathomable treatises on herbs and poisons, stones and stars. Finally, there is the immense legend of "Hasib Karim al-Din and the Queen of the Serpents": a delirious cosmogony that one feels rather presumptuous calling a "tale," unless we would give the same name to certain passages in Revelation.

We are now far from the delightful couple—the Caliph and the Vizier in merchant dress—linking story with story and night with night like Ursa Major, or the masked duke, "the old fantastical duke of dark corners," who links scene with terrible scene in *Measure for Measure*. We are far from the alleys full of fetid smells and adventures pursued in the tinkling footsteps of the Christian confidante or the Nubian slave. Far from the coolness of the secret courtyards, human lives bought back with a tale, and the "erotic pantomime of lovers." From the interior to the exterior—or from the exterior to the interior—once the lamps are doused and the moon has set, we proceed toward a land of relentless, overpowering sunlight, where nothing seems to cast a shadow. The enormous sensuality of the *Nights* has dissolved like incense smoke. Already, in the fourth and sixth adventures of Sinbad, we detected the odor of the tomb. But "The Story of the City of Brass" may be the only tale among a thousand in which the mortal whims of the senses are no more than a distant strain of melancholy music—the memory of a shadow that disappeared centuries ago from the face of a sundial. Only the eyes of the horsemen riding toward the city are continually entranced, but do they comprehend the reality of what, in the bewildering light, appears so much larger than it is? As in prophetic dreams, the air is but a boundless void, and at the same time as dense as a cloud of fire. Time and space have been "rolled up like a scroll," as they will be at the Second Coming, and in the purplish dark the Word revolves alone. We leave behind the crowded, sleepless cities and go out into the desert, the kingdom of God.

This—the desert—is almost the only reality experienced in this story, not only by the anguished soul but by the nostrils, the pores, the taste buds. There is an acrid smell of wool and hemp, and dust beneath the teeth, and sweat-scorched hides, all archaic and brutal (as in that other inconsolable journey to the City of Brass, *Seven Pillars of Wisdom*).

Almost the only reality, I say, because there is another: the reality of metal. The big abandoned armories, the Brass Horseman who stands guard along the way, the very walls of the city that suddenly rise "like a mass of iron cast in a mold," the funerary tablets made of iron and silver that wail, commemorate, and admonish in every corner of that lifeless place. Everywhere is metal, mystical and wild: almost the mark or the insignia of Solomon, the secret lord of this story. Indeed, the Holy Books say—and it is clear today from the mines of Palestine, where Eusebius chronicled the Christian martyrs whose eyes were gouged out and whose feet were mutilated—that the monarch was expert in every metal and that God set "the fountain of brass" flowing for him.

Where is the city found? Curiously, it is never named—not until it is so close that it acts like a magnet on the merry cavalcade traveling, beneath its white Damascene banners, toward a wholly different destination. No one in the group then seems to remember that they had set out in quest not of the City of Brass, nor of any other city, but rather of certain bottles, also made of brass, in which Solomon sealed up the genies who refused his authority before hurling them into the sea.

They started out from Syria heading "toward the West," and—though there was an uncharted West beyond the Maghrebi lands then ruled by the procession's leader and the hero of the story, Emir Musa—it is, in any case, a strange West, where the genies take the shape of sphinxes. But somewhere in the desert the towering Brass Horseman diverts the procession "in a direction other than that wherein they were journeying." But in *which* direction? Toward the deserts of Libya, Egypt, even Judea? Are they advancing on this journey, or retreating? "Two years and some months hither and back," the mysterious spiritual leader of the procession, Sheikh Abd-al-Samad, had predicted. Soon after, these years were contracted into days, then dilated again into an immeasurable length of time. But hadn't "the very ancient man shot in years and broken down with the lapse of days" uttered the formula familiar to all those who travel in such strange dimensions: "the road is long and difficult, and the ways few. . . . It is full of hardships and terrors and things wondrous and marvelous"?

A map of this journey, should anyone wish to draw it, would appear no less absurd, and no less reasonable, than the map drawn by the great medieval cartographer who pictured the earth "sometimes as a disc in the middle of the ocean and sometimes scattered upon the waters like leaves from a branch." Isn't this how the earth looks to us on every appreciable journey—like a circle, a spiral, a star, a few leaves from a branch? In time and space, the City of Brass does not seem all that different from the castle of Monsalvat where the Holy

Grail was kept; the Marquis de Villa Nova wrote that it resembled an island floating, now here, now there, on one point or another of the land or sea.

(In the course of her thousand nights, might Scheherazade not narrate certain events that won't take place until centuries later—such as this one, here, which we have before our eyes?)

Then there comes a moment when the City of Brass seems to double itself. The men think that they have already entered, but no, this is only the ante-city, a prefiguration of the real one, just as a trivial dream prefigures a meaningful dream, or a specious love a true love. Dividing the horsemen from the City of Brass is an impervious wall with twenty-five gates, "but not one can be seen, nor is there any sign of them." And it is only natural that everyone should notice this and no one say it. It is only natural that the funerary tablets, which suddenly shimmer on the far side of the wall, should be far away and close, seven in number and three, in Greek and in languages that have never existed. And the great forgotten names on the tablets, the names of fallen and scattered sovereigns, Persian and Amalekite and Indian kings, are the "last reports / of greatness fallen into dust and clay." One thing flows into another, and it all tumbles violently together: as in Emir Musa's "hard sob" as he stands unmoving atop the wall, or the crazed laughter of his soldiers who, clapping their hands, throw themselves over the side of the wall. So we often fall, weeping and laughing, into the center of life when "the living and the dead, the sleeping and the wakeful, the ancient and the new are within us and are all, once again, the same."

So we all fall—characters, reader, narrator—into a narrower, deeper, more interior labyrinth, in which Solomon's bottles are the only lodestone: like Proserpina's hyacinth or the first tale that Scheherazade tells King Shahryar, immured in his sanguinary dream.

In the erotic stories of the *Nights*, we proceed in a similar fashion: through alleys and squares, storehouses and courtyards, up to the innermost room and the longed-for bed. At the center of the city, too, there is a room and a bed, "and on the bed lay a damsel, as she were the lucident sun, eyes never saw fairer."

Now the bed on which the damsel lay, had steps, and thereon stood two statues of Andalusian copper representing slaves, one white and one black. The first held a mace of steel and the second a sword of watered steel which dazzled the eye...

But around this bed we will hear no tinkling glasses or lutes, no happy, luscious laughter. It is with the voice of an engraved tablet that the princess, too, recounts her own death, intones her great admonition, her pure and awe-inspiring *de contemptu mundi*. It is the most serious of the recitatives, the most heartrending of the arias in that majestic series of arias and recitatives that mark the travelers' passage into the sepulchral city. Quicksilver sparkles in her eyes "which seem to follow them from left and right." The void given form, the end of all vanity, she lies there, as though deep within the center of the human heart, which everyone must traverse at least once in his life, or, as the saints advise, at least once each day:

> O child of Adam, let not hope make mock and flyte at thee,
> From all thy hands have treasured, removed thou shalt be;
> I see thou covetest the world and fleeting worldly charms,
> And races past and gone have done the same as thou I see.
> Lawful and lawless wealth they got; but all their hoarded store,
> Their term accomplished, naught delayed of Destiny's decree.
> Armies they led and puissant men and gained them gold
>   galore;
> Then left their wealth and palaces by Fate compelled to flee,
> To straitness of the grave-yard and humble bed of dust
> Whence, pledged for every word and deed, they never more
>   win free:
> As a company of travellers had unloaded in the night
> At house that lacketh food nor is o'erfain of company:
> Whose owner saith, "O folk, there be no lodging here for you";
> So packed they who had erst unpacked and fared hurriedly:
> Misliking much the march, nor the journey nor the halt,
> Had aught of pleasant chances or had aught of goodly greet,

Then prepare thou good provision for to-morrow's journey
stored,
Naught but righteous honest life shall avail thee with the
Lord!

Probably it was necessary for the men to come this far in order to understand the futility of their journey. Neither Emir Musa nor the caliph who sent him will make use of Solomon's bottles, when these are finally found. Don't those who seek knowledge to increase their own power eventually discover that power is laughable? They become prisoners of their knowledge who can only free themselves by turning their backs on power and—like Emir Musa at the end of this journey—setting out on a pilgrimage to "the Holy City of Jerusalem." It happens, in every fairy tale, that when you set out to get one thing, you mysteriously receive another.

By this point, it will already be clear that "The Story of the City of Brass" is no more than a musical interpretation, or a dance, of Ecclesiastes. We know that the obedient genies constructed palaces of all sorts for Solomon, as well as statues, and plates as big as swimming pools, and that they dove down to pluck pearls from the seabed for him. Certainly, that prophet dominated the cosmos and "interpreted God in perfect truth" because he knew, as no one before him had known, the infinite vanity of domination: he, the great skeptic, perfectly detached.

Remember now thy Creator in the days of thy youth, while the evil days come not, nor the years draw nigh, when thou shalt say, I have no pleasure in them.... Or ever the silver cord be loosed, or the golden bowl be broken, or the pitcher be broken at the fountain, or the wheel broken at the cistern. Then shall the dust return to the earth as it was: and the spirit shall return unto God who gave it.

The wise king seems to have placed the bottles where they are sure to attract Emir Musa, a man worthy of seeing the truth, to the City of Brass. God-fearing and steadfast in his obedience (he is the only one to suggest abstention: from the city, from the body of the princess), as prompt to lament as he is to give praise ("Verily, we were created for a mighty matter!"), the noble Emir dies and is reborn in the city. The journey has journeyed with him, and the remote destination toward which he has traveled, beyond the mountains and the plains—isn't it precisely "the cavern of the heart"? Such is one of the names that Islamic mysticism gives the desert, "a place where injustice does not reign, a place of encounters, temptations, revelations." Afterward, it is entirely fitting—and immaterial—that he conquer Spain, as he historically did. (The inconsistent, or encoded, legend does not contradict this when it assures us, in stark contrast with the history books, that he remained in prayer until the end of his days in "the Holy City of Jerusalem.")

Only the man who set the whole machinery of the adventure in motion—the courtier Talib—will not return to Damascus. The labyrinth engulfs those who walk through it for profane purposes. Indispensable and useless, he will place his hand on the body of the princess and die the death promised, in "Hasib Karim al-Din and the Queen of the Serpents," to whoever dares touch the body of Solomon, seated on his throne in his green priestly vestments, wearing the sacred tetragram on one finger of the hand that lies open on his heart.

For the princess has momentarily become the Wise King. Who else looks out from behind those cold and sparkling quicksilver eyes? That her face is a simulacrum, the face of a well-crafted doll, is a thought that can't help but enter Talib's head. But his head and his voice alike abandon him a few seconds later. Such is the figure's reply:

He mounted the steps to the bed between the pillars, but when he came within reach of the two slaves, lo! the mace-bearer smote him on the back and the other struck him with the sword he held in his hand and lopped off his head, and he dropped down dead.

All the stories of Solomon, the Prince of Brass, insist on the other-worldly quality of his power, which extends (like that of Hermes Trismegistus, the Lord of Mercury) beyond the realm of life. Over the whole huge book of the *Nights*, one way or another, the great name casts its shadow. Whether or not this king was the author of Proverbs, Ecclesiastes, and the Songs of Songs, a pillar of fire certainly lit his way if these three texts, and the hundred legends that surround them, spontaneously coalesced around his name, like fragments of some marvelous Atlantis. The Spirit, as we know, bloweth where it listeth and composes its figures however it sees fit.

The city has twenty-five gates, "but not one can be seen, nor is there any sign of them." This reading is only one conjectured gate, and, naturally, the most obvious one.

2. FLYING CARPETS

The book of the *Nights* is piled high with carpets. Often they serve as a ceremonial center. Everything happens, as it were, on top of them. Solomon flies on a carpet to do battle with the rebel genies while the birds dart above him and the beasts walk below, in the carpet's shadow. A cunning lover rolls herself up in a carpet to enter her master's room, and corpses are concealed in another rolled-up carpet (the perfect horror of "The Story of the Three Apples"!). Men and women sleep, make love, play mellifluous instruments, and above all tell stories and pray on carpets. "And looking timidly in at the door, she saw a small chapel where a young man, kneeling on a carpet, recited the Holy Koran in a sweet-sounding voice."

Here we are dealing with the small, light prayer carpet pious Muslims carry with them on their travels so that no matter where they go they will, during their five daily invocations, always enjoy the purity of a privileged space, untouched by an infidelious foot. The curved arch of this carpet is the "prayer niche," which is to be turned in the direction of Mecca: a ritual synthesis of a mosque with a votive lamp suspended in the center, or a lustral amphora upside down and overflowing with flowers—usually three carnations. It is a little verse from the Koran that almost always provides the most bizarrely, lyrically eloquent decoration. Metaphysical rules bind the Islamic carpet in its aversion to representational images. Like any artwork of consummate wisdom, they imprison such images in the unforgiving beauties of a disdainful stylization: the price and fruit of a rigorously traditional contemplative education.

But why does the carpet fly? In Western tales, it is common enough for a princess to wake up "in her own bed, a thousand miles from her father's kingdom, in a palace she has never seen before." And the winged horse, an astral and fatidic creature, is familiar at many latitudes. But the flying carpet remains unique, and marvelously inexplicable.

There are some fascinating books about the art of the carpet that answer, like oracles, almost any question one could ask about the genealogies and meanings of these spaces made of wool densely knotted, then cut and shorn, which, finally, unfurl their fervent narrative tangles, their pure mental geometries, before our eyes. These books tell stories of carpets that are nineteen centuries old, like that perfect Persian carpet found in a royal tomb in the Altai Mountains, whose ten thousand kilometer journey allows us to credit completely the existence of the incredible Silk Road. As we turn the pages, we see the immemorial geography of the carpet expanding, and with it the geography of the *Nights*, whose stories were woven from the same migrations and minglings: Turks and Greeks, Jews and Persians, Arabs and Egyptian Gypsies, Syrians, Armenians, Circassians, Kurds, Turkomans, Tartars, Mongols. And the same geologic column stretches on for millennia—from the mythical carpet of Ctesiphon to the modern carpet, which is imperturbably similar to the ancient one.

"A harsh, dry climate, a copious abundance of wool and flocks, the need for fast and easy transport" bring about the aesthetics and techniques. The different levels of private and spiritual life blend together in the carpet, making it an exquisitely complete miniature of tradition, which excludes nothing as long as it is contemplated in its utmost purity.

Who, ordinarily, weaves the carpet? The cities of Persia—the carpet province of choice, although the art is as vast and diverse as the East itself—create and propagate carpet schools wherever there are sources of fresh running water. The "carpet masters," those itinerant bards of the loom, wander, like storytellers of old, from village to village and region to region, lavishing the local artisans with the treasures of their prodigious memory, stocked with countless compositional patterns. And everywhere there is the singular visionary, able to hold the dreams of the generations in the hollow of his hand: a nomad who has seen more than he could say and who has a good deal stored up in his heart; a weaver slave uprooted from his homeland whose nostalgia, served by winged hands, is worth his weight in gold; a poet who grasps connections and harmonizes figures with an irreducibly discriminating instinct for the rhythm of objects and spiritual styles; a mystic, finally, whose carpet soaks up prayers and fasts, who dedicates the symbolic ex-voto, dictated to him by his devotion, to He who, as he knotted and snipped the multicolored wools, deigned to grace the warp with a ray of his splendor. A genius, in a word, who is always a genius of the type indicated by his name: a mind inhabited by a demon, which boldly combines the biological, intellectual, and spiritual energies it has inherited. The superb human specimen capable of tying the Senneh carpet's ten thousand knots in one square decimeter of space without losing sight of an overall vision of bright herons and pink flamingos: "an eternity in microscopic space" that ought to dismay us, if we stop and consider what meditative beauties the regal anonymity of yore used to cover the ground where man walked and what our contemporary destitution now raises to the level of his eyes.

They reveal to us, these enchanting books, what we always seem to have known. For nothing that cannot be read in many ways is capable of holding our attention for very long. And the Oriental carpet is one of those objects that (following one famous definition of great art) a person could be locked up in prison with for many years without going crazy. Above all, the books reveal to us that the carpet is a language and that, if a person understands this language, he can read a Bokhara as a resplendent, blood-red poem, the way a heraldist friend of mine once started reading, with astounding speed, the tangled family sagas told by a suite of armorial bearings on the wall of a church.

Traditions have an unconquerable abhorrence of the vague, the sentimental, the gratuitous. Precepts and prohibitions passed down from generation to generation implicitly condemn, in the humblest craftsmanship, any sort of fantasy. Like the fairy tale or the parable, the carpet stubbornly refuses to engage with anything other than the real, and only by way of the real does it arrive at its spiritual geometries and contemplative mathematics. Talking about symbolism in carpets is no less puerile than talking about symbolism in fairy tales and parables, since senses and super-senses are woven together there just as tightly as warp and weft, and in them each man—as in that ancient teacher's stories that no person heard in full, yet every hearer felt to be perfect and complete—will read the message destined for him and him alone.

The mind contemplating a carpet can come gently to rest in this subjective objectivity, as it might in a forest animated by a hidden spring. The studied measurements, the concentric design, the restorative purity of colors distilled from nature and cooled in running waters, transform the carpet into a fulcrum of contemplation in some cases worthy of comparison with the sacred mandala. The inexhaustible combinations of a never-random chance make it, furthermore, a supremely living dead language: we possess the key to certain phrases but not to the whole discourse, which we cannot understand except by consulting other languages—and nomadism multiplies possible meanings to infinity. If in China the triangle suggests the fulfillment of desire, in Central Asia it can only represent the nomad's tent; the Indian scorpion is a salutary amulet that wards off leprosy, but in the

Caucasus it speaks of the disdainful courage of those who kill themselves before surrendering, and in China—secretly, elegantly—of the dissatisfaction felt by the educated. By forbidding the representation of animate beings, Islamic orthodoxy juxtaposes allusive symbols with natural motifs. In a transitory city of caravans, the Caucasian craftsman will, with thrilling nonchalance, incorporate Buddhist metaphysical symbols into the prayer niche, and make interpretation even more difficult when he takes it into his head to weave, with votive intentions, the tools of his trade: bone combs and wooden rods.

As in the old Gregorian liturgy, it is the colors that lay the symbolic groundwork of the carpet. The golden yellow extracted from the sumac, an ancient token of the fortune and grandeur the sun spreads at our feet, is offered to the Indian lord in search of rest. The green that shines on the Prophet's banner, as well as on the turbans of the faithful sanctified by the pilgrimage to Mecca, is, in Turkey, reserved for the prayer carpet. Blue, the essence distilled from indigo in Persia, evokes, if dark, meditation on the eternal; if pale, romantic melancholy. And as for the harsh, aggressive black symbolic of revolt, it is the virile hue par excellence, which the Mongol hordes chose as their emblem.

The discourse of the figures is woven on top of this primary poetic field: the divine acumen of the lizard, the spiritual regeneration of the pine cone, the capricious fortune that wings speedily away in the delirious flight of the bat. The Chinese vase contains spiritual happiness, and the orchid sweet death. The five-legged dragon recalls the formidable majesty that terrified Confucius at the sight of the emperor. The symbol takes ever tighter hold of the absolute: in the sacred cup of the lotus, the tree of life like a flaming candelabra (axis of the world, vertical path between man and divinity), the immortal peacock that so often opens the infinite circle of its tail on Christian sarcophagi of the first centuries. In the Christian provinces of Asia, where the animal world was excluded from the ceremonial carpets that decorated the churches, the prayer niche might feature a stylized cathedral door or bishop's miter. The cryptographies of the Oriental carpet, in turn, insinuated themselves into the adornments of the churches. Even in the lands of the Medici, whose disdain for exoticism limited the loads of their ships to Greek spices and books, someone has recognized echoes of the carpet: on the facade, for example, of the Badia Fiesolana. Those austere Florentines never wished to hide the ascetic elegance of their terra-cotta floors with Oriental rugs, it's true, but they had beautiful ones painted at the feet of their Madonnas.

The silent dignity of the carpet's geometric figures—both the simple ones (the Chinese square missing one side: a door left hospitably open) and the emblematic ones (three spheres arranged in a triangular pattern, alluding to clouds and thunder: the mark of Genghis Khan)—become marvelously complicated in the arabesques of classical Arabic script or its angular version, the Kufic, which so readily disguises itself as simple decoration. "Let her throw me at her feet and walk all over me, for I have wound a hundred glorious formulas from every tongue around my shuttle": so a sixteenth-century Persian carpet, preserved in Munich, covertly recounts its amorous exploits. Another, housed in Milan, speaks a different language: "Here is the path that leads to the wellspring of life, where even the wild animals have a refuge."

By its nature, poetry proceeds from shape to shape, and the motifs are indeed sometimes hidden one inside the other, or one behind the other, acrostically. In what appears to be the mere red-black fret of a border, the jaws of a fantastical beast emerge, and out of these jaws sprouts a sapling, where a goldfinch, about to launch itself gracefully into flight, is hidden by a leaf of the branch on which it perches. As in a poem, the transition is not only from shape to shape but from kingdom to kingdom: the illustrious, mysterious oval palmette so common in Oriental carpets, the *boteh*, now becomes an almond, now a flame, now a pearl, and, never symmetrical, graced with the slight, sublime distortions of nature, it curves here to the right, there to the left, combining in these delightful irregularities an essence common to all three kingdoms. Even the borders are eloquent. Even the *number* of borders, which can be as high as twelve or thirteen, expresses something—a wall within a wall, a discourse within a discourse. And a hierarchy of allusions governs them, from innermost to outermost.

Despite these paleographic complexities, it is not impossible to discern even now, in a wedding carpet made in Kis Ghiordes (a place known for its particular art of knotting carpets), the doubling, on a soft pink background, of the prayer niche and the prayer lamp directly opposite each other: all surrounded, in mellow earthenware tones, by auspicious tulips of prosperity and carnations of wisdom placed inside a green-rust border with large, serrated teeth that unexpectedly encloses the intimate square within the fearsome heights of a sacred mountain. In a Caucasian carpet, the theme of virile courage, developed with the utmost elegance, is revealed: a pointy, mesmerizing multitude of magnetically green-blue and dark red scorpions, bows, and flying arrows set close together harshly contrast with a velvet background of coarse tawny camel hair. In a carpet made in Asia Minor, an astringent ritual purity no doubt eliminated the lamp and even the amphora from the prayer niche, so that no representational figure might violate the indescribable watery, shadowy green at its center. The great song of praise was left to the pomegranate trees and the spiritual blues of the roses and fish in the vast borders surrounding this space.

But why does the carpet fly?

We are told that in the classical Arabic language "carpet" and "butterfly" share a common root, and this cannot be merely on account of their mesmerizing colors. Weaving and knotting in themselves allude to events ordained for mankind by invisible hands. And we know how the Greek word *kairos*, indicating a fleeting opportunity to be seized like a miraculous flower, is used to define something else indefinable: the momentary, flashing fissure between the warp threads, through which the shuttle passes fast as lightning, like a lethal blade between two pieces of armor.

But why does the carpet fly?

A book full of wisdom, which relates almost everything that classical Persia—and above all mystical Persia—taught about the threads that run between heaven and earth, perhaps also tosses us, as if by accident, the little golden key that can give us access to the innermost "chamber of the carpet": this tiny, ironic piece of ground capable of flight. This book alludes to a spiritual recomposition of Eden, indeed even of a world prior to Eden, where the stone and the star, the rose and the crystal, the spring and the thorn, the fierce animal and the meek one, are allied in a single dimension that encompasses them all (so it seems that the fourth is not the last). It speaks of emerald cities—"Jabalqa and Jabarsa of a thousand gates"—"where the various kinds of autonomous original images are infinitely realized" (just as in a Persian carpet), "forming a hierarchy of degrees varying according to their relative subtlety or density." Such cities are encircled, so to speak, by Mount Qaf, the center as well as the circumference of the world that is so often mentioned in the *Nights*, and the heart of that labyrinthine cosmogony called "Hasib Karim al-Din and the Queen of the Serpents." Again, as in the carpet, the shape of these cities is square—a sign of perfection and totality.

That the Oriental carpet is meant to offer a mirror of the divine freshness of a world without guilt, we are furthermore informed by the four paradisiacal rivers that sometimes stem from the prayer niche, flowing from there into Christian mosaics, where they are transformed into the crystalline springs of the Gospels, or pour down the rock on which the Lamb stands, or tragically traverse the cosmic mantle of the Byzantine bishop. The Christian mystics saw, in the mysterious garden of the Song of Songs, an image of the garden of innocence, where the soul no longer does anything but "watch the flowers as they grow, from the first day of spring."

Isn't the intrepid traveler who collects himself for prayer on the carpet moving, step by step, toward these transfigured lands, these lands seen in visions, whether Edenic or pre-Edenic? "Here is the path that leads to the wellspring of life . . ."

It is only reasonable that the meditations of these men should sometimes result in levitations—those flights in which the body seems to be shot upward by the taut bow of the ecstatic mind. Saint Joseph of Cupertino is perhaps the greatest proof of such states, which are quite common in the history of Western contemplation. The contemplative dance of Saint Dominic, hovering above the ground on the tips of his toes, with his hands extended and clasped above his head like an arrow, provides an even more graphic image of them.

The two enigmas would then seem to be unraveled together and at once: the carpet flies because it is a piece of spiritual land, and the designs of the carpet herald that land, which is found in spiritual flight. Not Iram of the Pillars—a dangerous attempt to imitate the inimitable—but the humble memory and adumbration of its model.

THREE

THE UNFORGIVABLE

Come, my songs, let us speak of perfection—
We shall get ourselves rather disliked.

—Ezra Pound

THE PASSION for perfection comes late. Or, better, it is late to manifest itself as a conscious passion. If at first it was spontaneous, and if in every life a moment comes when we must face the "general horror" of the world that dies around us and decays, the ineluctable moment will reveal this passion for what it is: the only wild and composed reaction.

In an era of purely horizontal progress, in which the human group seems more and more to resemble that line of Chinese men on their way to the guillotine mentioned in chronicles of the Boxer Rebellion, the only nonfrivolous attitude seems to be that of the man in line who is reading a book. We are astonished to see the others beating one another to a bloody pulp while they wait their turn, trying to curry favor with the executioners at work on the platform. We admire the two or three heroes who keep charging headlong at one or another executioner impartially (since it's well understood there's only one executioner, even if the masks do alternate). As for the man who is reading: he at least shows good judgment and a love for life.

It's wise to forget that, according to the chronicles, this man owed his head to the fact that the German officer escorting the condemned couldn't cope with his composure and had mercy on him. It's worth remembering the words that the Chinese man uttered when questioned, before he disappeared into the crowd: "I know that every line read is a gain." It's allowable to imagine that the book he held in his hands was a perfect book.

What do I mean by this? Not necessarily that it was a sacred book in the canonical sense. Everything that brings us joy is somehow or other divine territory, as one illustrious demonologist says. I can just as easily imagine it being a luminous treatise on the lives of mushrooms or the knots of Persian carpets, an accurate description of a great fencer or a collection of letters with a good number of words that go together well. Or even that "Essay on Knives" that someone, they tell me, is currently writing, and that seems to me well worth anticipating since the writer writes with perfection, and whether she is talking about knives, or Francis Bacon, or Anna Pavlova's thin big toe tensed in the agonizing arabesques of *Giselle*, she is responding in a way that does credit to the guillotine that lies in wait: which is to say, the miserable biochemical world of tomorrow, where thought, as has been reverently proclaimed to us, will be no more than a serum, and consciousness no more than an integument, but not even a serum or an integument man will be able to receive as an inheritance at birth, since everyone knows that an electronic impulse can deprive him of both at any distance, at any stranger's whim.

Meticulous, specious, and inflexible like all true visionaries, the poetess Marianne Moore writes an essay on knives. She writes about green lizards and Aldine ligatures, dancing girls and flamingos with "maple- / leaf-like feet." She writes about the pangolin, an "armored animal—scale lapping scale with spruce-cone regularity," "the night miniature artist engineer," and "Leonardo da Vinci's replica." She writes about the "dead fountains of Versailles" and the "noiseless music that hangs about / the serpent when it stirs or springs." Into her quick, ravenous quotation marks, hedged in between two hemistichs, she gathers up as much beauty as she can plunder, wherever she happens to find it: in Plato, at the zoological garden, in a catalogue of old courtly garments, in the natural history column of *The Illustrated London News*. She writes about all these things, drawing morals out of them like serendipitous arpeggios promptly dissolved by her punctilious hand. Only one thing, however, is her trade, her lodestar, and her psalm: arduous and marvelous perfection—that divine affront to be venerated in nature, to be touched in art, to be gloriously invented in our day-to-day behavior. And this is why her books make such good companions in the guillotine square.

There is one difference. It does not seem the Chinese man was interrogated either by the German officer or by the other men who shared his fate. Today he is interrogated constantly. Today no reader is allowed to read without justifying himself. But he, too, better hold his tongue. If he were to utter a single word about the reasons for his reading, he would, to say the least, be impeded from continuing to read. Why? Because, first of all, it's a pure miracle that this book has come into his hands. Marianne Moore says of an eminent contemporary poet: "He has naturally in some quarters been rebuked for his skill; writers cannot excel at their work without being, like the dogs in *Coriolanus*, 'as often beat for their barking / As therefore kept to do so.'"

2.

> But it is true, they fear
> it more than death, beauty is feared
> more than death, more than they fear death.
> —WILLIAM CARLOS WILLIAMS

Perfection, beauty. What does it mean? Among the many definitions, one is possible. It is an aristocratic characteristic—indeed it is, in itself, the supreme aristocracy. Of nature, of the species, of thought. Even in nature, it is culture. The refined, upright posture of a girl from the Costa d'Oro is the work of centuries of swimming, clay jugs balanced on heads, initiatory songs and dances more complicated than the purest Gregorian. Lacking only one of these three elements—reverence, free play, feminine arts—perfection would not bind those limbs in her chaste, imperious veil. Over the course of millennia, in a manner of speaking, the tree of paradise has expressed the lyrebird; hands interlocked for a long time have, gradually, been converted into Gothic arches.

Today all of this is insulted, disavowed and destroyed, irretrievable and yet always present, like the poison thorn beneath the nail—man has converted it into an object of sacred horror. Thus every memory of celestial time is banned and buried forever in the potter's field. More than anything, it is denied. For perfection is known to be, first and foremost, a thing of the past: abidance, quiet, quietude. The man in meditation, the woman at the threshold, the genuflecting monk, the prolonged silence of the king. Or the beast on the prowl or pursuing delicate tasks. This aerial and terrible weight—of silence, and waiting, and duration—man has rejected. And now here he is, living in paranoid terror of "feeling and precision, humility, concentration, taste." On the other hand, how could he be expected to summon the courage necessary for the excruciating cry: "Get away from me, beauty, you scare me, every time I think about you it tears at my soul, a curse upon your head"? Like the cry of Eve cast out from the Garden, all of this calls for veils and the darkness of the woods. Just consider all the indirect attacks on the handmaids of the irretrievable thing: grace, lightness, irony, keen senses, watchful and well-trained eyes. Or to make intellectual use of theological terms: clarity, subtlety, agility, impassivity.

This being the case, the poet especially is unforgivable. An august, modest old age protects the poetess mentioned above. But not long ago she was spoken about, and not without politeness, as a sort of medieval nun who embroidered memorable chasubles, more in love with the colors of her silks than with the holy faces she portrayed— as though a portrait could inspire veneration if an almost maniacal attention had not determined the materials needed to answer to the portraitist's vision. But the great poets are by now all dead or very old.

Even death is no longer a safe conduct. Publishing suicide was risked, and committed, when the essays of Gottfried Benn, those great laments for Quaternary man, were offered to the public with delirious precautions: Please, don't take them seriously; please, no one consider them more than a "phenomenon," a "sign of the times." Needless to say, not one critic laughed.

Benn is unforgivable, and certainly not because of the ashen sack-cloth he wears in his capacity as a political sinner (nor is it good manners to recall how often bad politics are forgiven in the name of bad writing) but because of the purple stole he wears as a high priest of the form: the author of a few poems that could only have been written by the greatest master the German language has seen in many years—for this is, finally, what it comes down to. Benn is unforgivable because he maintains that the poet should not be the historian of his time; on the contrary, he should be a trailblazer so advanced that he finds himself millennia behind his time, and an ancestor so traditional that he is able to prophesy the most distant future cycles. A witness only to what endures, forever immobile: a warrior, a star, a death, a rowan.

He offers proof of this almost inadvertently in a poem of two stanzas, "but between the two stanzas is a distance of twenty years." The two stanzas begin with the same chord, open out into different progressions, and flow back in circles to their source—which is only possible because the same mind has twice been moved in its enduring entirety. This is the little poem, of such feral beauty, which begins with the words *"Welle der Nacht"* and can be found in his *Statische Gedichte.*

> *Welle der Nacht—, Meerwidder und Delphine*
> *mit Hyacinthos leichtbewegter Last,*
> *die Lorbeerrosen und die Travertine*
> *wehn um den leeren istrischen Palast,*

Welle der Nacht—, zwei Muscheln miterkoren,
die Fluten strömen sie, die Felsen her,
dann Diadem und Purpur mitverloren,
die weisse Perle rollt zurück ins Meer.

Wave of the night—, sea-ram and dolphin seen
with Hyakinthos's airy weight borne high,
where laurel roses and the Travertine
around the empty Istrian palace sigh,

Wave of the night—, two chosen shells it bore,
in tidal stream from cliffs incessantly,
then, diadem and purple lost once more,
the white pearl rolls into the sea.

We, too, not long ago, had our writer indicted for refinement, liable to the lèse-majesté of the masses: the Prince di Lampedusa. Old-fashioned. Oh, he could hardly have been more so: with his titanic irony, his prodigious indifference to false problems, the full-throated happiness of his rhythmic melodies—like one of those famously insouciant arias that gentlemen used to whistle on the way to a duel. For what is the Prince di Lampedusa's book if not a duel à outrance between beauty and death, and *his* death, among other things? Unforgivable, this Lampedusa who leaves the grand ball with a smile just a moment before the chandeliers blaze, and explains away the pavane that, for the others, is such a feverish affair. Unforgivable, this Lampedusa who laughs at all ideological gloominess and sentimental solemnities—at all those insufferable, ancestral, national tendencies to "take things seriously." He is outrageously erudite. And he pays attention, never batting an eye, to the realities that are the poet's destiny: the glory and the destruction of the perfect creature, the ultimate irony of the dust. A ball, a star, a death, a rowan.

3.

Consider worthy only that
to which all a man's art has been applied.

—DANTE

But the masses, whether or not they feel aggrieved, read the Prince di Lampedusa. Bevies of boys and girls read Gottfried Benn and Marianne Moore. The unforgivable have disciples.

Who, then, abhors perfection? It would be tempting to suspect those who are aware of what goes into the making of perfection, what it costs to obtain it: the nightly vigils, the hard mornings, the vows of chastity, obedience, and poverty it imposes. Those, I mean, who couldn't stand the strain of it. If discussions about art are placed on their natural axis—the greater or lesser mastery of the artist—they are immediately shunted onto other, not very clearly laid tracks, such as the artist's "commitment" or "presence." It's telling that the very word "mastery"—as well as the humbler "technique"—has by now dropped out of critical language, as have the simple, unappealable definitions "beautiful" and "ugly," which today are the patrimony of the world of footballers and boxers, on whose technique there are discussions worthy of the poetry competitions of the Fujiwara court.

Who will remember that the ultimate goal of those great "essays toward a theory of childhood," those "pianistic preparations for death," Frédéric Chopin's twenty four études, was an irreproachable disciplining of both hands? Timeless, transparent children race between drops of sun and arrows of greenery through a timeless, transparent garden; the dead rise up, gentle and dreadful; love contemplates its own abyss; a village dresses in mourning. And the whole miracle rests on the simplest of intentions: to make the student flex his wrist at least six hundred times, thereby strengthening the joint of the ring finger.

Where, then, should we look for writers, given that time is not a matter for poetry and that what now seems to be asked of poets is a matter of time?

In Italy, the last critic was, it seems to me, Leopardi. Already with De Sanctis, the pure disposition of the contemplative mind was definitively disturbed and distorted by the obsession with history. Leopardi was the last to examine a page as it ought to be examined, in the manner of a paleographer, on five or six levels at once: from its feeling for human destinies to its ability to avoid discordant vowels. He examined it, that is to say, as a writer. For Leopardi the text was an absolute presence, and he did not proceed differently when breaking down a passage by Dante, Padre Bartoli, Homer, or Madame de Staël. Anything that did not lend itself to *multiple readings*, he ignored. I would rather not think of him examining a contemporary page. Even if it were among the most beautiful, I suppose he would note the almost total absence of the word "as" and the ablative absolute: the lack of the analogical, although by this I don't mean the metaphorical, and the wholly poetic—prophetic—ability to turn the real into the figurative or, in other words, into destiny.

4.

A poet does not speak language but mediates it,
as the lion's power lies in his paws.

—MARIANNE MOORE

Where, then, should we look for the writer? It's a question that begets questions, one after the other. For example: What is style?

The first image that presents itself is this: Style is a polar virtue thanks to which the feeling of being alive is rarefied and at the same time intensified. As a result of a simultaneous and contradictory motion, in which the artist distills an object by reducing it, like the Tang painters, to its unique profile, to an unbroken line that is, so to speak, the very articulation of the soul, a reader will feel it multiplied within him, glorified in innumerable harmonics. One example of tragic style and sublime horror concentrated in a single stroke is found in Pliny the Younger, when he writes about the chief vestal virgin whose dress snags as she is being lowered alive into the sepulchral chamber, and who pushes away a soldier's hand "with one last gesture of refinement, as if not wanting to defile her quite chaste and pure body." No less masterful was the innovation of a great Italian mime Moretti, as Harlequin in the scene from *The Servant of Two Masters* where two meals are served at once: at the apex of a miraculous progression of leaps and somersaults, he suddenly reduced his movements to a sequence of cadenced instances of stillness—legs crossed, arms open, arms crossed, legs open—until he dropped abruptly on his head, even as his legs and arms, very slowly, continued in that scissor-like motion. In the audience, the feeling of dizzying activity at that moment approached the image desired—the image of something *impossible*. He concretized, in a certain sense, the saying "There is nothing more motionless than an arrow in flight." Sir Laurence Olivier in *Henry V* added something to the weight of impending battle, with its potential wounds and future memories, by tugging an inch of sleeve up his wrist.

One finds such concentrated tension in very few writers—which is to say, in all of the great writers. The less great from time to time also manage lofty or exquisite moments. But these days it's easier to find such surprises and felicities in more or less anonymous texts where some inalterable passion is at work. Marianne Moore confesses the intoxication she felt at the "impassioned explicitness" of the Federal Reserve Board's letter regarding certain counterfeits that had been put into circulation. Leafing through a guide to the Ducal Palace of Urbino, I myself felt the sort of jubilation one experiences listening to seventeenth-century music when I discovered that the author—a superintendent fit to burst with decorous enthusiasm—used the phrase *ever so* instead of the word *very* in quite delightful and unusual ways: "All the doors of the palace must have originally been ever so precious . . . The elegant arches branch off from the capital and descend to ever so decorative corbels." Even the innocent sprezzatura of his reiterative adjectives ("From this very high window, it is clear that we are in a high tower") added, as he would have said, to the "heroic beauty." And I was not at all surprised when he was able to pull off an enormous description of the trompe l'oeil in Duke Guido-baldo's study—a showpiece if ever there was one—*ex corde*, by the sheer strength of his astonishment.

Nowadays we might seek similar pleasures in dictionaries and treatises. Without hoping for the splendors of a Buffon, it's rare that even in a modern treatise on zoology, or for that matter a nursery catalogue, one will fail to come across a few perfect verbalizations beyond the scope of most contemporary writers. (A description of a certain species of owl: "A deep but brief two-syllable howl, the second syllable fading slowly away, sometimes followed by a calm, guttural snicker . . . a high-pitched, sneeze-like bark . . . a clear and baying *uirro*," and so on. A description of a rose: "A slim and perfect, turbiniform bud, which opens into a solitary flower with velvety petals that converge at the edges. Their salmon-yellow color shades into chamois-auburn where it joins the stem. Bearing upright, foliage bronzed . . .")*

Spiritual devotion to the mystery of what exists produces style in and of itself, as demonstrated by the admirable language—now in the process of extinction—of peasants. A poet who paid attention to every least visible and invisible thing—like an entomologist endeavoring to express, precisely, the inexpressible blue of a dragonfly's wing—would be the supreme poet. In fact he existed: his name is Dante. Others have touched these forms of plenary attention at certain times, and still others, at all times, lesser forms of attention. This is perhaps the only nontemporal distinction between one poet, storyteller, or philosopher and another. (The mystic who has given us a technical account of every single instant of spiritual life, in treatises that have nothing to envy in the most perfect scientific catalogues—where the wing of the word never loses a hint of its purple—is Saint John of the Cross.)

Nothing less than a devouring passion for truth informs these

---

*Guido Ceronetti emphasizes the linguistic eminence of an enologist who "chisels out" a fine wine as follows: "Ruby-red color, deep and unambiguous; tends toward orange. Intense bouquet, definite violet tones (very old: tar). Dry, full, robust flavor; austere but not excessive; a strong backbone and broad structure that lingers; harmonic."

multiplied instants of life and, as I've said already, eloquence can pivot on a particle. Mozart's last (Italian) letter is an almost terrifying example of style when it has become one with nature. You will remember the great central phrase, the repeated lament about death approaching, wrapped in the black cloak of the stranger in the *Requiem*. And then: "Life was, indeed, so beautiful..." he bursts out. Try removing one of these five little words. Here is the workaday formula: "Life was beautiful." Or the nostalgic: "Life was so beautiful." Or the candid: "Life was, indeed, beautiful." But "Life was, indeed, so beautiful..."— only this is the dagger that pierces, drawn from its sheath by two monosyllables, arranged in a simple and inscrutable order.

5.

> Really solitary, you
> and words alone.
> —GOTTFRIED BENN

This miracle of life multiplied—which is finally nothing if not happiness, to which every reader aspires, always, like a child instinctively reaching out for a pink peach or a seashell—seems to happen all the more completely the greater the solitude of the poet, although it also depends on his leap out of the water, like the salmon nosing against the current, and his ability to remain, if necessary, "leaping up, up, out of water, at the full moon," without hope or desperation. There is no need to enumerate the holy hermitages: Ravenna, Recanati, the tower on the Neckar River, Amherst, the cork-walled room on boulevard Haussmann. But the great poets are by now all dead or very old.

Among the living, Djuna Barnes is the one who has most thoroughly embraced this Trappism of perfection. No one has any idea where she is, she sends a book to the presses every twenty years, and her name finds a way, every time, to drop out of the catalogues. As far as most people are concerned, she might as well be an unknown woman of the seventeenth century—a sort of Inés de la Cruz or

Countess of Winchilsea. And here, in the regal, ruthless, very long-deferred verses of her great tragedy, *The Antiphon*, we glimpse the secret of that infinitely demanding refusal:

As the goldsmith hammers out his savage metal
so is the infant axial to the dance.
Wrapped in metric, hugged in discipline,
rehearsed in familiarity reproved;
grappled in the mortise of ritual,
turning on the spirit of the play,
equilibrium else would be a fall
paid for in estrangement, each from each . . .

Hands off, you too near thing!
Would you that I leap into myself,
there dismiss me of my occupation
to set me in the slum of their regard?
Would get me clapped between the palms of their approval?
Get me rated in the general horror of the common mouth
and to the verdict of the vulgar stand me down
crying "I am a fool!" to ease a fool?

In the general horror, there is also this psalm that exalts and escapes. It is texts like these that serve as a bulwark for the boy who wants, as Benn writes, "to read Job and Jeremiah with his back to the wall, and carry on."

There are few, very few, of these little fortresses that allow themselves to be worn away by the sands and the winds rather than going to ruin in hotels and caravansaries. Sometimes it has happened I've been leafing through a magazine bristling like a porcupine with impeccably momentary poems—one surpassing the next in its ferocious temporariness, scrambling feverishly to embrace the hour of its death—when a silence falls, the page opens like a pale, sea-colored sky, and a garland of verses settles on it, as pure as Ursa Major. Here is a poet. Impassive and vertiginous, as far away as happiness and more remote than a tombstone. Once I know such a poem by heart, I cut it out and save it. Then begins a period of waiting, always long, for the book, always short, which contains the poem: that hour of Lent or Pentecost, that beseeching of the sea, those violet wheat stalks whirling in a spring rain as fervent as blood.

But let the poet vacillate only for a moment, since it's easy to tempt a righteous soul with the double lie of the "renewal of his resources" and his "duties toward the social" (as though, deep in the interior, the proper development of spiritual forces does not ceaselessly modify the exterior; as though the cenobite does not go further than the man of society, "for example is eternal and the rings of its extending influence are indefinite")—let that poet stop sitting with his back to the wall reading Job and Jeremiah for only a moment, and see what torment will follow. See how easily his most ephemeral confreres will beat him, at the first verse, on the ground of colloquial ideology and worldly fluency. Snatched up by the common maw, he is no longer capable of anything. He is *human* now. He is *in solidarity*. He is *consoling*. To put it plainly, he is no longer memorable. More than once we have seen such an albatross enter, out of politeness, into the cricket's cage.

What is a true joy to behold is the already elderly poet who, having sailed every sea and run aground on every atoll, shuts himself away more and more, as the days go by, in pure and inaccessible forms. For example Boris Pasternak, or William Carlos Williams, who ended his days as a literary pioneer writing in tercets. These writers—not the others—are unforgivable for those who read with the eyes of the flesh.

6.

> Blazing with refinement.
> —The Temple Hymns of Zhou

So what is style? We have said, first of all, culture, whether natural or mental. We have said a heightened feeling for life. We have said solitude, honey and locusts. And yet we've said nothing. We know "what it is cannot be said; / what it is not can be." Style is the Tuscan house like a lily—all light and loftiness and renunciation. Style is that other black-and-white lily, the benefactress of the Portinari altarpiece—half nun and half fairy—who worships her God with the most Florentine of smiles. Style was certainly the sacred dance of the great Watusi of Rwanda, so similar to the white priests of Dura-Europos and now destroyed by men of mediocre stature. Or the other dance ("hands clenched, wrists flexed") seen by a poet in a dying child's limbs, opening and closing slowly, like a corolla. All figures in which the eye has caught or transfused that second life which is the saving analogy (lily, corolla, dance, death, star) in which peace and horror are laid out in identical, innocent geometries.

Sometimes, on a train or in a waiting room, you see a human face. What sets it apart? Again, we can say what the face does not have— what its features do not betray. The eyes do not distrust or solicit, do not stray or investigate. Eyes that are never absent and never wholly present. Nowadays such faces, which are so common in ancient paintings, seem sealed by an invincible melancholy. Yet on the train, in the waiting room, they fill the soul with happiness—with a heightened feeling of being alive. No words will be spoken, but the pure, sudden smile offers flight into a peaceful place, vulnerable to the point of being inaccessible. The phrase that comes most immediately to mind is: "Conscious eyes." They are, in reality, heroic eyes. They have looked at beauty and not withdrawn from it. They have recognized that it is gone from the earth, and for this reason they have gained it in their minds. Not even photography can completely destroy these faces, which are more and more rare, it's true. The race is changing, now the species is changing; soon these faces will hardly be seen at all and when they are seen—for they, too, are unforgivable—it will be as something foreign to the context, to the system that contains them. Already they are beginning to become invisible, like Longinus's lance or the Grail, which they say a hand snatched back to heaven once men were no longer worthy of looking after it; like the Chinese man reading his book, on whom the crowd quickly closed again. For them, however, beauty, though banished, never ceases in its unnoticed circuit. Flower, star, death, and dance continue to resemble one another, and the resemblance continues to vanquish terror. Clarity, subtlety, agility, impassivity. Sit with your back to the wall, read Job and Jeremiah. Wait your turn. Every line read is a gain. Every line in the unforgivable book.

A Digression
ON LANGUAGE

SOMEONE has said, and it seems hard to disagree with him, that in a few years the subtle gradations of language used by the various characters in Proust will seem no less enigmatic than the Egyptian Book of the Dead or the Etruscan funerary stelae. In fact, we might go further and wonder how Proust is being read even today. Is there anyone who still laughs, for example, at Dr. Cottard when, welcomed into Madame Verdurin's box with exquisite politeness ("It is very good of you to have come, Doctor, since I'm sure you've seen Sarah Bernhardt many times, and, besides, I do wonder whether we're not a little bit too close to the stage"), he dutifully replies: "Yes, indeed, we are far too near, and people are beginning to think Sarah Bernhardt's a bit of a bore. But you expressed a wish for me to come and your wish is my command. I am only too glad to be able to do you a little favor..."?

You may remember that at this point Madame Verdurin decides Dr. Cottard is a scientist who lives in a world apart from practical existence, so that in his case it is pointless to depreciate anything they offer him simply for the sake of modesty. Monsieur Verdurin replies by saying that he'd never dared to mention it but he had noticed the same thing himself, and so, the next New Year's Day, instead of sending Dr. Cottard a beautiful ruby with an understated note, he will buy him an artificial stone for three hundred francs and let it be understood that it is something more or less priceless. Indeed, Proust's art is truly magic if this dialogue still provokes a smile, so thoroughly have such candid relations and remarks become the norm, and almost de rigueur, nowadays.

It was long ago said of a man of patrician bearing, Frédéric Chopin, that "nothing bothered him more than being believed because of his genteel manners and Slavic courtesy": an all too common modern complaint, alas, for well-born men in a world now barbarous (not barbarian), from which the serious implications of urbanity and the impervious modesty of grace have been banished: a horribly literal nightmare in which everything *is taken at face value.*

We are regressing, one might speculate, to an age of pachyderms, where it would not be fair to expect familiarity with crystalware: the understatement or courtly litotes, for example, and its fine complement, the noble hyperbole, so dear to Shakespeare, which is often a hyperbole in reverse—an "inverted overstatement." If there is still a Chinese mandarin, and he still possesses porcelain palaces, and he still invites an exalted guest to honor his lowly home, I fear he cannot expect in reply more than a quite serious, paternal, vaguely perplexed: "But, my dear friend, this isn't bad at all!"

As for mandarins still among the living, in the sphere of letters, I know of none but Borges. We open one of his books and happen on the marvelously civilized definition he gives of his own fiction: "the irresponsible game of a shy young man who dared not write stories and so amused himself by falsifying and distorting the tales of others." No sooner has the critic (infallible, jubilant) read this than he shouts: "Look! Here is Borges openly admitting his own lack of creativity!"

It does not seem at all unusual that Borges sometimes claims to have been interviewed by an "anthropomorphic gentleman." It would, however, be strange if no one asked him, as in fact no one has, whether the interviewer was not perhaps a monkey in civilian clothes.

If we let our minds wander this way, we reach a point where we begin to wonder strange things. With what feelings of indignant frustration, for example, a contemporary person would first encounter Dante's sublime litotes: the *Commedia* being called a comedy because, after so many horrors, it has a happy ending. Or what a curious individual Alessandro Manzoni would seem—a man whose work is nothing but a very dense weave of litotes, brightened here and there by some superb hyperboles. A hundred years later, the discretion with which he indicated the secret identities of some of his characters appears to have been absolutely wasted: Cardinal Borromeo and the Unnamed, above all, who are so patently the same man, as are Don Abbondio and Don Rodrigo—both of whom are moved solely by force, and it makes no difference if one of them is at the tip, and the other at the hilt, of the sword.

In the famous long dialogue between the cardinal and the "savage lord," Manzoni bewitches us with his artful ability to vanish behind a web of eloquent litotes which bring the two faces of the herm imperceptibly closer together ("These saints are always obstinate"—the cardinal's chaplain reflects—"[Borromeo] always does things his own way..." But two pages later Borromeo himself will be rebuking the Unnamed for "his impetuous willfulness and imperturbable fixity") and, simultaneously, to sketch the outlines of both of these impressive figures in a series of brief, impassioned, hyperbolic exclamations. Readers will remember how, by placing their two biographies side by side—calmly resigned to appearing as theatrical as ever, which allows him the utmost secrecy—Manzoni emphasized the radical solitude in which both characters had perfected the contrasting masterpieces of their separate lives. It is said that "the world" did not exist for the Unnamed, and that he was in fact so indifferent to it that Don Rodrigo didn't want it to be known he had connections with such a man, for that would mean giving up far too many things: the amusements and accolades of polite society, as well as the protection of his uncle the count.

Sometimes, as many have said, only such a pure ascesis of delinquency allows a person to change radically, in an instant, his direction and nature: like the turn of the rudder that alters, above the navigator's head, the meaning of the constellations. ("The great sinners," a famous old demon warned, "*seem* easier to catch. But then they are incalculable. They are, if things take the wrong turn, as ready to defy the social pressures around them for the Enemy's sake as they were to defy them for ours.")

The cardinal is so well aware of this—he so immediately recognizes the Unnamed as a man of his own stripe—he begins their conversation by reversing their roles, as is only done between men of equal rank on equal footing (which is to say, he exclaims that the Unnamed's visit gives him reason for remorse since he should have long ago paid him a visit of his own), and he concludes their conversation with a marvelous indiscretion worthy of angels and sovereigns: "My love for you devours me!" Whereupon the other man, thunderstruck and quick as can be, pays him back in his own coin: "Will I return? Were you to spurn me, I would stand as obstinately at your gate as a beggar. I need to talk to you! I need to hear from you, to see you! I need you!"

Now the door to the antechamber, mobbed with dumbfounded clergymen, opens. *"And the wonderful couple appeared."* The rest of the story—describing how that population (which was still a society) treated the Unnamed, who "went unarmed and alone" but "was no less inviolable than when he bore arms to ensure his safety," and the ecstatic faces of the men who "turned to look at him again as he went on his way," and so on—is only a long gloss on this majestically simple sentence.

Behind the wonderful couple comes Don Abbondio, *whom nobody pays any mind*, just as nobody will pay any mind to Don Rodrigo once the plague has knocked the sword from his hand. What delicate allusion can be addressed to Don Abbondio, what noble hyperbole, what fine and fiery rhetoric? The divine pastoral rebuke that Cardinal Borromeo will deliver to his curate is marked from the first by relentless, painstaking, barren explicitness—a telltale sign of desperation. With the Unnamed, the cardinal only needed to toss out a single hint, like a lit match tossed on a stack of well-seasoned firewood. With Don Abbondio, the cardinal keeps on despondently piling new logs in the hearth, already quite well aware there's no fire to burn them. The unfortunate curate does not understand. "Like a chicken in the talons of a hawk ... suspended in a region unknown to him, in an atmosphere he has never before breathed," he has the same sort of leaden innocence we find in animals of the less sensitive species: chickens, yes, or Dr. Cottard, or Don Rodrigo, or Borges's critics. Even if Borromeo is not accompanied by armed men, he scares Abbondio even more than the Unnamed, and the bond between the two scares him most of all ("to throw his arms around the neck of that fiend!"). In his head, at the end, he harbors only one petty, stale, unthinking thought, but that is precisely where Manzoni slips in (for those who haven't already discovered another) the last key to the secret of his herm: "Is it not an astonishing thing that the saints, as well as the wicked, always have quicksilver in their veins; and not contented with making a bustle themselves, they would make all mankind, if they could, join the dance with them!"

This is only one example among many. Manzoni so elegantly managed to conceal the secret symbolic implications of *The Betrothed* (its oblique, elusive construction; its games of mirrors, echoes, and silences) in claims to the contrary and excessive denials, he has successfully persuaded the world for more than a century that he was the first to write a realistic, moralistic, apological novel, a microscopic study of the celebrated "jumble" of society, and God knows what else. If anyone has read *The Betrothed* otherwise, he appears to have kept it to himself. Then again, anyone who today tries to offer a variant reading of this or any other book—or this or any other event—seems bound to a particular fate: something very much like the life of a caveman or, rather, since there's a good deal of joy to be had in such choices, like the life of that Theban painter who daubed his most dazzling ochers and his coolest blues on the granite and clay that were destined for the darkness of the tomb.

FOUR

WITH LIGHT HANDS

IF WE LOOK in the dictionaries for the word *sprezzatura*, we find various definitions, all very beautiful and very imprecise, for such noble words have no synonyms or equivalents. "Frankness, fluency," Fanfani offers, "the opposite of mannerism or affectation, it is sometimes of service to beauty." And Zingarelli, who likes to give words their intellectual crest, describes it as "a casual manner of speech or action," adding that it is "typical of a self-assured master." Petrocchi lists it, as one would expect, among the modes of behavior typical of the aristocracy ("noble sprezzatura"), but he classes it, admiringly, among the voluntary behaviors: "an attitude defined by magisterial nonchalance." From which he deduces a questionable axiom: "Sprezzatura is an art." Not one of the dictionaries—those marvelous compendiums of stylistic clairvoyance—forgets (how could they?) sprezzatura in dress, which, as already mentioned, "is sometimes of service to beauty" and, logically enough, "the definition may also be extended to works of art or genius."

It is immediately clear that these definitions do not quite account for Brummell's cravat, knotted in the dark to lend it the incalculable elegance of chance—nor, for that matter, the Japanese precept that refuses to recognize a garden as perfectly tended unless, at last, on the well-swept path beneath a tree, the gardener shakes out a casual embroidery of red leaves. Its sister word, *elegance*, doesn't seem to accommodate sprezzatura's creative qualities, its fresh, communicative flame; "tactfulness" limits it to conscious matters, and "casualness" dissolves it into gesture. "Nonchalance" comes closest, but it is only a negative, hollow, and therefore merely momentary instance of sprezzatura.

Sprezzatura is in reality a whole moral attitude that, like the word itself, requires a context that is almost gone from the contemporary world, and, like the word itself, is at risk of disappearing. Or rather, since nothing that's real ever disappears, it is at risk of languishing in those oubliettes where, in savage and more honest times, they used to chain up princes who'd provoked the ire of the people until their very names were forgotten.

In certain portraits—depicting faces now lost, faces that will very soon be unrecognizable, and if not unrecognizable, unforgivable, they will be so alien to the context that surrounds them—in certain portraits still hidden away in old houses, we see this light, arcane quality that is not, I think, inseparable from style. In a famous photograph of the last emperor of Russia dressed in the clothes of his saintly ancestor, Alexei the Quietest, the haughty symmetry of the wide purple velvet sleeves is mysteriously replicated on his chest by the golden wings of the two-headed eagle and crowned by the perfect, monastic, warlike circle of the collar. All of this (unexpectedly enlivened by the jaunty tilt of a fine black-marten cap) tells us more than any history book about the mystic audacity of that ill-starred sovereign, the last purely Muscovite tsar, who attempted—with no intellectual weaponry, or political genius, or help from a single human being—to lead the Enlightenment autocracy of the Petersburg Romanovs back to its traditional Russian religious destiny. If he had succeeded in adopting Alexei's tender, implacable sprezzatura as well as his clothes, perhaps he wouldn't have had to wait for the hour of his passion and death to impress history's pages with the image of a soul-stirring monarch. Empires crumble when the education of princes yields to bourgeois lethargy, with its scrupulous, superstitious ignorance of the spiritual roots of all power. Around the Russian tsar, encircled by sublime icons and marked with the holy *myron*, the empire collapsed in a heap of English novels, tea cakes served by English aunts, ponies, Maltese puppies, and chemical baths; and the sacred diadems had already fallen by the time the splendid creatures wearing them ceased to perceive the horrific incongruity between the tragic *epos* and the nicknames more appropriate to purebred poodles which appalls us in their letters. Nicholas's finest biographer tells us that this most Christian emperor, the prisoner of a court assiduously impervious to any simple or grandiose conception of power for at least two centuries, was no longer capable even of that sine qua non of sprezzatura: "the art of exercising vigorous and efficient authority over subordinates." And yet, until the last year of his reign, the people used to kneel as he passed and kiss his shadow, as in a painting of the age of the apostles, so completely did they sense, in that gentle man, a reverence for their own destiny.

(With some exaggeration, it may be said that anyone who has never had a sovereign above him—or a people below him—capable, at the slightest change of mood, of separating his head from his neck, will seldom possess the authentic gift of sprezzatura, a quality psychologically linked to risk, audacity, and irony, something akin to the haughty and indifferent exchange of looks between the tamer and the leopard ready to leap: "imprudent wisdom, courageous prudence.")

Sprezzatura is a moral rhythm, it is the music of an interior grace; it is the *tempo*, I would like to say, in which the perfect freedom of any given destiny is made manifest, although it is always delineated by a secret ascesis. Two lines hide it, like a ring in a case: "With a light heart, with light hands, / to take life, to leave life ..." It is allied—or, rather, it *was* allied—with high birth, but it is also native to the poet, with his deep-seated horror of easiness, prudery, euphemism, promiscuity, heaviness, undue haste. Neither the man of good breeding —if any still exist—nor the writer of good blood will imagine he can use oblique words when directness is required, or shrink from the worst, or cravenly curtail the inevitable. Both of them bear some resemblance to those gentlemen in Balzac who were neither ultramodern nor old-fashioned, who weren't at all flashy but who caught the eye—whose distinction today was the same as it had been yesterday and the same as it would be tomorrow.

Above all else, sprezzatura is in fact an alert and amiable imperviousness to the violence and baseness of others, an impassive acceptance—which to unperceiving eyes may look like callousness—of unchangeable situations that it tranquilly "decrees nonexistent" (and in so doing ineffably modifies). But beware. Sprezzatura is not kept alive or passed on for very long if it isn't founded, like religious vows, on an almost total detachment from earthly goods, a constant readiness to give them up if one happens to possess them, an evident indifference to death, a profound reverence for what is higher than oneself and for the impalpable, courageous, inexpressibly precious forms that are its emblems here below. Beauty (interior before becoming visible) above all, the generosity of spirit at its root, and a joyful way of being in the world.

This means, among other things, the ability to fly in the face of criticism with smiling good grace and a dignified eloquence born of total forgetfulness of self: a trait we find advocated in the precepts of both mystical education and worldly civility. The Trappist monk, in the chapter on culpability, is ordered to lie facedown on the ground, before he even knows what he is accused of, the moment the brother designated for the purpose speaks his name. If he happens—the rules are emphatic on this point—to express by any external sign that he has not done what he is accused of doing, even when in reality he has not done it, "at the first glimmer of an excuse, everyone else will prostrate himself for the sake of the accused, in atonement for such a serious attack"—on humility, or good taste.

Cosimo de' Medici was a master of both popular and aristocratic sprezzatura. When he realized the ambassadors arrayed in ermine and diamonds—whom he'd abandoned to attend to "an angelic little nephew of his" who had come in "with some switches and a little knife for Cosimo to make him a flute"—were taken aback, he raised his eyebrows with a smile we can easily imagine as enchanting: "Oh, my brothers and lords . . . I see you are surprised I should have made that flute. It's as well you didn't ask me to play it. Because I would have done that too!"

The great Florentine saga flows, all through the fifteenth century, between such affably unassailable banks. To those haughty merchants "with melancholy faces and pleasant, playful manners," the king of France offers the immeasurable privilege of boasting the golden lilies of Valois. For this, the *très chers et aimés cousyns* will not be quartering their shields. No, they will limit themselves instead to placing these lilies ever so politely over one of their six balls, which will be changed on this occasion from red to blue. At Cosimo's funeral, they will just as politely decline the offer of Louis XI's banner, "since their father had requested a modest funeral service." The whole life of Lorenzo the Magnificent will be tuned to this note, down to his final act of elegance, which shows us humanity in its purest state: his last smile at Pico and Poliziano, while—and who could have known it better than he?—the balance of Europe was about to be tipped: "I wish that death would have been so good as to spare me until your library was complete." (From Urbino, the placid ferocities of the pious Federico sing in harmony. A great flatterer, Galeazzo Visconti, whispered to him that he wished he could always undertake feats of arms with him, since in that case he could never lose. "The Duke of Urbino turned to him and said, 'I learned all that from His Excellency Duke Francesco, your father.'")

We find these unassailable, seemingly not even heroic (sprezzatura would blush) sayings scattered here and there over the globe as it turns with the times: in fifteenth-century Italy, in China, at the Temple, in the ancient capital of Montezuma—when the emperor, smiling sweetly at Cortés, opened his tunic and showed his chest: "They told you I am a god or make myself out to be one. But you can see for yourself, I am flesh and blood like you, and mortal, and palpable to the touch." Its heraldic symbol might be, in Russia, the little bunch of white grapes with which, in the dead of winter, the delightful Potemkin thanked Catherine II for the gift of a province, and even more so the sable cloak he threw down on the snow during a journey so as to die quietly, without inconveniencing any innkeepers. "With a light heart, with light hands . . ." The smile takes on a wild, mystical undertone in the reply an Arab gentleman gave a friend seeking to console him for the loss of his entire family: "Only the days keep us company…"

Literature is, curiously, not rich in examples of sprezzatura. Villon's whirling verses are the first to come to mind. In Shakespeare, the royal gestures cross "like blinding flashes" in a way that is supremely tragic, while the hallmark of sprezzatura is, as has already been indicated, both its verve and its tendency to understatement even in the occasional, mortal *flamboyance*. Cordelia's "salt" undoubtedly partakes of it, and above all, in *Richard II*, the darling wish made by the gardener whose plants the queen, in her great distress, has cursed never to grow. "Poor queen! so that thy state might be no worse, / I would my skill were subject to thy curse. / Here did she fall a tear; here in this place / I'll set a bank of rue, sour herb of grace…" Style and character, music and biography, all sometimes partake of this singular quality: as in Marcabru, Bertran de Born, Charles d'Orléans, and that man of the same stripe, who also stands at the source, in the first dew, of a language: Pushkin.

In his great treatise on *la théologie de la noblesse*, Proust would seem, from first page to last, to be in search of sprezzatura, although perhaps he is not as aware of it as one might think if the cruel and dreary snobbery of Oriane and Basin de Guermantes can still enchant him. In Robert de Saint-Loup, however, he has given us a captivating and almost perfect example. Almost: because some leprous spots have tainted the beautiful living frieze melodiously flowing along the walls of the restaurant—the loss, above all, of the feeling for its intellectual lineage. Humanitarian and *avancé*, Saint-Loup innocently believed in the supremacy of those poets whom the pathetic, prophetic Madame de Villeparisis would, and not without reason, have made eat with the servants. In the long run, damage to the aesthetic sense cannot fail to do harm to the moral sense as well. Saint-Loup's Croix de Guerre left its testimony on the most sordid of floors, and the marvelous silhouette of the golden bird lost its splendid, solitary contours. "Style,"

D'Annunzio once declared—unaware he was defining the ethic of sprezzatura in four words—"is isolating power."

Can we associate sprezzatura with the delicate, ferocious geometry behind the "Dance of the Dragonflies"? Or with the inflexible metronome in the études of Frédéric Chopin, by which tenderness and turbulence, rubati and turbati, ecstasy itself and piercing premonition were mercilessly measured? "Let the left hand be your choirmaster and always keep time," taught this Racine of the piano, intolerant of pedals, glissandi, rallentandi, crescendi, passions, revelations, proclamations. "Let nothing be seen of our innermost heart, let nothing be known of us but our smile." A musical Guermantes with his plumage intact, his feet winged, his expression "less dreamy than it was witty and sweet, and altogether devoid of bitterness"—but not of irony—he dryly called the glances he'd happened to cast into ossuaries and graves *Scherzi*. "*Facilement, facilement*," he would repeat again and again as he paced up and down the room, pressing a handkerchief soaked in eau de cologne to his mouth or sipping honey water so as to be able to speak, and drilled *The Well-Tempered Clavier*, that treatise on asceticism, into his students' brains. "*Facilement, facilement*": the hand had to fall from above, almost as though flung on the keyboard for the fun of it, never clenched over the keys with anxious obstinacy like a slave shoved up against a railing. A Cistercian in a tailcoat bought at Dautremont's, he himself refused to expose the white orchid of his visions to the mortal breath of the multitude without a period of contemplation and abstinence: Bach preludes and fugues before each concert were "the best way to exorcize lyrical inspiration, *that agent of darkness*."

The shame and pity of lies, a wave of joy, the innocent boldness of the boy on his pony out to conquer the world (the marvelous little polonaise composed at the age of twelve!), the iridescent veil of fountains in the sunlight, the swelling of the curtains inside a charming house. Grace and happiness without any qualms—not even psychological ones. And from time to time the horn in the depth of the woods, the irrecusable tolling of the hour, "O my Poland," all this and the dead, all this and my approaching death, all this and thy will be done, "let nothing be seen," a handkerchief, soaked in eau de cologne, over the voice as soft as a voice can be: "*Facilement, facilement.*"

Such an ascetic distrust of selfhood paved the way for the sovereign hauteur, the explosive, aerial staccato, the Lipizzaner elegance, of the *Polonaises.* It has been said that this majestic dance-parade, born in the halls of the Kingdom of Poland, was a sort of virile poem meant specially to exalt the sharp, violent beauty of the men and their courtly art, the prerogative of the Polish nobles of the past. (In the mazurka, the triple-meter dance of the Mazovian Lowland, the home terrain of the famous "tempo turbato," which was wrongly believed to be one of Chopin's discoveries, it was the women who triumphed "in the accentuated and prosodic sway" punctuated by the clicking of their heels: proud and nuanced, tender and provocative.)

Pure, terrible Frédéric Chopin took this dance of Catholic gentlemen perpetually on crusade—which was not a display of themselves but of their rank and vision—and led her away lightly, gently, without loosening a single one of her seductive coils, out of the hall and the palace and back to her genesis and her places of origin: the field of honor and feats of arms, of loss and funeral vigils. By tightening its rhythms in an incandescent mesh, he turned it into a model of moral sprezzatura, in whose most stylized instants the inspiration of a race can be measured in a man: a gauntlet thrown down with a smile at fate, a leap through the fire—the art of making light work of inalterable moments without batting an eyelid. All around, as in a story by Pushkin, there is the freshness of dawn; a robin rejoices in an elm; the duel to the death is transmuted into a contest of elegance and youthful beauty, almost tender in its speed and its pride (only the left hand keeps reminding us—very softly—that this is a duel to the death).

It is typical of sprezzatura to choose, as the messenger of the ineffable and the terrible, the least canonized form of all: dance, and almost always folk dance, not a society dance beaten out by the soles of three generations. And—obstinately—it maintains its disguise twice over: through the slim sonorous beam of a single instrument on one hand, and under the pretext of a light entertainment or technical meditation on the other—the duchess's album, Delphine Potocka's birthday; mastery of diminished sevenths or chromatic sixths. *"Facilement, facilement."*

The secret aristocracy of folklore, the intimate link between folk dance and noble style and the secret rhythmic figures of religious chants (that rubato has its roots in Gregorian does not seem doubtful), was the patrimony of the musicians of earlier eras. It is difficult to tell dance from liturgy in a Bach passacaglia or a Bull pavane. Courtly dance and folk dance converge, in every sense, in sprezzatura, and some splendid features of it survived as late as thirty years ago in the peasantry: in dance, yes, but also in courtship, in blood sports, especially in language, and even in infringements of the law, the people displayed traits of a momentary refinement that was neither fictitious nor superficial. The elegance of the hunter's velvet jacket was redoubled in the bandit by a provocative boldness that sometimes rose to the level of greatness. The legend of the famous "Passatore" of Romagna, still familiar to our grandparents, sprang more from the poetry of his sprezzatura than from his distributive justice, for he risked his life with a laugh, for a rose caught flying in a leap or on a reckless, bloody bet. The fable of the robbery at Forlimpopoli, with the bandits lined up on the proscenium of a theater full of beautiful women, whose jewels were unhooked from their necks and wrists with gracious partiality, was tinged with eroticism. It shone with all the caustic colors of an amatory provocation.

Sprezzatura, at its most secular, is certainly one of the characteristic traits of the adventurer—a mercurial, ambivalent, imponderable character, in which the seed of grace nevertheless persists. The people, with their atavistic horror of withdrawing into themselves, recognize the very principle of life in the good-humored imprudence of such a character. For millennia, they followed the course of his adventures in fairy tales and legends, where sprezzatura establishes absolute dominion starting with the sovereign use of language. In that brave, outspoken hero who liberates princesses, mocks ogres and giants, never runs out of tricks or innocent guile, but always remains childishly obedient to a fairy (a *fata*), they unconsciously saw a figure of the soul—a dove to the heavens, a serpent to the world—which hurls itself joyfully, enthusiastically, toward encounters with the divine.

At any time of life, sprezzatura is a youthful gift, inseparable from the smile that conceals youth's powerful inclination to asceticism, its insane and unthinking heroism. The fairy tale faithfully observes these laws, and only yesterday a young man already bereft of legends tried, with an effort of the imagination, to mirror the last inhabitant of the elven kingdom: the frail, radiant actor Gérard Philipe, who sped across the stage and started speaking with a smile and a slight trembling of the pupils "as if in the grip of a sudden inspiration."

The cold fear, the horror perhaps, of once more provoking the masses with its butterfly delicacy has stripped youth of this splendid mantle fit for Ariel—the bequest, even where strength and grace are lacking, of its innocence and spontaneity, which can so unexpectedly unfold its perfect flower: reverence. The cross of boastfulness to which the pitiable and serious young are now nailed has no more affinity with sprezzatura than the sulkiness that makes them ill and permeates their pensive sulks. The sullen, lifeless "charity" of some of today's young Christian extremists would put the cherubs to flight, covering their many eyes with their many wings. "*Facilement, facilement...*"

Good manners are the beginning of holiness, Francis de Sales assures us, and sprezzatura—this attitude that so often blooms on the tall stem of classical virtue—is perhaps only one step away from pure religiosity, of which it remains, in any case, the finest human equivalent.

In that little manual pertinent to the education of princes as well as the formation of saints, the rules of the Trappists, the chapter dedicated to "conferences" (the monks' recreations) contains an exquisite list of proscriptions that add up to a little poem of spiritual sprezzatura. In it, sentimentality and prevarication, self-contemplation ("for good or ill"), loquacity, the propensity to disputation, didactics, and anecdotes ("worldly events that have occurred in the last forty years are never to be discussed") are banned with equal scorn. But nothing—in that absolute monarchy of silence—is so firmly banned as the sullen and programmatic mutism that is the hallmark of this century's most loquacious Christians. "The young will have the good grace to speak less than the others, but they must, however, restrain themselves in this matter with the greatest freedom and not with shame. No one will excuse himself from speaking by saying he does not have anything to say, but when his turn comes, as best he can, everyone will say, if not something, at least a few words." ("Say whatever you like, my daughter," a Russian grand duchess echoes in a letter to her very shy daughter, "but talk to your neighbors at table! Nothing is more odious, or ridiculous, than a taciturn princess.")

"He has a sort of stoic stupidity, a coarse austerity," says Cardinal Bona, another master of stylistic and religious sprezzatura, who is not coincidentally a Cistercian, before going on to sketch the worldly profile of the saint: "Prompt to pay homage, unresponsive to insults, humble when honors are offered, reluctant to become indignant, affable, tractable, cheerful and playful within reason, sociable without scorn, appreciative, beneficent, and charming."

It would seem that grace is the raw material of Grace, and undoubtedly the holy adventurers, the brilliant heroes of legend who with a light heart and light hands cast their lives into the Immutable, were cut from this cloth. *Joy, largüeza, proeza*—the rules of Provençal courtesy completely suffuse Francis of Assisi's youth. His companions remembered him as "a prodigal man, a cautious merchant, but quite munificent, haughty, and generous, light and not a little audacious, with a generosity of spirit, a largeness of heart, and a liberality of mind that could not be matched." In the dream that prompted his conversion, all the symbols he saw were chivalric. After his conversion, he asked his father for his possessions and, when summoned before the bishop, displayed tremendous sprezzatura by stripping naked in the middle of the episcopal palace and tossing his clothes on the floor.

(The bishop admirably paid him back in kind by draping him with his mantle.)

Certainly, the man who, with angelic fury, hurled down tiles and bricks from a roof in Assisi to remind the straying spirits of the monks that all they needed was a roof of air and walls of light rushes that could be dismantled as easily as they were made; the man who, in a cell in Greccio, threw the pillow in which the Evil One had taken up residence at his brother's head; the man who, in the convent of the Poor Clares one Lent, drew a circle with ashes in the center of the chapter house, prostrated himself in the middle, and went away without saying a word, was that same man: a man become "simple not by nature but by grace"—which is yet another possible definition of sprezzatura, at its most transparent. And the same nobility that led him to "take every person's condition into account" made him a radiant lord of souls when, as will happen, he no longer cared about possessing them.

I could go on through the whole martyrology, down to the humblest, least-known names. The crystalline note of sprezzatura rings out from beginning to end—from the gentlehearted bishop of the first century, Polycarp of Smyrna, to the little Carmelite of the twentieth, Elizabeth of the Trinity—and it is hard to see how it could be otherwise, if the lives and deaths of this brilliant myriad were nothing but the glint and reflection of the very Source of light. It seems to me that not much has been said of Christ's sprezzatura, but I don't know what else we could call that thing we find on every page of the Gospels—especially in the latter pages, where human agony take tighter and tighter hold of the Word—that thing we are constantly encountering in the fabric of life, in its unquestionable, ineffable solutions, compensations, sanctions, economies, and ironies: the secret writing of God, and a clear reflection of heavenly piety. It has been said that a smile never played on the Redeemer's imperious lips, but with what other nuance at the corner of his mouth and between his brows could he have uttered certain phrases—certain remarks and questions, addressed to enemies and friends?

"Will ye also go away?" (John 6:67); "Does this offend you?" (John

6:61); "For which of my good works do you stone me?" (John 10:32); and the terrible: "Friend, wherefore art thou come?" (Matthew 26:50). Or: "Were there not ten cleansed? But where are the nine?" (Luke 17:17). And his remote, astral way of writing in the sand, then suddenly lifting his eyes, full of clement irony: "Woman, where are those thine accusers? Hath no man condemned thee?" (John 8:10). And more subtly, more intimately: "Martha, Martha, thou art careful and troubled about many things..." (Luke 10:41), or: "And if any man will sue thee at the law, and take away thy coat, let him have thy cloak also..." (Matthew 5:40). Even his most characteristic spiritual instruction ("let nothing be seen...") is couched in an aesthetic admonition: "When ye fast, be not, as the hypocrites, of a sad countenance: for they disfigure their faces, that they may appear unto men to fast.... But thou, when thou fastest, anoint thine head, and wash thy face; That thou appear not unto men to fast, but unto thy Father which is in secret..." (Matthew 6:16–18).

What is this if not an immense, unceasing invitation to the interior liberation that is utter forgetfulness of self—of the ego magnetized by the sideways mirrors of psychology and the social—stripping off what hinders and deceives the spirit in order to acquire the light step and radiant rhythm that disburses the happiness of the saints? Once all our clothes have been tossed on the floor of the episcopal palace, perfect love demands perfect freedom from all ties to the calculable and the apparent, the passional and the approved. For this alone is the ultimate meaning of giving what one has to the poor, denying oneself, taking up the cross and following the winged steps that precede us, turning the other cheek and forgiving. The famous litany called the litany of humility, composed half a century ago by a very high dignitary of the Roman Catholic Church ("From the desire to be esteemed... praised... honored... consulted... approved of... from the fear of being despised... rejected... forgotten... mocked... suspected... free me, Jesus"), should in reality be called the litany of regeneration, of joyful liberation, of that holy indifference whose central virtue—humility—is both a condition and a consequence, a seed and a finished fruit. The sprezzatura of certain beggars, in whose eyes there is a freedom so sovereign that giving them the smallest gift immediately becomes a grace received, is great and exquisite.

"With a light heart, with light hands..." A pure life is given its rhythm by this light and vehement music, composed entirely of forgetfulness and solicitude, smiles and pity. There was a time when the rites and the liturgy were the collective and geometric locus of this ineffable rhythm. In the simplest of the old ceremonies, there was the *grande allure* of vision: that elegance of the living flame, that heated dialogue in which the powers of the soul and the invisible succeeded each other in tempo rubato, that crash of interstellar silences—another, more pressing instance of God's writing, which opened, in the blind block of the world, a thousand points of escape to the realm of supernatural beauty: which is the realm of mirrors set upright and of shackles fallen, where living and leaving are an ecstasy, one and the same.

THE FLUTE AND THE CARPET

I.

> The wicked are estranged from the womb: they go astray
> as soon as they be born, speaking lies. Their poison is like
> the poison of a serpent: they are like the deaf adder that
> stoppeth her ear; which will not hearken to the voice of
> charmers, charming never so wisely.
>
> —Psalm 58

> The song of the reed flute is fire.... Those who do not
> hear this fire from the flute are as good as dead.
>
> —Jalāl ad-Dīn Rumi

WHAT DOES any examination of man's condition come down to today if not a list—stoical or terrified though the list-maker may be—of his losses? From silence to oxygen, from time to mental equilibrium, from water to modesty, from culture to the kingdom of heaven. And there really isn't much to offset the horrifying catalogues. The whole picture seems to be that of a civilization of loss, unless one dares to call it a civilization of survival, since, in such a postdiluvian condition, dominated by immoderate and universal indigence, a miracle cannot be ruled out: the survival of some islander of the mind still capable of drawing up maps of the sunken continents.

The loss of losses, the seed and circumference of all the others, is, however, what cannot be named. This is always the case. Besides, how could creatures who have suffered the mutilation of the very organ of mystery—Pasternak would call it the ear of the soul—realize that they have lost *their own destiny*?

The ancient mind seems to revolve solely around this irrecusable idea: Fate or the Sibyl's answer, Homer's daimon or Caesar's star, Sirius who churns up the sea from the depths or fixes Polaris in the sky—or that Spirit who governs the planets as the planets govern the human humors to which Leonardo subscribed, or what Christians always called by its name: vocation.

Even before all that, in any case, there was a book; there was an immense soliloquy and a personal canon that teaches us to trace the fate of every last man on this earth back to its source and forward to its end: the Psalter. One hundred and fifty times, with shouts, sobs, laughter, whispers, belly to the ground, dancing, ecstatic, the psalmist pleads simply to know, or to recognize, what has been his "for all eternity, and is therefore destined for him." He seems to give thanks solely for having sometimes known or recognized it. And merely to know or recognize it typifies the fine summit of his spirit, the intellect: "Lord, make me to know my end..." "Cause me to know the way wherein I should walk..." "God be merciful unto us, and bless us, and cause his face to shine upon us, that thy way may be known upon earth..." "Give me understanding that I may live..." He claims, finally, the only right of the human mind that is unquestionable before God: a perfect ear with which to perceive his own vocation and melodiously answer to it.

In Psalm 58, this mystery is contemplated in the guise of a musical simile. The wicked man is the deaf adder who stops up his ear to escape the voice of the charmer—the fakir expert in incantations.

According to the commentators, the text literally says "from him who ties magic knots," and the word for "wicked man" combines the attributes of the teller of untruths, the arrogant man, and the mocker of signs and mysteries to such an extent that the Vulgate could brilliantly inflate him into "the professor of pestilence" and a contemporary translator condense him into "the heretic." Doesn't all this depict, with poetic grace and majesty, the person who flees from venerable voices and covers his eyes before the invisible? The person who, in contrast with the saint, refuses to be tangled and untangled—gently, blindly—in God's writing on earth: in the cryptographies of a destiny?

Many poets and wise men have compared destiny to a marvelously complicated carpet whose other side—knotty and chaotic—the weaver never reveals. Only from the other side of life—or in moments of vision—is man capable of intuiting *the other side*: the inconceivable design in which he forms one thread and one knot, one brown or green corresponding to another brown or green, one fragment of an image, one part that typifies the whole. Even the obedient coilings and uncoilings of the adder are woven into this allegory, so simple and so rich with splendor: the flute of the charmer knots and weaves the adders as the weaver's hand does the woolen threads. But there is no allegory that reality does not already contain. The extraordinary "carpet masters," those bards and mystics of the loom who in ancient times traveled from village to village and could hold hundreds of symbolic patterns in their heads, "dictated" these figures to the local weavers in a slow, mesmerizing chant. And because those sprawling, rosy miniatures, the Senneh carpets, had to be made by the fingers of children—the only ones capable of tying knots of such magical smallness—the fiery voice of the flute would have enthralled their young minds and set the rhythm for their work.

The regal completeness of the carpet has made it a religious object in every era. A precious space, a transfigured piece of earth, in the East it is an image—or even replaces, like a small, portable mosque—the place of prayer. More modestly—simple primers of meaning—some old Italian prints in their own way suggest the fresh, meticulous universality of the carpet and the exquisite, incalculable uniqueness of every thread and knot. Stepping down from her carriage, in the silent square, a woman's black veil, crepe cloth, and silver cross announces her widowhood. The career soldier rides by jingling in the background, while the soldier of fortune strides to meet him. The peasant bristling with greens in no way resembles the blue trout fisherman. From a parvis, the bishop comes down covered with symbols, followed by some tonsured monks swathed in the three colors emblematic of their vows and a knight encapsulated by his cross. And the cripple, in his doublet and shirt, always sitting in the corner with his crutch beside him, is the universal cripple—a figure religiously recognized by the whole society, like the leper with his stick and bell.

Destiny is not separable from the symbol, and it is not at all strange that man has lost one in the very act of denying the other. In the old days, clothes constituted a symbol, or a language of symbols: you could tell at a glance what destiny a man was pursuing—by which I mean what destiny was pursuing him. The long processions of con-fraternities that wind across so many prints provided these holy maskers with the highest wisdom: flute notes that the craftsman was free to follow, consecrating the hours of his labor or the charity of his nights to a saint or a mystery no less than to the prince who served as a protector of the arts and a founder of charitable works. But at the altar of the saint or the mystery, the masks fell away, and each man wonderfully rediscovered his face and wove it most delicately with the other, which was altogether different from his. Until Napo-leon's cultural genocides, it appears that in the city of Rome alone there were more than five hundred of these confraternities. The entire population therefore participated in this spiritually adventurous life and oriented themselves in this exalting language of symbols. Their remaining churches (among the most beautiful in the city), books, paintings, and insignia still speak the language of ecstasy.

Once those mirrors were shattered, how could man not be deprived of a face? We do not need to be reminded of how terrifying a modern crowd can be, because of the total erasure, in such overwhelming numbers, of the human face and of the pure, heartrending images that human faces can sometimes compose. A collective face is an impossibility, and destinies are canceled out in the bone-chilling, illusory typologies that contaminate our lives if we so much as think of them: the man at whom all the walls of the metropolis shout which music he should like, which house he should desire, which woman he should dream of, relentlessly offering him a jumbled profusion of vicarious destinies: the actress who drank poison, the champion who died in an accident. There is no relationship, needless to say, between destiny and the misadventures of such personages who are, in turn, the product of a collective vortex that kept them from any risk of a vocation from the first. And the chain cannot be broken. All these lives turn in circles, one enticing the other, and "the wicked walk on every side," precisely as the psalmist warns.

2.

A certain sound of the divine instrument in the soul...
—SAINT ANTHONY MARIA ZACCARIA

Among those multitudes, as a peasant might say, there wouldn't be room enough to grow a grain of millet. And a grain of destiny? In reality, what makes destiny sacred is the same thing that distinguishes the sacred, the same thing that distinguishes poetry: its reclusion, its segregation, the ecstatic emptiness in which it is fulfilled. Already, half a century ago, Eliot showed us, in a ruthless cutaway, those houses and rooms full of nonlife, where the horrendous heap of newspapers, the gramophone, the unnerving randomness of the gestures had crowded destiny out, and where even eros was already a headless specter: "unreproved," "undesired."

The space of destiny is concave, silent, and resonant, like the case of a precious instrument; it is Poe's "suspended lute." Once upon a time there were places where people withdrew "in order to see into themselves more clearly," which to me seems to suggest they were retraining their ear to the sharp whisper of the flute and the faint tocsin of the weaver's shuttle. Ancient parlors that paved the way to and protected destiny the way shells pave the way to and protect the sea. Slowly, soundlessly, a pendulum would swing; the portrait of a founder would gather the honey of silence on his lips; a book would be placed, closed and alone, on the corner of a large, uncluttered table. What was it, in those rooms where the branch of a holm oak tapped at the window, that spoke of imminence and distance, of an inevitability coagulated drop by drop in the hives of a sweet, tetragonal patience? There, for centuries, hands had joined in prayer, the noblest gesture of them all; for centuries, eyelids had been lowered before the mouth dared to speak the sentence in which an eternity was at stake. Gestures of inconceivable delicacy—kissing a scapular, pointing a thumb at the heart or the brow—had given voice to silence during reunions and breathless farewells: gestures spaced and bounded by the motionless dance of the hours, the prohibitions, the rites (*you will perhaps be able to see him after evening prayers, during Advent he will be on spiritual retreat, women are not permitted in that part of the abbey*), as the most intoxicating inspirations are bounded by the pure cruelty of rhyme.

"We must stay out of the game of circumstances so that nothing reaches us except the inevitable," a poet once warned. And what is the inevitable if not precisely what is "for all eternity"? "Did you put it there?" a Desert Father said to his disciple, who as they were traveling the roads asked him if he could pick a sow thistle he had spotted on the wayside. "Then why would you want to pick it up?" Indeed, it is written (John 3:27) that a man can receive nothing, unless it is given him from heaven.

Like Saint Andrew's manna in the hollow of the vial, destiny is formed in a void by virtue of the same complementary laws that govern the birth of a poem: abstention and accumulation. The word that will need to take shape in that hollow is not our own. It is up to us to wait in the wilderness of patience, living on honey and locusts, for a very slow and instantaneous precipitation. When it comes, it is brief and will not be repeated. "The words of the Lord are pure words." It is again the psalmist who reminds us of this, and it is the story of the prophet Elijah, who did not hear the word of his destiny in the great wind or in a thunderclap but in a still small voice, and covered his head in terror. A visionary, Margery Kempe, whose enchanting prose is ignored by studies of mysticism and anthologies of English literature alike, at the end of her life heard the Holy Spirit speaking like "the voys of a lityl byrd whech is callyd a reedbrest, that song ful merily oftyntymes in hir ryght ere. And then schuld sche evyrmor han gret grace aftyr that sche herd swech a tokyn."

The adders fall under the spell of the subtlest of instruments, and the shuttle is no noisier as it casts its luminous beams of thread through the warp. An emptiness filled with silence, into which destiny will rush by a physical law, just as energy will rush into a vacuum: this is what Saint John of the Cross describes to us—and what else does the fairy tale whisper in our ears, through its regal unfolding of figures? The lost prince of the *Spiritual Canticle* can only be found by becoming a pilgrim and a beggar, or, for a man whose heart is empty, by becoming a man who has died from a terrible love: what in the East is called a dervish or a fakir (and the moment such mysterious nuptials take place, it is only reasonable that the charmer is called by the same name as the one who is charmed).

I have heard a man of the world recall one of the central moments of his life: how, having been locked in a Trappist monastery by mistake one winter evening, he preferred to risk spending the whole night there rather than speak to a monk who, completely unaware of his presence, had come out through the gates of the cloister and was silently advancing toward him in the darkness. The "violence" (so he said) of that God-immured destiny overwhelmed and terrified him. He felt himself an absolute *non licet*, to be mingling his uncertain destiny, even for a moment, with that of the Trappist—who could not, in any case, have answered him—without any preliminary purification or even the slightest authoritative sign of the invisible. In the world where he usually lived—a world of wandering beings who spoke a lingua franca and whose faces and clothes were interchangeable, who scarcely remembered whether they were coming from Casablanca or Tokyo, whether they had met in Washington or Dakar, a world of universal dissolution in which everything was possible and inconsequential: "unreproved," "undesired"—that Trappist advancing in the darkness had seemed to him like the last heroic demiurge intent on his work of daily recomposing the cosmos, daily separating the elements and the species...

But what constituted the violence of that destiny if not emptiness? At the start of their circular dance—led by the flute and symbolizing the motion of the spheres—those mystic Islamic dancers, the whirling dervishes, take off their huge black cloaks, images of the world. In the same way a man's clothing, country, memories, and language, and that essence of essences, his name (in which antiquity recognized fate itself, to such an extent that it imposed two names on each man—one evident and usable, the other secret and sacred; to expunge it was to expunge the man)—all these things fell from him. But God restores with the right hand what He takes with the left. In ragged, archaic, meaningful clothes, this man was now dressed like no prince ever before, and from his mouth deserted by words came the spirals of a song that, with no desire to mean anything human, was capable of taming wild beasts. His strengths—memory, desire, skill, rapacity—died, only to be gradually regenerated as powers: vision, intercession, aptitude, prophecy. The old name was wrapped up in an altar cloth and put away, and he was marked with a new name that served to seal his resurrection. A sacred mask was once more imposed on him. Again he assumed a celestial double. For with that new name a long-dead saint—now his daimon, the spirit responsible for his care—had become a fixed star in the firmament of his spirit, an unfading corolla in the nursery of his mind: *stella stillans claritatem, rosa rorans bonitatem*. And finally there was the predicate, which forever fixed his contemplation on a particular celestial mystery: the Cross, the Transfiguration, the Eucharist, the Communion of Saints. (How could we separate Thérèse of Lisieux from the two heraldic mysteries ineluctably placed on her path to perfection, the Childhood of Christ and the Face of the Dying Jesus?)

"To him that overcometh will I give to eat of the hidden manna, and will give him a white stone, and in the stone a new name." Until he accepted the name ordained from on high for his son John and wrote it on a writing table, Zechariah could not recover the power of speech. God is the baptizer, but how can we really know if the name Joseph signifies his righteousness or if righteousness gave the name its meaning; if Lazarus—Eleazar, he whom God has helped—did not receive his name so that the glory of the Most High would be tacitly manifest in him from birth?

The repudiation of the name and the divine predicate in Western

religious orders is perhaps the most dismal indicator of the renunciation of the holiest and most precious mandate of all: to confirm
and safeguard destinies. For religion is nothing other than a destiny
sanctified, whereas the universal massacre of the symbol, the inexpiable crucifixion of beauty, as I have said before, is the universal massacre and crucifixion of destinies. The hatred of the traditional
splendors passed down in figures and images is only one aspect, and
certainly the most significant aspect, of that profound suicidal impulse
that the great exorcists always discover at the root of every possession.

3.

Note the words, mark the mysteries.
—SAINT GREGORY THE GREAT

... secret warnings and mysterious invitations...
—LEO XIII

In a famous passage, Proust asserts that the principle of style is the
same principle that governs a traditional salon: renunciation. Abstention and interdiction are the sine qua non of destiny, as they are of
parlors and poetry. What are the Tablets of the Law but a long list
of abstentions (you shall not do, you shall not say...)? What is the
Book of the Dead if not a meticulous account of abstentions (I have
not done, I have not said...)? Virtue is negative, and poetry is nothing but the exercise of this global virtue, which it shares with nature:
the patient accumulation of time and secrets that suddenly becomes
that miracle of superior energy: a poetic precipitation.

It would seem that destiny, for the man of the word, and particu-
larly for the storyteller, was once the clay with which he worked. He
imagined, combined, and recounted destinies, from the epics and
chansons de geste to the sadly hypnotizing nets of psychology. In fact,
in the history of the Word, there are ironically few true masters of
the mysteries of destiny, and their patron may be John the Revelator

of Patmos: those who have traced, more or less on their knees, after years of vision, desire, and terror, the unique and universal story written "elsewhere" before being set down in their book—those who have been able to discern the pattern in the city's constellations, the golden bell among the bells of history—are very rare indeed. Such people are both the weaver and the carpet; they play the flute and answer to it, a bit like the Byzantine protodeacon who, in certain ceremonies, announces the divine event and at the same time recites it. They suffer, in their hearts and loins, the stories they tell, and therefore contemplate them like the dead, who look lucidly down at their tiny bodies with a rarefied, redemptive compassion. This is the way Lawrence of Arabia describes the horribly transitory actions of a group of men in the desert—as if the imperturbable eye of God were once more looking down on the plains of Troy or Joshua's camp; he gathered the sighs he heard in the barracks, when all the men were immersed in their sorrowful sleep, prisoners of the coffins of their bodies, and lifted them up to the highest summits of language. The search for the Arab leader—that modern fairy tale of the three emirs self-contained as a mandorla in *Seven Pillars of Wisdom*—proceeds according to the same inverted rules, from oasis to oasis, emir to emir, until, at the end of many marvelous paths, they reach the man who will be the very image and pledge of destiny, the prose slows to a dirgelike rhythm, and in the dark tent thick with presences, the traveler's tired, indefatigable eyes pause and isolate, with the monstrous magnification of a lens, two lowered eyelids, two delicate hands lightly touching, with tremendous determination, the hilt of a sword just drawn from its scabbard . . .

The tale of the three emirs puts me in mind of the tale of the three apples. In that famous story, told by Scheherazade on the eighteenth night, the clairvoyance of the people offered a thoroughly, scrupulously horrifying depiction of destiny. No wonder Hofmannsthal tried to reproduce its imperfectible horror in the ecstatic meditations of his brief, bone-tingling "The Golden Apple." But in fact, rather than dwell on those works that so consummately narrate destinies—"The Altar of the Dead," or "The Tale of the 672nd Night," or "The Beautiful Genoese"—I would like to linger on others that, like little mythological puzzles, present us with the very workings of their mystery. I am thinking, for example, of the terrifying verses of Cavafy— that desolate Alexandrian who was, with his ear so attuned to augural signs, a spiritual son of the great archons of destiny, Plutarch and Shakespeare—especially those verses in which the young Nero, whom the Delphic oracle has told to beware the age of seventy-three, smiles, for he is barely thirty (while far away, in Gaul, Galba "secretly musters and drills his army— / Galba, the old man in his seventy-third year"); in which Thetis, mourning Achilles, pleads and wonders, where was Apollo, his divine protector, although it is Apollo himself who had "gone down to Troy / and together with the Trojans had killed her son . . ." The black threads that weave these mortal convergences in Cavafy, in Borges give rise to other images: secret exchanges of masks and the mutual justification of destinies. Two theologians who hate and denounce each other unto death will appear, in the indifferent eyes of eternity, to be a single man, and Dante's one, long look at the divine ideograms inscribed on a leopard's pelt will justify the pure and total desperation of the poor captive animal.

Perhaps it is Pasternak's novel that reveals, with the greatest liturgical delicacy, the pain and glory of predestination such as it might be deciphered by a dead man: the words noted in fear and trembling, the reverberation of mysteries and signs, the steps and glances that sanction death in the very places where life was most intense—and, once again, God's writing in the arrows, the stars, the circles melted in the frost on the window glass. The exemplary code and classic map of destiny, however, had already been drawn by one of the great prose writers no one has read, owing to that law (denounced, I believe, by Ernest Hello) which states that the least scent of the divine will put the world to flight: the banker Marie-Alphonse Ratisbonne, in the brief account of his conversion. Ratisbonne, too, reveals the dazzling reverse side of the visible to the eyes of the living, but he does so in the manner of a man who, like Lazarus, is now contemplating an incredible world. His spellbound disbelief in a story that turns on something outside of the human sphere inspires him, in his literary innocence, to the most refined procedures of fatidic narration: the emergence, all through the story, of trivial circumstances that could foil a whole divine plan; the thrashings of the soul torn between conflicting temptations, as though, up until the very moment of revelation, it were the subject of a dispute between two warring presences; the thickening of the threads and the quickening of the melody as we approach the story's climax, while the sleuth-hound memory rushes to retrace his steps and recapitulates, in an almost terrified rapture, the twists and turns that seemed so random at the time: the train he did not exit, the carriage that blocked the road, the friend who showed up unexpectedly, the strange night, the bizarre and very wise wager. And all of this is braided together with dreams, objects, words heard by chance, "secret warnings and mysterious invitations," and as that dark pestering dog that barred his path is now revealed to be the specter of the past, so the dead stranger, laid out at dawn in the shadowy chapel—that luminous Comte de la Ferronays who had prayed for Ratisbonne without ever having met him—is revealed as a luminous propitiatory victim.

When a man is transformed, the world is transformed. Instantly, it is populated by figures and marvels he was always brushing against but never so much as suspected—things that have always existed, but only today are truly present. Everywhere he looks, as if they had just been restored to their physical form, he sees impossibly beautiful places and charming creatures whose mere existence is an implicit celebration, governed by stellar circuits, escorted by invisible choirs, graced with expressive gestures. The call of the flute conjures up some worlds and cancels out others. Even a writer with an extremely modest ear, Thomas Merton, was able to evoke for once in his life (during his first stay at a Trappist monastery) this law of interpenetrating worlds nested one inside the other. He says that he experienced the exhilarating feeling of possessing the whole earth, not because of what he saw, but because of the place toward which his sight was directed: that Archimedean point outside the world. Things not possessed and not coveted, things that—pure mirrors and echoes— allude to other things, are intoxicating. For destiny is not in the field you own, but in the pearl for which you sell that field. That the body applauds when the soul is wedded with its destiny can be seen soon after: the man who, as long as he lived in the world, was afflicted by a thousand ills becomes strong and vigorous once he submits to a life of unthinkable austerity. The body, an intelligent servant, refuses to obey those who don't know where their steps are directed. Indeed, in medical literature, the case of the anemic girl whose red blood cell count ironically increases once she can finally fast with pleasure on a longed-for Carmel is now classic.

It was the humble, majestic lord of the Italian language who bequeathed us the apostolic book of destinies, which is both a literary masterwork and a treatise in figures on the quasi-scientific notion of providence, which the ancients, I believe, called *economy*. Neither psychology nor passions nor characters form the basis of a classic—that patrimony that belongs to the people long before it belongs to the culture—but an overwhelming feeling for man's encounters with destiny. And in *The Betrothed*, there is no other protagonist. Royal destinies and vicarious destinies cross on every page: on one side, in Borromeo and the Unnamed—two faces on the same herm—the man is tethered to his daimon; on the other, Abbondio and Rodrigo— whose passions, whether fear or lust, decide things for them—are constantly diverting their intellects from the psalmist's "way." In that fervid, bitter gloss on the Psalter (though no doubt the whole novel could be called that) which is Borromeo's admonition to Don Abbondio, the Cardinal expounds the simplest and most important law of spiritual mathematics: how running away from a vocation leads, by mechanical necessity, exactly where the danger is most grave; how fidelity to a sacred mask is the only safe bet—and how by assuming it Don Abbondio would have been favored by fortune, but by refusing it he has been subjected to the rigors of blinder laws: the rigors of the laws of the world. These laws are incarnate in the Unnamed, an ascetic condor, the inverted instrument of an identical economy, with his infernal communions, his "secret league of atrocious deeds." "Sorcery and sanctity are the only realities. Each is an ecstasy, a withdrawal from the common life. Great people of all kinds forsake the imperfect copies and go to the perfect originals. The merely carnal, sensual man can no more be a great sinner than he can be a great saint..."

There is another glossator of the psalmist in *The Betrothed*, and it is no coincidence that her thread is so delicately, so virginally, braided with that of Borromeo. This is Lucia, whose melodious notes—always blended with "crooked ways" and "straight ways," with what "is or is not suitable to her condition," which is to say her destiny—are the same notes plucked on David's cithara: Lucia's shocking and unshakable modesty serves as a bridge between the perception of the saint and the refined instincts of the people, that choir of *The Betrothed* who are constantly declaring their aristocratic reverence for anyone with a destiny. Fra Cristoforo, Borromeo, Lucia, the Unnamed—all have this thing called destiny. But the people do not discriminate further; the other characters do not interest them, and they pay them no mind. And since they are still a society, they find joy in that supreme representation of destinies which the rite provides to all men who are not damned—and which can also, in moments of great upheaval, provide a sermon such as Fra Fedele's: a spiritual disquisition on destiny that is a miniature of the novel at the center of the novel, one of those tragic round mirrors in which Velázquez and van Eyck captured vast rooms momentarily invisible.

The people of that time and place were, besides, predisposed to the music of destiny. That was their natural province. Their language dripped with it: "that is not his star," "you can't bargain with fate," or "change your country and you change your destiny." Out of wisdom, as well as necessity, the peasant obeyed the precept of multiple meanings: "Never eat unless you're truly hungry, never drink unless you're truly thirsty." The canonical geometry of works and days, the votive order of crops, and the rhythmical reports from the stars ruled all things gratuitous out of his life. For him, they were the poet's meter, the monk's breviary. His was a world of admirable associations and heartbreaking fragilities: in honor of Saint Mark, begin rearing the silkworms; sow the beans when Venus's luminous beauty mark appears near the mouth of the moon; leave the dinner carved on the table at the end of All Saints' Day; do not give thanks for the loan of bread, yeast, or fire, for God alone is their Lord; never offer the Divinity a flower that a human nose has sniffed; during Lent, in the evenings after dinner, abstain from telling stories other than fairy tales or the lives of the saints ...

4.

> All of this hints at something, it means something.
> —SAINT AUGUSTINE

Lovers of destiny, the people preferred and were always re-creating that magnetic field of visions and prodigious symbolic economies: the fairy tale. What is myth if not a representation of destiny in which nature plays so integral a part that, when the landscape is condemned, myth is condemned also?

From its rings come dreams, the apparitions that the abyss, the caves, the waters, the full moon, and the coils of the wind weave around the mysteries and spells that the very spirit of the language draws from the ancient symbols of piety and horror.

One image of destiny is the great forest: in the fear that attends its threshold, its incalculable extent, its profusion of paths (which makes it possible to ride for centuries, like an ancient Nordic hero, and always find oneself in the same spot), the murky, tremulous light that is neither night nor day. And in that murk, the shuttle of encounters flashes between the trees: the hermit's chapel, the damsel weeping by the brook, or, at the farthest portal of this dark green gallery, the knight with his visor lowered, who brings his horse, and our breath, to a halt. And the castles that appear and disappear. And the sudden silvery lakes where there are no boats in sight, but a broadsword has been planted in the center of the waters.

The fairy tale is destiny in slow formation, a revival of water and spirit, and the fairy-tale hero, more than any other, is asked to be as pliant as the adder responding to the flute, which resonates everywhere and nowhere: in the inexplicable formulas and the dread of transformation, from the mouths of the Moirai weavers who do not even hide their name (*fata*), even in the wild, instructive silence of the creatures and places locked in the pure amber of a magic spell. Sometimes—as in a verse found in France and Romagna, Germany and Tuscany—it is the flute itself, the instrument carved from the bone of the murdered man, whose innocent voice survives and mourns a destiny:

> Oh shepherd, hold me in your hands,
> But play me softly lest you hurt my heart!
> They killed me in the Val di Sisa,
> They killed me for nothing at all,
> For a feather from the Griffin bird.
> If my brothers had asked me for it,
> I would have given it to them, out of love . . .

The negative virtue required of the fairy-tale hero is as rigorous as that required of the monk. And after stringing together shirts from nettles, after seven years, seven months, and seven days of silence, after the trials of beauty and fear, he will be granted comparable powers: he will be able to break spells, restore fabulous riches, and reassemble the beautiful mosaics of living creatures.

The knight's journey through a series of duels and illusions, as we are all well aware, is a mind's journey into God. But what do the scenes inside the castle and the nights of the holy watch represent if not life's liturgical moments: those sacred spaces inside and outside of time where men gather to reestablish, in stylized mimesis, their connection with God. The opening of the Arthurian saga—the hypnotic passage of the Holy Grail clothed in white samite through the breathless hall of Monsalvat (a scene that excites destinies, since immediately afterward the knights declare their wish to go in search of it)—has its origin and end in the deathly silent transit of the Sacred Chalice "which no one is permitted to behold," held by the priest and hidden by a purple veil in the Byzantine rites of Lent.

5.

> It is impossible to retain the Memory of the Encounter
> without entering the darkness of the symbol.
>
> —LOUIS MASSIGNON

Whenever a man, moved by the flute's faint, devastating music, responds to it with a pure intonation, "what is dictated to him is not a verbal form but an action, or rather a movement of the body in space." Thus Abraham had to migrate immediately, Moses to take off his shoes on the holy ground of the burning bush, the disciples to break bread, while the relatives of the resurrected were commanded to feed them without delay. In order to recover the terrifying intimacy of his encounter with destiny, man repeats this gesture, imparts and teaches it. So that there comes to be a daily resurrection, by means of an inspired stylization—allusive words, tragic vestments—of those moments that halted, in vertiginous stasis, the wheel of human time. The genesis of the Christian rite seems to have been, for man, much the same.

But there is more to it than this. For the rite converts, from memory into presence, the destiny of destinies and the fairy tale of fairy tales, which no undefiled ear can resist and to which all the fairy tales in the world affix themselves and covertly allude: the story of a god on earth. Like the fakir stripped of every possession, the redeemer God, in the guise of a slave and subject to death, sways to the voice of the other fakir, the creator God. The supreme Enchanter and the supreme Enchanted are united in a mortal offering, and the Gospel of John is only the long musical cartouche, the earthly score, of this dance of the divine Serpent whose shadow is cast on the earth by his celestial Double. "I can of mine own self do nothing: as I hear [the Father], I judge..." (John 5:30); "The Son can do nothing of himself, but what he seeth the Father do; for what things soever he doeth, these also doeth the Son likewise" (John 5:19).

The two Testaments do not seem to know the word *destiny*, but is there ever a question of anything other than this inalienable possession, *pars mea, hereditas mea in aeternum*? And again, as ever, it is Christ who strikes that chord as it was never struck before—drawing from it the deep, incandescent notes that echo through his whole life on earth:

"Woman, what have I to do with thee? mine hour is not yet come" (John 2:4); "I will not go ... my time is not yet complete" (John 7:8); "The hour is come, that the Son of man should be glorified" (John 12:23); "Now is my soul troubled; and what shall I say? Father, save me from this hour" (John 12:27); "then Jesus knew that his hour was come that he should depart out of this world unto the Father" (John 13:1); "These words spake Jesus, and lifted up his eyes to heaven, and said, Father, the hour is come" (John 17:1). When they wanted to take him where the multitude was headed, a formula falls from his lips (John 7:6) that establishes the distinction between vicarious destiny and royal destiny for all eternity: "My time has not yet come; but your time is always ready."

How could the destiny of the cosmos not be implicated in the destiny of the God a great baroque poet imagined as Zenith and Antipodes, with hands spanning the poles and tuning all the spheres, joining eternity and time and apportioning the quadrants that give geometric order to the seasons and feast days? The books in which the rites are recorded—those zodiacal, cosmological books—run motionless through the whole circle of the year, each canonical hour celebrating the passage of the light, a moment of creation, or the gradual transition from dark to dawn, from the chaos of the mind to its illumination. In the celestial orbit of the sanctuary, along the melodious ellipse of the eight modes and the innumerable tones ("the winter tone and the summer tone ... the tones of Easter, Christmas, and Lent ... the tones of the Pontiffs, the Doctors, the Confessors ..."), man braids the majestic slowness of the hours with the lightness of the dance. The ceremonial robes he wears, with their different colors, visibly convey different meanings to the eye: death, purgation, contemplation. Around a still sun—Christ—Christ himself, in the tragic mask of the priest, wheels with the zodiac. He shines, the first seed of light, in the dark womb of the winter solstice; he suffers through the cruelty of April, then springs from the rock like the whirling lilac from its hibernal branch; he mounts in the midday sun and later plummets down to earth in a fire that is, simultaneously, a gentle rain, igniting all things frozen and tempering summer with its slight chill.

In this time-within-time of the ceremony, the earthly destiny of the Sacrificed Sacrificer—"He who offers and is offered up, who receives and is handed around"—is linked with the destiny of the man who imitates him in a communion that theology will never be able to describe as well as the most formidable language of all: the supreme intellectual beauty of the gesture.

The vesting of the bishop, during the Byzantine papacy, was a marvelous narrative of destiny. He too, before anything else, is stripped of that "chapel" mantle where—with the amazing elegance God grants only to certain hypnotic lepidoptera, or to the mind of man after a thousand years of contemplation—the cosmos is depicted in its four quadrants; then he changed out of his monastic robes into a black penitential cloth. This figure of poverty and pain is then slowly revested among plainsongs and rhythmic offerings of incense, with all the powers and virtues of the Model: the scarlet of the monarch and the martyr, the stole of the sacrificer, the double-edged sword on Patmos coming out of the mouth of the Word: speech that judges and severs. On the four-lobed golden crown the very face of the heavenly King glows, the lost sheep rests in the pallium, while the many-eyed, many-winged cherubim flutter around the small round flabella singing the holy Trisagion at the throne of the Lamb. At the bishop's feet is a carpet covered in images: an eagle with its wings spread over a walled city, the episcopal totem—magnanimity, fortitude, eyes capable of staring at the sun of orthodoxy, guardians of the citadel of God. In the crozier shaped like a caduceus, the two serpents of prudence and wisdom face each other like golden pincers. A double and a triple candelabrum accompany him: the two Mysteries of faith encapsulated in his person, which is now the literal, central, magnetizing replica of the icon of the Pantocrator. The choir can now rightly call him by the name "despot." Later, from the fragrant cloud that hides him from view, his voice will sound a lower tone than the others: the Almighty speaks in a whisper...

But behold: At the end of the celebration of the mysteries—as if the divine bequest were soaring back up to heaven, like the Grail or Longinus's lance—all those splendid pelts are torn from his body one after another. The clergy, who for hours have circled him like planets dancing around the sun, escort him out and leave him—again all in black—at the threshold of the dark chapel. He has once more become a solitary monk, divested of everything, in an attitude of supplication, for, "Lord God, human nature cannot bear the essence of Divinity, and you have set on your throne, in accordance with your plan, despots who have the same passions we do…"

The liturgy weaves destinies in concentric circles. Fasting and retreat bind the bishop and the priest in terrible intimacy before the ordination, and afterward the priest will have to call this bishop's name every day of his life, whether the bishop is alive or dead, offering him a fragment of the Host. Messenger and psychopomp, with his long stole unfolded like a letter between heaven and earth, the deacon leads the dance of the sacred adders; he mediates between the destinies of the sanctuary and the destinies of the nave. He is the bearer of vocations: "The Master is calling you," he chants on Holy Friday, conducting the twelve priests, whose feet he will wash, toward the bishop. For the liturgy, according to tradition, is only the earthly shadow of that other liturgy that is ceaselessly being offered in heaven. In that shadow, the deacons are the angels and archangels, while the choir proclaims itself to be a mystical representation of the cherubim, escorting the heavenly powers "that now invisibly celebrate with us."

And in the outermost circle are the people, who weave their own destiny into the plenary destiny of God, the vertical destinies of the ministers, the destiny of the living and the dead, and the destiny of the loving spirits who keep watch from the vast firmament of the temple: painted in icons, raised on altars, incorporated into columns, shining in stained-glass windows, recumbent on sarcophagi, even spread, like a fine, dark scripture, on the marble floors. Each of those spirits is endowed with its spiritual blazon: a sword, a wheel, a palm, a mystic animal: imprinted with a destiny that is momentary yet apt to be revived, unique and universal as a rose or a star: *stella stillans, rosa rorans*. The five senses apprehend and absorb these concerts of supramundane and earthly destinies with a sort of ecstatic terror, in an ineffable rubato of voices, gestures, flames, and plumes of incense that turn the church into an incandescent vortex, a living loom where the shuttles sound like plectrums. (These are the moments in which the Ethiopian liturgy introduces cosmic instruments: the drum, the sistrums...)

I have said it before: In these instants, it becomes clear that an age of malediction, where any highly, subtly differentiated destiny is held in horror, gives rise to the long night of liturgical vandalization and the butchery of every rite.

What is the "Communion of Saints" if not a sidereal locus where destinies converge, share mysterious nourishment, trade in fluid coins? The regal peasant of Molise who can still offer the stranger the treasure of her enduring love—her nine "first Fridays"—shows she is well acquainted with the law of ineluctably interconnected destinies, which flow together, as the Scriptures tell. The law that says that if someday the weary find rest, it is because a peasant prayed in a field. It was this same law that permitted Francis de Sales and Jane de Chantal to see each other four years before they met—the Bishop of Geneva praying in his chapel, the young widow with the light brown hair crossing a clearing. Being very attentive adders, the two of them then organized their entire lives around this inexplicable encounter.

6.

> The Master is come, and calleth for thee.
>
> —JOHN 11:28, 10:3

> Every man seeks to understand his true name.
>
> —SAINT ANTHONY THE GREAT

Certainly, the voice of the flute is remote. It is almost always imperceptible. Interwoven with the thousand voices of the age, it blends with the discordantly bewitching music of the mundane concert. Its delicate lament is like a sound heard in a dream, like the voice of the little nightingale whose diamond dart will cause every sound in the forest to fall silent.

Anyone who flinches at that slight stabbing pain has known the contemplation of the audible. But the ascesis of attention requires a keen persistence, because that sound is continually being drowned out, cut off, and dissipated by the hiss of the perceptible, and nothing is easier to believe than an auditory fata morgana. Other voices, other flutes, are continually simulating this fire that dies if it is not heard, and no doubt the spurious concerts have seldom been as persuasive as they are today.

Counterfeit destinies, orgies of possibilities, are proposed and solicited everywhere we look. Invitation follows invitation, wink follows wink. Who said you can't be a poet and a man-about-town, a mother and a siren, a priest and a jet-setter? Why not get a taste of that terra incognita, those unfamiliar customs and aromas, that language, that fountain, that adventure: right now, blindly, within arm's reach? Why Shanghai and not Borneo? Why not the Antilles? Why one totem, one daimon, one name? Why should there be one destination set aside for us "for all eternity"?

Pasternak exorcised this grand illusion in a quatrain:

> Leave blanks in life, not in your papers,
> And do not ever hesitate
> To pencil out whole chunks, whole chapters
> Of your existence and your fate.

Teach the young adder not to loosen her coils unless she is responding to the sound that has legitimate authority over her. Teach her never to eat unless she's truly hungry, never to drink unless she's truly thirsty. There is no education worth receiving or imparting except an education of this kind.

For every wayfarer, there is a melody that is his and his alone —a melody that he has been seeking from birth, since before the centuries began, *pars, hereditas mea*. But how and where are we to discern it?

In, first of all, the voices of the dead, whose bones, like the whistle fashioned from the murdered man, sometimes seem to sing softly in our ear. In the four treasures that the dead bequeath us: landscape, language, myth, rite. Treasures for which it does not seem unreasonable to throw one's own life away, if life without them is a dead star. At the sound of the flute, the four sister sphinxes raise their heads in our blood and begin to murmur beneath the sand of our thoughts, like the water of a well deep underground. And in the signs and mysteries, the warnings and invitations: the similitude that keeps returning to us through the years, a pestering visitor with her hood pulled down to cover her eyes. When we are children, it is the distressingly pleasurable fairy tale that we are always asking our grandparents to tell—that we act out in our games and revisit in our dreams: the heraldic fairy tale that is the pride of every child, almost as if he recognized in advance his future blazon, so that the child with a difficult destiny, beset by painful transformations, will always want to hear "The Ugly Duckling," while the little girl who awaits a saga of secret diadems and unspoken glories will never get enough of "The Goose Girl" ("Farewell, Falada, who hangs up above! / Farewell, young queen, who passes down below…").

Why do our steps blindly, ineluctably gravitate toward one road and not another? Why is the eye magnetized by the map of an unremarkable city? Why does the maiden Alacoque's heart leap in her breast at the sound of the unfamiliar name Paray-le-Monial? And what about the last Russian tsar, when he set foot on the threshold of his martyrion, the house that belonged to the Siberian merchant Ipatiev—he, the last of a line begun three hundred years earlier in the old Ipatiev Monastery in Kostroma? Did the tsar recognize what was to come?

There can be no doubt that the gentle bishop Polycarp recognized it when he was getting ready to flee persecution for the sake of his flock. As he prayed, he grew drowsy and saw the pillow on which he prayed surrounded by flames. "This is pointless," he said, "whatever

I do, I am going to die at the stake." And when his flock tried to wave away the premonition, he smiled and told them the name of the centurion who was already waiting below: Herod. And there is no doubt the Christian catechumen recognized it who, in his childhood, felt his heart stop beating when the holy of holies opened, so as to savor the indescribable disillusionment he felt when he saw *only* the scrolls of the law... Plutarch and Shakespeare, Borges and Cavafy, Hofmannsthal and Pasternak have spoken of nothing but these instantaneous pronouncements. Above all, those supreme confessors of destiny, the spiritual teachers, have spoken of them. These teachers have never grown weary of tracing, in the constellations of moments, the writing of God.

It was precisely so that this decipherment would not be doomed to failure, so that seeing might change into perceiving ("of the discernment of inspirations"), that the subtle game of limits, the magic net of the hours, prohibitions, and duties, was conceived, evening prayers, and the tone of doctors, and nothing will reach you except the inevitable, for a man can receive nothing, unless it is given him from heaven.

Around us, it's true, there are fewer and fewer destinies. But truly God knows more about it than we do if, in the places of horror and vast solitude assigned to us, a boy in a suburban columbarium can still stay up all night reading an immemorial text, if among twenty thousand workers one girl can still have visions, if the death-hungry junkie can end up at Mount Athos. Those who have no masters do not always have the devil as their master. We live in an age of substitutions, and we are still granted some prodigious surrogates. The portion, however, of the psalmist's inheritance is assigned elsewhere than on this earth.

> It gives me such comfort to drift
> And feel that my life and my lot are
> Thy priceless and wonderful gift...
> I feel how Thy hands are ablaze,
> The hands that have made me and hold me
> And hide like a ring in a case.

FAIRY TALE AND MYSTERY

DEER PARK

IF I WRITE sometimes it is because certain things do not want to be separated from me any more than I want to be separated from them. In the act of writing them down, they enter me forever—through my pen and my hand—as if by osmosis.

In joy, we move into an element that is entirely outside of time and reality, but whose presence is perfectly real.

Incandescent, we walk through walls.

Marvelous story of Pharaoh Menkaure, whom the gods condemned to die young. His clemency, which had broken faith with the tragic destiny of Egypt following the tyrannies of Cheops and Khafra, curried him no favor with the gods. And so he has his palaces and parks lit by thousands of lamps. He will turn nights into days and thus live twelve more years instead of the six remaining to him.

This is, there is no doubt about it, a parable of the poet—that involuntary enemy of the law of necessity. What can the unjustly punished poet do but turn nights into days and darkness into light? To keep alive what life has promised us in vain, as Hofmannsthal would say.

Love, in its essence, is tragic because from it—and only from it—the arrow of our present flies and instantly plants itself in the future: so that all the space we will have to travel through slowly is spanned in a single moment, and an unknown end, which our soul will be utterly unable to escape, is fixed in place.

"I had set foot in that part of life beyond which one cannot go with any hope of returning."

"La grande énigme de la vie humaine ce n'est pas la souffrance, c'est le malheur."

It is a discovery that few make, and it is perhaps the only bedrock on which we are permitted to set foot. One could divide the realm of human suffering into misfortune of the right hand and misfortune of the left hand. The ancients knew these holy metaphors, beyond which no definition is possible. Misfortune of the right hand is to misfortune of the left hand as a sword wound is to the grip of quicksand or dying of thirst in the desert.

Poverty, parting, persecution, even death itself may be misfortunes of the right hand. A great deal of poetry, some of the most beautiful, has flowered from such misfortune. Whereas the misfortunes of the left hand almost always remain silent. Few escape to tell them, like Jonah from the belly of the Leviathan. Here we find the miracle of *Philoctetes* and *Richard II*, "The Setting of the Moon" and Hölderlin's last lines, *Un amour de Swann* and *Stephania*, Gaspara's extraordinary sonnet "Sir, I know that I no longer live in myself."

Very few things, with many centuries separating them. But as with the phoenix, life glows in them long after the ashes have gone cold.

The critic is an echo, yes. But isn't he also the voice of the mountain, of nature, to which the poet's voice is directed? Isn't the critic as intent on his poet as the poet is intent on the pleas of his own heart? That is why, when he comes to talk about it, he must already have undergone it completely. He must give it back not like a simple mirror but like an echo: laden and suffused with the long road traveled, in nature, by both voices.

A poet's means of drawing illuminations new to his consciousness from the work he has already done is like Münchhausen's means of reaching the moon: cutting the rope beneath him in order to lengthen it above.

Pure poetry is hieroglyphic: decipherable only with the key of destiny. One returns ecstatically year after year to the beauty of ducks, archers, gods with the head of a dog or a bird without suspecting their fateful disposition. How many times have I repeated certain lines or stanzas to myself: "Oh city I have written your name in the palms of my hands," "This day I breathed first, time is come round...," "being dead gives us no rest." But around their secret position, until my own destiny gave me the key, I turned blindly, as if around a historiated column in which I could make out only one image at a time: the scribe, the snake, the eye.

Hieroglyphic poetry and beauty: inseparable and independent. One senses the justice of a text long before understanding its meaning, thanks to that pure timbre we find only in the noblest style, which is in turn born of justice. "My mind, transfixed and robbed / by my thieving thoughts / that promised me time and did not bide..." As in nature, which is beautiful only out of real necessity, so in art, too, beauty is an outgrowth: it is the inevitable fruit of an ideal necessity.

Deep streets carved between lightless houses and crowded with Masaccio's poor. I walk them every day. They are the streets of the neighborhood around San Frediano. But in the fresco they are the Streets of the Poor, whether in Florence or Jerusalem, Rome or Palmyra. And yet it would not be so if they weren't, to begin with, and down to the last crack in the stone, the streets of San Frediano where, on certain winter mornings, the shadow of the boy who took the steps of the Carmine four at a time still seems to scamper.

I can't think of any universal poetry that does not have precise roots: a fidelity, a return.

Saveur maxima de chaque mot. Reflecting on these words, it struck me that to achieve this "maximal flavor," all the elements of the vital and spiritual forces must be brought to bear: violence and gentleness, slowness and quickness, the unexpected and the unavoidable, the deep-rooted and the light as air.

We never find much flavor in unusual or conventional words—words that have no precise citizenship, words that Machiavelli accused of being "pimped out," but only in pure or original—in real—words, when they are driven by a vital force and bloom like flowers in the clear light of the spirit. Word-corollas, articulated by their vowels and consonants as well as by their petals and veins. "*O mein Herz wird Untrügbarer Kristall an dem das Licht sich prüfet...*" Or: "Tearful city / whose stars / of matchless / splendor / and / in brightedged / clouds..." Or again: "*dans l'air liquide et glacial... comme dans une coupe d'eau pure, les narcisses, les jonquilles, les jacinthes...*" (Or simply: "*Je demandais à Albertine si elle voulait boire. 'Il me semble que je vois là des oranges et de l'eau,' me dit-elle, 'ce sera parfait.'*")

Harun al-Rashid: an eternal, enchanting image of the artist. He wanders through the night dressed as a merchant, identifies with every last porter, sailor, and brigand, and like them risks losing his life or his hand. But the caliph is still the caliph. In the morning he will take his seat on the golden throne of justice and have to assume the destiny, the meaning, of all those existences.

The strength of his scepter lies in casting it away each night, like Prospero's staff.

The truth, which is always something a little greater than what is true. The truth, which speaks in *exact hyperboles*. "Take my corpse away," says Oedipus.

2.

Poetry does not sustain life except by virtue of pure beauty, which is to say by virtue of nature. The Chinese sustain life: their private universe is expressed in the visible universe, the dark night in the weight of snow on the bamboo, in the extreme length of a pheasant's tail. The Tao itself shines there, "in the garden hedge."

The youthful, wide-eyed poetry of P. sustains life. "My heart will be covered with peach skin / so that it will be the color of your face." At sixteen we behave, without realizing it, like the Chinese. Overwhelmed by the modesty of innocence, we see eternity in a cloudburst or a windfall of persimmons. Later, we should be able to do the same thing deliberately. But the modesty of perfect consciousness is very difficult.

Proust: the long poem of the primitive manna, of vital energy elevated to a magic power. A tidal poem: people, places, words, melodies, first full and then drained of their powers. Under the bright and terrible waves of manna, the rocks speak, the sand turns to gold, everything moves, responds, changes, envelops man and dominates him, with the right of life or death. When these waves dry up, everything returns to the condition of the fossil, dry as a desert, immobilized in skeletal whiteness.

The marvelous ceremony of Proust is the evocation and resurrection of the manna obtained by the sorcerer with the aid of sacred objects: the hawthorns, the *bille d'agathe*, the *petite phrase de Vinteuil*. So in the Polynesian rituals the bone fragment, the print of a human foot in clay.

All the unsayable things, all the most elusive and subtlest strands in Proust's analyses, arise from syntheses and return to syntheses. Their vast circle shifts from object to object—a similitude of glaring concreteness—as the genie, released from the bottle, must return to the bottle if he wishes to be of service to man. It is not for nothing that the whole immense book is born from a sip of tea: Lethe in a cup.

This enormous and ceaseless motion within the figure is what makes it possible to read Proust on every level of existence, without exception, even if he does not allow himself to speak of many of these levels. And this is what places him in the constellation of the poets rather than the novelists: he is a mediator and seer more than a witness.

Proust's work is above all a feat of the highest nobility, a knight-errant's *geste* in defense of a cult on the verge of disappearance, a beautiful and empty tomb. This is not only to be attributed to the world on the wane that he describes. For it is above all perceptible in the supreme beauty of the language, the perfection of a language in which the purest aristocratic and popular modes (the French that can only be learned from the Duchess of Guermantes or the peasant Françoise) are constantly mixed with the passion of a final farewell. A language saved at the last moment and made an instrument of salvation for the very things it signifies, including the less than noble ones, placing them, with its strength and purity, on a plane where nothing can defile them anymore.

Often this farewell is patently organized in symbols, as in a long and sorrowful ceremony: "*Tous les beaux noms éteints et d'autant plus*

ardemment rallumés ... de sorte que ce fut devant la porte comme une
récitation criée de l'histoire de France."

Once the poet's task was to name things: as for the first time, as we
were told when we were children, as on the day of Creation. Today,
his task seems to be to say farewell to them, to remind men of them
tenderly, sorrowfully, before they are extinct. To write their names
on the water: perhaps on the same rising wave that will soon over-
whelm them.

A shady park, the green mirror of a lake plied by beautiful golden
ducks, in the heart of the city, amid a blizzard of reinforced concrete.
How not to think while looking at it: Is this the last lake, the last
shady park?

Anyone who is not conscious of this today is not one of today's
poets.

In poetry, as in relationships between people, everything dies the
moment any sign of technique rises to the surface. The true education
of the mind has never had any other end since the world began but
the death of technique, of that sad savoir vivre that the child, who
does everything so naturally, was one day taught by adults. Through
this instruction in the art of living, every man is torn from the
threshold of his innocence, just as the princes of old were torn from
their father's house by the mottled flowers or the deer at bay. It is a
necessary journey, and it will need to lead him far beyond the rose
or the deer, deep into the heart of caves and terrors, where savoir vivre
will melt like wax on contact, real and metaphorical, with the four
elements.

One can then become natural on the far side of technique, as
children are natural before it arrives. But for some time now, man
has seemed immured in his technique like an insect in amber. The
paths leading to water and fire—and even to earth and air—are now

all closed to him. Around his garden, there is a high wall within which nothing new can grow—"if a bird in flight doesn't drop a seed."

Small children have mysterious organs, sensitive to omens and correspondences. At the age of six, I used to read fairy tales all day long. But why did I always return, fascinated, to certain images that later on I would *recognize* were almost recurring emblems for me, almost heraldic devices. The dialogue, under the dark city gate, between the goose girl and the severed head of a horse. "Farewell, Falada, who hangs up above! / Farewell, young queen, who passes down below..." A story that I discover in every corner of my life, ready to be reinterpreted on new levels and opened with new keys.

Thus, in poetry, the image preexists the idea that will slowly seep into it. For years, it can haunt the poet, whatever it may be: fabulous or domestic, dismaying or familiar, often an image from early childhood, the strange name of a tree, the insistence of a gesture. It patiently waits for revelation to come and fill it. In Proust, this mystery of the image suddenly flooded with torrents of meaning and then reappearing, time and again, as though seen from switchbacks still higher than a mountain, is the very essence of his poetry.

Yet I love my time because it is the time in which everything is failing, and perhaps precisely for this reason it is truly the time of the fairy tale. And I certainly don't mean by this the era of flying carpets and magic mirrors, which man has destroyed forever in the act of making them, but the era of fugitive beauty, the era of grace and mystery on the verge of disappearance, like the apparitions and arcane signs of the fairy tale: all those things that certain men refuse to give up and love all the more, even as they seem to be increasingly lost and forgotten. All those things we must set out to find, albeit at the risk of our lives, like Belle's rose in the dead of winter. All those things that, as time wears on, are concealed beneath ever more impenetrable disguises, in the depths of more horrible labyrinths.

Maturity: that mysterious instant that no man arrives at before his time, even if all the heavenly messengers come down to help him. Thus the series of apparitions, in the old tales, who all speak eloquently but to no avail: the dove, the fox, the old woman with the bundle of brushwood. All of them say the same thing, repeat and reiterate the same warning. It should be easy to see, beneath their feathers, their red fur, or their rags, the blue flash of the Moirai's gowns...

Maturity: a matter of neither thunderbolts nor "voices." Only a sudden, I would almost like to say "biological," collapse—a point that must be reached by all the senses at once if truth is going to become nature.

It is to wake up one morning knowing a new language. And signs, seen and seen again, become speech.

Maturity is to be continually extricating from the world, which solicits and surrounds us on every side (including and above all the world of beauty), only what is ours for all eternity and is "therefore destined for us."

It is a continual response to the Tempter on the mountain.

The love songs of Saint John of the Cross. If he hadn't written those three immense treatises explaining their meaning, what would we have made of them? His description of the conjugal bed "*de cuevas de leones enlazado / de mil escudos de oro coronado.*" This is the same way the narrators of fairy tales describe their dark nights and their ascents of Carmel. Only they omit the commentaries. It is up to us to recompose them.

"*Los ojos deseados / que tengo en mis entrañas dibujados.*" Mystics are so happily and obstinately at ease with erotic language. Whereas so few lovers dare to use supernatural language.

In a non-imaginary relationship—a relationship not ruled by the game of forces—no feeling or thought can remain isolate for long before rapidly reversing into its opposite. Thus deprivation immediately becomes nourishment, desire consent, grief the consummate feeling of presence, and humility a crown of grace ceaselessly received and restored. Only feelings and thoughts such as these, which do not have time to be corrupted by their results, are allowed to endure and develop in all their purity. The continual and harmonious clash of opposites leads the spirit into a state of ardent stillness, fills it to the brim with a life that does not overflow because its own movement restrains it. "From the center to the circumference and from the circumference to the center / the water moves in a round vase / depending on whether it is hit from without or from within."

Only in this way and within such a circle can love shimmer uncontaminated. *Mais une amitié pure est rare.*

Like a pure poem. Which lives by identical laws.

3.

"Every great painting is painted against painting—in fact, it destroys all painting."

So it is every time I read a great book: I witness the destruction of the language, I watch the language levitate above all languages and not lie down *in ullo*, the way the language of Dante levitates above spoken Italian.

What a mysterious secret binds the great writer to his reader, and what an abyss there is between them. It is the quite familiar tone of a private conversation, such as only kings can grant: full of arcane allusions and delicate questions, which everyone who hears it will remember into old age and recount to his grandchildren, like the encounter with Henry V on the field at Agincourt. From the first lines of the *Commedia* to the last letter of Pasternak, for example, we find the same sublime nonchalance, the same confident, serious, gentle detachment.

That is the way with the sovereign writers. We submit to them before we understand them. We know their meanings must be caught on the fly because we sense that, while they are speaking to the individual, they are also answering before God for an entire community.

What is missing in X.'s beautiful prose that keeps it from truly being writing? I can find no word except *ceremony*. Noble writing without ceremony has never been possible, even if the ceremony was concealed in a conventional whisper. There is supreme ceremony in the great Gothic tercets of Dante, as there is ceremony in Chekhov: a rustic chapel where the rain-soaked boots of the faithful—distracted hypochondriacs racked by boredom and misery—is suddenly superseded by a Byzantine chant, incarnating centuries of gestures. (And it makes no difference if it's a question of a guitar in an orchard threatened with destruction or a breath of wind interrupting a smile.) It was no less ceremonial for Williams to describe a crimson cyclamen's journey from budbreak to death than it was for an ancient Taoist monk to cook rice, eat it, rinse his three bowls in the waterfall, and then place them one inside the other, all with the gestures prescribed.

Marvelous moment in the parable of a poet. When he no longer needs to summon the legions of angels and demons from the four cardinal points and set them clashing in celestial lamentations. When the lightest touch on the strings is enough to have us in tears at his feet. Two words: "*Thymesou soma* ... Body, remember..."

But for this to happen, the voice must speak—like Cavafy's voice—from the far side of death.

Unnamable desolation of a painting: Carpaccio's *Two Venetian Ladies*. Where does it come from? Another perfect work composed of opposites.... On the graceful terrace, every form of beauty has been gathered, as in a heraldic image: flowers, puppies, tamed white turtledoves, peacocks with precious tails, pomegranates more ardent than rubies. The sky is very calm, almost bronze in the amazing depth of its blue. It is the profoundly beautiful, motionless hour, which one would like to hold still forever. But "What's the use?" This is what the ladies' two mild, lost, objectless gazes, their two pure and empty profiles (equivalent as two things, like two minerals in a treatise, or two aquatic plants, robust and confined), seem to ask.

Homer proceeds no differently, enumerating all the joys of life—including that hot bath prepared by beloved hands—when he wants to make us feel the horror of Hector's death.

But in the ladies' expressions there is no trace of youthful death or amorous lament. They tell us nothing but a "profound story of emptiness" whose horror has been muffled by idleness and ground down by boredom: the horror of pointless beauty, which is emptier than an empty shell. "Unhappy monsters," a gentleman of their own time called them. And this was what Carpaccio managed to say in silence: through enumerations and repetitions, and by placing in one corner, where no one would see him, a dreadful and desperate-looking dog who is gnawing on a scrap of wood.

It is a long apprenticeship that teaches us to strip away veil after veil, skin after skin, and get down to the core of a relationship. We cling to our belief in tact, discretion, reserve, delicate veils—and it is only right that this should be so, until the moment they are perceived as veils: enticing pitfalls and impalpable dangers for the wide-eyed student of love.

Job, God's best friend, had no respect for Him, no reserve or discretion. He wouldn't stop shouting about himself or accept an answer except from Him: *Voca me et ego respondebo tibi, aut certe loquar et tu responde mihi.*

If each lover were absorbed only in his own love, if he were sweetly heedless of the feelings of the other and, at the same time, for this very reason, forgot himself, submerging himself like a happy fish in the reality of the other, no love would ever end. "May I never have to ask you for your love" ought to be the vow both lovers take, the sacramental formula pronounced at the wedding ceremony.

It is an impossible balance. But what else does love need in order to live? "As long as you are unable to hear the sound of one hand clapping..."

Every love is a walk over the waters of Galilee: one doubt, one fear, *one look down*, and we sink. The eyes must always be lifted on high, fixed on the peaceful god who holds out his hand to us.

Mediocrity, fear, subjugation to the world. All this appears to me today as a two-way mirror that the prince of the world has slipped like a diaphragm between the roots and the summits of the soul: so that it is no longer possible for them to reflect or nourish each other, happily, like heaven and earth.

Not only does this mirror attempt to separate the two parts of the soul, it attempts to isolate them both in stubborn self-contemplation: the roots of the roots, the summits of the summits. Thus two languages are born in two airtight compartments. Down below: "Life's a different story, let's maintain a healthy sense of proportion, let's not make literature." Up above: "The sublime mission, the sacred name," and so on. The rhetoric of the roots and of the summits is established, and life and thought alike become frozen in place.

Perhaps we were given freedom of choice only to be able to destroy that mirror (which people very often call freedom of choice).

Whom God would destroy, He first makes mad, says the proverb. But how cannily He makes the ones He wants to save mad too. How else could He lead them through the dark night, the forests full of bears and snakes, past the specters of the dark and the face of their own sins—the whole endless procession of horrors necessary for the encounter?

It is always a "moment of madness" that shows us the way out of the labyrinth of deceptive appearances, where diamonds look like snail shells, gravel pearls, and hell yawns under every step we take through the lovely Elysian meadows.

Youth is the first and most fatal of these labyrinths. Even dreams come to her in reverse; they coax her into going astray with divine words; messages written backward in a house where there are not yet any mirrors.

Those are the days when the god covers our eyes with his hand—otherwise we would quickly cover them ourselves, in terror.

The inexorable, inexhaustible moral of the fairy tale is victory over the law of necessity and absolutely nothing else, for there is nothing else to learn on this earth.

The heroes of fairy tales are called upon to face many obstacles, and the only way they can overcome these obstacles is to exit the game of forces once and for all, seeking their salvation in another order of relationships.... The brave little tailor, to win the contest with a horrible giant, capable of breaking all his bones with a single breath, throws a bird instead of a stone into the air...

There is no giant, in the game of forces, that a bigger giant cannot face down; no treasure is sure to be the only treasure; and how easy it is to upstage one marvelous princess, if the king promises the throne to whoever finds her, with another princess even more alluring.

More fatal still are the rigged scales (if my enemy is on the left, then I must be on the right; if my rival is rich, then I must be poor) in the unstoppable, pendulum-like game of the law of necessity, whose oldest ally is simple guile.

When the cadet prince makes his entrance into the throne room and says, "In all my travels I did not find one princess worthy of my attention, but I have here a little white cat *qui fait si bien patte de velours*," we know right away that he will get the crown.

Horoscope. One after the other, the fairy godmothers come to the little princess's baptism. They are the seven planets or the twelve constellations, propitious or adverse depending on the parents' merits: Did the queen send out all the invitations she should have? Did she remember the fairy who had shown herself to be a true friend and not pass her over in favor of more powerful fairies? They may all be benevolent fairies—auspicious planets and happy constellations— but more often than not an evil Saturn (the neglected, spiteful fairy) will come darken the sky with her bat-drawn carriage, subverting everything, all the precious gifts of the others, and delivering an inauspicious verdict: the princess will die when she is twenty years old. Supplications are useless, everything seems lost, when one last fairy— a jovial being who, as it happens, hasn't yet had her say—intervenes with her own little promise. She will not be able to undo the curse, but she will alleviate it by changing its nature: the princess will not die but will sleep for one hundred years, before her destiny is fulfilled. Delay, then, not disaster, will preside over the princess's life . . .

Such is the relationship between the errors of the parents and the destiny of the children, the imponderable time necessary for a life.

Just as horoscopic is the scene of the round dance—what Madame d'Aulnoy, in a popular and arcane idiom, calls "*le branle des fées.*" It may be the young fairies' celebration at the spring equinox or, on the contrary, it may be the Secular Council that is held every hundred years in the clearing of Brocéliande: fate renewing its ties with nature or a sort of conjunction of spectacular stars.

Many fairy-tale heroes, born deformed or very small, are thrown by their mothers, determined to dare all, into the center of the round dance, into the thick of their own destiny. Usually the child, after a few moments of foreboding perplexity, is picked up by the fairies. His deformity will not be removed, only elevated to a power: the little man will be granted the ability to penetrate impenetrable places; the armless to discover treasures, veins of gold, and the whole extent of the underworld, a mirror of the heavens.

His misfortune will be a key for others.

In the legend of the ghost ship, those who died in mortal sin are forced to return to the scene of their crime every night and repeat, without rest, the *final scene* of their damnation. This is a recurrent theme in legends all around the world. Hell represented not as an arbitrary punishment but as the horrible, interminable repetition of a gesture.

Already it provides a perfect image of neurosis, with its hellish compulsion to repeat. Neurosis, which must have existed even then, but, like everything else, was robust enough to end up as a story rather than a symptom.

The fairy tale, like the Gospels, is a golden needle suspended from an imponderable, oscillating north, which is continually tilting in different directions, like the mainmast of a ship on a rough sea. How are we to choose, case by case, between resignation and cunning, naivety and wisdom, memory and salutary forgetfulness? One wins because in a country of dupes and schemers, he was skeptical and secretive; another because he childishly put his trust in the first person to come along, or even in a band of criminals. The enigma is new every day, proposed and never solved except in the decisive moment, the pure gesture—which is not dictated by anything but is nourished, day after day, on patience and silence.

It is worth noting that a writer who attempts a fairy tale almost always produces his best prose: almost as if language, when it comes into contact with symbols so universal and particular, cannot help but distill its purest flavor (so that a classic book of fairy tales opens not only the atlas of life for a child but also the atlas of language).

Or perhaps those symbols can only be fully mastered by those who have a feeling for their own language as liturgical as that of the Sunday Mass and as familiar as an everyday meal.

In this light, the "daily bread" of Luke, which in Matthew becomes "supersubstantial bread," would reveal itself to be not a philological obscurity but a natural ambiguity.

In old books (those written before the early nineteenth century), I do not remember ever having read any such phrase as "the happy kingdom of childhood," "the paradise of the paternal house." These expressions seem to have been born around 1850, and clearly a book like the *Recherche* could only have been undertaken in the era of the first automobiles. An earlier author—Montaigne, for example—would instead have said "carefree childhood," like someone referring to something delicate and as yet without form: clay yet to be shaped by the potter's expert hands. The primer of a prince of the House of Este contains, on every page, pictures of that child fulfilling all his future duties: battles, triumphs, tournaments, court balls.

It is clear, then, that the myth of childhood does not have, for modern man, the private meaning he would like to give it. What he is looking for, behind him, is not his own childhood but the world's childhood—the childhood of his whole lineage—so as to survive himself. Proust testifies to this on every page and appears to affirm it most explicitly in *Le temps retrouvé*, where, in writing about realist art, he is in fact writing about a whole way of life that is the perfect opposite of deep reality. That complex, solid, unfathomable reality which, even if we have not been permitted to experience it, is revived in us, too, by the madeleines called old photographs: those houses and gardens, those teas on the grass, those children with perfect cheeks and conscious eyes beside a wooden horse that is a real horse in miniature, a doll that is a small woman or a girl, never an allusive puppet; and the unapproachable beauty of the old people, who have all the modest majesty of ancient trees; and the clear dedications that could not be more precise: "to my darling husband," "to my beloved brother."

A syntax of life still in force and intact lent those simple dedications the utmost decorum, as musical syntax allowed Chopin to approach the most sorrowful places, the most secret chambers, without violating them. A syntax of life that stops us cold when, among our own disorganized, miscellaneous snapshots we suddenly come upon an old house shaded by its linden or its cedar of Lebanon, with a dog lying by the door and the curtains raised. If we happen to have spent some time there, when we were very young children, every other token of our past is abruptly distorted, bleached with unreality, and no longer speaks to us of anything—except our guilty attempts to freeze moments fleeing from our distracted memories, instead of leaving the image its inward permanence.

Marlowe and Proust. Marlowe's *Edward II* is a tragedy whose sole object is the total and radical transformation of all its characters. The tragedy revolves slowly around them as around a dark star, but with such spectral naturalness it misleads the spectator, minute by minute, regarding the degree of that transformation. So that when all the light is in shadow, and all the shadows have been brought into the light, it is no longer possible to remember how things stood at the start.

This is an utterly tragic sense of life, such as not even Shakespeare could presage. The possibility of finding ourselves in a world, a situation, that is completely unrecognizable, completely different from the one we believe we inhabit—and inhabit to such an extent that we no longer have any consciousness of it. The horror of the letter addressed to a dead man. Of decrepit faces immured in the lugubrious hairstyles of twentysomethings.... The havoc of time outside, and the halt of time within.

Like the sepulchral reception in *Le temps retrouvé*, where the petites bourgeoises have taken the place and names of the fabulous duchesses—and no one present is what he was to the others at the start, or what he was later on, or even what he was yesterday.... But only Proust has been able to blend the appalling downward motion of time (the methodical descent of the law of necessity, the *vanitas vanitatum*) with the ascendant, unremitting counterpoint of language—as in certain passages for piano by Beethoven, where the melody continues to rise higher and higher into the light while the bass descends deeper and deeper into darkness.

> *Ce n'était pas que l'aspect de ces personnes qui donnait l'idée de personnes de songe. Pour elles-mêmes la vie...était de plus en plus devenue un songe. Elles avaient oublié jusqu'à leur rancunes, leurs haines, et pour être certaines que c'était la personne qui était là celle à qui elles n'adressaient plus la parole depuis il y a dix ans, il eût fallu qu'elles se reportassent à un régistre, mais qui était aussi vague qu'un rêve où on a été insulté on ne sait plus par qui. Tous ces songes formaient les apparences de la vie politique où on voyait dans un même ministère des gens qui s'étaient accusés de meurtre ou de trahison. Et ce songe devenait épais comme la mort chez certains vieillards...*

The deer confined in the park—misplaced and graceful objects penned there for distracted eyes—do not ask themselves "Why are we no longer free in the great forest?" but "Why are we no longer hunted?"

A young hand sometimes caresses them. "King Arthur is dead," the children explain to the deer, "and hunts and tournaments, prodigious duels and sacred feasts died with him. Never again will a stag be pursued by the twelve knights. Never again will he wear a golden crown around his neck or bring the dogs to a halt by lifting up the cross of the Savior among his antlers. Never again will his body be eaten at the supper of the Holy Grail. Nothing threatens you now, sweet deer—and here, you shall have food and drink from our hands."

The deer bow their heads and beat the fence lightly with their antlers. But at night they are overcome by a gentle fever and call to one another. They hear, or believe that they hear, Arthur's horn. "He is not dead," they say, "he is not dead. He will return. And again our life will hang upon an arrowhead."

ATTENTION AND POETRY

Truth did not come into the world naked but in symbols and images. There is rebirth, and there is an image of rebirth, and it is by means of this image that one must be reborn.

—Gospel of Philip

IN THE old books, the just man is often given the heavenly name "mediator." Mediator between man and God, between man and other men, between man and the secret laws of nature. The role of mediator was given to the just man—and the just man alone—because no imaginary or passionate tie could constrain or deform his ability to read. "*Et chaque être humain* (one might add *et chaque chose*) *crie en silence pour être lu autrement.*"

This is the reason so much importance has been placed on the freedom of the heart. Every church recommends it as a kind of spiritual hygiene: vigilance against turmoil, readiness for divine revelation. However, no church has ever explicitly said: Keep yourselves pure in your works and thoughts in order to reconcile men and things in an unshadowed gaze. Here poetry, justice, and criticism converge: they are three forms of mediation.

For what is mediation if not an utterly free capacity for attention? Set against it is what we, quite improperly, call passion—that is, feverish imagination and fantastic illusions.

We might say, then, that justice and imagination are antithetical terms. Passionate imagination, which is one of the most uncontrollable forms of opinion (that dream in which we all move), can in reality only serve an imaginary justice. This is, for example, the essential difference between Electra's passionate justice and Antigone's spiritual justice. Electra imagines she can proceed from blame to blame, shifting the weight from one link to the next in an unbreakable chain. Antigone moves in a realm where the law of necessity no longer holds.

Indeed, contrary to what is typically asked of him, the just man does not need imagination but attention. We are asking a judge for justice by the wrong name if we ask him to "use his imagination." What, in that case, could the judge's imagination be except an inevitable abuse, an act of violence against the reality of things? Justice is a fervent form of attention, and completely nonviolent. It is as remote from appearances as it is from myth.

"Justice, a golden eye, looks." An image of perfect immobility, perfectly attentive.

Poetry, too, is attention. In other words, it involves reading, on multiple levels, the reality around us, which is truth in images. And the poet, who takes these images apart and recomposes them, is also a mediator: between man and God, between man and other men, between man and the secret laws of nature.

The Greeks were disdainful of imagination: fantasy had no place in their minds. Their heroic, unswerving attention (of which Sophocles provides perhaps the most extreme example) continually established relationships between things, separated and united them, in an unceasing effort to decipher reality and mystery alike. The Chinese meditated for millennia, in the same manner, on the marvelous Book of Changes. And Dante is not, however scandalous it may sound, a poet of imagination but a poet of attention: to see souls writhing in the fire and the olive tree, to recognize pride in a cloak of lead, is a supreme form of attention, which leaves the elements of the idea pure and uncontaminated.

Art today is largely imagination. In other words, it is a chaotic contamination of elements and levels. All of this, naturally, is opposed to justice (which is, in any case, of no interest to artists today).

If attention is a patient, fervent, fearless acceptance of reality, imagination is impatience—a flight into the arbitrary: an endless labyrinth navigated without Ariadne's red thread. This is why ancient art is synthetic, whereas modern art is analytic and, for the most part, concentrates on breaking things down, as is appropriate to an era brought up on fear. For true attention does not lead, as it may seem it would, to analysis but to a resolving synthesis, to symbols and images—in a word, to destiny.

Analysis can become destiny when attention, successfully performing a perfect superposition of times and spaces, is able to recompose them, one after the other, in the pure beauty of the image. Such is the attention of Marcel Proust.

Attention is the only path to the unsayable, the only path to mystery. In fact, it is firmly anchored in the real, and only through allusions hidden in reality is that mystery manifested. The symbols of the Holy Scriptures, myths, and fairy tales, which have nourished and consecrated life for millennia, are clothed in the most concrete earthly forms: from the burning bush to the talking cricket, from the apple of knowledge to Cinderella's pumpkins.

When it is confronted with reality, imagination recoils. Attention, on the other hand, grasps it, directly, as a symbol (think of Dante's heavens, the divine and detailed translation of a liturgy). It is thus, finally, the most legitimate, absolute form of imagination. The one to which the old alchemical text no doubt alludes when it recommends dedicating "the true imagination and not the fantastic imagination" to the work. By this, clearly meaning attention, in which imagination is present but sublimated, like the poison in medicine. Due to one of the many ambiguities of language, it is commonly called "creative imagination."

It hardly matters if long and painful pilgrimages lead to such a creative instant, or if it comes in a flash. Such bolts from the blue are only the spark (whose origin and nature become increasingly mysterious as little by little it gives us the key to everything) that attention solicits and prepares: like the lightning rod the lightning, like the prayer the miracle, like the search for a rhyme the inspiration that may flow from that rhyme.

Sometimes it is the attention of an entire lineage, a whole genealogy, which suddenly flares up in a godlike spark: "I had set foot in that part of life beyond which one cannot go with any hope of returning."

Such an individual, whose attention is ravishing and definitive, the world defines, with a very beautiful abbreviation, as a genius, meaning a person inhabited by a demon, a person who incarnates the manifestation of a spirit unknown.

Attention frees the idea from the image, like the genie from the bottle, then gathers the idea back inside the image: once again in imitation of the alchemists, who first dissolved salt in a liquid, then studied how it re-formed and solidified into figures. It is a matter of decomposing and recomposing the world in two distinct but equally real moments. And so justice is served, destiny is fulfilled, through the dramatic decomposition and recomposition of a form.

The expression, the poetry that is born from it, can only, of course, be hieroglyphic: something like a new nature. That is why only a new attention, a new destiny, will be able to decipher it. But the language instantly reveals the degree of attention that produced it, through its earthly and spiritual weight: the more consummate it is, the more space and silence that surround it, the more intense the poet's attention must have been.

Every word is offered in its multiple meanings, like the strata of a geologic column: each one differently colored and differently inhabited, each one reserved for the reader whose intensity of attention will allow him to discern and decipher it. But for everyone, when a poem is pure, it comes as an abundant gift that is simultaneously partial and total: beauty and meaning independent yet inseparable, as in a communion. As in that first Communion, which was the multiplication of the loaves and fishes.

Everyone who heard the master speak, says a Hebrew tale, felt they

were hearing a secret destined for his ears alone, and so everyone felt
the marvelous story the master told in the squares belonged to him
and was complete, although every newcomer heard only a fragment.

"*Souffrir pour quelque chose, c'est lui avoir accordé une attention ex-
trême.*" (So Homer suffers for the Trojans and contemplates the death
of Hector; so the Japanese sword master does not distinguish between
his own death and that of his adversary.) And to have given something
extreme attention is to have accepted suffering it to the end, and not
only suffering it but suffering for it, placing ourselves like a shield
between it and everything that can threaten it, both inside ourselves
and outside ourselves. It is to have taken upon ourselves the weight
of those dark, incessant threats, which are the very condition of joy.

Here attention attains perhaps its purest form, its most precise
name: responsibility, the capacity to respond on behalf of something
or someone, which is equally vital to poetry, understanding between
beings, opposition to evil.

Because truly every human, poetic, or spiritual error is nothing,
in essence, if not inattention.

To ask a man to never be distracted, to be continually turning his
faculty of attention away from the errors of imagination, the laziness
of habit, the hypnosis of custom, is to ask him to realize his highest
form.

It is to ask him for something very close to holiness in a time that
seems to be pursuing, with blind fury and bone-chilling success,
nothing so much as a total divorce of the human mind from its capacity for attention.

THE MAXIMAL FLAVOR OF
EACH WORD

ON WILLIAM CARLOS WILLIAMS

... constant in its swiftness as a pool.

A WILLIAM CARLOS WILLIAMS anthology (however small or quasi-private it may be) is a rather difficult thing to put together. The poet's whole oeuvre is in fact configured a little like a very long, detailed cosmic diary, composed day by day, section by section, in that kaleidoscopic rhythm of breakdown and recomposition that he himself defines in a well-known letter:

"Now life," Williams writes, "is above all things else at any moment subversive of life as it was the moment before—always new, irregular. Verse to be alive must have infused into it something of the same order, some tincture of disestablishment, something in the nature of an impalpable revolution."

This poetic procedure is not only carried out in Williams's technique—in the wild, subtle unfolding of his syntax and the irreducible naturalness of his metrics, all governed by laws at once lofty and crude but (like the laws of life) exquisitely wise.

It begins much earlier; it originates in the eyes: fixed, with marvelous constancy, not on the object but on the metamorphosis of the object.

Revolutions, as he has said—of the bud and the terraqueous world, of seeds and eras. Faces, cities, events built up and broken down. Tender tragedies, which Williams witnesses hourly, with a dedication that sometimes makes him—the apostle of American poetics par excellence—a Chinese master of the classical age.

Williams's geography can therefore only be a geography of archipelagos. Only a complete panorama of his work would be capable of revealing the shadow of the volcanic land from which his innumerable Antilles emerge.

But as the flower (that delicate hero of Williams's saga) testifies to the invisible tree, so each of the poet's verses offers us the pure elements of his art. Chief among these is the rather rare combination of extreme lightness and powerful rootedness that is the very substance of poetry—a sense of the *maximal flavor of each word*, of which Williams is one of the few living masters.

Some years ago, this short preface was printed in a tiny collection of translations of Williams, dedicated to him on the occasion of his seventy-fifth birthday; these are now interleaved, in the present volume, with Vittorio Sereni's versions. Titled, after one of Williams's lines, *The Flower Is Our Sign*, that earlier book was in fact a sort of herbarium, chosen with care from that immense botanical garden—forest, field, kingdom of "growing things"—called *The Collected Poems*.

Without thinking twice about it, I'd written the adjective "Chinese," which, applied to Williams, seemed to provoke some surprise. Whereas it would have seemed legitimate, I suppose, for the young Pound or the later poems of Brecht.

More than Pound and at least as much as Brecht, however, Williams to my mind fits this description. If by "Chinese" we mean, as I think we do, the archetype of the artist who is freest in his own time and space, which is to say freest *from* his own time and space— adept at yielding to the wheel of the seasons with the same purity with which the old man of the waterfall, praised by Zhuangzi, bowed to the furious caprices of the water; at conducting back to the rhythms of the zodiac the very slow emergence of an Indian shot bud from its hard sheath of sepals; at seeing the heartbeat of an insect, as Shen Fu tells us he was able to do, with eyes capable of staring at the sun. Eyes like those of the engravers who decorated the books made by the Ten Bamboo Studio or the *Manual of the Mustard Seed Garden*, in whose retina a piece of cork tossed up by the sea, a piece of limestone, a lemon rind, or a walnut shell take on an appearance as horrible and heavenly as the petrified crystal of a rapid or the fossil whiteness of a desert of cliffs.

That Williams is also, as Randall Jarrell phrased it in four words, "the America of poets" does not much conflict with this, nor does the quasi-totemic cult that the sect of "hipsters" has been dedicating to him for years and years now.

What they find in Williams consciously (but how to apply this rejected word to them?), this pathetic, inarticulate group who scream at the top of their lungs in a state of ecstasy far too reminiscent of weeping, hardly matters to me. Banging around, looking for a nail, at the four blind walls of their prison—highways, peyote, cool jazz, promiscuity—they'd already stumbled onto Zen. And in that case, too, it hardly matters whether, looking at those sweet and terrifying old men, they are more interested in seeing the stroke of the spatula that fixes the ritual fly whisk on the rice paper than the innumerable Guanyin goddesses: immersed in the white landscapes of the lotus, illustrated down to the daintiest petal, those goddesses made it possible for the old men to deliver their mad, conclusive stroke with the spatula.

It is the same, I think, with Williams. His graphic mimesis of luminous signs, the syncopation, the jargon, the brutally spoken long prose sections that separate the songs of that immense epithalamium called *Paterson*: all this can only fascinate them—no doubt much more than does the tireless chronicle (I was going to say hagiography) of "The Crimson Cyclamen": a Passion of the Flower followed, in a sort of limitless dilation of the pupil, from birth to old age, and mirroring another and more mortal passion: that of human thought.

With the monks and Williams both, whether they're conscious of it or not, the "Beat" generation is contemplating strange beings who do not need drugs, stuporous music, or mad trips on transcontinental trucks to discover, in the real world—in a sea rock, a face, a garbage can—the Himalayas and prairies that "amaze and delight," the vast, forgotten landscapes of the mind. In the one as in the other, these apostles of forced imagination hail the untroubled masters of attention, the artisans whom Sereni says "stand facing the abyss."

In Williams's *Selected Essays* (an infinitely surprising and savory book, written with savor and surprise), there are two dialogues—one revolving around the mystery of marriage and the other around faith in art—which would not be at all out of place among those Zen koans that counsel you, for example, not to trust your own perceptions until you are able to hear the sound of one hand clapping.

That isn't all, of course. Defined in so few words, so swiftly, Williams might seem to be a case of flagrant poetic schizophrenia, so contradictory are his various different sides: the indefatigably "human," the categorically "American," the "avant-garde" under pain of death. All of this does, like any steadfast or ingenuous resolution (one always thinks in this regard of Proust writing about Vinteuil), sometimes lead him to make things that are beneath his destiny as a poet. I would not advise anyone who has loved his poems, his essays, or *In the American Grain* to read his *Autobiography*, nor the majority (but *only* the majority) of his stories. All those pages were written in shirtsleeves, and with his heart on at least one of those sleeves: his protagonist is always the little man who is all men, such as the specious photographs of Edward Steichen have been showing us for years.

Here it seems that Williams *wants* to forget what is in fact a subject rich in trepidations in his letters and poems: the perfectly dosed mixture of his blood: Caribbean, Judeo-Spanish, pure English. Which is to say: Indian, Arab, and Protestant. The blood of a man born of contrary winds or, so to speak, of a man against the wind. The ten memorable pages of "The Destruction of Tenochtitlan," "The Discovery of the Indies," and the bewitching little study on the *Libro de Buen Amor* by the Archpriest of Hita would be enough to shed a very particular light on the book that contains the first two and is surely, along with the lyrics, Williams's great work: *In the American Grain*.

The grace that comes with abandonment to chance and the waters of the waterfall (a quality proper to mixed blood), as well as a cunning innocence worthy of the dove and the snake, rescue Williams from all these passionate misunderstandings: they merge them in the "streamlike purity of purpose" he speaks of when writing about Columbus. But it is in Montezuma's incomparable profile that he has perhaps put the better part of himself and his ultimate vision: tracing the reasons and contradictions of a sublime nature in the chilling abdication of a man and of his world.

"From its music shall the best of the modern verse be distinguished," Williams has written in more than one letter. And his long series of notes on prosody, justly entitled *Measure*, is not very different from a treatise on composition: a work that is, indeed, almost written in code, so many of the terms are so mysterious and almost esoteric; but all of it illuminated by the brilliant selection, and the supremely passionate examination, of certain texts: Spenser, Chapman, *Antony and Cleopatra*, Sidney Lanier, the hymnal—down to Hopkins and contemporaries.

In reality, a poem like "Perpetuum Mobile," just to mention one— this sort of early Schoenberg solely for strings, alternating with jazz drumbeats (the two policemen walking to the bank)—nevertheless remains a timeless composition. Its beauty is so tragically unreal and so subtly fluctuates from one to the other of its three movements that it remains elusive: "music that flows beside you on the water," on that spirit arisen from the waters that is a big city at night.

(And how strangely the "tearful city" runs to meet—an upside-down mirage, in the heavens of the opposite hemisphere—the "unreal city" of the poet whom Williams, up until a few years ago, believed he had to battle against. On the contrary, they are united by the bow of one of his phrases: "the classic is the local fully realized: words marked by a place.")

Alongside this poem, there is another born from the same seed— the attempt to enucleate words from the capsule of syntax: stars detached from their galaxy, but not scattered, only isolated—so as to form more unusual constellations—in their ecstatic, humid rings of light. The poem is titled "To an Elder Poet"; but of this poem I'm once more unable to say anything, except that I seem to see it written "on the wall of the inn" by a rarefied Po Chu-i reborn.

Because of its collective nature, the avant-garde is monolithic. Williams's journey through his own language (his own land) has perhaps been the most solitary in contemporary American poetry. More solitary than that of Malraux's two heroes, who machete their way through the "*écoeurante virulence*" of the virgin forest, following the traces of a very ancient Royal Road.

Only his great friend Marianne Moore can be compared to him in terms of solitude; but she remains impassive in her porcelain garden, intent on her invaluable work as a paleontologist-taxidermist, in which she goes about enclosing tiny and exquisite prehistoric creatures in limpid blocks of amber: apart from life and apart from air. It is their gemlike immobility that preserves them from time.

For Williams, it is the opposite. Like Saba, like Cavafy, like Brecht, he battens on his own continual transmutation, his tireless return; like a salmon, he swims against the current toward the sources of speech and the "maximal flavor of every word" of which I spoke at the start. These are precisely the poets, the masters of the joyous mysteries of the word, who continually immerse it, "so that it lives," in the mournful waters of Parmenides. "Masterpieces are only beautiful in a tragic sense, like a starfish lying stretched dead on the beach in the sun. A touch of the unknown.... A passionate statement about death."

"A Testament of Perpetual Change" is the pre-Socratic title that a studious nun, Sister Bernetta Quinn, has given her long essay on William Carlos Williams.

ON JOHN DONNE

for Jaffier

I.

> For oh, to some
> Not to be martyrs is a martyrdome.
> —JOHN DONNE, *The Litanie*, X

"I HAD my first breeding and conversation with men of a suppressed and afflicted Religion, accustomed to the despite of death, and hungry of an imagin'd Martyrdome."

John Donne will spend his whole youth in this atmosphere of opprobrium and exaltation, mortal secrecy and painful spiritual refinement common, in every era, to proscribed religious communities long martyrized in both body and spirit. All his life will be a restive tugging against the chain of this terrifying legacy, and then a rushing back to it the moment he feels the chain go slack.

Children who, for years, at the table, never hear adults talking about parties or business, family imbroglios or court positions, but only Real Presence and Propitiatory Sacrifice, anathemas and apostasies. Children roused while the bands of sleep still bind them tight because a pale young man, in clothes not his own, has arrived in the dead of night from Douai or Reims, and at dawn, with the doors and windows of the study locked, will don his priestly vestments; and already friends from all over London are gathering, in small silent groups, to attend the forbidden Roman Mass. Children who are made to take a long detour through the city so that they will not see the crowds congregating and the squadrons of horsemen dragging the same pale young man (or another), trussed up with his head to the ground, toward a heap surmounted by a gallows—or perhaps lifted above the crowd so that the bloodless, upturned, ecstatic face might be engraved in the tender young mind.

In what amounts almost to a series of initiation rites, the relic of a great dead member of the family, that completely unforeseeable martyr, Lord Chancellor Thomas More, is shown to these children; the letter written by their uncle, a monk, on a night of execution is read out yet again, horrendous in every particular; a book by the wonderful Edmund Campion, once the jewel of the university and the court, who threw his life away to enter the lethal priesthood, so that the island would not be bereft of Sacrifices, as in the prophecies of Daniel.... And every moment, in the lives of these children, is moved and governed, like the tides, by the phases of that cadaverous moon, that Chimera in a red wig, the daughter of the dropsical king and the twelve-fingered sorceress, the Queen Pontiff anathematized by Rome—whom Donne, years later, when she delivers the gallant Earl of Essex to the cleaver, will in turn anathematize in a long poem.

Donne's own intellectual life was to be governed by the phases of that "cold, aged moon," so that at Oxford he kept shifting from one discipline to another so as not to have to sign the Thirty-nine Articles and the Oath of Supremacy and graduate with a degree that would have made him an apostate. As a boy, he resembles Miris, the voluptuous adolescent celebrated by Cavafy, who leads his life like everyone else his age—is quarrelsome, prodigal, refined—but whom they all know is a Christian and, after his edifying death, will lead them to ask themselves whether they ever really knew him. His eyes are clear, hungry, skeptical; his knuckles taut on a sword guard. In costly and profitable company, he indulges every lust—not least of all the intellectual one. "A great visitor of ladies, not dissolute but very neat," nothing human is alien to him; he is versed in every language and is a diligent theatergoer. But at dawn, in the six matutinal hours he devotes to study before granting himself "the greatest liberty," he reads and reflects, annotating Saint Thomas or Cardinal Bellarmine's *Disputationes de Controversiis Christianae Fidei* from first page to last.

He holds up poorly under such pressure. The revival of persecutions, his brother's death in prison, the death of Essex and then of another charming mystic in frivolous clothes, the Earl of Arundel; the throbbing ambition to win rank by his wits alone; those many years of agony that he never was able to convert, with the simplicity of his elders, into spiritual energy: all this made the "suppressed and afflicted religion" an unbearable burden for Donne. It demanded too much of his lineage and his worldly patience. It is likely that in 1597, when he enters the service of the Lord Keeper of the Great Seal, Sir Thomas Egerton, and is initiated into the life of the court, Donne's Catholicism, if he has not yet formally abandoned it, is already sepulchered in silence like the Catholicism of William Byrd, or John Bull, or Shakespeare—that taciturn prodigy who never uttered a word about faith except when hidden behind a mask, a *persona*.

Not even this decision brings him happiness. In Donne's work from these years, there is a mysterious apology for suicide, *Biathanatos*, and it is plausible that some of this poem's lines, which have always been interpreted as a rebuke against Catholics, conceal a personal torment: "For oh, to some / Not to be martyrs is a martyrdome." It is a hard knot to untie: Donne is a man upright enough to refuse a benefice from the Church of England, but not upright enough not to merit it for having helped draft indictments against Catholics, including, it seems, against Mary, Queen of Scots, herself.

When at the age of twenty-eight, he meets, falls for, secretly marries, and runs off with Ann More, the niece of Sir Thomas Egerton and daughter of Sir George More (who will make him pay for the marriage by having him thrown in prison), Donne has already abandoned the erratic, planetary destiny of a Catholic recusant. Predictably, he longs for one of those thin magic circles that allow a man to travel to another time and place. The *imago mundi* is finally reduced to the dimensions of a room, a face, a pupil in which, as in the round, concave mirrors of van Eyck and Velázquez, everything is safely stashed. And just as his love affairs now seem to him no more than the prehistory of a subtler and more accomplished state of existence— poor risible types prefiguring authentic history—*affectio coniugalis* will become, in its turn, a still-timid type prefiguring a future *dilectio Dei*. Breaking loose from the earth, this perfect pre-theological love will point like an arrow in the direction of theology: "Here the admiring her my mind did whet / To see thee, God; so streams do show the head . . ."

This love lasted for seventeen years and was gladdened and grieved by twelve children; a desolating poverty froze every flower of this garland, one after the other. In dire need, ambition again comes to his aid. Donne becomes a courtly poet and a courtier, and, in excessively beautiful poems, assigns the masks of worldly courtship to the powerful, sorrowful feelings that obsess him. An illness or death in the house of Herbert or Bedford or Drurys will serve him as a tenuous pretext for his magniloquent fugues on death: his own death, the death of his loved ones, the death of the world he holds dear. Does Donne, himself, weep during these years? Since the days of Homer, the slaves of Achilles have known how to mourn "under the pretext of Patroclus / each for his own," and Simone Weil has authoritatively described the slave who, forced to sing his master's praises, ends up loving him sincerely.

It is on the advice of King James I—or at least so he would have us believe—that Donne finally decides to be ordained in the Church of England. His deep knowledge of the two theologies and his remarkable eloquence soon make him a well-known priest, then a deacon who will leave his mark on the history of St. Paul's Cathedral. The first natural impulse of renegades is intolerance of those who, despite everything, hold to their faith. In his poems, prose, and sermons, Donne marshals quite a few criticisms of the "suppressed and afflicted religion." And from time to time—for the wish to reconcile the irreconcilable is a trait typical of contradictory characters—he tries to convince himself that, after all, the two Churches are really one.

But here, in Donne's later years, we find a new and different contradiction: his short-lived disapprobation of certain Catholic customs—monastic life, for example—more and more yields (and with increasing formal beauty) to those purely ascetic meditations that Helen Gardener has called "Ignatian" and that, quite unexpectedly, ally the English poet with the writers of the Counter-Reformation: the pale Knights of the Cross and the Four Last Things. Sin and death become the dominant note of the Holy Sonnets and the basso ostinato of the sermons. In a gesture straight from the great mystic theater of Spain, he has himself painted standing, with a winding sheet knotted on his head—just as he will stand, blind and vigilant, on his own tomb, his face turned toward the East in the tradition of the apostles, ready for the final call. Daily contemplating this image in an etching that stood on his night table; giving his last sermon before the court, his face already cadaverous, *de morte sua*; laying himself out for burial and closing his own eyelids in the presence of his friends, as in the scenography of El Escorial: everything, in the last cycle of Donne's life—and, as we shall see, in his poetry— participates, in the midst of the Reformation, in a singular process of assimilating conflicting forms.

2.

> ...the meditation and modulation...
> —JOHN DONNE, Sermon 2, Preached in the Evening
> of Christmas Day, 1624

The emblematic landscape of Donne's poetry is like the landscape in Dürer's *Melancholia I*: a symbolic catalogue and compendium of all the human and occult arts—books, globes, scales, retorts, armillary spheres, hourglasses, compasses, and telescopes. In the background, the ruins of cathedrals and illustrious monasteries now overgrown with weeds and ivy, scraps of liturgical chants that have survived in processions to ancient shrines: as in John Bull's sublime Walsingham Variations and Philips's Pavans and Galliards, to whose rhythms, at court balls, the queen shuffles her skeletal feet. Here tolling bells and hunting horns mingle with "flourish and fanfare," funeral marches, and clavichord tones; here is the jargon of the market and the tribunal, dissecting-hall nomenclature and bedroom babble, the subtle, marmoreal lexicon of theology and the susurrus of the fountains in English parks, the mythological scream of the mandrake root and the refrains of the litany, the specious sophisms of the lascivious courtier and the grave tenderness of the spouse. It is all tackled and tumbled together with the potent, offhand verve of the great dramas of the era: the poem's curtain opens abruptly on a scene already in progress, on a plausible and piquant story completely unexplained, whose first word tells us all we need to know. It is the "Who's there? / Nay, answer me . . ." that stops the heart in the first scene of *Hamlet*. It is the placard they used to set the scene at the Globe or at Blackfriars with a scant few words: A room. A door on the street. A garden. And even that was more than enough.

Virginia Woolf has noted that what is most attractive in Donne "is not his meaning, charged with meaning though his poetry is; it is the explosion with which he bursts into speech. All preface, all parleying have been consumed; he leaps into poetry the shortest way," as a lover jumps through a window into a room, shutting everything else out: the time, the place, the universe. He stops us with a gesture: "'Stand still,' he commands. . . . And stand still we must." His cycle of love poems for Ann More reminds us of Rembrandt and Saskia's domestic scenes, painted only a little later. We know every stick of furniture in their room, every glint in their windowpanes, every gleam in the glasses they hold up to toast, every fold in their bed curtains, but they don't bother to tell us a word about the world outside.

The presence of the imperious, urgent visitor accelerates the rhythm of our life, sharpens our perceptions, and illuminates objects one after the other like a restless torch, giving them a more exciting, substantial life: "The 'bracelet of bright hair' burns in our eyes." Often the process of illuminating object after object is so hurried the images are telescoped. However, this hurriedness is only feigned: object responds to object, echo to echo, and the distances between them are geometric and carefully calculated. By the end of the poem, we realize that the flamboyant, hot-tempered speaker is, in reality, a very subtle rhetorician well acquainted with all the games of symmetrical correspondence and hidden allusions. Ideas from the most disparate arts and disciplines are deployed with consummate elegance; the alchemical metaphor responds to the scholastic innuendo, and the juridical proposition to the military terminology, according to a planetary system of indestructible solidity. Yet the verbal games, the contrasting combinations, the wide range of allusions do not interrupt the soaring arc of the stanza, or the unruffled naturalness of the diction. Neither the breath of the human voice nor the subtle asymmetry of the vision are lost in that single line, from top to bottom, from one stanza to the next, which is the mark of a poem's necessity, so that sometimes—as happens with Cavafy or Eliot—we begin to wonder what meter he is writing in.

All these elements come to a head in the poetry he is thought to have written for Ann More: the envois, the aubades, the celebrations, the ecstasies, the whole long and haunted "dialogue of one voice." Two classical and yet quite unusual components are in play here: the sense of destiny that unites two beings against the horror of a world (Pasternak will make a great novel by choosing, strangely enough, the same ritual masks Donne uses in the poem "The Relic") and the sense of *status*, the initiatory rank that isolates, elevates, and crowns lovers. Realm, investiture, baptism, canonization, relic are their daily language; heaven, earth, thrones, and dominions their daily testimonies. We will find something very similar in a poet who brooded over John Donne: Emily Dickinson. But Emily, in the mystical vacuum of a total absence, burns one world after world; she leaps from one dead star to another still-living one; she journeys through madness and death with "a Chamois' Silver Boot." Donne, even as he shrinks the space, "the point in time" at which he lives and speaks, as far as it will go, seems to take possession of the world, as if it were a huge, marvelous, purely emblematic map he unfurled with both hands and spread like an imperial mantle, completely covered with symbols, under the footsteps of his love. Sometimes he appears to be playing with the terrestrial sphere like a Divine Child playing with the globe— or else he performs a risky and recondite trick worthy of a Chinese magician: a rotation of spheres that chase each other in double, contrasting circles of thematic words, like the stars in an astrolabe or the souls in the mystic rose. In these concentric, decentric compositions, the most abstract idea is dressed in images as visually precise as the illustrations in a scientific treatise, so that an arbitrary nuance in the translation can shift the angle of vision by ninety degrees. Donne, during this period, brims over with treasures, discoveries, formal rarities like a ship back from the Antilles, and yet, for the first time, he is divinely innocent; he is as simple as a child, and no less adorable.

What Emily called "the Etruscan experiment"—and we find in Donne the same image of a couple lying in their sweet sarcophagal pose—reveals to Donne the principles that make every supernatural relationship a propaedeutic to spiritual experience. Such a relationship liberates him from all the Old Alliances of sentiment: the law of necessity, the game of forces, pure psychology; it reveals to him the sacrament of distance, the mysteries of silence, the miracle of "mutual certainty of the mind," and the regret—which is already quite religious—for all the ways he formerly squandered his soul.

All of this can be found—distilled a thousand times, "hammered out until it forms the keenest blade"—in the theological and contemplative poetry he wrote after Ann's death. This is, indeed, all that remains. The coronas of spheres and intricate astrolabes used to adorn the slender neck of a brave and trembling girl now give way to otherworldly cosmographies. The connection between microcosm and macrocosm is still quite close, but the splendor multiplied by the facing mirrors is now concentrated on a single object: the one that the poet chooses, ascetically, as the subject of his meditation. Time is of the essence. Space, once more, is shrunk. But it is no longer a matter of condensing whole worlds; it is a condition for spiritual infinitude. Once more Donne tries to recover his prehistory, and this time the recovery is total: just as, when he contemplated love, he regretted his earlier love affairs, so the whole itinerary of his past suffering now strikes him as insufferable, and he disavows everything that has taken away from the ultimate realities. The Holy Sonnets are stripped down to the spirit; Donne's "massive music" is funneled into one chaste, piercing sustained note: the thunderous monotone of the mystics, who so often plead for death. He wants to cease to exist so that only the Other might exist. So that he might exist only in the Other. "Batter my heart, three person'd God.... That I may rise and stand, o'erthrow me."

The whiteness of an ivory crucifix, the *nave*-nave that breaks the blood-red waves, the dying body of the great cartographer of poetry itself like one last map, over which the scholars hunch, searching for the liberating strait: all the expansive, sparkling, fierce allusive imagery has changed. An inscrutable dignitary perpetually on the verge of death—so medieval he pictures himself in the pulpit "clad in the vestments as in a holy cloud," meditating on the virgin Sophia in the pristine tradition of the sapiential books—Donne is now spiritually and literarily wrapped in the winding sheet in a way we will not encounter again in Protestantism, except in the sublime, tragic pastors of New England transcendentalism. Around him is the dark glow of cathedrals robbed of tabernacles, where religious ceremony and state ceremony have the same dry and pompous polish: that aura "of Bible and war" in which his already fading voice sets the pure, otherworldly tone. And all of this, in a certain sense, bears a resemblance to this man who, in spite of everything, never knew the other side of the desire for martyrdom: that sweetness, that honey dripping from the rock and flowing, *gemitibus inenarrabilibus*, into the intoxicating *neumatizare* of the ancient jubilations, which had surely been tasted, for example, by George Herbert, or that free-and-easy Earl of Arundel—Saint Philip Howard—who wasted away in prison from the poison.

Underneath all of this—or above it—there is the enduring mystery of an art informed and illuminated to the end by a more or less arcane symbolism that walks along with him and follows him and is inseparable from him, like the shadows of the lovers in "A Lecture upon the Shadow," written in his youth. According to recent criticism (which Baron Pastor preceded by many years), the secret of the art of the Counter-Reformation lay in an occult return to the unfathomable religious cosmologies of the Middle Ages, such as they were codified in the masterful work of Guillaume Durand. The tremendous leap into the air, like salmon swimming upstream, the truly metaphysical passage from quantity to quality that, for a century, held back the surging deluge of Renaissance naturalism, begins with a determination to project the forms of the era onto symbolic substances that infinitely transcend them. The plans of churches returned to the ancient Greek cross. Asceticism and mysticism went back to their sources: the Scriptures, the Desert Fathers, the monasticism of the early centuries. Pomp itself changed its meaning quite dramatically. It went from being a show of longing and earthly domination to being an image of vanity—an intoxicated offering of things destined to perish. The appearance of Ignatius of Loyola, a pure specter proceeding toward his own tomb of gold and lapis lazuli; the heavy pontifical ornaments of the skeletal bishop in Valdés Leal's *Finis gloriae mundi* (ornaments placed on the hopelessly light plate of a scale whose other plate is weighed down by a heart aflame with love for Christ); the sepulchral dampness that chills the lace in *The Burial of the Count of Orgaz*: all of this stems from the same spiritual and aesthetic postulates that give life, under the thrones of Elizabeth and James, to John Bull's stunning innomine on Gregorian themes and the divinely dark Donne of the Holy Sonnets. A poet who, perhaps more than any other, courted the mortal dangers of the late Renaissance, Donne burns brightest when the outward forms of his era are underlain by a root system of cosmological and ascetic symbols (secretly tended by his own hand) that are ultimately the same as those of Dante Alighieri, the monastic breviary and the ancient cathedrals overgrown with weeds and ivy. Perhaps, if we want to read between Donne's lines, we would do better to reread Durand's *Rationale* or Autun's *Gemma Animae* rather than attempting yet another literary exegesis.

There is no doubt that this "lord temporal," whom chance or destiny—"rude Fate, Commissioner of God"—wished to make a "lord spiritual," served English poetry with a purity no less superbly atavistic, and no less frankly surprising, than the purity that led to the decapitation, for a "suppressed and afflicted Religion," of that great skeptic and utopian Lord Chancellor Thomas More.

A DOCTOR

A VERY taciturn psychiatrist, who was in some ways reminiscent of the doctors depicted by Anton Chekhov, used to advise his depressives to read the book of Job. He had a high opinion of these unhappy people, most of whom were afflicted, like Andersen's princess, with eyes that saw things too clearly, and he assured them that this arduous meditation on the order of the world would do them good; they would come away from it refreshed. The critic who wrote the following sentence about Chekhov must have understood the power of reading in a rather similar way: "He is the only one whose work we can press against our aching flesh without causing ourselves further pain."

Indeed, Chekhov belongs to that small minority of poets who have laid, in the foundation of their works, a perfect consciousness of the order of the world: the laws of necessity that govern us, the irreducible quantity of evil on this earth ("something irreparable, hopeless, which it was impossible to set right and to which it was impossible to become accustomed"). He was thus also conscious of the importance of living according to completely opposite and complementary laws—according, that is, to the risky "madness of love" that people are continually trying to stifle in both themselves and others.

The terror of a man confronted with the power of his own spirit, that irresistible need—as Simone Weil defined it—"to cover one's eyes with the veil of the flesh the moment one sees the smallest sign of the good": This, and nothing else, is the subject of all Chekhov's fiction. A perfect synthesis can be found in a short paragraph from the story called "A Nervous Breakdown," where the young student Vassilyev, who has suffered so much from his discovery of prostitution that he is now on the brink of madness, is relegated to that madness by the fearful world.

> "That I should have taken my degree in two faculties you look upon as a great achievement; because I have written a work which in three years will be thrown aside and forgotten, I am praised up to the skies; but because I cannot speak of fallen women as unconcernedly as of these chairs, I am being examined by a doctor, I am called mad, I am pitied!"...
>
> The [doctor], with the air of completely comprehending the tears and the despair, of feeling himself a specialist in that line, went up to Vassilyev and, without a word, gave him some medicine to drink.

This is the same bromide that will reduce the protagonist of "The Black Monk," too, to idiocy. That a man feels himself to be a "specialist in that line" and can find no better way to treat it than to administer a few drops to deaden the attention is something that happens every day, every hour. We could begin with Chekhov's critics and their by now mechanical attempts to induce narcosis with their talk of his Leopardian pessimism and irreducible sarcasm, the bankruptcy of his era and culture. This web of acquiescence, which envelops those who weave it as well as those who become entangled in it, can only be broken through with the old saying: "Close your eyes and you'll go blind."

Like any free spirit, Chekhov has his eyes wide open. He has heroically attentive eyes. It is this total presence—with no evasions or lapses—that gives the immense Chekhovian narrative its unity of representation, and almost of mystery, through all its innumerable acts. Tolstoy used to say that, up close, Chekhov's brushstrokes look random but from a distance reveal wonderful correlations of form and color. An observation we can expand and say that each of Chekhov's tableaus appears isolate from up close but from a distance finds its place in the vast fresco he intended to create—not of Russia at the turn of the century, or of any other land, but of the *cité d'ici-bas*, where, in ancient fashion, all the houses appear to be open on one side and, on the other, immersed in that fluid, insidious element that is the common human condition. The gaze that encompasses this world and recomposes its scattered meanings from above is no different from the gaze of Shakespeare: the terrible inventory of the evils of this earth made by Hamlet in his monologue is the wall that surrounds the city of Chekhov.

It is this gaze from above that gives the fiction, which is apparently so nervous, exuberant, and casual, the brimming sweetness of natural cycles, as well as that vertiginous sense of time, in which the characters' existences seem to unfold with stuporous slowness and, simultaneously, with terrifying speed—in which the day that never ends is suddenly a life that rushes by, already slipping through your fingers, lost: an irretrievable nothing for those who lived it just like that, like a day without end.

Chekhov is well aware—and how obstinately patient he is when he tries to demonstrate it—how the closed, immobile circle of habit is the wheel that carries the soul most quickly away to death. And what can counterbalance this habit (which he often, rightly, calls "satiation"), what can be prescribed to remedy and redeem it, if not its opposite: attention?

Chekhov assumes all of attention's risks, or rather its only serious risk, which gives the game its high stakes: the risk of a clear-sightedness that exhausts the trusting soul, saps it of the mysterious forces of fervor, leaving it unprotected against the enormous number of things that are unacceptable, which are the very core of the order of the world. For attention, like any form of extreme hope, can abruptly transform into despair and, turned against itself, take on the features of the most lethal of habits: inert resignation to human misery.

It is the risk run by the university professor in the marvelous "A Dreary Story"—the risk run by all those bitter, passionately good people, whom he often stops to describe at length, like a scientist testing his own serums on himself, for all these men have, more or less, his features: the subtle doctor in "Enemies," the coarse one in "The Princess," the splendid memoirists of "My Life" and "An Anonymous Story," the prisoner in "The Bet" (that brief, blazing variation on the great theme of Ecclesiastes). The psychiatrist in "Ward No. 6," a good, intelligent, cowardly man, whose fear makes it impossible for him to exercise attention, will reach, and overstep, the outermost limit of this risk. When a series of events burns away the barrier that his amiably stoic demeanor has for years placed between him and his patients, and he finds himself on the other side of horror, where life is really *impossible* and yet is lived, hour by hour, year by year, by thousands of beings much better than he, the doctor can only die, affirming what he had so long denied: the *impossible* miracle of life in misfortune.

Chekhov thus assumes attention in all its mortal fullness and all its mortal risks. The span of each of his stories is like a new day, when a man who spent the previous night brooding on the strength of his spirit now measures it in the most searing proximity. Chekhov's incomparable human sympathy, which makes him so lovable and consoling, is truly the sympathy of a doctor: the one who bears within himself a conflux of countless sufferings but doesn't waste words and "sometimes whistles without thinking." He goes in and out of the houses and knows how very little he can do for his patients; he believes very little in his own art; but he sits at their bedsides and lingers there. With him, he brings the only real drug: the unmistakable gaze of one of those people who are prepared to sit up with us the whole night through; the discreet, modest, "gentlemanly" language of the man who has learned to remind himself and others, continually, what pain might be worth, if it were reflected in a mirror of unshadowed love.

Deceit, mediocrity, compromise, satiation, ugliness: all this, too, must be endured, like the rest and more so, because they are even more deeply affecting and offensive, because an exercised attention is like an embrasure open to every arrow—a kind of continuous passion. It requires an enormous effort to give each presence an equal measure of presence while preserving, in one's inner depths, a sense of what alone really matters.

> The bedclothes, the rags and bowls, the splashes of water on the floor, the little paint-brushes and spoons thrown down here and there, the white bottle of lime water, the very air, heavy and stifling—were all hushed and seemed plunged in repose.
> The doctor stopped close to his wife, thrust his hands in his trouser pockets, and slanting his head on one side fixed his eyes on his son. His face bore an expression of indifference, and only from the drops that glittered on his beard it could be seen that he had just been crying.
> That repellent horror which is thought of when we speak of death was absent from the room. In the numbness of everything, in the mother's attitude, in the indifference on the doctor's face there was something that attracted and touched the heart, that subtle, almost elusive beauty of human sorrow which men will not for a long time learn to understand and describe, and which it seems only music can convey.

This is the polar opposite of "curiosity," of literary "disinterest," of that "objective observation" invoked in "A Nervous Breakdown" by the student's friend, Mikhail, who has just finished beating a drunk whore.

Such is the way Chekhov moves around the earthly city, hemmed in by the insurmountable walls of its evils ("Th'oppressor's wrong, the proud man's contumely, / The pangs of despis'd love, the law's delay, / The insolence of office, and the spurns / That patient merit of th'unworthy takes"), between houses whose doors stand open on one side and yet are guarded, like a wild duck's nest, by a sinister concord of silence. Inside, there are men who could help themselves and do not because they are tired, satiate, or fearful, because no one taught them how to express themselves, or because their capacity for reciprocal attention has been destroyed by unhappiness ("unhappiness does not bring people together but draws them apart, the unhappy are egotistic, spiteful, unjust, cruel, and less capable than happy people of understanding each other"). Chekhov's many women—Veroshka, Katya, Olga, Zinaida—dwell in these places: they are the different faces of a single question to which a convincing answer is never given. And the children, the boys, the pure lymph that will soon turn into blood sweat. And outside, in the open air, the solitaries and the exiles: the purehearted fallen prince who aims at a pheasant and shoots too high because even when hunting he cannot see the use of a mediocre act; the young monk on the night ferry mourning his dead brother; along the empty path, between the guards silent out of habit, the deportee who does not understand his punishment, that enormous punishment inflicted on him by people who expressed themselves with such noble words. The horse thieves joust around the fire, the old men lament the old age of the earth, the sledge drivers confide their griefs to their horses (since no one else listens to them). In the little train forgotten on the steppe, the abandoned bulls die of thirst, and the stray puppies dream, with yelps of nostalgia, of the blows of an imaginary master.

To take such routes every day, to risk such encounters, is the stuff of stoics. Chekhov, "delicate as a girl, gentle as a Japanese," carries only two talismans: the ability to smile and the presence of nature. When the reasons for discouragement threaten to cloud his vision, when nausea rises to stifle his tongue, Dr. Chekhov smiles. In their misfortune, his characters sometimes appear so intensely stupid that they display traits common to all the species that swarm on the globe: "He stared at me like a rooster at some grain: 'Now you'll finally be persuaded I'm an intelligent person.'" "A hundred times you've tried to drag me out of the pit, but nothing came of it. . . . Give it up! You can't coax a dung beetle to a rose."

Only what is pure seems to remove even the shadow of a smile from his face. Then we see his anguish, his almost religious anxiety, over everything that represents the eternal here below, in humble and mysterious code, and is nonetheless destined to perish. Whenever he comes to pass a judgment or establish a comparison, Chekhov gives his language over to these light, solemn, perishable presences. And a central space opens in the tangle of the narrative, a sort of deep, luminous "eye of the storm," which, as in Giotto's frescoes, instantly creates a fourth dimension:

"Life went on as before: even, sluggish, and free from sorrow. The shadows lay on the earth, thunder pealed from the clouds, from time to time the wind moaned plaintively, as though to prove that nature, too, could lament, but nothing troubled the habitual tranquillity of these people. Of Susanna Moiseyevna and the IOUs they said nothing."

"One could feel the approach of that miserable, utterly inevitable season, when the fields grow dark and the earth is muddy and cold, when the weeping willow seems still more mournful and tears trickle down its stem, and only the cranes fly away from the general misery, and even they, as though afraid of insulting dispirited nature by the expression of their happiness, fill the air with their mournful dreary notes."

The earth, like a ruined woman sitting alone in a dark room and trying not to think of the past, was brooding over memories of spring and summer and apathetically waiting for the inevitable winter. Wherever one looked, on all sides, nature seemed like a dark, infinitely deep, cold pit from which neither Kirilov nor Abogin nor the red half-moon could escape....

In such pauses, the innumerable possibilities for redemption from the laws of necessity are gathered in and secretly protected (as the servant in "An Anonymous Story" protects the tears of his mistress): the signs and presentiments of a natural charity, an obstinate and forgotten love. Then the space closes, soldered by the fatal circle of habit, but it is precisely this circle that is most cruelly incised around the soul of Chekhov's reader, isolating there, like a lost homeland, a place of unrealized and still-possible beauty.

"Fortunate is he," Chekhov writes of a confessor, "who is given the power to forgive." But in the last great stories, the extreme purity his gaze has attained makes it increasingly difficult for him to grant absolution. This is now a gaze capable of following—and describing—a life that is the shame of a nation, of a world—the life of the soldier Gusev—to the bottom of the sea, where his corpse has been thrown. In "An Anonymous Story," the rarefaction of the air in which the process takes place is that of the highest altitudes. He reduces the number of characters to three, seen almost as three archetypes, three creatures who have almost been destroyed: the first two by ardently aspiring to a life free from deceit and the third by the poisonous ooze of egotism. The unknown man, a young conspirator, has infiltrated the life of the powerful parasite Orlov by posing as a servant. One is undermined by tuberculosis and the fear of not being able to rise to his ambitions, while the other is satiated to such a degree he no longer knows how to savor even the most fragrant of gifts: the loving presence of Zinaida, who has left her husband for him.

Having failed to carry out the plan that brought him to Orlov's house—and at the same time having penetrated to the heart of himself, his illness, the world around him—the unknown man writes a letter to his master:

> You and I have both fallen, and neither of us will ever rise up again... Like Samson of old, I have taken the gates of Gaza on my shoulders to carry them to the top of the mountain when my youth and my strength were exhausted... But even if my letter to you were eloquent, terrible, and passionate, it would still seem like beating on the lid of a coffin: however one knocks upon it, one will not wake up the dead! No efforts could warm your accursed cold blood.

Orlov replies exactly as expected, with a letter that the entire contemporary world could sign:

> The more objective we remain, the less risk we run of falling into error.... But the fault is neither yours nor mine; we are of too little consequence to affect the destiny of a whole generation. The causes of this phenomenon are probably countless and of a biological nature. We are neurasthenics, flabby, renegades, but perhaps it's necessary and of service for generations that will come after us.... Everything has its cause and is inevitable. And if so, why should we worry and write despairing letters?

Between these two masculine archetypes, a feminine archetype: the fragile and natural spirit who pays for the clash between irreconcilable forces with her life after entrusting both men with her need for truth. Zinaida followed Orlov because she imagined he was alone, wise, and unhappy. When things go south, she clings to the unknown man the way a vine torn from a ruined wall clings to a young cypress. She will not survive the discovery that even this trunk is hollow: exhausted and hungry for peace and quiet, the young man is no longer able to fulfill his own ideal form. And what's more he wants her, he desires her ("like the other one").

> "The world of ideas!" she said, and she looked into my face sarcastically, "the world of ideas... Then we had better leave off talking. What's the use? Tell me, what am I to do? Teach me! If you haven't the strength to go forward yourself and take others with you, at least show me where to go. After all, I am a living, feeling, thinking being. To sink into a false position... to play an absurd part... is painful to me."

The unknown man, too, will not live for very long past the last page of his memoir. But in the dark sky of that page, Chekhov has re-formed the two passionate constellations, divided by the formless game of unhappiness, back into one. ("The thoughts and desires of living creatures are not as important as their sufferings.") But there is no absolution for Orlov. He is the only one who goes unscathed by all of this. He will drift into old age playing cards and devouring books, Baltic sturgeon, and human existences. Closing the lid of the whitewashed sepulcher once more, the unknown man exits his life.

Here, Chekhov's sense of justice shows itself to be quite similar to Dostoevsky's sense of justice at the end of the very long debate in *The Idiot*: Myshkin and Rogozhin, the two poles of human love, the two opposing and complementary forces, come together under the vault of a single crypt, like the ancient kings after a duel to the death. But under that vault there is no room for Totsky, the seducer with immaculate gloves, the root cause of the novel's catastrophe: the man of "curious experiences" and "interesting phenomena" (a vocabulary identical to Orlov's or Mikhail's friends, whom Vassilyev did not hesitate to call murderers). Half a century later, Pasternak will stage the trial for a third time: Totsky and Orlov will be reincarnated in Komarovsky, Myshkin and the Unknown Man in Zhivago, Nadya and Zinaida in Lara.

In his late stories, Chekhov often secretes his own voice in the voice of one of his characters. And it's telling that the character he chooses is never beyond redemption, never the man who's gone blind from having closed his eyes too long, but always someone who has preserved at least one last freedom: consciously suffering the distance that separates him from the good.

Under such masks, his sense of justice can be commemorated, rigorous and pure, without shattering the sphere of silence or betraying the difficult prospects of attention. Chekhov's famous pessimism is, finally, the only possible optimism, the doctor's optimism when he becomes a mediator: seeing the world as it is, our fellow men as they are, and at the same time attempting to "read them otherwise," to decipher their gigantic hieroglyphic meaning with the only key we're given—the strength to accept both the order of the world and all that ceaselessly surpasses it. Pasternak read Chekhov along these same lines, as a writer who "inscribed man in a landscape on equal terms with trees and clouds ... [and rendered the true simultaneous resemblance to] life in the far broader sense of a unique vast inhabited frame, to its symmetries and dissymmetries, proportions and dispro-portions—to life as a hidden mysterious principle on the whole."

HOMAGE TO BORGES

Consideré que estábamos, como siempre, en el fin de los tiempos.

EVERYONE knows that Rome, the enormous hybrid, has everything: basilicas below water level, a pyramid, hanging gardens—even a sanatorium on which a tall iron tower burns black oil from dawn to dawn. But not many people know that in a very sad square—among the most disfigured by the century, urban planning, and life—Rome has a "circular ruin."

This little earth-brown ruin is shaped like a sunburst or, more accurately, like a palm leaf: several lines, which were once perhaps corridors, converge on a small door. The whole thing used to be a tiny alchemical temple, a chapel for Christian kabbalists built in the seventeenth century by the Marquis of Palombara and frequented by, among other more or less unknown personages, Christina of Sweden. Today, all that remains intact is the door. And in fact this monument is now remembered solely as "the Magic Portal."

In reality that portal, blocked up with red bricks, no longer leads anywhere. It is a sealed page, and only around the edges, along the bright marble frame, can we read a few words, like the black-and-white birds that hang midair, between earth and sky, on their motionless wings: *Quando in tua domo nigri corvi parturient albas columbas tunc vocaberis sapiens.... Qui scit comburere aqua et lavare igne facit de terra coelum et de coelo terram pretiosam....*

I have spoken of the square where this ruin can be found. But I have not mentioned how close it is to the central train station, which is as good as saying, in a metropolis, how close it is to one of the foulest urban drains. The square itself is a spiral of Dantesque circles. At the edges there is the wall of red meats, damp feathers, scales, and dirty aprons (but also corollas of pure ice, glaucous leaves, and roots) of a permanent market. Farther in, there is a park for children: nothing, on what remains of some flower beds, but a crudely painted pasteboard village fully intending to be humorous (children today must understand at a glance that a toy is no longer a vision but only the incarnation of a wink). These wobbly cartons offer children of ancient lineage sad little fantasias of faraway places (most of which are as dead as this one): the Texas saloon, the gold-nugget bank, the miniature miner's train, and so on.

The square is furthermore inhabited, in its crisp, cold branches, by a rotund constellation of cats, sustained by the ruins, the market, and above all the train station (those who live near such a station, who arrived and could not leave, who could have left and did not know how, who prosper on these impossible stays and departures—the fortune-teller, the astrologer, the healer, the usurer—observe, according to tradition, a whole Leviticus of taboos: chief among them respect for the arcane, vaguely dangerous life of the cat).

Finally, in these precincts, there is a prowling and omnipresent population of young men: mysterious and obvious adolescents standing on the corner with their hands in their pockets, or lying on one of the branching lines of the ruin with their caps over their faces—or carrying a bucket of bloody water covered with blue scales, or else a broom they use to channel a brown, ammoniacal effluvium toward the sewer drain.

This square might seem the ideal place for those whom Proust called collectors of the masks of the real: writers of appearances, realist writers. It is all here: the cats' sharp teeth tearing at yellow viscera; the smell of feathers, salt, and humors mixed with the sickly, virginal odor of the milks and cheeses; and the slightly mortuary aroma of the early hyacinths. In a sulfurous and decaying atmosphere of children screaming, hard looks, and cigarette butts spit as far they will go.

Here, however, is where one finds the Magic Portal. It is clear that it would immediately render itself invisible to such writers, and it is even clearer that, without the Magic Portal, the entire square would disappear. Of the cats perched high in the branches, soon nothing would remain but laughter—like the laughter of Alice's Cheshire cat, or the laughter that the alchemists ascribe to Mercury. Of the putrid sediment of the market, there would be only a spray of snow left in the air: the soul of a white Prunus. And of humanity, there would be merely a funerary statue overturned on one of the branches of the ruin, and the cap on its face would have become a mask of gold. (*Horti magici ingressum Hesperidum custodit draco et sine Alcide Colchicas delicias non gustasset Iason.*)

In this visceral and Pythagorean square, I thought of Borges. I thought of his hierophantic gesture replicating the gesture of the man who figures, as he himself recounts, at the top of the Gnostic map: one index finger pointed up at the sky, the other down toward the earth. I recalled the heartbreaking, impassive words with which he has perhaps sealed the lips of contemporary poetry for many centuries to come, just as the Magic Portal was one day sealed: "Every language is an alphabet of symbols whose use presupposes a past that the interlocutors share."

(Who shares that past today? Who shares that alphabet of symbols? Is there a past? Are there symbols? Where, then, is our language?)

Blind and almost imperceptible in his lost alphabet, like the little Magic Portal, the princely Borges remains: the walled-up center of a circular ruin that the eye, now reduced to a single dimension, brushes past without suspecting its presence. (*Est opus occultum veri sophi aperire terram ut germinet salutem . . .*)

Foreigners still come on pilgrimage to the Magic Portal and transcribe its lofty sentences in notebooks small enough to be tucked into a pocket. They are well aware, these people, that the square derives its virtue and measure solely from the Magic Portal. The square—a mortal present that will destroy itself like the portal, abjectly and innocently.

"I considered that we were now, as always, at the end of time."

SUPERNATURAL SENSES

INTRODUCTION TO *SAYINGS AND DEEDS OF THE DESERT FATHERS*

To Father Irénée Hausherr S.J.

An old man was asked how to visit Abba Anthony. "A
fox lives in a lion's cave," he replied.
　　　　—Sayings and Deeds of the Desert Fathers

THE CHRISTIAN masters of the desert flourished, exploded, in a
moment that lasted for three centuries, from the third to the sixth
after Christ. Constantine had only recently restored the Christians'
right to exist, breaking with the doctrine of Commodus—*Christianoùs
me éinai*, the Christians are not—and gently removed the young
religion from the marvelously moist ground of martyrdom and the
incomparable seasoning of the catacombs.

Needless to say, this meant consigning it to that mortal danger
which has remained in force for eighteen centuries: accord with the
world. While the Christians of Alexandria, Constantinople, and
Rome reentered the normality of rights and days, a few ascetics, terrified by the possibility of that accord, ran from it and sank into the
deserts of Scetis and Nitria, Palestine and Syria. They sank into the
radical silence that only their rare sayings would have furrowed, like
fiery comets in a fathomless sky. In reality, most of these sayings were
uttered in order *not* to reveal anything, just as the existence of those
men strove to be the existence of "a man who does not exist." ("It was
said of the Scetiots that, if any person caught them at their practice,
which is to say came to know of it, they no longer held it for a virtue
but for a sin.")

The sayings and deeds of the Fathers (*lo'goi kai érga, verba et dicta*) were at all times collected with extreme devotion, for they were almost always very hard, uncrackable nuts, to be carried around for life and crushed between the teeth, as in fairy tales, in the moment of gravest danger—and furthermore the Fathers, for the most part, flatly refused to write. They were collected on parchments in Greek, Coptic, Armenian, Syriac. And these parchments perpetuated not only the prophecies and wonders of the Fathers and their disciples but also those of certain secular unknowns who secretly practiced their precepts and, hidden in those metropolises that the Fathers abominated, were sometimes masters to their masters.

A few of the Fathers were anchorites. Such was Anthony the Great, father of all monks, the Egyptian master who over the centuries came to be venerated as the lord of animals because, having returned to pre-Adamic innocence, he enchanted the wild beasts. Others were anchorites who had brief moments of communal life in a church, at an oven or a well. Still others were cenobites in a monastery or some tiny laura of dazzling white cobbles coagulated between the cliffs and chasms. In majestic and skeletal mountains, they move into animal caves or dug-out cellars that looked like giant dovecotes: in every dark mouth of stone, a human body. Wild animals and corpses appear to have been their models. ("Abba Pastor, make peace with the idea that you have already been buried in the grave for a year.") Or else they were wild animals and angels, like their only archetype, that inconceivable creature covered in shaggy fleece with large brown wings, feeding on locusts and honey, John the Precursor—and in the archetype of that archetype, the prophet of fire, Elijah. Inside the cave the beast, and at the mouth of the sepulcher the angel: Arsenius sitting at the threshold of his cell, a thin linen cloth on his chest to collect the endlessly flowing tears; those tears in which the self dissolves like salt in living waters; those supremely mysterious tears for which the Roman Church composed a votive mass.

Apart from John and Elijah, it really does seem the Desert Fathers have no ancestors. Among the Christians, no one who preceded them resembles them. Their doctrine seems to spring forth entire and already armed from the head of Anthony the Great and continues undaunted, unchanged, for eighteen centuries, all through the Christian East: the whole mystical Church of the East is built upon it.

From the spiritual loins of Anthony sprang the regal progeny of the ancient Fathers: Arsenius the Roman, who had been a pedagogue at the court of Byzantium before becoming a monk for forty years (during which time "no one could ever say how he lived"), as well as Macarius of Egypt, Evagrius Ponticus, Hilarion, Pastor, Alonio, Sisoes, Poemen, Paisios, John the Dwarf, Moses the Ethiopian. From these came multitudes of others, down to the masters of the Gaza desert of the sixth century—Seridos, Barsanuphius, John, Dositheus—and the sublime Syrian masters of the fifth century, Isaac and Ephrem. Their teaching informed that of their friends and disciples, bishops and doctors of the East: Athanasius, Chrysostom, Basil, the two Gregorys. Through Cassian the Roman, the foundations were laid for the patriarchal rule of Benedict of Nursia and every form of monasticism in the West. Later, another Latin, Nikephoros the Solitary, and Gregory of Sinai drew from these teachings the doctrine and practice of the Jesus Prayer, the purest unbroken prayer, which is at the heart of the Greek and Russian *Philokalia* and the narrative that edified an entire people, *The Way of a Pilgrim*. The whole of Mount Athos still stands upon it today—with its anchorites whose number no one knows, its ecstatic birds nested in the caves above the sea at Karoulia—as do the Slavic monastic communities, the few remaining Russian sketes.

In the West, this teaching, after only apparently being stifled in the universal disaster of the Renaissance (for among the contemplatives of ancient stock it had never stopped being handed down), reemerged in the mysterious Counter-Reformation. It is reincarnated unchanged in Cardinal Bona, a Cistercian monk, in Saint Anthony Maria Zaccaria, and in Lorenzo Scupoli (whose writings, in a celebrated Russian translation, became a central ascetic text throughout the Slavic world). Not to mention John of the Cross, builder of the system. In that era so full of unknowns, if anachoresis was not reborn in the West, *xeniteia* within the world, or interior migration, reached the heights of perfection in many men.

Speaking of the Desert Fathers, as has been previously observed, is in fact no less difficult than getting them to speak. To do so, we would have to be them, but then we wouldn't speak either. We do not have, or no longer have, the senses needed to understand them. The very space that isolates them is so enormous it cannot be crossed. Men greater than the true, as the Truth is always greater than the true, could only come about in places of extreme solitude. Nothing except the "bare, burning desert" could contain them. "What is most remarkable about the Desert Fathers," an English theologian, Bryan Houghton, has noted, "is that they obstinately remain in the desert. It is no longer possible to reach them. They reveal absolutely nothing about themselves. They do not even seem to care very much whether anyone succeeds in questioning them. They know very well that they will get the last laugh. They had reached the point where the self had simply vanished. There was no more psyche on which to hang any psychology. When they suffered the divine charismata—and I phrase it this way without irony, for divine charismata are terrible things—what did they think? Silence, silence ..."

Their physical movements are themselves so scarce and secret we can only compare them to geological wrinkles or interpret them as we do the great symbolic movements of the heroes of the Scriptures. They tread the burning earth by the bush (undressing and throwing themselves facedown on the ground is one of the very few gestures in which we continually surprise them), proceeding in a pillar of cloud that hides them from view and ought to lead them to the land of milk and honey. But they never breathe a word about this land. For them, what counts is the exile, the crossing, and the lesson they have come to teach with their silences: how to be absolute strangers on this earth, how to exist anywhere precisely like "a man who does not exist."

The Desert Fathers let us know only one thing about themselves beyond a shadow of a doubt: their cell is a *martyrion*, they have come "to fight for every death"—the death of the body, the death of the man, the death of the mind itself (*nous*)—"so as to become alive with God unceasingly in silence." The angel seated at the entrance to the

sepulcher never tires of repeating: "The man you are looking for—
Anthony, Arsenius, Macarius—is not here."

This is the *hesychia*, the divine quietude or holy impassivity that—
as is reasonable—made these immovable men like fire, so that their
raised fingers emitted flames, and their speech was "like a sword
stroke." It was important that, while they prayed, a disciple kept watch
at the door so that no one could see how, in reality, that door was the
mouth of a furnace.

Having said this—having given up once and for all "knowing" anything about the Fathers, let alone interpreting them—it should be
possible, if our courage suffices, to sit motionless at their feet and
contemplate—between sayings, and above all between silences—the
doctrine that sprang armed and ready from Anthony's brain. We are,
at the feet of the Fathers, very close to those "springs" so celebrated
in all ages by revolutionary archaeologisms, and here, in fact, we find
the things that these archaeologisms have repeatedly attempted to
banish, all those things that they have more and more successfully
banished, so that almost nothing remains of them in a world that, as
never before, goes about celebrating the imaginary—romantic, sentimental—splendor of the springs.

I do not think it is even necessary to mention the fundamental
steps of the Fathers' *scala coeli*: the total amputation from the world
and the extreme refinement of one's powers—which are themselves
simple tools for transforming the inner man—through silence, fasting, the singing of psalms, manual labor. All these rules remain rather
plainly constant through the whole history of traditional Christian
monasticism. But with the Desert Fathers a particular light, which
their taciturnity does not soften, falls on elements that later on and
elsewhere will be only implicit, later on and elsewhere practically lost,
and that are, nevertheless, the cornerstones of their teaching and their
teaching alone.

The supernaturalization of the five senses, for example—or rather
the existence of those "supernatural senses" that the *hesychia* has

called to life, whereby a still-living body can become something very close to a glorious body: the water in which some Fathers have simply washed their hands can exorcise a novice tempted by an impure spirit. Hands that, when raised, pour forth flames, and that must be quickly lowered in prayer so as not to be overwhelmed by ecstasy. Bodies on which a fiery eagle descends during synaxis, a sheet of fire covering the vestments. The radiant, menacing autonomy of the scapular, the psalter, and the girdle, so immersed in the life of the saint that they can burn the enemy like a red-hot iron and make him scream.

The same arena where everything is played out—the mind—has a life of its own, even, according to Isaac, a body of its own, which consumes every last act and action, neither more nor less than the other body, while the other body is deserted: a tomb guarded by demons. ("Whosoever looketh on a woman to lust after her...")

It is Anthony the Great who defines once and for all this fierce, feral relationship between the human body and the human mind, in one of those sentences that shoot from him like lightning bolts from the steep slope of Sinai: "Demons are not visible bodies, but we become bodies for them when our souls accept dark thoughts from them. For, having accepted these thoughts, we accept the demons themselves, and make them corporeally manifest." In this light, the image of the devil or possessed man who wanders "in the deserts, among the graves" acquires a new and chilling meaning. (Gregory the Great gave this wandering mind a feral appearance: *lupus qui sine cessatione quotidie non corpora sed mentes dilaniat, malignus videlicet spiritus.*)

In the pure and unified mind, God can dwell. From the torn, multiplied mind, God wants to escape. This is the only reason for doing everything in one's power not to sin and the only real motive for relentless purification.

The techniques of this purification are infinitely varied and infinitely contradictory. Every precept is constantly reflected in its opposite, in a game of facing mirrors, a vertiginous explosion of antinomies that renders any sense of possession or success impossible in this matter, and even especially in this matter. But these acts of purification always depend—like the attitude toward the exterior

world—on a preliminary and radical inversion of all natural psychological laws. This is, after all, a common denominator among all
spiritual athletes at whatever point in time or space we find them.
The dispute with the dark powers that besiege the mind is won by
reversing all the usual tactics, following a kind of spiritual aikido in
which the enemy's aggressive energies are used, so to speak, rather
than repulsed—their violence indulged until it becomes its opposite.
Such is the holy sprezzatura of the Gospels and those little gospels
called fairy tales. "And if any man will sue thee at the law, and take
away thy coat, let him have thy cloak also. And whosoever shall
compel thee to go a mile, go with him twain." If a man or a demon
accuses you, you double the accusation; if a man or a demon threatens
you, you let him know you are avid for an even more terrible threat.
"What will you do, old man, for you still have another fifty years to
live [and suffer]?" "You have distressed me greatly, for I had been
prepared to live for two hundred years." To the evil one, when he
manifests himself: "Well now, this is really something!" And twelve
years later, seeing him go away defeated: "Where are you running off
to? Stay a while!"

The technique of the Buddhist koan is by no means alien to these
sweet and terrifying Christian lands. "Is it good to go and visit the
aged monks, or is it better to stay in one's cell? The rule of the ancient
fathers was to visit the aged, whom they rightly ordered to remain in
their cell."

"Like the sound of one hand clapping," the densely knotted mysteries of destiny and divine providence ring out in melodious opposites
all through the Desert Fathers' sayings and deeds. What is a blessing
for Sisoes will be a prohibition and a danger for Hilarion. If the scribe
is not fast enough to record Barsanuphius's words exactly, it means
that he inscribes them as God wishes them to be recorded and, recorded in this way, they will do their work. And if the pestilent oil
were not mysteriously destined for the sick old man, the distracted
disciple would have put the honey in his lentil cake instead.

"Providence," Anthony teaches, "is the Word of God, who brings
himself to fruition and gives shape to the substance that constitutes

this world." Into this divine carpet, a man may weave himself with the magic thread of love which bears the strange name "Communion of Saints." All the wonders, conversions, and graces that the stories of the Desert Fathers tell are bestowed on someone "for the punishment someone else has assumed" or for the privation and humiliation someone else has accepted. So it is that Apa Bane, abandoning all acts of corporal charity for a life of pure prayer, is able to cause "the barley to grow in abundance throughout the world and the sins of a whole generation to be remitted." Any other form of charity, toward God or a brother, would appear justifiably laughable to the Fathers— as sentimentality or complicity.

Around these great recumbent lions of the spirit, the world of forms, like the world of the word, is nearly abolished and therefore more terribly violent. Their heraldic objects—the psalter, the leather belt, the sheepskin, the wicker basket, the bowl, the small loaves, the salt—look almost menacingly lonely, like dinosaur bones, whether in blinding light or in total shadow. Their sentences are iron-tipped arrows that hum through the air before lodging themselves vertically in the disciple's heart. God plummets into these cells and bodies with a tremendous, solitary batting of wings. And within these bodies, rooted in the sky as they are, there is a frightening strength: visionaries and thaumaturges tempted for a hundred years or more, fragile young men who burrowed into mountains.

The stripped-down, boiled-down story whose clauses are always the same—like Homer's poems—whose psychological audacity and verbal frugality make all profane narrative sound like the hollow rustling of reeds that kept Arsenius from his meditations, offers us, time after time, a portrait of a man who can seemingly never be portrayed, for he dwells beyond every enigma: the spiritual man. Abba Moses the Ethiopian, who had been a slave and a thief; Paul the Illustrious; the two little martyred brothers; the handsome officer who became "like an ancient leper." Only the great Russian prose, which begins with *The Way of a Pilgrim* and is by no means exhausted, has something of this style, which was handed down through Byzantium and Eastern ecclesiastical literature.

And yet in that story of a Desert Father whom Tolstoy wished to resurrect, "Father Sergius," there are no deserts or wild animals or angels; there is only a heroic, pathetic Russian prince. "A man who does not exist," each one of the Desert Fathers is all of the Fathers and none of the Fathers precisely because, once more, he is an unrepeatable, inconceivable Father. From the hundred tesserae of sayings and deeds that make him up, can an Arsenius be reconstructed, reassembled? Arsenius hidden behind a pillar in the church, "handsome, with a white beard, a lean and well-built body, his eyelashes drooping from his copious tears"; Arsenius, the ex–imperial tutor perpetually immersed in the stench of rotten leaves "in return for the perfumes and odorous oils used among the people"; Arsenius who "had decided never to write or receive a letter and in general practically never to say anything"; Arsenius "aflame" at prayer and so ravaged in his cell by his "great affliction and sadness" that his disciples went away terrified; Arsenius begging, if they hear that he is somewhere, not to go there; Arsenius who, having returned to the disciples he had abandoned for months, asks them why they did not go looking for him and adds, with gentle tears: "The dove has not found a place to land and has returned to the nest..."; Arsenius, dying, who confesses his terror and threatens to sue before the court of Christ anyone who tries to make relics of his body. "'And how would we do it, Abba? We don't know how to prepare the dead.' 'What, you can't tie a rope to my foot and drag me to the top of the mountain?'"

Show me the poet sovereign enough to sketch such a profile, the poet pure enough to invent those minimal scenes that literally break the heart, like the sudden cry of the sick old man when he is handed some wine: "I didn't think I would taste wine again before I died..."?

That school of heavenly peasants, the painters of northern Russia, saw in visions and projected on the surface of the icon the divine childhood of the Desert Fathers: a childhood that transfixes and terrifies like Wisdom herself, like the inexplicable majesty of animal innocence. The old anchorite who "grazed with buffaloes," in one of the briefest and greatest pieces of prose that a human hand has traced, was found one morning with the buffaloes in a net. "The hunters were terrified when they saw him." And they released the old man, who, without saying a word, "set off running after the buffaloes."

And so, having said and thought of them everything we could possibly say or think, we, too, are forced to let every one of these men go—touching our brows in silence to their holy footsteps—if grace has led them to cross our paths for a moment in the desert.

INTRODUCTION TO *THE WAY OF A PILGRIM*

I.

"By the grace of God, I am a Christian, by my deeds a great sinner, by vocation a pilgrim of the lowliest origins, wandering from place to place. My earthly possessions are a bag of dry crusts on my back and, in the inside pocket of my smock, the Holy Bible. Nothing else."

This opening, one of the most captivating in the literature of any country—comparable to the opening of *Hamlet* or "The Porter and the Three Ladies of Baghdad"—inaugurates at once a great spiritual treatise, a picaresque novel, a resplendent Russian poem, and a classic fairy tale.

In the mysterious anonymous text transcribed on Athos by Abbot Paissy of the Monastery of Saint Michael the Archangel of Cheremis near Kazan around 1860, the fairy tale is, for once, unmasked, which is to say it reveals what all great fairy tales covertly are: a quest for the kingdom of heaven, the pursuit of an unknown and inexplicable vision, often only of an arcane word, for which the hero abruptly deserts his beloved homeland and all good things in order to become a pilgrim and a beggar, a holy fool with a heart of fire, whom the whole world will mock and that "the world behind the real world" will help and guide with marvelous signs and wonders.

Like that Nordic hero who wanted to "learn to shudder" at any cost, the Russian pilgrim is determined to walk on and on, beyond the steppes and forests, the towns and villages—beyond the endless curve of the globe if necessary—provided that the meaning of three words spoken by the apostle Paul, which he has heard by chance upon entering a church, is revealed to him: "Pray without ceasing." The pilgrim soon finds the key to this command, which instantly strikes him as all-important and hyperbolic (how is a person supposed to pray without ceasing, busy as we are with living almost without ceasing?). A charming spirit—a *starets* whom it is hard to say whether he meets in the flesh or in the spirit, since the death that parts them soon after is revealed to be a trifling incident, not even momentarily interrupting their ecstatic dialogue—gives him an ancient and powerful sacred formula, a very brief prayer containing "the Name which is above all names and to which Heaven, Earth, and Hell show deference": "Lord Jesus Christ, Son of God, take pity on me." Two other talismans accompany this gift and have, like the slave in Aladdin's lamp, the responsibility of teaching their own use: a book with a singular title, *Philokalia, or The Love of Beauty*, and a ritually intricate rosary—each knot is made up of seven knots—on which to chant the formula unto infinity.

The story of the Russian pilgrim is the chronicle, no more and no less, of his dazed and euphoric cohabitation with the Jesus Prayer. This prayer is the wondrous jewel whose radiance protects the body and illuminates the mind, reveals distant things and tames wild beasts, conquers all hearts, satisfies all needs, and transmutes all landscapes. And not only that. It is also a presence, so alive and sweetly imperious that one fine morning "it is the Prayer that wakes him up." Later, it will also be the prayer that urges him onward and keeps him within its ring of miracles, its blissful mandorla. Held tight in the arms of this invisible prince who enraptures him everywhere he goes, the pilgrim begins to enter the most delightful state in the world: it is not he who prays the prayer but the prayer who prays him. He does not experience it; it experiences him. It is not his heart that enunciates the divine words but he who is divinely enunciated. At the entrance to the celestial labyrinth, the apostle Paul, giving that strange command of his ("Pray without ceasing"), knew exactly what this meant: *Vivo autem, iam non ego, vivit vero in me Christus. . . . Ipse Spiritus postulat pro nobis gemitibus inerrabilibus . . .*

And so the pilgrim walks on, accompanied by the deep declamatory voices of the twenty-five ancient Fathers who, in the *Philokalia*, bequeathed the insights of their experience of the Jesus Prayer. The old book is the dazzling theory; the pilgrim's story the biography, the transition from the masterly "you" to the trembling "I" of the newly initiated disciple. From method to life. From Saint Augustine's majestic treatises on grace to the lyrical purity of the *Confessions*.

Around this intoxicating story of love between the pilgrim and his prayer, a multitudinous, marvelous world is unveiled at every step. A world which is not all that different, at first sight, from another metaphysical Russian poem, Gogol's *Dead Souls*. But here we are witnessing the "living souls" concealed behind the dead ones like "the world that is concealed behind the real world." Here we are witnessing the sublime, vertical, ascetic Russia of the people, which revolves around the lauras and the sanctuaries, the hermitages of its thaumaturges, and the holiest liturgy—the Russia that, because it is completely Russian, conserves within itself, like an imperial seal, "the precise form of Byzantium."

Wherever the pilgrim goes, he sees this ecstatic Russia emerge from the shadows. Loving lizards crawl out of every crack and crevice, gently surging toward that regal ray of sun: the Name repeated in the prayer—the miraculous, mortally silent masonry of devotion. In the posthouses, among the deportees, on the doorsteps of the taverns, in the luminous patrician house radiant with icons and expensive books, whose lord bends down to put fresh bandages on the dusty feet of the "wandering Christ,"* there is no need for questions. A light, constant trembling of the tongue moved by ceaseless invocation, a visionary joy in the eyes, a few words spoken with excruciating sweetness: the recognition is instantaneous, there is the total intimacy that springs up between two men smitten with the same great adventure, and one story emerges from another, like the old concentric Russian

---

*This episode, which seems so fictional, occurred in a noted house, belonging to a relative of one of the Kapnist counts, as a descendant of theirs has attested. Further proof, if proof is needed, of the historicity of *The Way of a Pilgrim* and of the reality of this Russia.

dolls, each one more extraordinary than the last and yet with no sense of surprise, just as in *Dead Souls* none of the "soul sellers" marveled at the inconceivable exchange proposed. Gogol himself, as many readers will know, aspired to compose a poem about the other Russia—about the living souls concealed behind the dead ones. If he inexplicably decided to abandon it, perhaps this was because at that very moment, somewhere, the pilgrim's hand was already writing it.

In the whole miraculous affair, probably the most incredible miracle is that the adventure became a story with structural continuity, august and innocent Homeric refrains, and all its narrative mastery dedicated, mirabile dictu, to spiritual intuitions. The briefest of its chapters—the one, for example, in which the pilgrim's books are stolen, or the other about the healing of the frostbitten legs—are no less literarily incandescent than the carriage scene in *Anna Karenina* or the confession of Madame de Clèves. It is, finally, miraculous that this supremely defenseless book exists at all; that someone thought to write it and wrote it; that, against all odds, the great spiritual secret of Eastern Christianity has been wrapped in this candidly determined, unconsciously lovely literary form.

2.

Father Irénée Hausherr of the Society of Jesus, to whom we owe many exalted pages on the spiritual teachers of the East, writes that the pilgrim is simply "the faithful disciple of a six-hundred-year-old doctrine called *hesychasm*,* just as the *Philokalia* that nourishes him, although published in Venice in 1782, is no more than a compendium of manuscripts dating from the golden age of this teaching, in the first centuries." Whether or not the manuscript was compiled by the Abbot of Paissy on Mount Athos based on the testimony of another monk of the holy mountain who had known the pilgrim, "this at

---

*From *hesychia*, meaning "perfect quietude of the soul, holy impassivity" (I. Hausherr, "Hésychasme et prière," in *Orientala Christiana Analecta* [Rome, 1966], 176).

least demonstrates that the monks of Mount Athos did not forget the method of 'physical and scientific prayer' once espoused by Nikephoros the Monk and Gregory of Sinai."

In order to speak without irreverence of this aspect of the pilgrim's book—its capacity as a treatise, which is especially evident in its second part—we would do well to pause for a moment on the very concept of prayer, which in the West seems to be in full eclipse, and not only in the brief, recent, hellish hegira, in which the very idea of prayer has been radically extirpated from human consciousness. Misunderstandings have been gathering on it like dust for at least the last hundred or so years. Despite all the great spiritual autobiographies and all the great classical texts of mysticism and asceticism, for those still practicing it, prayer no longer seems to have, except in certain cloisters, any expression except the voluntary one of petition. Who, anymore, admits what prayer really is—a royal road to the transmutation of the soul, a preparation for union with God and assimilation to Him? Not an action but a state. The mystic's prayer "of pure adherence." The perfectly selfless litanic or exclamatory prayer favored by the saints. The "My God is my everything" that Francis of Assisi repeated with his face pressed to the earth through the long night.

For those who want to dive into the ancient mysteries of prayer and rediscover its marvelous freshness, a long reading of *The Way of a Pilgrim* may suffice. It is a book that has played a part and still plays a part, after all, in the spiritual education of many Orthodox Christians. A reader will find, first recounted in the story and later analyzed in the dialogues, the premises, developments, and prodigious effects of prayer: for the person praying, for the body and the soul, for those he encounters on the road, even for those who pray without knowing what they're doing, like the child forced to recite the prayer under his uncle's whip—even for the wolves and the elements, "since," Father Hausherr observes, "perpetual prayer returns a person to the state of primitive innocence, including the happiness of this state and its power over nature."

There is still the enigmatic teaching that is the hinge on which not only the whole *Way of a Pilgrim*, but all Byzantine contemplation, turns: "to go down to the bottom of one's own heart," "to return the mind to the heart," "to redirect the attention of the mind to the heart," since that is where God dwells and where we must go to meet Him. This appears to be the perfect opposite of Western mysticism's "escape from self," its "placing the heart and the mind in God" in order to leave behind the body like a house abandoned. In the West, an ecstatic rapture separates the soul from the senses, and the body is uprooted from the earth in moments of levitation, almost as if it were being sent up in pursuit of the mind on high. In the East, the body inhabited by God, in the secret chambers of the heart, glows with light and almost with glory, like the body of Saint Seraphim of Sarov, who shone like a sun before a very terrified Mr. Motovilov. But since in such dimensions there is neither high nor low, neither outside nor inside, since the center of the heart is not separable from the infinity of the heavens any more than the atom is separable from the galaxy, and words lose all precise direction, the two experiences are in reality one. Perhaps we could speak of a double and simultaneous movement of the spirit, which withdraws in search of God into the secret chambers of the heart and discovers in this center the infinity into which it leaps.

On the other hand, there are mysterious reciprocities, and it is fascinating to hear repeated, in the melodious theology of a young French Carmelite of the nineteenth century, Elizabeth of the Trinity, the pure doctrine of the Eastern Fathers exactly as it was instilled in the pilgrim: "My occupation is to retreat into my heart and lose myself in Them [the three Divine Persons] who dwell there." "Bury me in the depths of my soul so that I might find God." "All I have to do is pray in order to find him here, inside me, and he is all my happiness." "It is the secret that has transformed my life into a paradise in advance—the belief that a being called Love dwells within us at every instant of the day and night and asks us to live 'in fellowship' with him."

Thus the great Russian lineage of *yuródivyy* and *stranniki*, holy fools and vagabonds, has its Western counterpart, even more than in the ancient palmers and pilgrims, such as Roch of Montpellier, in that joyful, tender, and inflexible mendicant perpetually "wandering from place to place," from Compostela to Bari, from Loreto to Montserrat, and from basilica to basilica until he died on one of their steps, Benedict Joseph Labre, among whose relics—pure rags hardened by mud—there are a rosary and two books: a breviary and the *Lives of the Holy Fathers*.

Those same Fathers that the pilgrim finds in the *Philokalia*. Those same *Lives* that—transmitted by Greek, Coptic, and Syrian scribes, through Byzantine and Slavic ecclesiastical literature—somehow founded the purely Russian narrative style that runs from *Pilgrim* to Gogol to Dostoevsky to Chekhov. A narrative style that shows no signs of dying out, since much of its monumental innocence and dignity can still be found in Pasternak's liturgical language, Solzhenitsyn's stern fables, and Andrei Sinyavsky's blank notebook pages.

SUPERNATURAL SENSES

vita mutatur, non tollitur

ANYONE who comes in from the secular streets and approaches, with excitement and terror, the sacred enclosures, is inevitably overcome by two complementary anxieties: the terror of "losing" his five senses (since, explicitly or implicitly, he has been taught that they are all he has) and the fear of still being too carnal for these enclosures. That such intimacy with the divine may be the supreme occasion for the five senses—*the occasion for metamorphosis*—will not be easy, as it has not been easy for at least two centuries, to communicate to him. Recently—in accordance with the unfailing contemporary preference for the suicidal solution, both for the body and the spirit—he has been encouraged to believe that his five senses, exactly as they are, can serve him very well even in supernatural life. Between nature and the supernatural, there is no longer any gap: the Incarnation of Christ would have proceeded to level all distinctions, destroy every enclosure, and tear the veils of the sanctuaries.

Among the Christian clergy, potential initiators to a spiritual life of the body now survive only on the margins, in caves completely imperceptible to those who pass by. The liturgy, the sovereign initiator, now shines like a cupped candle on only the most inaccessible rocks—Mount Athos, a few Benedictine peaks—or in the most minuscule pigeonholes, lost and forgotten in the metropolis.

Who will be left to bear witness to the immense adventure, in a world that by confusing, separating, opposing, or superposing body and spirit has lost them both and is going to die of this loss? In the prophesied era when the old will see visions and the young dream dreams, the only remaining witnesses may be the poets, who have dual residency in old age and childhood, dreams and visions, the senses and that to which the senses perpetually allude. It is a poet, the only religious poet living today, Andrei Sinyavsky, who has succinctly defined the lost gesture it seems increasingly imperative for us to remember: "It is not a question of overcoming nature *but of replacing it with another nature unknown to us.*"

1. In the longest pause of a slow journey that would lead him to his death, a first-century Christian bishop, Ignatius of Antioch, wrote and sent a letter. All through Asia Minor, "chained to ten leopards"— a detachment of praetorians—he was slowly translated to Rome, where, *ut digne populo romano exhiberi possit*, the amphitheater awaited him. The doomed man feared above all else that the church of that city might rescue him from the wild beasts. At the heart of his letter to the Romans, two times intersect, like the vein and the artery:

> I am the wheat of God and I shall be ground by the teeth of the wild beasts, that I may be found the pure bread of Christ. Do nothing for me, but let me be offered as a libation to God.... I desire the divine bread, which is the flesh of Jesus Christ of the seed of David, and the drink that I long for is his blood, which is incorruptible love.

The style of this lamentation is undeniably wonderful. An august spirit, gripped by a sheer agony of love, shines there with all its dark fires. The contents, however, are nothing more than the commonest matters for the second generation of Christians, the generation that had read the Word under the gaze of those icons—*mimèmata*—of the Word: Peter, John, Paul. The vertiginous canonical lexicon of theophagy pours into them directly from the original Rock: "Whoso eateth my flesh, and drinketh my blood, hath eternal life; and I will raise him up at the last day..." And reciprocally: "With desire I have desired to eat this Passover with you before I suffer..."

In order to be devoured and assimilated by divinity, man must devour divinity. In order to be offered to God as food and drink, he must eat and drink Him.

Three centuries later, this arrow of the Word that pierces the heavens and causes them to drip with blood seems to have penetrated still deeper. Another bishop, John Chrysostom, from his see, says to the people of Constantinople:

> He permitted those who desired to do so not only to see him but to touch him, to taste him, to bite his flesh.... We taste Him who is seated in the heavens and adored by the Angels, but the Angels dare not admire him while we eat of him.... Let us therefore return from the Eucharistic table like lions breathing fire from their nostrils, dreadful even to the devil.

More than a millennium later, in Geneva, we hear, in the voice of a third bishop, Francis de Sales—one of the most mysterious characters of the exorbitantly mysterious Counter-Reformation—the last echo of the sharp Eastern cry that reverberates back through the ages, to Ignatius: "Jesus, our sustenance, over which we exercise the greatest of dominions.... How could it not be our desire that He possess us, eat us, chew us, swallow us, do with us as He pleases?"

But the murmur of the "rivers of living water," pouring forth from the bellies of those men who were still so close to the divine Water Carrier, has become increasingly muffled over the centuries. Angela of Foligno, Catherine, Teresa have, yes, celebrated the blood that filled the cup, which filled and dripped from their mouths when they received the sacrament, but theirs was already the language of ecstasy and charisma. In the early Christian world, the miracle itself was tautological. The marvelous carnality of divine life had no need of wonders. They remembered the Word—"the one we have seen and touched," "the one that, resurrected from death, ate and drank with us," "the one on whose chest John rested"— trembling at the thought of him laying hands on bodies sealed by sickness, his fingers stuck into their ears, his saliva laid on their tongues, rubbed on their nostrils, mixed with mud in order to unstitch their eyelids. And the breath of the divine mouth that passed through the half-open mouths of the apostles like the breath of the Creator into the still-closed form of Adam. They remembered how, before each miracle, deep sighs and sometimes groans issued from his chest, and how before the greatest of them—the resurrection of a young man who had already begun to rot—his eyes were red and swollen with tears, and after two long shudders that had looked like anger—*embrimásthai*—he finally exploded in a tremendous scream. They remembered how powers burst forth from his body if they so much as touched his woolen tunic, woven from top to bottom in a single piece, like lightning from a cloud. The lovely, inexplicable hands of the Word, whose memory, through the central act of their cult, would have been preserved for eons and eons. And His mouth, from which John, in the revelation on Patmos, had seen the double-edged sword emerging.

The touch, the breath, the saliva of God, transmitted to these men by the mouths and hands He had given new life, as though He had brought them back from the kingdom of the dead, still pulsed on the skin of these ecstatics, whose eyes, for this very reason, never blinked as they stared in contemplation of the inconceivable heavens. The mysteries that sent them flying facedown on the ground were still wrapped in their prenatal caul. The first and only condition of any reality of a very high degree is transcendence, and the opposite is equally true. The Second Person of the Trinity is not conceivable if one does not believe that His body was mangled in the unparalleled torture reserved for criminals subject to common law. And no one can contemplate the Third, in the tender mockery of its incarnation as a dove, if he has never covered his head before the celestial arrow that impregnates an adolescent girl initiated into the secret of the Temple.

2. All this remained written in the Gospels, as well as in those apocryphal books where, in spite of everything, so many official feasts have their roots. All this the church embraced and generously gave, reproducing it literally in the laying on of hands and insufflations of

the Spirit, in the insalivations and administrations of sacramental food, or, indirectly, in luminous oils, in the complicated chrisms where countless plants and buds macerated for days and days to the sweet rhythmic chanting of the Scriptures; in the incenses and balms that were allusions or commemorations (conjuring holy anointment, Magdalene's angelically sensual gesture, which it was said would be remembered until the end of time). And there were objects, kisses, acts, words, which were called "sacramentals" because, one way or another, they prolonged the healing power of the sacraments. The church jealously guarded in its atria, and projected into the universe, the "new creation made by God with his own saliva" of which another Father, Saint Ephrem, spoke.

This subtle, sublime circulation (of *pneuma*, of *prana*, I dare say sometimes of manna), which is the very lymph of a religion, was perpetuated in doctrine and daily worship, but in the vicarial teaching, through a slight alteration of the structure of the language, it was separated from Christian life as though being placed behind thicker and thicker glass. The truth remained visible, but to touch it became difficult. In the texts of the Latin Mass, they immutably celebrated a sacrifice; they continued to beg, with ancient sublimity, for the swallowed body and blood of the Word to adhere to the viscera now purified from the stains of villainy; they still made their offering over the bones of the murdered, of those who "had washed their stoles in blood," and the spirits of the murdered were twice evoked, Stephen and Barnabas, Linus and Cletus, Clement and Ignatius, Perpetua and Felicitas; and the kisses would fall fast and hard on that other body of Christ, marked by the wounds of five crosses: the altar. But the corporeal elements of the *tremendum* seemed to have disappeared from all the homilies and all the books of meditation for Mass. The ancient definition itself, *tremendum hoc mysterium*, with its immense, phonic weight, almost dropped out of the liturgical books. The sacrifice, although always faithfully commemorated, was evaporating into the spiritual. How many still recognized the priest's fearsome stature as the *sacrificer*? The bishop's palms, twice stigmatized with oil, continued to rest a long time on the priest's head during his ordination, in a coursing current of grace that bound and permeated both bodies utterly, but how many saw in this, so many centuries on, more than the mere sign of an election in which the power of the man played practically no part? It is no accident that the profoundest treatise on the mysteries of the sacrifice and the priesthood, by Father de Condren, has never been well known except among a select few clergymen and, in less than a century, disappeared from libraries, seminaries, and the memory of man.

Something of the ancient sensuality was much better preserved in certain popular passions that are so hastily labeled "superstitions": in the people's need to touch relics, press their lips against images and statues, or crawl on all fours on the floors of sanctuaries (just as the woman who suffered from a flow of blood for twelve years crawled like a worm through the crowd to touch the hem of the Lord's garment) to offer the divinity something of their own bodies: severed braids, for example.

The Renaissance, the Reformation, the incessant necessity of theological disputes, above all the Enlightenment: all of these trials were promptly overcome by doctrine, but each time it seemed to tear away another strip of the radiant corporeality, the vivid skin of the old Christian life: that life afflicted with infinity in every cell of its theandric body.

In the cell of a monastery, in an order founded—and not for nothing—by the fathomless Bishop of Geneva, God suddenly manifests himself to a rapturous young girl in the mystery of blood and water. He reveals his own heart—that center of the body and the cosmos, that cup of "incorruptible love"—as a fiery pit where other hearts, hearts that are human, go out like sparks. Devoured once more, assimilated by that God who offers, to mortal eyes, the supreme defenselessness of an open breast.

Every syllable of these conversations, which the humble girl recounts in her admirable, antiquated French, gives us goose bumps. God knows if a meditation of this kind permits such adventurous juxtapositions, but it is sometimes impossible not to think of Shiva, the destroyer and regenerator.

But behold, not long after she is dead, or perhaps while she is still alive, the Christian world is flooded with images in which this mystery is pictured in the person of a blond-bearded dandy fresh from Louis XIV's *petit lever*, who—this is very curious—proffers on his palm not a vial of perfume but an ovoid object, presumably made of red porcelain, and decorated with a flamelike plume.... And so it continues, down to those Sulpician ghosts made of plaster and papier-mâché positioned, among the sobs and denials of the seers, in the rocks and caves, among the springs and thorns where, traditionally, the *Sedes Sapientiae* had rested her dainty feet. The real miracle—and there's no doubt it was a miracle of faith as well as of grace—is that through fifteen generations men and women have been able to sanctify themselves by contemplating these images, laboring to pray "little crowns" and "little flowers," exciting their sympathies and sentiments by reading booklets so unexciting that it is often a mystery whether they are supposed to accompany a Via Crucis or a Te Deum. Today, such images and books are suddenly beloved and revered, in the light of what has happened to them, and what continues to happen to them—which would not even be worth mentioning if it weren't clear that the atrophy sown by the plague does not spread except to those places where a mortal emaciation already awaits it. What has for centuries been forgotten by bodies is easily eliminated from souls.

3. In a cry for mercy that he offered after receiving the Eucharist, a Greek mystic, Symeon the Metaphrast, prayed as follows (the italics, here as elsewhere, are mine):

> Thou who art fire, thou who burn up the unworthy, burn me not, my Creator, but rather *pass through all my body parts, my innards, my heart.* Burn thou the thorns of all my transgressions, purify my soul, hallow my thoughts, *make firm my knees, and my bones likewise; enlighten as one my five senses*, establish me wholly in thy fear.... Purify me, cleanse me, *make me beautiful....* Make me a Tabernacle of thy Spirit only, and in

no wise the dwelling place of sin, that from me, thy habitation, through the entrance of thy Communion, every evil deed and every passion may flee *as from a fire*.

It is perfectly apparent, in such a supplication, that the acquisition of supernatural senses demands the natural senses be sacrificed: the latter must be cast into the former, and be kindled and burned up by them, like the precious resins mixed in the holy chrism. "*Eros* is nothing but the spray of myrrh," writes one commentator on Ignatius, "that must be burned up and disappear in the fire of *agape*." To speak here of sublimation or repression is degrading, and even a perfectly canonical word like *mortification* seems somehow mortifying.

"Let the saints rejoice in honor. Let them sing for joy on their beds," a modern contemplative recalled the first night his limpid body was seized by a divine visitation and levitated a few centimeters above his bed. Nothing is solely metaphorical in the domain of the invisible, where the word is the condition of substance and substance of the word—and least of all the nuptial theme. A theologian instructs us: "The Holy Communion is an act of love consummated with God, body to body, flesh to flesh. It is a preliminary condition of this act of love that we render ourselves able to be loved. This is *ascesis*." Again and again, the mystics endeavor, singing and moaning, to remind us that in order to be united with such a spouse the natural senses are themselves as laughable as those of a newborn baby. The senses of the newborn are to our senses as our senses are to those of the glorious bodies endowed with clarity, subtlety, agility, and impassivity, capable of walking through walls and closed doors. But is it perhaps unreasonable to believe that still-mortal members, made supernatural through divine encounters, may already in some sense partake of such glory? It is Irenaeus of Lyon (a generation after Ignatius of Antioch) who decrees it: "Our bodies, when they receive the Eucharist, are no longer corruptible." Ignatius himself had defined the sacrament as *phàrmakon athanasìas*: the medicine of immortality. ("Living water, flowing water," to be precise, "which gushes forth *into eternal life*.")

"If a body," says John Climacus, "coming in contact with another body, subject to its influence, undergoes a transformation, how could a man not be transformed who, once he has been purified, touches the body of the Lord?" And hence the flowering, the flourishing of those new organs and senses, and the unimaginable subtlety that comes with them: the eyes that see what others cannot see, beyond the veils of space and into the caves of consciousness; the ears that catch inexpressible words and music; the nostrils that can sniff out horror and grace; the taste buds that find in the Host the flavors of manna, blood, honey, and nectar. The skin exudes a light like phosphorus or fluorine, as people have seen and painters attested, for the halo and the mandorla of light are not a symbolic invention of sacred iconography. The pores distill the scent of flowers, myrrh, incense; the soles of the feet rise above the ground; the regenerated body is gently carried upward by the same fire that feeds it.

One day before Mass, such a ruthless trembling in body and spirit, such a foreboding and fear that he would levitate in the presence of the people, overcame Philip Neri, that it was impossible for him to prepare with the usual prayers. In the deep, sculpted sacristies, through the high-ceilinged halls of the old Roman churches, he tried to distract himself by playing with animals: kittens, sparrows, and the famous little dog, Capriccio. The chalices with which he celebrated Mass all bore the indentations of his teeth, so eagerly did he drink the "life-giving blood." He held the heads of the sick and pressed them to his burning chest, which smelled of moss and ermine, instructing them in the virtue of chastity. Kisses, caresses, and laughter punctuated his healings. He would wind his rosary around the sick person's neck; at times he would administer disciplinary slaps and blows; or he would put his cap on the other person's head, with one hand over his eyes and the other on the heart of the afflicted.... "One soul in love with God" remarked: "it gets to [the point] where one must say, 'Lord, let me sleep.'" How could such a body not lift up off the ground? In a corner of his tiny room, in Rome, a little piece of paper commemorates the moment when his prayers filled him with such extreme and uncontrollable joy, his heart expanded and broke two of his ribs: *Cor meum et caro mea exultaverunt in Deo meo.*

When there is no such double exultation, like the exultation that made the baby leap in Elizabeth's womb, it may appear the threshold has not been crossed. But vision and rapture are not required. In medical literature, the case of the anemic girl whose red blood cell count ironically increases once she can finally fast with pleasure on a longed-for Carmel is now classic.

(That, for decades now, the clergy have not believed disease has its roots in spiritual disorder speaks volumes about the sidereal distances that separate them from the Word: "Go, and sin no more, lest a worse thing come unto thee.... It is the spirit that quickeneth; the flesh profiteth nothing.")

4. A Syrian Father, Isaac, succinctly describes the regeneration of the senses: "When, through grace, [a living creature] *acquires the senses of the inner man*, he receives the milk of a region located beyond the [natural] senses.... He becomes a *visible creature of the Kingdom of the Spirit* and comes to perceive the new world, which is a world free from the multiple."

There is an allusion to this same milk, it seems to me, in the Introit of the Sunday Mass in Albis, the day when the neophytes, having been born again in the baptismal lustration, cast off their white tunics: *Quasi modo geniti infantes, rationabile, sine dolo, lac concupiscite*—a quotation from Saint Peter. Since the days of Pythagoras, milk, along with honey, has been a divine drink, perfect for assimilating the new, virgin reason. The mountains shall drop with sweet wine and the hills shall flow with milk and honey, says the Prophet of a world made fecund by the Word.

We always find eating—this most essential of carnal activities, which assimilates a part of nature to the body and unites microcosm with macrocosm—at the head of spiritual alphabets. One priest recounted how the words of the reader, poured into his ears at the seminary refectory while his mouth was tasting his food, had worked their way into his mind like no other language before or since. Didactic wisdom that proceeds straight from the Founder: the image and substance of the Father, he bequeathed of himself, as an image and a substance, a meal.

The churches, and before them the traditions, closely linked food and death. Funeral libations, offerings of food to the dead, feasts around the corpse. But that supreme funeral banquet, the Last Supper, is something else. It is, theology tells us, both a telescopic prefiguration and an immediate realization—in which the progress of time is abolished—of the separation of body and blood that is taking place now, that will take place soon, that will take place forever and ever. Another poet, Nikolai Gogol, meditated on this beautifully: "Suddenly the funereal table disappeared, leaving behind only a sacrificial altar.... The word has given rise to the eternal Word. The priest, raising the Word like a sword, has completed the sacrifice."

At this death feast, the deathless dead man is eaten while he is still alive. He himself eats, so to speak, himself, even as the others eat him—and what food can God taste if not his own divinity? Isn't this the eternal circle of "incorruptible love" in which man is only a conduit, a mere opportunity, a pretext for God to love God? For which man has always been the goal, if we consider that, "since the beginning of the world," the Word is killed solely for this: "With desire I have desired to eat this Passover with you.... For I say unto you, I will not any more eat thereof, until it be fulfilled in the kingdom of God."

Even in the prayer for the dead, there is food—and such is the true food of the dead. Again, metaphor is changed into reality, as the natural senses are changed into supernatural ones, since all nature is nothing but a metaphor for the supernatural. The Mass for the Dead looked dazzling in the crypt of an abbey where a monk, before offering the sacrifice on behalf of the two dead men in the presence of two living ones, placed, on top of the large Host, the two fragile, smaller Hosts destined for the two couples who stood on opposite sides of death. The living would eat the immortal food for the dead, and the fragment of the Host that is dipped and dissolved in the wine was, this monk explained, the life that dissolves but is not lost in death: *vita mutatur, non tollitur*—a phrase in the Preface for the Dead.

Who is poorer and muter than the dead among the poor still

present at the meals of the living—the dead, who need the hands and mouths of the living in order to eat? Reciting the prayers for the dead, a saint from southern Italy, Pompilio Maria Pirrotti, used to roam among the skulls in the ossuaries, placing pieces of bread between their teeth: "Oh, this one is so hungry!" Slowly leaving the refectory after giving thanks, with their hoods lowered and their hands in their sleeves, the monks recite the De Profundis, while the Eastern clergy, two days after Easter, announce the resurrection of "incorruptible love" to the world of the dead by crumbling a cake made of wheat and grapes on the tombs.

5. The saint is the man in whose person it seems impossible to recognize any trace of the original wound, by whatever name one wishes to call it. "Make me beautiful," Metaphrast prayed, and in fact anyone who has had the good fortune to meet a saint will find it hard, for the rest of his life, to utter the word *beauty* without the utmost circumspection.

The man with supernatural senses exists at the crystalline source of the species, in that adamic condition that Antonio Abate defines as "the pure original essence of the soul." Its seal is a precious, fresh, radiant body even at a venerable age, and strange powers over animals, who come running and meekly obey: as in the divine afternoon breezes of Eden, or the mysterious forty days of solitude during which a celestial court of wild beasts surrounded the Second Adam. An uncontaminated innocence, from which every last trace of animality has fallen away, cannot fail to magnetize the animal world. Wild creatures do not usually attack children, not because children are saints but because they are the saint's model. To close the circle you must remake yourself, through "incorruptible love," as "one of these little ones." This and nothing else is the "new heaven and new earth" of the Apocalypse, which so many people are so naively speculating about today: a new body and a new mind, microcosm and macrocosm united in ecstasy, free from the multiple. A new creation "made by God with his own saliva." Nothing else justifies the veneration of relics, which still radiate the power of the transfigured senses and have become a dwelling place for sublime guests.

The imagery and phraseology of the recent past were anemic, but, like fragile eggshells, they still contained the substance intact. The latest stage in the process has, however, involved a sudden subversion. All the substance is draining from the ignominiously shattered forms. They are already practically unrecognizable or have become so corrupted their nature has changed. The inexpiable crucifixion of beauty, the universal martyrdom of the symbol—which announced both the presence and the elusiveness of the tremendous—has robbed us of our ability to perceive what is above all unique to the tremendous: the divine realism that surpasses any created reality. Thus the bread, the loaf that is supposed to be broken and distributed at random, however and wherever, like an ordinary meal, has, with terrible retributive justice, gradually lapsed into being a mere sign and from being a mere sign to being a mere abstraction—and all the while, people more and more naively believed they were sinking their teeth into it. But the transcendent, again, shows itself to be an inescapable condition of the real: once the notion of it is suppressed, the teeth sink into the void. It was not only physically that the Byzantine chalice, which during the penitential ceremonies of Lent "no one was permitted to behold," held the whole mystery of theophagy; it was not only physically that it shone in the delicate Latin Host made of white and transparent flower, the pure veil of something else entirely, round like the circle of infinity, the center and circumference of the cosmos, offered, in the shafts of sunlight, to the eyes before the mouth. "The vicarious victim of the universe," Charles de Condren called Jesus Christ, the Sacrificed Sacrificer, the High Priest, in whose body creation is immolated and we feed on the infinite.

The canonical image of the Byzantine Pantocrator—with skin the color of a date or a lion, with a large bifid vein in the forehead, with a split chin akin to the two hemispheres—was simultaneously a stylization of the cosmos and of that other consummately realistic image, with the broken nasal septum and the swollen cheek: the *rex tremendae maiestatis* of the Holy Shroud.

Only if they live, as they have lived for millennia, in this extreme and terrifying realm apart do the splendors of the rite have meaning: the flames, the incense, the tragic vestments, the majesty of the gestures and faces, the rubato of the songs, the steps, the words, the silences—the whole vivid, luminous, rhythmic symbolic cosmos that never stops pointing, alluding, referring to a celestial double whose mere shadow on the earth it is. In the face of this distinction, reason itself retreats to the modest place set aside for it by nature, and the body instead is called to recognize, welcome, and receive the invisible. "Our body"—it is again Anthony the Great who instructs—"is the altar where our spirit must immolate the soul and all its passions so that God can descend into it." In the Eastern churches, where, thank heaven, the people do not utter a word, a powerful and constant current blowing in from the golden doors of the sanctuary passes through the upright bodies taut as bows and bends them into deep bows, brings them to their knees, prostrates them like a bolt of lightning, so that their brows and bellies are pressed against the floor. It is a "corporeal prayer," the only kind that Angela of Foligno did not distrust; it is Saint Dominic's ecstatic dance in fourteen attitudes of contemplation. The wild, erotic incense transfigures the breath; at the deliberate crash of the silver chains thrown high into the air, the ears "open" with a start; the incandescent vortex of chants, icons, and flames unifies and amplifies perceptions. All five senses are thrown out of the body—out of the "demonic space of the world"—and into a state of heightened vigilance that is consciously induced and perpetuated, and that puts them on the path to transmutation. It is worth saying again: Anyone who has ever been present for an inspired celebration of a traditional liturgy will not easily be persuaded to traffic, even in the face of the most consummate art, in the word *beauty*.

To expect that the regeneration of the profane, the "consecration of the world," can take place anywhere other than in vertiginous regions—on the peaks of Sinai—is puerile. Eating a symbolic meal with friends, wherever and however imagination dictates, in memory of an ancient philanthropist—even if he did have an exceptional ear for language—represents both the decay of the sacred and the loss of the profane, and if this convivial and commemorative theme is yielding day by day to a purely political theme, it is not at all clear why this shouldn't yield to a different and darker theme in turn, once people's curiosity to experiment with the present one is exhausted. Heschel reminds us that, if we stop calling God to our altars, demons will ineluctably occupy them. The baleful homeopathy that advises treating a world insanely sick with squalor, anonymity, profanity, and license with squalor, anonymity, profanity, and license is not practiced with impunity. It makes perfect sense that the Eastern Church, the Church of triumphal glories, is the enclosure whose fasts are the strictest and whose ascetics are draped in heavy chains.

Sinyavsky speaks of an old Russian woman who, coming back from the bath, refuses to let her "hooked and monstrous nails" be cut. "My hour has come," she says: "how am I supposed to climb up God's mountain without my nails?" "It is difficult to believe," he observes, "that the old woman has forgotten her body is going to be food for worms. But her figurations of the kingdom of heaven are real to her to the point of being tangible. And she thinks of her immortal soul as having nails, as having its shirt stuck to its body—as if it were another barefoot old woman..." In the face of so many noxious humanitarian and sentimental rationalizations, Sinyavsky naturally applauds the old woman's genuinely spiritual attitude—and, besides, it is a classical image she has in mind: the "holy mountain of God," who gives us wings, and prehensile fingernails, so we can cling to that formidable little fantasy. Apparently, only a man brought up in scientific atheism for thirty years has been able to grasp the vital knot, the obstructed central vein that is separating, as well as stifling, the human body and the human mind. Even as his footsteps were erased beneath the snows of the Arctic world, he closed the circle opened by Ignatius: "Christ is risen literally, concretely, in the flesh. He drank and ate with us at the same table.... Apart from this, there is nothing."

Amid the consternating silence of the religious world, it will once again be up to the person who dwells in symbols and images to cry out without relent, so that the power of the real goes back to imprisoning his heavens and the absolute to transmuting his earth: in that new nature unknown to us, made with divine saliva, which exudes the milk and honey of sweet reasonableness.

Note. I would not have dared to write about the subject addressed in these pages (*mulier taceat in ecclesia*, as is also expressed elsewhere, as indirectly as possible) if it were not, as it is, merely a series of quotations from some old Christian texts, linked together by a few notes made in the margins. I would like to acknowledge these texts because at all times, but especially in times of horror, the only point in writing an essay of this kind is to send the reader back to its univocal, imperturbable sources. The Holy Gospels according to Luke and John; *The Letters of Ignatius of Antioch*; *Philokalia* and *Early Fathers from the Philokalia* (Faber & Faber); Athanasius of Alexandria's *Life of Saint Anthony*; Father Charles de Condren's *Idée du Sacrifice et du Sacerdoce éternel de N.S. Jésus-Christ*; Saint Francis de Sales's collected works; Veragno Magni's *Life of Filippo Neri*; Marguerite-Marie Alacoque's *Life and Works*; Nikolai Gogol's *Meditations on the Divine Liturgy*; Andrei Sinyavsky's *Impromptu Thoughts*. Metaphrast's prayer is quoted in full in a little Ordinary of the Divine Liturgy of Saint John Chrysostom and, in part, in Paul Evdokimov's *The Art of the Icon: A Theology of Beauty*. The passage on the loving encounter with God is part of Most Rev. Bryan Houghton's still-unpublished volume *Arms Outstretched in Mercy*, a chapter of which was published in the first issue of *Conoscenza religiosa* as "Prayer, Grace, Liturgy."

OTHER WRITINGS

INTRODUCTION TO KATHERINE MANSFIELD'S *A CUP OF TEA AND OTHER STORIES*

BEYOND all the conquests of style, every literary work that merits the name "art" always projects, on the screen of the page, whatever element predominates in the author's personality. There is spirit work and heart work, brain work and blood work, nerve work and memory work.

Katherine Mansfield's work, however, is consummate creature work. It has blood that circulates, nerves that receive, a brain that filters, a spirit that transforms. Each of her books, if it is not all of life, is—completely—all of *a* life.

We have, in addition to her fiction, a journal and some correspondence. Between these and her fiction there is no essential difference. The journal and the letters read like research, the fiction like realization, but all of it reflects, with lucid force, her one and only aim: to re-create life. And for Mansfield "to re-create" means profoundly "to welcome," the way a plant welcomes the nourishing sap and the warming sun: it means to accept and understand an existence in all its significance, so as to be able to give it over completely to art.

Such is the tormented and fortunate gestation whose labor is recorded in her journal and letters. The short stories, in parallel, will gradually become the finished fruit, the synthesis. One work would not be possible without the other, and for those who have not already read the former, the latter may seem odd and in need of an introduction.

Katherine Mansfield was born in Oceania, into a family of French pioneers. Latin blood, then, which had been transplanted for a time in a rich young land. These two elements are the basis of her existence:

the one as a factor above all stylistic, evident in her classical sense of taste and form; the other as a physical essence, the absolute need for a native spontaneity, for a pantheistic virginity of heart that is always new. "Out of technique is born real style, I believe. There are no shortcuts," she writes in a letter. "I . . . have a passion for technique. I have a passion for making the thing into a *whole* if you know what I mean . . ." But also: "The artist has no problems . . . when you come to think of it, what was Chaucer's problem or Shakespeare's? . . . The artist takes a long look at life. He says softly, 'So this is what life is, is it?' and he proceeds to express that. All the rest he leaves."

Only suffering, pitiless pain, will perfectly develop these two forces inside her—forces that will later be released with a purity worthy of a mystic: "One must submit. Do not resist. Take it. Be overwhelmed. Accept it fully. Make it *part of life*. Everything in life that we really accept undergoes a change. So suffering must become Love. This is the mystery. . . . It is to lose oneself more utterly, to love more deeply, to feel oneself part of life—not separate."

She wanders through the world alone, ill, on edge. Even her brother Chummie, the very picture of a happy existence, is violently torn from her. Agonizing pain drags her down sometimes to "the bottom of the sea," it spreads through her every fiber like a poison; but she does not give in, and does not fight either: She makes something of it. She will have to take this all-consuming pain, served like a sentence, and relive it in her prose, where it is not an ingredient so much as a presence, indispensable to pathos.

> *Everything has its shadow.* . . . In a way it's a tragic knowledge— It's as though, even while we live again we face death. But *through Life*: that's the point. We see death in life as we see death in a flower that is fresh unfolded. Our hymn is to the flower's beauty: we would make ourselves immortal because *we know*.

On page after page, her journal and letters only quietly repeat this; sometimes the day begins drained of strength and shades into evening dreadful of solitude. She writes, not to tell her own story, nor even to make a confession to the person she loves, but in search of something within herself—the solitude and suffering of a self—in almost therapeutic fashion.

> Supposing I were to die as I sit at this table, playing with my Indian paper-knife, what would the difference be? No difference at all. Then why don't I commit suicide? Because I feel I have a duty to perform to the lovely time when we were both alive. I want to write about it, and he wanted me to.... Very well: it shall be done. The wind died down at sunset. Half a ring of moon hangs in the hollow air. It is very quiet...

Here is salvation: the sea, the evening colors stretching out to the horizon, the thousand soft sounds that come before sleep, a woman crooning a song—particulars that quiver like frail, miraculous little flames on a background of shadow and seem to draw their life precisely from her death. Everything inside her goes out to meet them, and the moment is consummated in all its meanings, becoming, so to speak, eternal.

Landscapes, figures, interiors. She is able to make every detail essential in an exquisite bustle of rhythm and color. The short stories of Mansfield do not present events. They have nothing to do with Maupassant or Pirandello, for instance: perhaps they take off from Chekhov and develop his methods. For what interests Mansfield is creating an atmosphere, which may be a three-dimensional representation of a state of soul or a state of things, while constantly avoiding psychological introspection. There is nothing symbolic in this. For her, these observations of things in themselves naturally predominated, as if the reality surrounding her, emotionally infused with whatever had determined it, were the most important truth and the sole justification.

Consider the significance of the little enamel box in "A Cup of Tea," the antique furniture in "The Doves' Nest," or the barrel organ in "This Flower" (a credo more than a story). They are signs, metaphysical indications of a drama in which they have played an accidental yet fatal part.

From her earliest stories, when New Zealand was still prompting her to a youthful and hearty impressionism, to the perfection of the last ones, her method is clear: no subjective narration, no sentimental passages in which one character is thinking about another. The writer must exist only as writing. She does not recount the story of an individual but becomes the individual and the story. "Pearl Button," "Millie," and that tragic seafaring ballad "Ole Underwood," with its wind and fugitive colors, are nothing other than the autobiography of a character and the country seen by that character. Let us put them in the first person: Pearl is a child, the sea she has never seen will thus be "a great big piece of blue water"; for Ole, the pilot, the pine trees roar "like waves in their topmost branches, their stems creaked like the timber of ships." And this is true up to the end, up to the penetrating and extremely subtle ambiguity of "*Je ne parle pas français*"—where it is the tragicomic protagonist's very essence that renders the complicated game of self-analysis necessary.

The reader will perhaps be surprised that *A Cup of Tea and Other Stories* includes two of Mansfield's unfinished texts. But to omit these final pages, in a selection that follows Mansfield's trajectory almost step by step, would have meant omitting her last word, which already bears within itself the miraculous serenity of death.

A TRAGEDY BY SIMONE WEIL
VENICE SAVED

THE SPANISH plot to sack Venice in 1616, as recounted by the Abbé de Saint-Réal, is the subject of the tragedy Simone Weil composed near the end of her short life. Death prevented her from finishing the transitions that would have linked one essential scene to the next. But this does not at all diminish the huge importance of this tragedy, into which all the veins of Weil's thought flow together, as into a delta, making it a kind of poetic translation of her famous essay on *The Iliad*, that marvelous compendium of insights into the human condition.

Nearer in time to the events in Venice, the Elizabethan poet Otway was the first to intuit its dramatic force. In his *Venice Preserv'd*, he captured some of the most stirring aspects of these affairs: the great theme, dear to Shakespeare, of friendship and honor, debated by the loyal conspirator Pierre and his weak companion Jaffier (who out of love for a young Venetian reports the conspiracy to the Most Serene Republic). Hugo von Hofmannsthal takes up the same theme again three centuries later, in a sketch called *Venice Preserved* that attempts, with consummate delicacy, a first apology for Jaffier—who acts as Pierre's complementary compeer and almost the other half of his soul.

Weil, as usual, redresses all the perspectives and, from one angle or the other, brings them back to the center, for, as has previously been observed, "Simone Weil is always moving in a single direction because she is always searching for a single thing"—and this thing is nothing if not the center of gravity in any given situation, which for her can only be of a spiritual nature, however violently it may erupt into action.

Like her spiritual masters, the Greeks, what interests Weil in a tragic event is principally action: not as an occurrence, and still less as psychology, but as the eruption, the extreme projection, of a consciousness: action that is, so to speak, "immobile." Or to use her own words: "Action would be like a language. As works of art, etc. On the stage—the slow maturation of an act, with the universe around—then the act rushed into the world."

In *Venice Saved*, the relationship that is closest to Simone Weil's heart cannot then be the relationship between Pierre and Jaffier, or between Jaffier and Violetta, the young woman who has, simply by appearing, showed him Venice. Nor can it be the traditional conflict between the warring semblances of fidelity and honor. The relationship that interests her, here as elsewhere, is none other than the relationship between the law of necessity and supernatural love ("directed even to the things of this earth"), a love that she calls by its other name: the faculty of pure attention.

She therefore needs to create a protagonist of outstanding stature, who is capable of acting as a fragile yet powerful counterweight to the law of necessity. "Take up again," she writes in her notes for *Venice Saved*, "for the first time since Greece, the tradition of tragedy in which the hero is perfect." We then see that to fill this exceptional role, she calls on precisely the man whom historians have branded with infamy: Jaffier, the disloyal.

At the center of Weil's tragedy is Venice: a perfect city, "a human milieu of which we are no more conscious than the air we breathe. A contact with nature, the past, tradition." And there is a man, Jaffier, the most influential and prestigious of the conspirators, who knows he can crush the city simply by closing his fist, uttering a single word. But this man, unlike all those who surround him, unlike almost all men, is a creature capable of pure attention. He alone is thus in a position to *see* this city, to perceive its real existence, to think of it, suddenly, beyond his "furious zeal," which is to say beyond his desire to possess it, sack it, destroy it. The moment this "supernatural distance" is established between Jaffier and Venice, the imaginary values of glory and power are replaced with the real and unspeakably precious values of the *milieu humain*, and it becomes necessary for Jaffier, as though it were a special and inescapable duty, to obstruct the horrendous destiny hanging over the city. But in order to do this, he has no choice but to "stop time"—and this is as good as agreeing to let the city's destiny fall, later and with greater violence, on his own head: it is as good as agreeing to be destroyed in place of Venice.

So Jaffier reports the conspiracy, demanding a promise of pardon for the conspirators, however, from the Council of Ten—a promise we get the sense will not be kept. Indeed, all of them are put to death except for the informer Jaffier, who will, in a gesture of extreme contempt, be given some gold shekels for his betrayal. The last act of the tragedy—the one that Weil described as "a horrible, interminable period of idleness, after the furious zeal of the first two acts"—unfolds in the state prisons.

Jaffier, "a pure, invariable being," is the only one who has never been overwhelmed by the hunger for conquest. His companions, on the other hand, as Simone has portrayed them in the first acts, are merely a concatenation of secondary effects: a handful of adventurers, pirates, and mercenaries torn from their natural roots and hurled onto the scene by a series of brutal shocks. "He who has been uprooted can only uproot." Up to now, they have lived in the realm of unreality, nourished by the obsessive thought of a "glorious compensation" for their past humiliations: a compensation that by now has become identified with Venice, that priceless prey. Jaffier's act obstructs their blind impulse, which shackles and imminent death violently constrict. Their reactions are various, but in the dreadful vacuum created by their arrest, each man is instantly reduced to the condition of an object: he can no longer retrieve his own identity, he can no longer bring himself to believe in his earlier real existence now that it has been stripped of its dreams. Here are the words of the conspirator Renaud, who had dreamed of a kingdom:

Who are they, who are they who have stolen my destiny?
That part in which I have a right to power and glory?
Do I have to die here? For then I shall never have lived.
I have never lived, because I have never governed.
No, this isn't possible, you must live before you die.
They will kill me there, in prison, before the break of day;
and so I shall not reign; no, I shall never, ever reign!

Jaffier's passion, which takes place on quite a different plane, is also of quite a different nature. Jaffier has never lived in the imagination, and he does not fear death. But the false promise made by the Council of Ten has robbed his act of all valor and humane pity. Now the world—that world which he alone had been able to *see*—turns to stone around him. The city that he saved now strikes him as unrecognizable, and indeed as unreal, in the terrible light of his companions' fall. His transformation into an object occurs slowly and takes him through all the phases of spiritual diminution—revolt, threats, supplications, delirium, lifelessness—and at last ends in the loss of self-consciousness. His companions die hurling curses at him and destiny, feeling they have been plundered and trampled by an intolerable injustice. But this prideful illusion is not permitted to Jaffier. Gnawed at by remorse, and a horror of himself "that would perfectly suit a criminal and that is on the contrary experienced by the victim," he has now become Jaffier the traitor—not only in the eyes of his friends and enemies but in his own:

Which man is there so low that I might dare, without trem-
    bling,
even to raise up my eyes to the level of his knees,
traitor that I am?
Am I the one who has come to this?
Was I once not laden with honors,
surrounded by the highest respect?
Have I not been cherished by a friend?

I was dreaming. All that was only a dream.
I was always vile. I am vile now.

Now Jaffier, too, is operating in the realm of the unreal. And now the sorrowful, mute spirit of his past as well as his future (thus of all possible dimensions of feeling) seeks refuge in the "veil of the flesh." Not in order to hide the truth from himself but to escape his own shame.

God, my soul has need of flesh, in order to hide its shame.
Flesh that eats and sleeps, with no future and without a past.

Old Renaud had behaved no differently in the first act, when he planned and preordained the destiny of Venice, if the conspirators prevailed, in a speech to Jaffier that Weil herself described as "lessons in high politics" (and which it is difficult to read today without trembling):

Tomorrow they must no longer know where they are. They must no longer recognize anything that surrounds them. They must no longer recognize themselves. The local people must feel like strangers in their own home. This has always been and always will be the policy of conquerors: to uproot the conquered. We must kill this city to the point where the citizens feel that a revolt, even if it were successful, would not be able to bring it back to life; therefore they will submit.

There is thus no difference between the agony of a populace and the agony of one man. It is always a matter of the most total and irreparable misfortune: the misfortune of being uprooted. In *Venice Saved*, Weil shows us this misfortune as it is: absolutely bitter, without any sort of halo—Jaffier, the perfect hero, reduced to a vegetative life, while the circle of his humanity closes over him forever.

But his act, this act he believes he has wasted, lives on elsewhere.

Already, far from him, it has completed its journey. The dawn has risen over Venice, unconscious and intact. The sun will bathe the feast of Pentecost with its beams, and Venice will be wedded with the sea. This indescribably precious reality—the rejoicing of a people, in all the grace and richness of their traditions—is expressed in Violetta's luminous song: a blossoming of youth, hope, and joy nourished on Jaffier's bitter blood.

> Loveliest day, now suddenly you're here,
> on my city and its thousand canals;
> those humans who receive your smile
> see how sweet you are!

In the period during which Weil was composing this tragedy, she wrote to Joë Bousquet: "To arrive at understanding absolutely that things and persons *exist*. To achieve this, even just once before I die, is the only grace that I ask."

Only such an undivided sense of reality has the power to create, in a work of poetry, a corresponding measure of truth, and with it the possibility of an absolute reading (on every level of life and consciousness) of the symbols and figures it sets before us. The importance of the existence of a work like *Venice Saved*—and our capacity for comprehending its parables—will not be lost on anyone who nowadays still tries to live, as much as possible, at the level of attention that Simone Weil advocated: the level where problems rediscover their center and the barriers erected by nonexistent values fall away.

GRAVITY AND GRACE IN *RICHARD II*

...To cheat time, I've been writing a little essay on Shakespeare's *Richard II*. For a thousand reasons I think it's less than nothing, but still I'd like you to read it. It's full of references to S.W.—and, ideally, oriented toward her—because I thought, reading *Richard*, that if she hadn't died so early, S.W. would have written about it eventually. Please accept this *babillage*, in lieu of S.W.'s wonderful language, as a token of our shared love for her.

The essay, though brief, is not finished. It's missing a second, shorter part, in which I'd like to recall the figures of Northumberland and Carlisle, to whom I allude in the first part (the animal-man and the saint, exceptions and buttresses to all human laws), and dwell on the *noche oscura* in which Shakespeare must have written this tragedy. Many other quotations, all gorgeous, will illustrate this brief inquiry into Shakespearean malheur.

—Cristina Campo, in a letter to Remo Fasani,
January 20, 1952

In the opinion of Simone Weil, *King Lear* was the only one of Shakespeare's tragedies completely permeated with a pure spirit of love, and therefore on a level with the "immobile" theater of the Greeks. Perhaps *Richard II* never caught her attention at an auspicious moment. It is, anyway, very difficult to grasp and wrest into the light this mysterious tragedy, the most silent of all of Shakespeare's works—this path that is constantly covering its own tracks, this voice that doesn't want to raise any particular problem or to support any particular thesis. A story recounted with eyes downcast, slowly and, one might say, in the dark: *en una noche oscura.*

> For God's sake, let us sit upon the ground
> And tell sad stories of the death of kings;
> How some have been deposed; some slain in war,
> Some haunted by the ghosts they have deposed.

For five long symphonic acts, full of returns and rigorous reprises, confined in the very tight mesh of unbroken blank verse, not a single laugh, in this drama of young people, not one gallantry or a pleasantry, even a lugubrious one, from a clown. Not one of those great breaths of spring or autumn. Not one of those gratuitous songs as natural to Shakespeare as the circulation of the blood. In *Richard II*, everything falls inexorably down. Everything obeys the law of gravity. And yet it is in *Richard II*, more than in any other work since Homer, that the royal gestures "continually cross like blinding flashes" and grace blooms, a pure, pale flower, on the dark foliage of necessity. Never, I think, have "gravity and grace" been more exactly encapsulated in a play.

If *Hamlet* is the tragedy of irresolution, *Richard II* is the tragedy of relativity, or rather of reversibility. A group of young princes, united by ties of blood, and profoundly divided by this same blood (which has many times been spilled by their ancestors), whose consciences are extremely refined and whose spirits are ardent and melancholic, unremittingly clash in an attempt at loyalty and unity that is continually frustrated. Behind them two old men, John of Gaunt and the Duke of York, grow feeble and obscurely fall into the same strain, already tinged with defeat or with a presage of death.

> Call it not patience, Gaunt; it is despair.

By the end of the play, not one of these characters (except two of the most peculiar, Northumberland and Carlisle)—not one of these men striving toward a solemn, absolute assertion of self—will still wear the ardent expression he wore at the start. The law of gravity will transform them, one by one. It will give them different expressions, different gestures, different absolutes. It will convert them all into the common absolute of misfortune—already familiar to the old, but terrifying to the young—and at this somber threshold they will slowly turn around and say a final farewell to grace, in sorrowful, loving remembrance of those they have lost or will have to lose, according to the law of gravity.

> For Mowbray and myself are like two men
> That vow a long and weary pilgrimage;
> Then let us take a ceremonious leave
> And loving farewell of our several friends.

The very slow fall of Richard II, immersed little by little, as into boiling oil, in his own essential grandeur; Bolingbroke's ascension to an irresistible throne, which overpowers his pure, law-defending temperament; the foolish loyalty old York shows to the new king in an effort to make up for his heartbreaking disloyalty to the old one; the terror of death in the heroic boy Aumerle—the fatal fruit of his boyhood: In this chivalric drama, there is not a single chivalric situation that does not eventually fall back on necessity—and that, from this necessity, does not reach out toward the most spiritual chivalry—which is to say, toward grace. Gestures of grace that the poet pauses midair, when they are just about to fall. The grievous and chastened sorrow of each individual voice, isolated and yet flowing into the others,

> Like an unseasonable stormy day,
> Which makes the silver rivers drown their shores,
> As if the world were all dissolved to tears . . .

Certainly in no other tragedy by Shakespeare, or by anyone else, have aversion and rancor been so perfectly ignored—absent from the depths of the soul and the envelope of the language alike.

Each of the characters, once he has finished with his moral violence, redeems it by means of respect. York, who has become a traitor by the law of gravity, speaks of the fallen Richard:

> As in a theatre, the eyes of men,
> After a well-graced actor leaves the stage,
> Are idly bent on him that enters next,
> Thinking his prattle to be tedious;
> Even so, or with much more contempt, men's eyes
> Did scowl on gentle Richard; no man cried "God save him!"
> No joyful tongue gave him his welcome home:
> But dust was thrown upon his sacred head:
> Which with such gentle sorrow he shook off,
> His face still combatting with tears and smiles,
> The badges of his grief and patience,
> That had not God, for some strong purpose, steeled
> The hearts of men, they must perforce have melted . . .

The vanquished king hands over the crown of England to his rebel cousin, whom he had earlier banished, then dispossessed, according to the law of gravity. The conscience of "the Lord's anointed," which is as strong in him as it is in all the others, even after he has lost the throne, here dissolves into a miraculously clear-eyed meditation on his own misfortune:

> Here, cousin, seize the crown . . .
> On this side my hand, and on that side yours.
> Now is this golden crown like a deep well
> That owes two buckets, filling one another,
> The emptier ever dancing in the air,
> The other down, unseen and full of water:
> That bucket down and full of tears am I,
> Drinking my griefs, whilst you mount up on high.

An unmerited offense, called down by the law of gravity, can still be redeemed by grace, and in this case without any effort at all, in perfect purity. A gardener has imprudently spoken to a servant of Richard's fall. The Queen, in the shade of a tree, overhears him, and in her despair hopes that the plants tended by this messenger of misfortune will cease to grow. Left alone, the gardener thinks aloud:

> Poor queen! so that thy state might be no worse,
> I would my skill were subject to thy curse.
> Here did she fall a tear; here in this place
> I'll set a bank of rue, sour herb of grace:
> Rue, even for ruth, here shortly shall be seen,
> In the remembrance of a weeping queen.

Bolingbroke, the new king, is finally brought his "buried fear," which is to say the corpse of Richard, who has been killed by a courtier who had heard that the new king desired his death. To the murderer, who is in any case already repentant and full of reverence for the royal blood he has spilled, Bolingbroke responds with the loyalty that is the basso continuo of the entire tragedy, the constant of all its characters:

> They love not poison that do poison need,
> Nor do I thee: though I did wish him dead,
> I hate the murderer, love him murdered . . .
> Lords, I protest, my soul is full of woe,
> That blood should sprinkle me to make me grow . . .

It is this marvelous consciousness of the core of human tragedy, the reciprocity and the simultaneous incompatibility of the elements that compose it—influence and destiny—that bonds these men's souls so closely together. Actions have only a sad, intermediary function. Beauty alone can affix a seal on words or deeds.

So it always is and always has been, since the immobile first act (to which the memory repeatedly returns), when the two young knights, Mowbray of Norfolk and Bolingbroke, were presented to the King and accused each other of treason. The weight of truth was already shifting continually: at first it was Norfolk, then Bolingbroke, who was convincing—and the King subtly doubted, not them, but the truth itself. It is only natural that he should have tried to pardon them, even if at the risk of his own life; and their refusal is just as natural, their wish to fight so that death itself might condemn or absolve them. Unlike all of Shakespeare's other tragedies, *Richard II* has its longest and most seriously significant pause in the first act. This is in the very slow heraldic episode, where the loveliness of the young, indomitable figures is entirely enshrouded in the bluish gray of dawn, the inexpressibly pathetic bell-tolling of a chivalric cere-mony—and the sadness of the reciprocal respect that, in the most intense instants, is transformed into a naked silence, already stripped of all hatred and conscious only of the misfortune to come.

> For Mowbray and myself are like two men
> That vow a long and weary pilgrimage;
> Then let us take a ceremonious leave
> And loving farewell of our several friends.

With a graceful gesture, interrupting the duel, Richard has for an instant halted the law of gravity—but only to be doubly overwhelmed by it, since the measure of gravity and grace is always and inevitably equal. It is the spared life of Bolingbroke that, following a concatena-tion of events rigorously alternating between influence and destiny, will naturally bring about Richard's death.

Is it important to ask ourselves by what paths Shakespeare arrived at this perfect equilibrium of spiritual perceptions, which has no prec-edents and which we will not find so purely distilled in any of his later works? Perhaps it would not be if the tragedy itself were not continually breaking away from us, its spectators or readers, and soaring to that zone of profound mystery I have called *la noche oscura*. A zone of mystery that (as in the duel scene in *Richard II*) is the first and perhaps the most charged of all the great Shakespearean plays. Indeed, according to a chronology as sparse as it is rich in illuminations, before *Richard II* Shakespeare had only written comedies and one grim exercise: *Titus Andronicus. King John* was quite probably written later, and there is no proof that the first two parts of *Henry IV*, which are set a little nearer to this period, preceded it. But all this hardly matters. Only one thing is certain: *Richard II* is the telltale pause that declares the first great experiences of the soul. Everything in this pause is eloquent—the scarceness and austerity of the images, all subjected to the greatest spiritual tension; the unusual sense of time, mercilessly and minutely measured by the verse; and above all the attempt, which is even more unusual considering this is Shakespeare, to keep everything within the confines of the purest sorrow. The image of the man, as the work elusively proceeds, seems so close and so immobile it makes us think of an optical illusion—the result, perhaps, of that veil of tears that he continually suspends between himself and us.

> Each substance of a grief hath twenty shadows,
> Which shows like grief itself, but is not so;
> For sorrow's eye, glazed with blinding tears,
> Divides one thing entire to many objects;
> Like perspectives, which rightly gazed upon
> Show nothing but confusion . . .

But where the glaring identification between author and character lets us see the whole tragedy as a pure meditation—a secret tribute or a secret apology—is in the fallen Richard's lamentations. Here is the mark of misfortune out of reach for mere imagination; the mark of that misfortune "which has nothing to do with unhappiness" and which alone reveals to us the monotony of horror; the immobility of time, in horror, that swallows up everything; the sameness, in horror, of all human losses. Thus Richard feels, in prison, his own person has been transformed into time:

> how sour sweet music is,
> When time is broke . . .

> For now hath time made me his numbering clock:
> My thoughts are minutes...

Thus he imagines the mere falling of tears will be enough to dig a grave:

> We'll make foul weather with despised tears...
> As thus, to drop them still upon one place,
> Till they have fretted us a pair of graves
> Within the earth; and, therein laid,—there lies
> Two kinsmen digg'd their graves with weeping eyes.

Thus he feels the blood of twenty thousand soldiers pouring down his face:

> *Comfort, my liege; why looks your grace so pale?*
> But now the blood of twenty thousand men
> Did triumph in my face, and they are fled;
> And, till so much blood thither come again,
> Have I not reason to look pale and dead?
> All souls that will be safe fly from my side,
> For time hath set a blot upon my pride.

No less, and perhaps more, than the Sonnets themselves, Richard II's fall bears witness to Shakespeare's *noche oscura*—that compulsory passage in human existence through moral violence out of which, dead or alive, a new man cannot but emerge. That the tragic emotional parable of the Sonnets is begun during this same period in Shakespeare's life may mean a great deal or very little. The report of the death—also around this time—of Hamnet Shakespeare, his twelve-year-old son, or the story of Shakespeare leaving London to retire, at the age of thirty-two and at the height of his adventure in acting, to the small town of Stratford may also mean a great deal or very little. The one thing we know for certain is that the violence was converted into suffering, and that the suffering divinely blossomed into love.

THE GOLDEN NUT

Ave, viaticum meae peregrinationis.
— Cicero

Creatures born on Sundays have the gift of seeing the
fairies that preside at their baptism.
— Carlo Felice Wolff

Every afternoon at half past four, for several long and glorious
summers, the watered gravel crackled with a special secrecy, almost
ceremoniously, under the tires of the blue Dilambda that had driven
up from the dark, blazing-hot portico on the ancient Via Cavaliera,
flashing through the light and the shade, by the lindens on the Via
dei Cappuccini, past the outrageous noble gates of the Villa Revedin,
before reaching our hill. And at the cold roar of the tires in the heavy
afternoon alive with cicadas, I threw my tricycle down on the English
lawn and Luigi, cassocked in his red jacket, quickly opened the little
glass-paned door in its bronze arc of ivy, while my beautiful older
cousins Zarina and Maria Sofia hopped down from the car like birds.
Suddenly the pure white of the last meadowsweet, which was already
shedding its petals on the gravel, echoed these new whites: the long
gloves of my big cousins, their small, pointed cloches, the freshly
washed fur of their old Sealyham terrier, and, above all, their bags:
those deep bags made of linen or canvas in which, afternoon after
afternoon, up from the dim, massive rooms of the Via Cavaliera, they
brought me their old toys.

Gone were the days, for me, of nervously shouting "What did you
bring me?" and hanging on to these bags. Smiling silently, though
my heart pounded, I now walked between them, while they held my

hands, toward the green iron table under the cedar of Lebanon already set for tea, with its tall wooden chairs likewise painted green and studded with hard little bubbles of paint. My mother came down, as soon as she awoke, in a purple kimono, carrying two or three scratchy canvas pillows printed with yellow roses. There were kisses and little exclamations ("But why did you get up so early?" "For goodness' sake, I've been awake for hours." "You didn't sleep? But you look beautiful. Like a rose." "Oh, don't say that. I hardly sleep at all anymore." "But what a beautiful afternoon." "Oh, yes, isn't it like a dream to be here again?"), then my mother would see me, a smile would flit across her lips, and on the round table, with a little laugh, the beautiful bags would open like corollas beneath the radiant faces: the two velvety peach-brown faces of my mother and Maria Sofia, who, although younger, looked exactly like her, and the golden-freckled Japanese face of Zarina, whose real name was Maria Cesarina, but who had translated her name in memory of the ill-starred empress of Russia. And in the heavy silence of an afternoon alive with cicadas, small objects emerged from the bags and were arranged in a circle on the table.

It is perhaps perverse, but it can be useful for a child to be brought up among people who are at least twenty or thirty years older than she is. There is no doubt, in any case, that my own childhood, which was in many ways already asymmetrical, overlapped with indescribable tranquillity another that had already gone by: that of my older cousins and their brothers: the last children dressed in straw Pamela bonnets and high blue belts, whose childhoods had not, in effect, been stolen away by the world. I wouldn't want to dwell too long on those somber, bewitching toys that, afternoon after afternoon, I was inheriting: those dollhouses whose dark walnut rooms were so sweetly, warmly funereal, with their ornate headboards, their stout little rocking chairs, the washbasin like a calyx with a small blue jug, a closed bud. And the tiny green wool carpets and quilted bedspreads, and that incongruous bench, firmly planted on curlicue legs, which belonged to the room but reminded me of the taste of long siestas outdoors, and inspired me to create a whole series of minuscule gardens patiently fenced off with sprigs of meadowsweet in the most secret corners of the garden. These toys had been through a war. They had crossed, with a heroic, immeasurable leap, the abyss that ought to have shattered a century and come to rest on the fragile edge of the final outcrop, where we were still holding out—but for how much longer? The last toys, the last little dying tokens of a time when childhood was not yet a world of winks and nudges, when youth was still prophetic and preparatory: that singular and always insufficient *répétition générale de la vie* which is, in fact, childhood. The carriage that is only a smaller carriage. The wooden horse that is a real horse in miniature. The doll that is a little woman or a child, never an ambiguous, allusive puppet. Like the three-year-old girl in pendants and bandeaux holding a rose, who, framed in a corner of my room, looked more than anything like a plump little grandmother—and yet she was the one creature I yearned for in my girlhood populated solely by adults. ("It's an old portrait of the Princess di Linguaglossa, Prime Minister Crispi's daughter," I heard it said, cryptically, at home, "the poor thing. She's no longer of this world . . .")

One of those summers, when I was brought back to the house on the hill, I had learned to read. Walking with my young father (who carried his walking stick straight up like a saber, the handle tucked into the pocket of his coat) through the streets of the city where we spent the winter, I would follow the tip of that walking stick which abruptly rose up toward signs for antiques or pastry shops, and I quickly grasped the relationship, the gravitational law, that bound letters together. The news reached my godmother, the solitary Gladys Vucetich, and she, too, traveled up the hill that summer from her house on the Via dei Cappuccini, darkened by huge cedars and her own radical, permanent state of mourning for a whole family of heroic soldiers; she, too, went up with her black veils and heavy tread weighed down by an almost mythological illness (for it hadn't prevented her from "spending the entire war with the Red Cross") and punctuated by the blows of her rubber-tipped black cane. Her very bright eyes—so bright the sockets seemed empty—were fixed in a somewhat maniacal stare, a sort of motionless omen of catastrophe. Gladys Vucetich had, in her turn, found in this big, impenetrable house (where the silence was such that, in the darkness of the dining room, you could hear the faucets dripping in the faraway kitchen filled with copper pots and pans) the books of her childhood. And now she, too, came with her oracular gift, no less fateful than the golden medal she had placed around my neck on the day of my baptism, engraved with all four of my names: Vittoria, Maria Angelica, Marcella, Cristina.

They were books with very hard covers, some of whose pretty, faded colors looked quite Gothic. I remember, on one of these covers, a tall female figure with a yellow ribbon around her forehead, carrying a scepter, guiding a little girl whom she held by the shoulders. But where was she guiding her? The small space conceded to these two figures didn't afford an answer. The image exuded a sort of gentle horror, above all in the face of the little child, who was, in miniature, identical to the woman. She had the same ribbon, but green, around her forehead, the same long pointy sleeves. Her hair was just a bit blonder. Eyes wide with astonishment, she leaned back, with an anxious reluctance that revealed, like a mirror, extreme fascination, against the person bending over her. FATA NIX was written underneath, in seven big Gothic letters—and nothing else marked that female image of the journey toward the earliest mysteries.

As it was for toy designers in that antediluvian era, so it was for the illustrators of books. They would never have understood if someone had suggested they "help the child" accept the mystical characters she was going to encounter (and thereby, inevitably, ensure she would not believe in them). Later, under that same vile pretext, came the programmatic deformation of characters which followed the irreparable glaciation of the animated cartoons: the grimaces of gnomes who looked like puppies, the bulging eyes of the ogre ("Come now, don't believe in him, you can see he doesn't believe in himself"), the iridescent insubstantiality, as though they were beetles, of the princes and princesses ("In place of these particular characters, who are face-less, you can substitute whoever you like: yourself, for example"). Gladys Vucetich's books belonged to the time of her childhood, the Liberty style of the fin de siècle, and during the Liberty style of the fin de siècle artists had illustrated fairy tales extremely seriously—in the same equanimous, meticulous black and white they would have used for *Demetrio Pianelli* or *Le Crime de Sylvestre Bonnard*, and yet not lacking the subtle intoxication that would have guided their hand in designing, for example, scenery for *The Tempest*. The result was a grimly adorable mix of Anna Pavlova in gauze wings and starry crowns with a Spanish reception circa 1880, held at a Habsburgian Court—an atmosphere of demure deathliness in which the wasp-waisted princesses looked as though they might be wearing both corsets and wigs, in vast, gloomy-gray palaces rife with potted palm trees, balconies, curtains with heavy silk tassels and braids as wide as your hand. I discovered then, with a thrill, that these fateful places and characters were not very different (all things considered) from the troubling yellow photographs of my young grandmother and several beautiful relatives now dead which my mother took with her everywhere, in green leather cases, when she traveled—those smiling photographs in which the smiles always seemed so remote and distressing to me because, behind the lady standing on feet that looked quite fragile beneath her mass of hair, beyond the raised curtain, the mist and leaves, there was always a thunderstorm threatening. Now, the princess in the book that had belonged to Gladys Vucetich wore a crown on her head instead of a feathered toque, but one could at last grasp the wonderful, painful secrets of the threat that loomed behind her frail shoulders. Vertiginously, through the ornate mullioned window, a big black-and-white swift might dart into the room, between her hands, carrying a tiny Elf King on its back. Or, from under the raised curtains, slowly, tragically, in would crawl none other than the Beast—that desolate and amorous nightmare, the nocturnal visitor of pale slender Belle, who was, for me, my grandmother's youth incarnate, entirely exposed to horror. And the Beast, as those good and gloomy artists had depicted him, was really nothing but a Beast, a pathetic and unnamable chimera, half griffin and half snake, drawn with manic care, scale by scale, coil by coil—and precisely because of this frenzied exactitude, it was unspeakable torture for me to see big tears gush from those eyes as he lay there on the ground, poor Beast, with his crown on his head, and Belle at the table, at the ceremonial hour, the time of dinner and music: alone, petrified, undismayed.

This image remained especially important to me, as did another, for a completely different reason: an illustration of "The Shoes That Were Danced to Pieces." In it, a soldier of fortune stands guard outside the bedchamber of twelve princesses who'd raised their father's suspicions with the perpetually scuffed soles of their shoes. This soldier, carefully pouring the drugged wine the girls give him every night into his beard, has been able to discover the wet, lacustrine, subterranean realms to which the princesses descend at midnight through a trapdoor, down a swirling spiral staircase, to go dance on an island with their young lovers. And the image showed the twelve young women, with their shoulders uncovered and their lustrous hair held down by headbands, no less fascinating or touchable than the most beautiful of my older cousins, who, at that very moment—shoulder blades, hips, and small breasts visible beneath her white dress in the sun—walked to the tap, hidden beneath a small iron hatch, which magically released, as if from the center of the earth, a jet of gushing water on the English lawn. You could believe, then, in every word—as though the story were being acted out a second time in front of you—listening to those enchanting creatures with velvety skin and almond-shaped eyes murmuring under the cedar of Lebanon, in the green chairs covered with bubbles, sipping their tea with ladyfingers and cat's tongue cookies (certain, in their naivety, that no one would understand them): "We had some fun last night, didn't we?" "Oh, how we laughed behind that poor guy's back!" "As long as Papa doesn't find out!" "Don't be silly, he has no idea . . ." In the book, of course, they have very different voices; they breathe a different air. Certainly, my beautiful cousins' real life is a charming life, as dark as midnight. The hour when, like the poor drug-addled sentry, I have to sleep between the two high rails of my brass bed. An hour of defiance and of sweet delirium, which I am only allowed to savor the next day: sounding out the words with my finger on the page, sitting by a bed of rust-colored zinnias, so absorbed I feel a thread of saliva running from the corner of my mouth. I am following the coils of the spiral staircase, the twelve girls that descended, like the twelve hours, toward the center of the earth, toward the dark, liquid midnight of life.... But all of a sudden, from the garden, comes the voice of my mother, softly questioning the cook who has been standing at the kitchen window. "Cook, is everything ready? You know how important it is for the professor..." And I imagined her big, bright, anxious eyes, and without distinguishing one anxiety from another, listened to that other sweet, bewitched creature, the duck in "The Love for Three Oranges," floating in the castle moat beneath the windows of the royal kitchens:

"Cook, O my Cook, what are they doing in the castle?"
"Duck, they are asleep."
"Cook, O my Cook, please help me. Just one more day and I'll never come back."

And what were the royal kitchens if not our kitchen, with its deep dark pantry and the red-brick oven into which Fernanda was just then placing a timbale of macaroni, and into which later, bound hand and foot, the wicked Queen Mother would fall? Flowing water, as I went on reading, replaced the zinnia bed and the meadowsweet beneath our kitchen windows—so concretely that even now, when I return to that lost kitchen for a moment, I find the zinnias and meadowsweet beneath the windows outlandish, as if I were seeing them suddenly appear in the middle of a Venetian canal. And on those summer mornings dazzled by liquid sunlight, embellished by the click of Riccardo's shears among the boxtrees, the crisp scampering of the dogs on the gravel, the golden cooing of the turtledoves in the cedar, a voice called to me from a French door opened so suddenly that it made me jump like a gunshot, exploding out of my own skin, which remained on the ground like the King Serpent's when the spell was broken—my golden skin, which was the book. The book, where the hatch in the middle of the English lawn led down to the underground lakes and islands where a moat flowed beneath the kitchen windows; the book, from which the hatch and the kitchen were now suddenly sundered, brutally robbed of their coat of arms, their secret noble weapons.

Around that time, I began to think that any incredible thing might befall my relatives in their undeniable double lives, so that the whole house, which was already mysterious in and of itself, gradually became doubly full of enigmas. The simplest things, such as the prohibition against talking at the table, especially when my uncle was present, my mother's handsome, taciturn brother around whom the whole house gravitated as though around a dark sun, shrouded all our time together behind a veil of magical interdictions. Above the white oval of the table, on those summer evenings when the French doors were thrown open to the garden, silence assumed its true value, which is the hoarding of powers. And when my uncle, who was often very tired from the many surgical operations he'd performed during the day, fell into a mild reverie no one dared to disturb, and his elegant hand, whose pinkie was adorned by a golden serpent with an emerald eye, absently came to rest on the Baccarat bowl, and he slid his finger around the rim, making a muted sound, like the groan of an incarcerated soul, the fond atmosphere of the room transformed into a cave where a wizard, like the Wizard of Latema, was raising his lantern to the pale faces of the prisoners he was about to save or condemn: something that my uncle in fact did every day, and several times a day, but whose impenetrable implications only I, there in those silences depleted by the cry of the crystal, refined by the glow of the serpentine ring, could presage.

Among Gladys Vucetich's books there was one slightly more modern than the volume by Fata Nix, illustrated by a brilliant artist who drew only the eyelids of his characters, leaving those empty sockets full of aquatic and sepulchral light—the eyes of sirens or statues. So the very presence of Gladys Vucetich, with her eyes so bright they looked empty, was laden with new mysteries, as her title of godmother ("Who is Gladys Vucetich, Mama?" "She is your godmother") inevitably evoked that horoscopic baptismal scene, so frequent in fairy tales, in which each of the twelve fairies—the fairy godmothers—brings her gift to the cradle of the newborn princess. But the gifts alluded to in the fairy tales were certainly not the dolls that Gladys Vucetich gave me; they must instead have been certain surprising phrases that escaped her while her watery eyes stared at me unblinking and her cane cleared the way like the fairy Gambero's wand in the clearing of Brocéliande, on the night of the Secular Council: "Do you know you were born on a Sunday? You will see many things others do not see." Or, placing a hard finger on the small blue vein still visible between my eyes: "You're lucky, child. You have Solomon's knot."

But there were scenes in fairy tales that, according to those illustrations, took place under the immense vaults of crypts, which were also decorated with palm trees and curtains, although they were really too monumental to remind me of any familiar figure. Behind those images was then inserted, like the second slide in a magic lantern, the big town, the great walled land of the *certosa*, the metropolitan cemetery, where for years I'd been taken on All Saints' Day. It was an imposing expanse of funerary habitations and, because it had been a vast seventeenth-century convent, a cemetery unlike any other: a shadowy palace with huge flights of arcades, corridors, courtyards, like the scenery of a Spanish tragedy put on in the days of Alfieri— pure romantic madness vowed to ineffable pain, forbidden love, and redemptive warfare, but always and only, for me, a shadowy palace of fairies.

In the great noble chapels that opened on either side of the arcades, in the immense covered passageways, from one cloister to another, from one wing to another, imploring hands of marble stretched out from the sepulchral monuments where the garlands were still decaying and the flowers still dying. The white hands of women in tears, embracing truncated columns or stone medallions, their heads veiled by one arm or by a shroud. Oh, how I knew those hands. Palms lifted in prohibition ("Do not sit on the lip of a fountain, do not buy meat from a condemned man..."), fingers sealing lips ("And you must not speak or laugh for seven years, seven months, seven days..."). Tall, stooped figures, often holding a child and leading him despite his reluctance, protecting him with their immense wings, the way the stranger with the yellow ribbon— the godmother, Fata Nix—led the child, the fascinated and terrified little neophyte, toward those secret places, and their eyes too were empty, like Gladys Vucetich's. But even here one could not stop or ask questions. My mother was in a hurry. She was running in the pure winter air, which glowed a bright, wet blue—the only color in that world of grays—under the arches of the arcades. With her veil pulled down to her fur collar, and the little bunch of roses held in her hands, she whispered, "Soon, here, *we will be at the end*, beyond the last cloister." It was impossible to catch those words exactly. All I know for sure was that our destination was elsewhere, at the end of something, beyond the vaults and gardens, beyond the great mossy arks of our more distant relatives, whom I had never met and who had made a name for themselves in the sciences, in literature, in the army—who now lay beneath immense sepulchral statues—Grief, with her broken zither; the Mourners, who were nothing but tears solidified in drapery; somber Time with his hourglass raised (here he is, the Wizard of Latemar, holding up his fatal lantern in our face)—which some of them had carved.

At some point, we would meet up with my older cousins and their fresh little noses, Zarina's laughing Japanese eyes, their kisses and their perfumes—blending with the strange aroma of fresh coffee, which everyone seems to carry in that city—and all of it woven into an even more heartrending scheme in that realm of dark angels, that enormous stone horror perfused with icy breaths, and the marvelous good cheer of that morning out of the city, the fragrance radiating from their bouquets of white carnations, the memory of the big, shadowy rooms from which they had come and to which we would return for breakfast: with the delightful flowery table where cupids dived into small silver tubs, and the deep walnut cabinets that doubt-less still held treasures.... Arm in arm with my older cousins, my mother would forget my presence and no longer even rush to reach her destination, whatever it was. From time to time, passing by one of the larger tombs, we would pause for a moment to read the inscrip-tions—*Laudomiae Rizzoli, spe lachrymata*; *Federicus Comes Isolani sibi ipse et suis aedificavit*; *Vale, cara anima!*—which I found no more or less shocking than other harrowing addresses:

> Farewell, Falada who hangs up above!
> Farewell, young queen, who passes down below!
> If your mother knew,
> she would die of sorrow!

Or:

> I wait I wait in the dark night
> and I open the door if someone knocks.
> After bad luck comes good luck
> and comes with him who does not know the art...

And everything took on terrifying life in the little comments being made around me, behind veils or furs: "Anna Pepoli, the poor wretch! How much she had to suffer for that scoundrel..." Or: "Fabrizio and Bianca...a tragedy for the entire family, a moment of insanity," which conjured up visions of abstract, paradigmatic mas-sacres, Bluebeard, his seven wives bathed in their blood, and Anne, sister Anne, the poor girl who, from the tower, scans the horizon in vain.

And suddenly that world of arcane sayings and petrified gestures that froze the heart (those gestures that, I knew, if one day we had really gone *to the end*, in silence, without once looking back, would have broken the spell of the palace and changed it into a vast illumi-nated ballroom)—that world suddenly opened, turned a corner, into the bright courtyard, and then into the semicircle of a small chapel surrounded by a wrought-iron gate, and then onto a white wall, as blank and conclusive as the end of a horizon. That was where the miracle occurred. The ciphered names and hieroglyphic inscriptions were suddenly replaced, on the soft marble, by *their* names, by my own names, which I had worn around my neck all my life on the gold medal given to me by Gladys Vucetich: Vittoria, Maria Angelica, Marcella, Cristina.... That little chapel where the carnations and roses made the air even more radiantly fresh, as morning were being added to morning, was the enigma, the true and only enigma—the node, not merely of the huge charterhouse but of everything: the little girl led by the shoulders toward the mysterious ball, the flower bed that changed into a moat, the empty eyes, the serpentine ring, the underground realms and the blood, the silence and the prohibitions, the little girl with the rose in whom childhood and old age tacitly tied the knot of their mutual secret.

My mother uttered the gentle, ritual, horrific words: "Here is Grandma, and there is Grandpa. Pray for them." And I read, under the name of the woman I had seen look so helpless in her portrait as a girl—with the huge, stormy curtains ready to let bestial love crawl inside, to let the Divine Prince penetrate her—I read under her name, which was also mine, Maria Angelica, two words: *suavis anima*. And next to them, under the name of my grandfather, Marcello, which was also mine: *animas fortis*. "Pray for them," my mother said again, with the look of someone who needs, with the sheer strength of her heart, to liberate the imprisoned couple—the heroic, enchanted love. And at those abstract and reverential words, the great velvety curtain of filial piety finally closed on me too, and a cloud of tears darkened my vision. The fairy tale was there, terrible and radiant, resolved for a moment and insoluble; the eternal, which is always returning in dreams, viaticum for a pilgrimage, the golden nut that must be kept in the mouth, that must be crushed between the teeth at the moment of gravest danger. I was looking for my little handkerchief, holding back my sobs, when my mother, with a faraway look in her eyes, placed her gloved hand on the back of my neck.

NOTES

Many of the endnotes below were written by Cristina Campo. Those composed by me are indicated by page numbers in italics. Dates of first publication are taken from Monica Farnetti and Filippo Secchieri's bibliography of Campo's work, which is included as an appendix in *Sotto falso nome* (Milan: Adelphi Edizione, 1998).

—A.A.

THE FLUTE AND THE CARPET

A ROSE
First published in *Fairy Tale and Mystery* (1962).

7   *have sight and not perception*: Ernst Jünger's *Vierblätter*.

IN MEDIO COELI
First published in *Paragone: Letteratura* and *Fairy Tale and Mystery* (1962).

10   *In medio coeli*: at midheaven.

10   *the gates were at first the end of the world*: Thomas Traherne's *Centuries of Meditations*.

13   *On the island of the Children of Kaledan, there lived a blind king who did not believe in death*: Allusion to the tale of Camaralzaman and Princess Badoura in *The Thousand and One Nights*.

13   *There is one fairy tale, and not even a very old one...*: Camille Mallarmé (Stéphane's niece), *La Légende Dorée de Mie-Seulette*, illustrated by Constant Le Bretton (Paris: Les Éditions G. Crès, 1923).

15   *essays toward a theory of childhood*: Boris Pasternak, "Chopin," in *Selected Writings and Letters* (Moscow: Progress Publishers, 1990).

15   *El Inca*: Garcilaso de la Vega, *Comentarios reales de los Incas* [Royal Commentaries of the Incas].

16   *as an Indian once put it*: Carlos María de Bustamante, in his preface to Fernando de Alva Cortés Ixtlilxóchitl's *Horribles crueldades de los conquistadores de México*.

17   *la fin du parc*: "the end of the park," Marcel Proust, "On Reading."

17   *Oh, incompetence!*: Jorge Luis Borges, "Dreamtigers."

21   *unlearned seeking*: a loose paraphrase of two lines in one of Nietzsche's poems.

21   *A Renaissance prince*: Pier Francesco Orsini (1523–1583), who commissioned the Garden of Bomarzo.

22   *locus absconditus, hortus conclusus, fons signatus*: "hidden place, enclosed garden, a fountain sealed up" (Song of Songs 4:12).

23   *Now you will come out of sleep*: Motokiyo, *Nishikigi*, in *Certain Noble Plays of Japan*, translated by Ernest Fenollosa and "finished" by Ezra Pound (Dublin: The Cuala Press, 1916).

ON FAIRY TALES
First published in *The Flute and the Carpet* (1971).

27   *what a mystic claims of prayer*: Bryan Houghton, author of the essay "Prayer, Grace, Liturgy," *Religious Knowledge* (January–March 1969).

29   *a little white cat qui fait si bien patte de velours*: Madame d'Aulnoy, "The White Cat," "a little white cat who has such velvety paws."

32   *le branle des fées*: Madame d'Aulnoy, "The White Cat." The phrase is translated as "the Fairy Brawl" by James Robinson Planché, who adds in a note: "The brawl was the dance with which balls were generally opened. The company took hands in a circle, and gave each other continual shakes, the steps changing with the time."

34   *Est-ce vous mon prince? Vous vous-êtes bien fait attendre!*: Charles Perrault, "Sleeping Beauty," "Are you my prince? You sure have kept me waiting!"

34   *A tale obscure, a medlar hard*: From a fairy tale by Luigi Capuana.

36   *Et in Deo meo transgrediar murum*: Psalm 18, "And by my God have I leaped over a wall."

LES SOURCES DE LA VIVONNE
First published in *Paragone: Letteratura* (1963).

39   *les sources de la Vivonne*: "The source of the Vivonne," the river that runs through Combray. Marcel and Gilberte see the "rectangular basin" near the beginning of *Time Regained*. The quotations from Proust are adapted from the Moncrieff and Kilmartin translation.

39   *the wild fig tree*: *The Iliad*, Book 6, from the Robert Fitzgerald translation. Andromache tells Hector to draw up his "troops by the wild fig tree; that way / the city lies most open, men most easily / could swarm the wall where it is low; three times, at least, their best men tried it there…"

39   *washing pools*: *The Iliad*, Book 22, from the Robert Fitzgerald translation. "Near these fountains are wide washing pools / of smooth-laid stone…"

40   *an English gentleman*: Sir George Reresby Sitwell, *An Essay on the Making of Gardens*.

40   *But the shrewd, sibylline fairy tale knows better than he*: We find the same magic art in ancient ceremonies. A litotes of enormous tragic power was created according to the same procedure at the consecration of the Russian tsar. The imperial cortege that arrived at the cathedral in a stunning crescendo of splendor brusquely gave way to an almost intolerable emptiness—and the emperor appeared alone, without an escort, on horseback, "in the simple field uniform of a colonel of the Guard, with a single decoration."

40   *The realm of the fairy tale, as someone has said*: Marianne Moore's essay "Anna Pavlova" ("Fairyland! It may be ecstasy but it is a land of pathos…").

41   *In the books that collect what still remain of these sagas*: Above all Karl Felix Wolff's inexhaustible *The Dolomites and Their Legends*. Followed by Aurelio Garobbio's *Leggende delle Alpi Lepontine* and *Leggende dei Grigioni*.

42   *of the highest station*: An allusion to Hofmannsthal, "An Episode in the Life of Marshal de Bassompierre."

43   The troubadour and crusader Jaufré Rudel is said to have died in the arms of Hodierna of Tripoli, his *amor de lonh*, or "distant love."

43   The volcanic lake Averno (Avernus) near the modern-day village of Cuma and the ancient Greek settlement of Cumae is described as "foul-smelling" (*olentis*) in *The Aeneid*, Book 6.

NIGHTS

1. The Story of the City of Brass

First published as an introduction to *Storia della Città di Rame*, translated from the Arabic by Alessandro Spina (1963).

All quotations come from "The Story of the City of Brass" [translated by Richard Francis Burton], the Bible (the Book of Kings), the Koran, Hofmannsthal, and Borges (whose presence, in my reading of the *Nights*, is constant). There are a few exceptions:

48 *the great medieval cartographer*: Cosmas Indicopleustes (who died in Alexandria in the middle of the sixth century). The quotation describing how he pictured the earth comes from Lucio Bozzano's *Antiche carte nautiche* [Ancient Nautical Charts] (1961).

49 *the living and the dead, the sleeping and the wakeful*: Torquato Tasso, in a letter to Dorotea degli Albizi.

51 *interpreted God in perfect truth*: Ibn Arabi, *The Wisdom of the Prophets*.

53 *This reading is only one conjectural gate*: Alessandro Spina has glimpsed another, which, in turn, leads us to an altogether different city: "In one place in the text," he writes, "a line of Dante's is smuggled in. It is a literal translation and at the same time a key (one of a thousand) with which to open the story, if we imagine the reader as Sheikh Abd-al-Samad struggling with a barred gate.

"If the *Commedia* had enjoyed special popularity and this popularity had expressed itself in imitations (but it probably came a bit 'late' to solicit imitations), and if popular poetry is high poetry vulgarized, the City of Brass might also strike us as an imitation—a decayed *Commedia*. It is pointless to insist on the parallels: Emir Musa and Dante, Abd-al-Samad (versed in all languages and scriptures) and Virgil, the City of Brass and the Inferno. Not to mention the characters they encounter, such as the djinn half entombed in the pillar, who narrates trickeries and battles with Solomon's ranks like any number of Dante's men of arms.

"Dante is in reality contemporary with much Arabic literature. Indeed, he is perhaps more contemporary with Arab literature than Italian literature. We have here a world that is perfectly organized, all the way to the vanishing point: God and his long arm, death.... It is true, as Hofmannsthal said, that the presence of God is the one, uninterrupted surprise in this tale (and the poverty of means by which very powerful effects are obtained is staggering). But in this series of monologues (for each sheet of metal is someone's monologue), the most touching thing, as with Dante's characters, is again and again the love of life:

But if you escape from these dark places
And come to rebehold the beautiful stars...

"The presence of the divine does not lead to contempt for the world. The divine is understood, essentially, as the end (or the destination) of everything. And the things that have been lost, the things one knows one must lose, the friends, the houses: all of it is loved all the more intensely. Death exists in order to stamp out the satisfaction of possession, which debases things.

"An Arab friend 'of the highest station' whose entire household was devastated by the Host, replied to my ritual words of condolence ('The good is in you,' 'Praise God no one lives forever'): 'Only the days keep us company...' There was no contempt in his voice, only love for this ephemeral gift." (Translator's Letter, in *Storia della Città di Rame*, 1963.)

2. *Flying Carpets*
First published in *Il Giornale d'Italia* (1966).

54 *some fascinating books about the art of the carpet*: In particular Robert de Calatchi's *Oriental Carpets*, from which almost all of the quotations in this section are drawn.

59 *a velvet background*: Not to be confused with the fabric of the same name, "velvet" here refers to the shorn wool, the fleece of the Oriental carpet that—especially in Kurdish carpets—may be a velvet made of camel hair.

60 *A book full of wisdom*: Henry Corbin, *Spiritual Body and Celestial Earth: From Mazdean Iran to Shi'ite Iran*, translated by Nancy Pearson (1960).

60 *the four paradisiacal rivers*: For the disquieting symbolic and familial poetic affinities among the carpet, the moth, and the episcopal mantle, see "The Flute and the Carpet," page 119, and the accompanying note.

60 *watch the flowers as they grow, from the first day of spring*: Madame Cécile Bruyère, *La Vie Spirituelle et l'Oraison* (Solesmes: Abbesse de Solesmes, 1960).

THE UNFORGIVABLE
First published in *Elsinore* (1965).

65 *Come, my songs*: Ezra Pound, "Salvationists."

65 The episode from the Boxer Rebellion is mentioned by Hofmannsthal in *The Book of Friends*.

67 *But it is true, they fear / it more than death*: William Carlos Williams, *Paterson*.

68 *feeling and precision*: Marianne Moore's essay "Feeling and Precision."

70 *Wave of the night*—: Gottfried Benn, "Wave of the Night," in *Primal Vision*, translated by Christopher Middleton (New York: New Directions, 1971).

71 *Consider worthy only that to which all a man's art has been applied*: Dante, *Convivio*.

72 *A poet does not speak language but mediates it*: Marianne Moore, "There Is a War That Never Ends."

73 *a guide to the Ducal Palace of Urbino*: By Professor Pasquale Rotondi.

73 *impassioned explicitness*: Marianne Moore, "Humiliation, Concentration, and Gusto."

74 The screeches are described in Peterson, Mountford, and Hollom's *A Field Guide to the Birds of Europe*, introduced by Julian Huxley, and the rose in a catalogue of the Sgaravatti nursery in Rome.

74 *Ruby-red color, deep and unambiguous*: Ceronetti glosses this profile of a Barbera (Riserva del Marchio), which evokes certain tawny portraits of seventeenth-century marshals, in appropriately inexorable fashion: "I would like to propagandize for Veronelli, the winemaker... because everything in his pages is exquisitely, abnormally aristocratic. The selection, the style, the descriptions, the recommendations, the classifications, the denominations, the set price for tastings: all of it holds itself apart from the vulgar and is proud of its apartness. Wines, like poems, do not allow for democratization. That's why they're so impossible to find. The feudalism of the small privileged reserves is a challenge made by a few refined men to centuries of reforms endured and accepted by the earth and the brain. The Vine is a disdainful aristocrat Desmoulins would have hanged from a lamppost. If the angelic Corday had whispered in Marat's ear the name of the Mersault-Santenots white or the Château de Chamirey red, that wild man bedeviled by cravings would have been quick to request them from the Widow's sharp hand and so merit the Girondine dagger twice over." (Regarding *Catalogo Bolaffi dei Vini d'Italia* and *Catalogo Bolaffi dei Vini del Mondo*, edited by Luigi Veronelli, 1970.)

75 *Really solitary, you / and words alone*: Gottfried Benn, "Words."

75 *leaping up, up, out of water, at the full moon*: A variation on Eugenio Montale, "The Shade of the Magnolia" (here translated by William Arrowsmith): "a mullet / leaping up, up, out of water, at the new moon."

77 *for example is eternal*: Letter from T. E. Lawrence to Lionel Curtis.

78 *what it is cannot be said*: The description of the experience of God *via negationis* in Jacopone da Todi.

78 *hands clenched, wrists flexed*: Williams, "Danse Pseudomacabre," in *The Doctor Stories* (New York: New Directions).

78 The style of styles is expressed by the liturgies. But this would lead the discussion away to another aspect of language altogether.

A DIGRESSION: ON LANGUAGE
First published in *Elsinore* (1964).

80 The passages from Proust come from *Swann's Way*. The quotations from Manzoni's *The Betrothed* are for the most part taken from the 1876 translation published by G. Bell & Sons.

81 *the irresponsible game of a shy young man*: From Borges's 1954 preface to *A Universal History of Infamy*, originally published in 1935.

82 In *The Betrothed*, the Unnamed is a highborn criminal based on Francesco Bernardino Visconti, who was converted by Cardinal Federigo (or Federico) Borromeo. Don Rodrigo is a villainous Spanish nobleman who tries to prevent the marriage of Renzo and Lucia, the titular betrothed. Don Abbondio is the priest bullied into refusing to marry them.

82 *The great sinners ... seem easier to catch*: This is the pedagogical devil in the immortal little treatise on demonology, C. S. Lewis's *The Screwtape Letters*. Let me add to the sentences quoted the following: "It is in some ways more troublesome to track and swat an evasive wasp than to shoot, at close range, a wild elephant. But the elephant is more troublesome if you miss."

WITH LIGHT HANDS
First published in *The Flute and the Carpet* (1971).

87 The title phrase comes from Hofmannsthal's libretto for Richard Strauss's *Der Rosenkavalier*: "*Leicht muss man sein, mit leichtem Herzen und leichten Händen, halten und nehmen, halten und lassen. Die nicht so*

sind, die straft das Leben, und Gott erbarmt sich ihrer nicht." "One must be light, must be one with a light heart and light hands, to hold and take, to hold and let go. Life punishes those who are not so, and God shows them no mercy."

88 *marked with the holy* myron: The tsar, at his coronation, was anointed (on the forehead, eyelids, nostrils, lips, ears, chest, palms) with the holy *myron*, a chrism composed of oil, balm, and wine boiled with forty-five species of precious plants and odoriferous gums for three days and three nights during Holy Week, over a fire fed by the wood of old icons, while the four Gospels are ceaselessly chanted. The *myron* can be blessed only by the Patriarch and is used solely for confirmation, the consecration of churches and antimensia (Holy Communion cloths) and, once upon a time, for the anointment of the tsar. It was both a sacrament and a mystery, which not only gives the monarch sacerdotal rights—making it possible for him to commune with the body of Christ without the mediation of the clergy—but episcopal rights as well, such as blessing the waters of the Neva on Epiphany (in addition to the charismata and thaumaturgies of the popular persuasion). However one views it, there is in any case no doubt that the association of the *myron* and the duma must seem as illicit to the tsar as the association of Rublev's icons and radars—in one of Yevtushenko's poems—seems to Andrei Sinyavsky. As for the Anointed as a divine projection and a sacrificial figure ("a sort of Russian Christ," as Bakunin defines him), in Russia there was a whole theology (or paratheology) which was not exclusively popular. One can form some idea of all this—a profoundly distorted but thorough idea— by reading the diaries of the Enlightenment ambassador Maurice Paléologue: *La Russie des Tsars pendant la Grande Guerre.*

89 *Nicholas's finest biographer*: After the admirable Julie Danzas, Robert K. Massie, author of *Nicholas and Alexandra* (1967).

91 *Federico* is Federico da Montefeltro, Duke of Urbino. The quotation comes from *Lives of Illustrious Men of the Fifteenth Century* (*Vite di uomini illustri del secolo XV*).

91 *They told you I am a god*: Moctezuma II, quoted in Cortés's second letter to Charles V. See also William Carlos Williams's "The Destruction of Tenochtitlan" in *In the American Grain*.

93 *Style . . . is isolating power*: D'Annunzio, *The Flame*.

94 *Pure, terrible Frédéric Chopin*: For Chopin's extreme restraint regarding politics and Polish nationalism, see Camille Bourniquel's study

of Chopin, the biographies by Edouard Ganche and Liszt, and especially the furious letters of the woman who was so displeased (*myron* and *duma*, Rublev and radar) to have to associate with Chopin: George Sand.

96 *as if in the grip of a sudden inspiration*: Julien Green, *Vers l'invisible: Journal, 1958–1967*.

99 *the litany of humility*: Composed by Cardinal Raffaele Merry de Val (1865–1930), secretary of state of the Vatican.

THE FLUTE AND THE CARPET

First published in *The Flute and the Carpet* (1971).

102 *for all eternity, and is therefore destined for him*: A phrase from Simone Weil's notebooks.

104 *The long processions of confraternities*: See Matizia Maroni Lumbroso and Antonio Marini, *Le Confraternite romane e le loro chiese* (1963). Until the liturgical reforms of the 1960s, Roman life in these neighborhoods was still filled with the sublime echoes of that world.

106 *We must stay out of the game of circumstances*: From a story by Hans Carossa.

106 *Like Saint Andrew's manna in the hollow of the vial*: The Cathedral of Amalfi guards Saint Andrew's body. In his sepulcher, a substance similar to oil, but as colorless and light as quicksilver, believed to have curative properties, is formed, and mysteriously fills a vial suspended in the void.

107 The Trappists, who, as everyone knows, take a vow of silence, after the canonical hour of compline, cannot break this silence for any reason. They cannot—or they could not. It is obvious that, when referring—here and elsewhere—to Catholic things, I am always referring to the period from year 1 to 1960 AD.

108 *stella stillans claritatem, rosa rorans bonitatem*: From an emblematic blazon of Saint Bridget of Sweden, in her rooms at Piazza Farnese, Rome. ("Star, pouring forth brightness, / Rose, distilling the dew of goodness.")

108 *To him that overcometh will I give to eat of the hidden manna*: "Vincenti dabo manna absconditum et nomen novum." Antiphon of the lauds for the Feast of Corpus Domini (Revelation 2:17).

108 The religious name and the divine predicate are now being suppressed almost everywhere. The predicate of Saint Thérèse of Lisieux was "of the child Jesus and of the Holy Countenance."

110 *"The Altar of the Dead"*: An 1895 story by Henry James.

110 *"The Beautiful Genoese"*: A story in Goethe, *Recreations of the German Emigrants.*

111 The translations of Cavafy belong to Edmund Keeley and Philip Sherrard.

111 *Two theologians*: Allusion to Borges's "The Theologians."

111 *Dante's one, long look at the divine ideograms* is described in Borges, "Inferno 1, 31."

112 *up until the very moment of revelation*: Ratisbonne had a vision of the Virgin in Rome at the Church of Santa Maria delle Fratte in 1842. He narrates this experience in *Conversion de Marie-Alphonse Ratisbonne, relation authentique par M. le Baron Th. de Bussière, suivie de la lettre de M. Alphonse Ratisbonne à M. Dufriche-Desgenettes, Fondateur et Directeur de l'Archiconfrérie de N. D. des Victoires* (Paris, 1930). The mortal remains of the Comte de la Ferronays, who had died suddenly the night before, were laid out that morning in the empty church. Like running water in classical visions, these remains interposed between Ratisbonne and the apparition.

113 *Sorcery and sanctity*: Arthur Machen, "The White People."

114 On Italian peasant life before Napoleon (but my father said that most of these customs persisted even during his childhood), I would refer the reader to the heartrending monographs written by M. Placucci and L. de Nardis in *Romagna tradizionale* (1963).

114 *Never eat unless you're truly hungry*: Moral precept of the orthodox theologian Plato, the Metropolitan of Moscow (1737–1812), in P. Tyszkiewicz, *Moralistes de Russie* (1951).

116 *Oh shepherd, hold me in your hands*: P. Toschi, *Fiabe e leggende romagnole* (Bologna, 1963). The text of the fairy tale—*"La penna dll'usell granflon"*—is in the ever so musical dialect of Castelbolognese.

117 *what is dictated to him is not a verbal form*: Hélène Lubienska de Lanval, *La liturgie du geste* (1958).

117 *pars, hereditas mea*: Psalm 16:5, "[The Lord is] the portion of my inheritance."

118 *a great baroque poet*: John Donne, in the poem "Good Friday, 1613: Riding Westward."

119 *He who offers and is offered up*: From the great sacerdotal invocation to the Offertory in the Byzantine Mass.

119 *certain hypnotic lepidoptera*: Entomological treaties tell us that butterflies and moths—the least well-armed creatures—have no defense except flight, mimicry, or so-called "flash coloration": for example, the sudden unfolding of the wonderful carmine "petticoat" when the *catocala* (underwing moth) takes off, produces an instant of astonishment that allows her to preserve her life. The *mandyas*—the Byzantine episcopal mantle with a purple background spanned by the big red-white stripes of the rivers of Genesis and four cosmic silver quadrants at its four corners—can produce an analogous effect when it is unfolded by the deacons. The butterfly, everywhere and in every era, is an image of the spiritual soul. It may also be an image of the supremely defenseless liturgy.

119 *the episcopal totem*: During his consecration, the Byzantine bishop is led from an image of the eagle's tail, to one of its heart, to one of its head. These three moments of identification with the eagle are marked by three increasingly profound professions of faith. The Armenian bishop, for his part, crosses three symbolic rivers: three regenerations parallel to those of the eagle.

120 *Lord God, human nature*: A prayer said by the Byzantine clergyman during the consecration of the bishop.

120 *painted in icons, raised on altars*: Western and Eastern liturgical elements are combined here. The broad strokes of the celebration are the same in all churches, but obviously in the West, and not in the East, there will be statues, sarcophagi, etc.

121 *her nine "first Fridays"*: The first Fridays of nine consecutive months, dedicated, traditionally, to the worship of the Sacred Heart.

121 *the young widow with the light brown hair*: Francis de Sales described Jane de Chantal on first seeing her during his Lenten prayer, as follows: "*Quelle est cette jeune dame claire-brune, vêtue en veuve, qui se met opposite au sermon et qui écoute la parole de verité si attentivement?*" (Abbé Bougaud, *Histoire des origines de la Visitation*, 1886.)

122 *Leave blanks in life*: Boris Pasternak, "It Is Not Seemly to Be Famous," translated by Lydia Pasternak Slater.

123 *the maiden Alacoque's heart*: The first time she heard the name of the place she was to receive the revelations familiar to all, Saint Marguerite-Marie Alacoque wrote one of her unfathomable and innocent pages. In them we find the following passages: "Several convents were proposed, but I could not make up my mind about them; as soon, however, as they mentioned Paray, my heart was overjoyed and I consented at once.... But in spite of all that was said, my heart remained insensible, and was more than ever confirmed in its resolution, ever repeating: 'Either die or

conquer.'. . . But I will pass over all the other conflicts I had to sustain, in order to arrive more quickly at the place of my happiness, 'my dear Paray,' where, as soon as I entered the parlor, I inwardly heard these words: 'It is here that I would have thee to be.'. . . Thereupon it seemed to me that I began a new life, so great was the peace and happiness that I felt. . . . I understood that Our Lord had cut off the sackcloth of my captivity and was clothing me with His robe of gladness. In a transport of joy, I exclaimed: 'It is here that God wills me to be!'" (*The Autobiography of St. Margaret Mary*).

124 *It gives me such comfort to drift*: Pasternak, "In Hospital," translated by Lydia Pasternak Slater.

FAIRY TALE AND MYSTERY

The following two essays were published in *Fairy Tale and Mystery* but were not revised or re-collected in *The Flute and the Carpet*.

Fairy Tale and Mystery contained: "Fairy Tale and Mystery" (later incorporated into "On Fairy Tales"), "A Rose," "Deer Park" (some of which was also incorporated into "On Fairy Tales"), "*In medio coeli*," and "Attention and Poetry."

DEER PARK

First published in *Fairy Tale and Mystery* (1962).

128 *I had set foot in that part of life*: Dante, *Vita Nuova*, translated by Barbara Reynolds.

128 *La grande énigme de la vie humaine*: Simone Weil, *Waiting for God*.

129 *Oh city*: Isaiah 49:16.

129 *This day I breathed first, time is come round*: Shakespeare, *Julius Caesar*.

129 *being dead gives us no rest*: Mario Luzi, *Primizie del deserto*.

129 *My mind, transfixed and robbed*: Dino Frescobaldi, "Morte avversara, poi ch'io son contento."

130 *Saveur maxima de chaque mot*: A phrase from one of Simone Weil's notes on poetry.

130 *pimped out*: In the dedicatory letter of *The Prince*, Machiavelli calls certain rhetoric *lenocinio* (which figuratively means "pompous" or "overly ornate" but at its root means "pimped out").

130 *O mein Herz*: Hölderlin, "Vom Abgrund Nämlich..." ("From the Abyss, Namely...").

130 *Tearful city*: William Carlos Williams, "Perpetuum Mobile: The City."

130 *dans l'air liquide*: Proust, *Chroniques*, "in the liquid, freezing air... as in a bowl of pure water, the narcissi, the jonquils, the anemones of the Ponte Vecchio."

130 *Je demandais à Albertine*: Proust, *Sodom and Gomorrah*, "I asked Albertine if she would like something to drink. 'I seem to see some oranges over there, and water,' she said. 'That will be perfect.'"

132 *Tous les beaux noms éteints*: Proust, *The Guermantes Way*, "all the beautiful names—extinct, and so all the more glowingly rekindled... with the result that there followed, at the front door, a sort of stentorian recital of great names from the History of France."

135 *de cuevas de leones enlazado / de mil escudos de oro coronado*: Saint John of the Cross, "hidden among the lion caves...and capped with thousands of gold shields"; translated by Willis Barnstone.

136 *los ojos deseados / que tengo en mis entrañas dibujados*: Saint John of the Cross, "the eyes I most desire! / I feel them in me like a scar"; translated by Willis Barnstone.

136 *Mais une amitié pure est rare*: "But a pure friendship is rare," Simone Weil, *Waiting for God*.

136 *Every great painting is painted against painting*: Goya, *El sentimiento de la pintura* (paraphrase).

139 *Voca me et ego respondebo tibi*: Job 13:22, "Call me, and I will answer thee: or else I will speak, and do thou answer me."

139 *As long as you are unable to hear*: A koan of Hakuin's.

145 *Ce n'était pas que l'aspect*: Proust, *Time Regained*: "It was not only in appearance that these people were like dream figures, their youth and love had become to themselves a dream. They had forgotten their very resentments and hatreds, and, to be sure that this individual was the one they had not spoken to for ten years, they would have needed a register which even then would have had the vagueness of a dream in which they have been insulted by a stranger. Such dreams account for those contrasts in political life when people who once accused each other of murder and treason are members of the same government. And dreams become as opaque as death in the case of old men..."

ATTENTION AND POETRY
First published in *L'Approdo letterario* (1961).

147 *Et chaque être humain*: Weil, *Cahiers*: "And each human being" [Campo adds: "and each thing"] "cries in silence to be read otherwise."

148 *Justice, a golden eye, looks*: Sophocles, *Fragments*.

151 *Souffrir pour quelque chose*: Valéry, quoted by Simone Weil. ["To suffer for something is to grant it the utmost attention."]

All of the notes in this and the remaining sections of the book were compiled by the translator.

THE MAXIMAL FLAVOR OF EACH WORD

ON WILLIAM CARLOS WILLIAMS
First published as an introduction to a collection of Williams's poetry (Torino: Einaudi, 1961).

155 *constant in its swiftness as a pool*: William Carlos Williams, "A Marriage Ritual."

ON JOHN DONNE
First published as an introduction to *Poesie amorose. Poesie teologiche*, translated and edited by Cristina Campo, 1971. Most quotations are from Donne's poems and sermons.

164 *under the pretext of Patroclus*: *Odyssey*, Book 4.

166 *is not his meaning, charged with meaning though his poetry is*: This and the following two quotations are from Virginia Woolf, "Donne After Three Centuries."

167 *a Chamois' Silver Boot*: Emily Dickinson, "Ah, Moon!—and Star!"

168 *massive music*: T. S. Eliot's description of Donne's sonics in "The Metaphysical Poets."

169 *of Bible and war*: From Borges, "New England, 1967."

169 *gemitibus inenarrabilibus*: Romans 8:26: "indescribable groaning."

169 *neumatizare*: Literally, an offering of *pneuma*, or breath. Historically, a way of singing liturgical sequences (according to the musicologist Lori Kruckenberg, who is in turn interpreting the thirteenth-century writer Guillaume Durand) "by singing certain phrases melismatically or by vocalizing the entire sequence without words."

A DOCTOR

First published in *Paragone: Letteratura* (1960). All Chekhov quotations are taken or adapted from Constance Garnett's translations.

180 inscribed man in a landscape: From one of Pasternak's 1959 letters, written in English, to Stephen Spender and published in *Encounter* the following year.

HOMAGE TO BORGES

First published in *Elsinore* (1964). All of the Latin comes from the Magic Portal, and the opening and closing sentence from Borges, "The God's Script," translated by L. A. Murillo.

SUPERNATURAL SENSES

INTRODUCTION TO *SAYINGS AND DEEDS OF THE DESERT FATHERS*

First published in 1974.

191 scala coeli: "ladder to heaven."

192 lupus qui sine cessatione quotidie non corpora sed mentes dilaniat, malignus videlicet spiritus: "a wolf that, daily and without ceasing, tears apart not bodies but minds, which is to say, an evil spirit."

INTRODUCTION TO *THE WAY OF A PILGRIM*

First published in 1973.

I have consulted *The Way of a Pilgrim*, translated by Anna Zaranko, though in many cases I worked directly from Milli Marinelli's Italian translation, which Campo quotes, and to which this text originally served as an introduction.

198 Vivo autem: Galatians 2:20: "Nevertheless I live; yet not I, but Christ liveth in me …"; Romans 8:26: "The Spirit itself maketh intercession for us with groanings which cannot be uttered."

199 the precise form of Byzantium: T. S. Eliot, "Lune de Miel" ("*la forme precise de Byzance*").

SUPERNATURAL SENSES

First published in *Conoscenza religiosa* (1971). Campo lists most of her sources at the end of the piece. *Vita mutatur, non tollitur,* from the Preface for the Dead, means "Life is changed, not taken away." The Heschel she mentions is the Polish-born American rabbi Abraham Joshua Heschel, for whose *Man Is Not Alone* Campo had written an introduction in 1970.

OTHER WRITINGS

INTRODUCTION TO KATHERINE MANSFIELD'S *A CUP OF TEA AND OTHER STORIES*
First published as an introduction to Mansfield's *Una tazza di tè e altri racconti*, translated by Vittoria Guerrini (Campo's birth name), 1944. All quotations come from Mansfield's fiction, journals, and letters.

A TRAGEDY BY SIMONE WEIL: *VENICE SAVED*
First published as an introduction to *Venezia salva*, translated by Cristina Campo, 1963.

I have consulted Silvia Panizza and Philip Wilson's fine English translation of *Venice Saved*, but in most cases I have translated directly from the French: *Venise sauvée* (Paris: Rivages, 2020).

GRAVITY AND GRACE IN *RICHARD II*
First published in 1952 or 1953.

Campo's friend and longtime correspondent Remo Fasani (1922–2011) was an Italian scholar, poet, and translator of German and French.

THE GOLDEN NUT
The text of this story exists—in the words of Monica Farnetti, editor of *Sotto Falso Nome* (the volume in which the Italian text was first published)—thanks to Campo's friend Ernesto Marchese, who received it directly from Campo. The typewritten copy includes, at the bottom, the note "(1951)—revised in 1969." A long gestation and multiple revisions can also be inferred from a pair of letters addressed to Margherita Pieracci, in which we read: "while I had the flu, I also wrote a 'Viaticum peregrinationis'... an essay-story about the presence of fairy tales in the life of a seven-year-old child. It might become beautiful, beautiful" (March 1963). And later (May 1963): "At times, the desire to write makes my chest feel like it's going to burst (for example, that story of mine I told you about, 'The Golden Nut')."

During Campo's lifetime, "The Golden Nut" appeared only in a Spanish translation by Hernán Mario Cueva, in the Argentine magazine *Sur* (1970).

241   *Ave, viaticum meae peregrinationis* does not seem to appear in the works of Cicero, but it does appear in a Catholic context in Johanne Benedicto Mitarelli's eighteenth-century *Annales Camaldulenses*: "And as we kneel, lifting up the body of Christ, we say: 'My Lord and my God, hail the beginning of my creation, hail the price of my redemption, hail the viaticum of my pilgrimage, hail the beginning of my retribution.'"

241   *Carlo Felice Wolff*: A folklorist of the Dolomite Mountain regions. Also known as Karl Felix Wolff.

243   *répétition générale de la vie*: A "dress rehearsal for life"; appears to come from the writings of Maryse Choisy, a philosopher, sometime occultist, patient of Freud, and critic of the surrealists.

244   *Fata Nix*: The pseudonym of Attilia Montaldo Morando (1866–1933), a children's book author whose retellings of fairy tales were published by the German Genoese publisher Antonio Donath and often illustrated in the art nouveau style by Pipein Gamba and Alberto della Valle. The cover Campo describes is the cover of *Per voi, piccini!*, a collection of eighty fairy tales first published in the 1890s.

252   *suavis anima . . . animas fortis*: Sweet soul . . . strong soul.

OTHER NEW YORK REVIEW CLASSICS

For a complete list of titles, visit www.nyrb.com.